To Kai

Behind the Sun

Sue Nielsen

*Best wishes
Sue Nielsen*

Copyright © 2008 Sue Nielsen
All rights reserved.

ISBN: 1-4392-1354-2
ISBN-13: 9781439213544

Visit www.booksurge.com to order additional copies.

For

My mother
Sarah (Sally) Eleanor Vince
Live forever!

My grandson
William Mitchell Taylor

and Earth's deaf community

Part One

The Pillars of Hercules

Prologue
c04 BCE

Gabriel stood on a hill overlooking Bethlehem, his wings drawn tightly in and concealed beneath a luxurious cloak. High above his left shoulder the brilliant light of a huge star burned strangely in the pale twilight sky. For forty nights the light from the distant dying star had remained dimmed by heavy cloud, but this evening it shone forth in all its powerful radiance. Its revelation in the heavens over Bethlehem at the precise moment of the event in the town below seemed to Gabriel an unlikely coincidence. It certainly deserved investigation.

He turned his head at a loud jingling sound. A caravan was making its way southwards along the narrow path. The leader, an elderly man with a pale olive complexion, was dressed in the richly embroidered robes of a wealthy Persian. He halted his camel and looked around as though surprised to see Gabriel alone. He leaned his turbaned head down and saluted him.

'We have come from Jerusalem today and will stay here this night. Will you join us, friend?' he asked.

Gabriel returned the courtesy, shook his head. 'Thank you, no. There is something I must attend to. Perhaps I will meet you later. Where are you bound?'

'We follow after the truth, now more than ever.' The man smiled enigmatically. 'May the light be with you.' He hupped his camel into motion and slowly descended the hillside.

Gabriel watched closely as the caravan passed by. Two men of similar appearance followed the first. They smiled and touched their foreheads politely but did not speak. Several servants followed their masters, leading heavily laden camels. An aroma of expensive spices and oils filled the air as they passed.

Nothing in the caravan aroused Gabriel's suspicions and he continued his close examination of the surrounding hills. Streams of people were still descending the slopes and making for the gates of the town, hurrying to meet the curfew for the census. Even so, many of them stopped every few moments to gaze up in wonder at the brightly burning star. Where small crowds developed, soldiers in their distinctive Roman uniforms urged the visitors towards the town. Hawkers milled around the gates, selling food and accommodation and when they pressed too hard, the soldiers turned their attentions to them.

The town, nestled amongst the upland hills was more brightly lit than usual and crowds surged through the streets. Gabriel surveyed the scene for several minutes and then he raised his eyes to the sky. The evening was calm and clear, but few stars were visible against the great light of the supernova.

He pulled his cloak more tightly around him and made his way down the hill towards the town. When he reached the gates the soldiers glanced at him curiously but he passed them without question and entered onto the wide paved street. Vendors were gathered there, lighting their oil lamps and calling out to passersby. They noted Gabriel and his fashionable attire, but did not offer their wares to him.

He walked through the small colonnade that faced one side of the main street. The arcades were lined with trestles and many people were eating in the open air. The smell of cooking made Gabriel grimace and turn his head away. He glanced into several alleys but they led to dead ends.

The busy streets allowed Gabriel to make his search without attracting attention. Many of the townsfolk had crowded on to their roof gardens to gaze up at the star, now even more brilliant in the darkening sky. Very few of them took any notice of this tall, aloof young man, dressed in the manner of a rich merchant. Those who did, looked twice at his unusually handsome face and then averted their eyes. Gabriel paused in front of one of the few tall buildings, and then mounted the external stairway. From this vantage he could see most of the town and he looked carefully around for many minutes. The Persian caravan had stopped outside an inn near the southern wall.

His survey completed, Gabriel descended from the rooftop and started toward the centre of the town. He increased his pace and his eyes moved purposefully from left to right. After a few minutes he halted abruptly. Five very tall men walking several yards ahead had caught his attention. They wore their dark curly hair uncovered and their complexions were pale and clear. They were clothed in the manner of wealthy Greek gentlemen, but their athletic gait and muscular physiques suggested otherwise. As the five men pushed through the crowd, the people nearby fell back and cleared a path for them, as though their expressions as well as their appearance commanded respect or fear. Gabriel moved forward quickly and laid his hand on the shoulder of the nearest man. The whole group stopped and turned around. Their faces paled further at the sight of Gabriel. He tightened his grip as the man started to speak. 'Not here,' said Gabriel quietly.

He glanced around and then urged the group into a narrow, deserted alley. He looked at each of the men in turn. Two of them avoided his gaze, but the others stared back resentfully. The tallest was a huge imposing man, older than the others and obviously their leader. He met Gabriel's eyes steadfastly, his face quickly becoming red with anger. Gabriel held his gaze and for a few moments there was a dreadful silence.

Finally Gabriel spoke. His voice was calm and even. 'Why are you here?'

None of the men replied. The tallest of the men folded his arms and stared insolently at Gabriel. His face had lost some of its awful flush.

Gabriel appeared unmoved by their attitude. 'You should not have come,' he continued. 'We made an agreement.'

The leader clenched his fists and thrust out his chin. 'Yet you are here. Explain that!' He spoke angrily but quietly as though unwilling to attract attention.

Gabriel's voice became colder.' I do not need to explain myself to you. That you are here is sufficient reason for my presence.' He paused and looked briefly to the side. 'I ask you again. Why have you broken the contract? Why are you here?'

'I changed my mind,' the man replied furiously. 'And what of it? We will stay as long as I please.'

'You will not stay.' Gabriel's voice was calm again.

'I will not answer to you!' The man leaned forward aggressively but stepped back in alarm as Gabriel pushed his cloak back over his shoulders. The cloak rose slowly in the air and a steel blue glowing light spread upwards in a fan shape over Gabriel's head. A soft rustling noise grew louder, like a thousand knives sliding gently over fine china.

The older man stepped back even further and the rest of the group huddled behind him.

'You would not do that, surely?' he asked in a shaken voice. His face was white with fear.

'Enough is enough,' said Gabriel in a cold, hard voice. 'Give me your hands.'

The rush of wind prompted a woman nearby to look around the corner. The alley was deserted except for some feathery leaves fluttering slowly to the ground.

1
More than 2000 years later

The alien, yet strangely familiar figures with their stocky bodies and heavily browed faces disappeared as the mist crept up the hill. Sally wondered if they were still standing there behind the white veil, or whether they were returning to their caves, taking with them the gifts she had brought. The Neanderthals had shown very little curiosity at her sudden arrival; no fear or aggression as she watched them go about their daily routines. When she had signaled that she had to leave, they made their elaborate gestures of farewell. She felt regretful but calm as she waited; but she jumped in alarm when something touched her shoulder. She fumbled with her eye mask and stared up at the blonde flight attendant leaning over her. 'We've landed, Doctor Burns,' the young woman said pleasantly, and turned away to assist another passenger.

Sally rubbed her face and yawned. She raised her left wrist and squinted at the small screen on her watcher. Four pm Sydney time. For a moment she did not know where she was. Then her stomach gave a nervous lurch. 'Geneva time,' she muttered, but the screen did not change and she recalled that the watcher was still on standby mode. It must be about eight am local time. She hated arriving early in the morning – a whole day fighting jet lag loomed ahead.

She stood up, ruffled her short dark hair, pulled her cabin bag down from the overhead locker. She checked the flap on the back of the seat in front of her and pulled out the document her boss had handed her in Sydney. Her stomach jumped again as she remembered his farewell.

Steven Andrews had looked at her closely. 'I know you're tired but we need you to go. You don't realize yet how important this discovery is. It's a once in a lifetime opportunity for you as well as for Lifescape.' When Sally did not reply, he had continued. 'There's no need to be nervous. Security will be very tight and anyway, you're not likely to make it to the final team. Australia's not important enough to be guaranteed a place. But think what it will do for Lifescape, just having you at the conference.'

Sally suddenly recalled her dream. She had always been fascinated with the distant past when mankind shared the planet with other human species. After completing her controversial PhD on why Neanderthals had not developed spoken language she had been offered a job with a film company. Her latest documentary 'Why We Are Alone' was the best work she had ever done. She had just signed off on the postproduction, and would probably be nominated for an Oscar.

For two years she had worked on nothing else. No wonder she had strange dreams; she was mentally exhausted. She felt irritation rising in her. What was she doing in Geneva? She should be home in Sydney, enjoying a long overdue holiday.

Most of the passengers had disembarked and it took her only a few minutes to reach the immigration checkpoint. She stared into the iris identity scanner, the machine beeped and the door in front of her swung open. She was surprised to see another checkpoint ahead. An official scanned her international identity card, looked briefly at her face and nodded for her to proceed. She wondered why the ID check had been set up again. She gave the man her most charming smile, but his grumpy expression did not change.

'I'm staying. You can go back home if you want to!' Ahead in the queue, two men glared at each other. As she moved closer the older man replied, arguing that they should fly back to India immediately. The younger one, a very handsome man in his early thirties shook his head. He noticed Sally watching them and his face lit up. He smiled as if he knew her. The older man nudged him and he frowned again.

'I respect your feelings, father, but I'm not leaving,' he repeated in Konkani. 'Now that the news is out, they might speed up the selection process. I want to be here when it happens.'

'What about your family? Don't you care how we feel?'

'It was you who persuaded me to put my name up in the first place. I'm not going to throw it all away now. Anyway, this is Switzerland. The security here is excellent. Nothing's going to happen.'

The older man's voice was urgent. 'You know how it is. Every lunatic group will see this as yet another Western conspiracy.' He looked around suspiciously.

The conversation made Sally uneasy. She wanted to ask them what they were talking about, but someone in the queue behind her gave a small nudge towards one of the customs desks. As she lifted her flight bag on to the counter, she glanced around. There was the usual mix of people – nothing out of the ordinary except for an air of preoccupation, almost of anxiety. She thought there were more airport marshals standing around than usual. Perhaps there had been a bomb scare.

'What?' The customs official was asking her whether she had anything to declare. 'No nothing.' The man unzipped her bag anyway and expertly rummaged around inside. He scanned her card and handed it back to her.

'Thanks,' she replied in German. 'Have a nice day.' The man grunted and did not return her smile.

She remembered to switch her watcher on as she passed into the arrival lounge. A message from Steven Andrews blinked, but she ignored it. She paused for a moment and looked around. The secretary at Lifescape had assured her she would be met. She hoped so. The airport was very crowded.

As Sally hesitated, a group of people surged through the doors behind her carrying her forwards. She heard a loud crashing noise, the sound of shattering glass and several shouts. She was suddenly surrounded, buffeted from all sides. A marshal pushed past her, she stumbled, lost her balance, and felt a sudden stab of alarm. Someone grabbed her arm and she turned to see a WorldSecure guard, a gun held above his head. She instinctively pulled away but the guard yelled at her and tightened his grip. As he thrust her forward, she caught sight of the two Indian men ahead. There were several more shouts and the younger man glanced back as if to see where she was. To her surprise, he smiled slightly and shrugged, then disappeared behind several guards who were also pushing towards the exit. Something slammed against her shoulder and she was almost knocked down. The guard tightened his grip again and to her amazement fired a shot above his head. The people around her pushed away frantically.

Sally could hear a loud voice over the PA system as she was thrust towards the exit, but she couldn't make out what it said over the increasing noise. One of the tall glass doors was cracked and broken glass crunched under her feet as they exited onto the concourse. Ahead, a uniformed man was helping the two Indian men into a black limousine. Sally glanced back and saw another WorldSecure guard pushing two more men forward - a very tall blonde man in a grey suit and a shorter Chinese man in a white tracksuit.

Behind them, more guards blocked the exit. Frightened faces stared at her through the glass doors.

The Chinese man waved and gave a rueful grin. The blonde man stepped towards her and put out his hand. 'Sally Burns! I'm Thomas Beecham. Sorry about the mess.'

As he took her hand Sally felt a strange jolt and for some reason she leaned towards him. He looked intently into her face, her knees gave way and she toppled forward. There was a deafening cracking noise and the Chinese man fell against her. Someone grabbed her from behind and the track suited figure slumped to the ground. Thomas Beecham kneeled down and turned the man over. As he felt for a pulse he looked up at Sally, a peculiar expression on his face. 'He's dead!'

Someone screamed and a man nearby retched violently. Sally stared down at the red stain spreading across the white tracksuit and instinctively touched her own chest. She raised her hand. It was covered in blood. The world went dark.

A strange smell filled the air, strong and bitter. She struggled against it and opened her eyes. She was in the limousine and Thomas Beecham was leaning over her. His face was so close she could see the fine lines around his eyes. He offered her the refresher towel he had been using to wipe her face but she jerked back, suddenly repulsed. She heard him say. 'It's all right. She's ok.' His voice sounded strange; a clipped English accent devoid of emotion.

The two Indians were seated opposite her. The older man slumped in the seat, as the limousine accelerated. His eyes were closed, his face pale and sweating. She heard someone curse and the younger man twisted around and stared out the window. Sally leaned forward to follow his gaze but she could not understand what she saw. As the limousine slowed to enter a roundabout, a group of people holding placards ran out onto the road. She fell back in her seat as the car swerved to avoid them.

'I told you how it would be. We'll be lucky to get out of here alive.' The older man straightened up and looked angrily at his son.

'What do you mean?' Sally automatically spoke in Konkani and the two men looked at her in surprise. 'Why did...?'

'God! I don't know...' The younger man's face contorted. 'His name is, was, David Liu - one of the psychologists.' He paused and continued in Konkani 'I'm Mohun Patel - zoology, and so on. This is my father.' The older man nodded and turned away. 'I assume you are Sally Burns? The linguist? I thought I recognized you.'

Sally nodded. 'What the hell's going on?' She looked down at the blood on her shirt and tasted bile in her throat.

The young man glanced at Thomas Beecham and continued in English. 'Haven't you heard? A German journalist got the story. It's all over the news.'

Sally shook her head. 'I've been traveling for almost twenty four hours. We got held up in Singapore. We weren't allowed to leave the plane and the vidscreens weren't working; some technical problem, they told us.' She clenched her hands to stop them shaking.

'Someone's leaked the whole thing; when and how it was discovered and of course, about the meeting here.' Mohun glanced at his father. 'We saw the newscast when we changed flights at Frankfurt. Apparently someone hacked into the project and sold the story to the highest bidder.' He scowled. 'It was stupid to keep it secret for so long.'

Thomas Beecham interrupted. 'The sponsors wanted to choose the right time to announce it.' His voice and face were still unnaturally calm and Sally felt again a faint sensation of revulsion.

Mohun frowned. 'Well, they chose wrong.' He continued bitterly. 'Why did David get shot? Just bad luck I think.'

His father interrupted, his eyes still closed. 'Some people will do anything to stop the project.'

'Why? I don't understand.' Sally shook her head again. 'I didn't know anything about it until my boss put me on the plane in Sydney. Why would people get so upset? Dozens of new planets have been discovered.'

Mohun grimaced. 'This is not some remote rock out past Pluto. The newscast called it "Earth 2"; same size, same orbit as earth, out of sight behind the sun. Just think about the implications; a new planet, the solution to all our problems, global warming, overpopulation. Why would they keep it secret? How long have they known about it? Some people are bound to think it's a conspiracy.'

His father interrupted. 'That's not all. What if you find intelligent life there? What if they already have and they're just not telling us.'

'That's not likely, is it?' Sally stared at the two men.

Mohun shrugged. 'Not at all, but a lot of people would like to believe it.'

As the car slowed, Mohun pointed out the window. Across the top of a building, a huge news sign flashed; - "WE ARE NOT ALONE."

2

'I really don't know what I'm doing here!' Sally looked down towards the wide boulevard and watched the large black bus discharge yet another troop of WorldSecure guards. 'And we're practically under house arrest,' she added.

'I'm sure you're exaggerating.' Steven sounded irritated. Sally glanced at his frowning face on her watcher screen.

'It's true. We're not allowed outside the hotel complex. I thought I was just here to give advice. I've told them I'm not interested in going, but they insist on putting me through all their stupid psych tests. It's a waste of time.'

Sally stared down at the hotel gates. A young man arguing with a guard was picked up like a toy and thrown into the back of an armored van. In the distance she could see the barricades holding back the growing crowds. Several burnt out cars remained from yesterday's conflict.

'I've heard in a roundabout way that the team will definitely include a linguist. It's likely that you and Pierre are on the top of their list.'

Sally smiled slightly. 'Well, that lets me off the hook. Pierre can charm his way into anything.'

'Aren't you the least bit intrigued? Think what it would be like – making contact with a new species. Would you really refuse to go if they picked you?'

'I agreed to come to this talkfest, Steven, and that's all. Anyway, everyone here is convinced that the chances of any intelligent life on Earth 2 are a billion to one.'

'So why do they want a linguist?'

'Who knows? No one here knows who the sponsors are or why they are doing this. Or if they do, they're not letting on. All I know is that they couldn't have caused more trouble if they'd planned it.'

Steven was silent for a moment. In a more pleasant voice he said, 'Anyway, there's still plenty of time to think about it. Don't make any rash decisions.' He ended the call before she could reply.

Sally sighed in exasperation and turned away from the window. A deep armchair faced a huge picture of snow-capped mountains. She slumped down into the chair, and gestured. The picture melted into the hotel logo and a list of news programs appeared on the screen. She scanned them quickly and selected Lehrer's Hour. An anchorman was summarizing the headlines and a list of the most recent terrorist attacks appeared on the screen. Sally didn't listen to the commentary. It was too depressing. She looked up again when she heard the man's voice mention Earth 2.

'We will return to those stories in a few minutes. But first, here is Wan-Ju Lee with a special on the Earth 2 developments.'

The Earth 2 consortium logo appeared briefly on the screen and then a smart middle-aged woman with shoulder length dark hair introduced herself.

'This special edition on the Earth 2 story is in response to the thousands of requests from viewers worldwide.' She turned to the screen on her left. 'On our panel today we have firstly, Doctor Loren Wellington, who made this astonishing discovery. Doctor Wellington is an Australian who works in London with EARN - the European Asteroid Research Network.'

Sally hardly recognized the young woman from the press conference three days earlier. Loren was sitting composedly with her hands lightly clasped in her lap. She was wearing a smart black trouser suit and her newly streaked hair gleamed. Sally smiled to herself. Someone had given Loren good advice.

'On my right is Doctor Neil Griffith, who oversaw the Earth 2 probe. Doctor Griffith works with JPL, the Jet Propulsion Laboratory at the Californian Institute of Technology.'

Wan-Ju paused to smile at the burly, pleasant faced man seated next to her, before looking to her left. 'Major John Armstrong from NASA. Many of you will remember that Major Armstrong was selected to command the Millennium on the Mars Mission which was cancelled last year.'

Sally looked at John Armstrong with interest; a tall, strongly built African American with a calm, handsome face.

'We also hope to hook up with Professor Pierre Meyer who is currently in Greece.' As Wan-Ju spoke one of the screens behind her lit up and Sally couldn't help smiling at the photo print of Pierre's cheerful face.

The camera returned to Wan-Ju Lee's face. 'We invited the firm of Edgerton and Mackenzie, who are acting on behalf of sponsors of the Earth 2 mission. However, they declined, stating they had nothing to add to their media release.'

Wan-Ju Lee turned to Loren and smiled. 'Now; first Doctor Wellington. Can you tell us a bit more about how you made the discovery? I understand you were trying to locate meteoroids behind the Sun, using data from the Ulysses project?'

Sally remembered that Loren had looked subdued and nervous at the press conference. Now her face glowed with enthusiasm.

'I've always been fascinated by the Ulysses project.' She smiled. 'I hoped to join the programming team for the next phase but I got sick during my PhD and missed out. Anyway, I had some spare time before my fellowship started so I asked for access to the final set of Ulysses data. You know, from the final pass over the North Pole of the sun. I wanted to see if my software could detect objects behind the sun, and ...'

Wan-Ju interrupted politely, 'We understand that your supervisor and some of your senior colleagues objected to you carrying out this project?'

Loren leaned backwards slightly and looked defensive. 'Well, yes. No one believed that my software would be fine grained enough to find small asteroids, and certainly not meteoroids. But my uncle is a senior researcher at the Vatican Observatory in Rome and he thought it was a good idea.' She smiled. 'Anyway, I was right. I've found several new very small objects behind the sun - fortunately none on a collision course with earth. And if this mission goes ahead, my software will be installed on early warning systems around Mercury and Venus as well as Earth 2.' She looked annoyed for a moment. 'With all the fuss about Earth 2, people seem to forget that. The sun won't be a blind spot for us any more - we'll know what's coming, and we'll have time to act. No more catastrophes, no more mass extinctions.'

Loren paused and Wan-Ju Lee took the opportunity to steer her back to the topic. 'So how did you feel when you first saw Earth 2? Didn't you think it was an amazing coincidence; an Earth like planet on the same orbit?'

'I couldn't believe it. I thought there was a major bug in my software, that all my results were crap. But I contacted my supervisor and he confirmed my findings.'

'Isn't it strange that it's not been discovered before this?' Wan-Ju Lee asked.

'Just luck I guess. Nothing's been pointed in that direction; not till Ulysses and that wasn't designed to look so far out into the heleosphere. So no one else has taken a close look at that data.'

'So what did you do then?'

Loren looked surprised at the question. Wan-Ju Lee leaned forward again. 'Doctor Wellington, one of the mysteries surrounding this discovery relates to the conduct of your supervisor - Professor Belboa - and the delay in getting your findings to proper scientific bodies.' Sally saw Loren's mouth tighten, as Wan-Ju continued. 'Can you tell us why the European Asteroid Research Network didn't announce this discovery right away? Weren't you worried that you might not get proper credit for it? Especially given the recent leak?'

Loren frowned. 'Everyone who counts knew that it was my discovery. I guess Mackay - the guy in charge of the supercomputer - was desperate for money.'

Wan-Ju Lee's eyes lit up and she glanced down at her notes. 'Many people wonder how it could have been kept secret for so long; considering how difficult it is to prevent hacking. Do you have any comments on that?'

Loren shrugged. 'Not really. I guess you have to suspect that something exists in the first place to figure out where to look. The scientific community is pretty tight lipped when it wants to be.' Her voice trailed off. 'Hacking's not really my area.'

'I believe that Doctor Mackay will be charged and that other possible breaches of intellectual property rights at the Vatican Observatory are being investigated. Were you aware of any problems like this, while you were in Rome?'

'I can't comment. I was only there for a few weeks and then I was transferred to London.'

'That was after your supervisor disappeared?'

'He didn't disappear. As far as I know, he went into retreat. That's not unusual in the priesthood. You might not know that Professor Belboa is also a Jesuit, like my uncle?'

'Yes of course.' Wan-Ju paused. 'But it was you, not Professor Belboa, who contacted EARN about your discovery wasn't it, some two weeks after your work had actually been completed? Have you any idea what happened to the data that you turned over to Professor Belboa, or where the Professor is now?'

'I have no idea. And since NASA and EARN are making the data available now to anyone who wants it, I don't think it really matters.' Loren sat back in her chair and folded her arms across her chest.

'Tough lady,' thought Sally.

'Well, congratulations on your great discovery and thank you, Doctor Wellington.'

Loren nodded and turned away as though someone was speaking to her. Her image on the screen was replaced by the man sitting on Wan-Ju's right. Sally was not surprised that Neil Griffith was no longer smiling.

'What can you tell us about this mission and how it's being funded?'

Neil Griffith's smile returned. 'The big picture is this. The probe sent to confirm Dr. Wellington's findings was adapted from one built by NASA as part of the Mars mission. The Earth 2 mission will not cost taxpayers a cent apart from a very small amount for some additional instrumentation. Everything that NASA and the European Space Agency and so on are providing was already under construction for the Mars Mission. The sponsors are paying for everything else.'

'We understand that there was a problem with the data sent back by the probe?'

'Well, yes; but a lot of the data got through before we lost contact with the probe. And that was a great deal.'

'So, what do we actually know about this planet? How is it different from our own world?'

Neil Griffith's smile widened. 'It's very exciting. When the data started coming through we could hardly believe it. A human stepping onto the surface of Earth 2 would feel quite at home. The gravity, atmosphere, and temperature ranges are almost identical to earth. There are indications of large bodies of water, like our oceans. And most amazingly, the rotation period is almost identical. The main differences are that Earth 2 has not one but two moons, with a total mass slightly larger than our moon. Also Earth 2 is tilted at around 45 degrees on its axis.'

Wan-Ju looked at him questioningly.

'So, the polar ice caps would be situated near Earth 2's equator.' A computer image appeared briefly on the screen, showing a spinning orb, with the north and south poles slanted at a steep angle. Neil Griffith continued. 'And there would be greater variation in temperature between the seasons than we experience here on Earth: because of the tilt.'

Wan-Ju Lee leaned forward again. 'Of course the question which everyone is wondering about is this. Will we find life as we know it on Earth 2?'

'Well, the data did confirm that Earth 2 has the equivalent to our Van Allen belts.'

Wan-Ju Lee raised her eyebrows. 'Which means?'

'That Earth 2 has a similar electromagnetic shield to the one that protects life on earth. Without this, we would all be blasted with solar radiation. So it's likely that the geology of Earth 2 is very similar to our own planet. Since we are on the same orbital plane and the same distance from the sun, that's not so strange.' Neil Griffith paused. 'But it certainly contradicts some of our current theories about gravity, as well as how planets were formed in this solar system ...'

'So Earth 2 might be suitable for human settlement?'

Neil Griffith shrugged. 'It's very hard to say until we get there ...' His voice trailed off.

'Thank you Doctor Griffith.'

'You're welcome.'

Wan-Ju was turning to the African American astronaut. 'Major John Armstrong, you were chosen to command the Mars mission. Tell us a bit about the space craft – the Millennium.'

John Armstrong looked relaxed but his tone was brusque. 'You could say that the Millennium is over engineered for this flight, which minimizes risk. And, of course the antigravity technology, the AGD, reduces the payload required for conventional rocket fuel - which frees up space for accommodation and equipment.'

John Armstrong straightened in his chair and Sally noticed again his strong physique.

'So, in your opinion, safety is not an issue?'

'The Millennium is equipped with two AGD shuttles. Each of these can provide accommodation for the whole crew and in an emergency could even be used to bring the crew home - though it would not be a pleasant trip.' He smiled lightly. 'Even the names we've given the shuttles - Radon and Xenon - were chosen because of their extreme invulnerability. They were built to Mars' specifications. You'd have to land in a volcano to do them any damage.'

Wan-Ju nodded. 'But some people have argued that problems with the antigravity drive are responsible for the probe's disappearance?'

'Not correct. One advantage of current AGD technology is that the drive can function as a deflector shield against collisions with space debris. But the AGD deflection drive was not installed on the probe to Earth 2 due to the probe's configuration and the limited window of time for launching the probe. However, we have used the AGD on more than twenty shuttle flights now without a single incident. You probably know that it's the AGD that's enabled mass tourist access to the space station.'

Wan-Ju Lee pressed the point. 'You can understand the speculation. This whole project has been cloaked in secrecy, even though the lawyers insist that the sponsors will gain no commercial value from the mission.'

John Armstrong's expression remained neutral. 'WorldSecure is hack proof. No doubt other agencies have the same technologies. And you are correct. The United Nations will be the administering body for this mission and all members will have equal access, including media rights. With regards to the secrecy, I understand that the sponsors were planning to announce the discovery within the next few months. JPL and NASA have been working to locate the probe. I assume they were hoping to get further information before this went public.'

'So there's no possibility that the sponsors or some other group have already sent a mission to the planet?'

John Armstrong's composure disappeared. He looked at Wan-Ju in amazement. 'What a ridiculous idea!'

'You must have heard the rumors?'

'I don't listen to wild speculation. There's no agency on earth which could have mounted an expedition of this magnitude in the time available.'

'Thank you Major Armstrong.'

John Armstrong muttered a reply.

Wan-Ju Lee turned back to the camera. 'Finally, we will now try to get Professor Pierre Meyer on the line.' As she spoke the TV screen once again revealed the slightly blurred photograph of a blonde man smiling cheerfully at the camera. Wan-Ju was pressing her earphone and frowning slightly.

'OK, we have voice but no visual. Can you hear me Pierre?'

Sally was surprised to hear the newsreader address Pierre by his first name. Then she remembered that Pierre had been getting more media exposure in the last year or so for his work on the excavation of the ancient Greek city of Helike and the Bronze Age settlements beneath.

There was nothing to prove that the Helike was the lost city of Atlantis, but interest in the site had been revived when Pierre found traces of what he believed was an unknown language on some of the classical Greek pottery. Sally had first seen the strange symbols when Pierre called her and sent pictures of the pottery shards. So far, no one had been able to decipher them.

'Hello Lily. How are you?' Pierre's voice came over loud and clear and Sally couldn't help smiling again.

'I'm fine. How are you Pierre?' Wan-Ju responded warmly to Pierre's use of her pet name. 'Still digging?'

Pierre answered in his charming French accent. 'I think we have taken up everything that is left of Helike and the ruins beneath it.'

'We'd like to ask you your opinion of Earth 2. Do you think that we will find life there and if so, how would we communicate with it?

'I have not much hope that it will be intelligent life. But I surely would like to find out.' There was a short pause and then he continued. 'If you want to know what it would be like trying to talk to intelligent aliens, you should speak to Sally Burns. I understand she is in Geneva at the Earth 2 meeting right now. I'll be there myself next week.'

Sally started back as though Pierre had jumped right out of the TV screen.

Pierre's voice was lost in static and Wan-Ju Lee smiled regretfully. As she started to thank her guests, Sally exited the TV. She stared thoughtfully at the image of snow-covered mountains for a few minutes. She felt a strange sense of relief. Pierre had worked with Lifescape on several projects. If he wanted to go to Earth 2, she wouldn't stand in his way.

3

From the office above the clean room, Ben Sorensen gazed at the image of the setting sun in the glass of the high-rise buildings. Most of the companies in Brisbane's high tech precinct were closed for the weekend, and the office lights had been dimmed or shut off. The smoke from distant bush fires fanned by the strong September winds had transformed the sun into a large red sphere, and its reflections in the darkened glass walls gave the impression that the buildings were floating and vibrating.

Suddenly this spectacle made Ben feel uneasy and he turned abruptly towards the more tranquil view of the Brisbane River. The city skyline only a kilometer away, was a blurred outline in the smoke-darkened twilight. Ben hoped there would be no fires along the freeway to the Sunshine Coast, when he drove home to Caloundra that evening.

'I'll drive back with you, if that's ok.'

Ben swiveled round in his chair. 'That would be great. Fiona hoped you could come.'

'Your mother in law is very sweet.' Victor Steiner was Ben's financial manager and business partner. Having no relatives in Australia, he was pleased that Ben's family made him so welcome.

Ben's watcher buzzed loudly, making him jump.

'They've arrived!' Ben recognized the voice of Brian, one of the two security men in the lobby.

Victor opened the door and followed Ben onto the balcony overlooking the lobby. A large group of armed personnel entered and dispersed quickly to secure the area.

Five men walked in single file up the wide curving stairs to the balcony. The first two wore the distinctive WorldSecure uniforms. The other three were dressed in smart casual trousers and short-sleeved shirts. They were tall and powerfully built, with short, crisp haircuts.

One of the guards stopped about a meter away from Ben and Victor, and after scanning them, announced 'Clear!'

The other three men stepped past him and the tallest smiled. 'Ben Sorensen and Victor Steiner I presume?' He spoke English with a slight accent. When Ben nodded the guard waved a smaller scanner across their faces. 'Confirmed,' he said and took up a position at the top of the stairs.

As Ben led the way into the office, the tall man continued, 'My name is Brown, Jack Brown. Could I please have the CD with the specifications?'

Ben answered: 'I suggest that we complete the identity procedure first. May I have your ID strips?

Ben turned towards the desk and the small ID unit that had been especially provided for this project. He inserted Jack Brown's ID strip together with the ID strip he had been sent via courier, and pressed the 'GO' button. The small screen flashed the message: 'CORRECT MATCH.' He repeated the process for the other two men.

Victor took the CD from his shirt pocket. Jack slid it into a slim plastic sleeve and after a moment nodded. 'The CD readings indicate no changes or copying. This CD is cleared. We'll also require the ID unit.' Ben nodded and handed it over.

'Excellent, and now for the watchers,' said Jack Brown.

Ben led the three men towards the large double glazed window overlooking the clean room below. He pointed down. 'On the left of the door you'll see the strongbox.

Inside are eight cases, four red and four blue. The red cases contain the Level One security watchers.'

Victor stepped forward. 'And here is the swipe card for the strongbox.' He held out the plastic card to Jack Brown. 'You just ...' Victor stopped. For a very brief moment the two men gazed at each other, then Victor turned abruptly away.

Jack Brown smiled blandly. 'We know your layout so we'll take it from here. I assume that you'll have no reason to leave this room.' He gestured to one of the guards. 'If you need anything Fred Carter will be right outside the door.' He gave a faint smile as Fred closed the door behind them.

Ben repressed a feeling of irritation and walked back to the window. Spotlights from the River Festival wavered through the smoky air. The river was dotted with dozens of lights as small boats and ferries crisscrossed the water. After a few moments he went to sit down at the long wide bench by the window overlooking the clean room. He felt uneasy about having armed personnel in the building. His firm had an A1 rating. What had happened to escalate security? Perhaps all the fuss about Earth 2. He thought briefly of his brother in law, and his endless scramble for funding for his research in planetary science. Perhaps Earth 2 would revitalize Alistair's career.

A few minutes later he saw Jack Brown and his two assistants enter the clean room donned in the white outfits. Jack went straight to the strongbox, swiped the card and opened the lid. Ben noticed that Jack positioned himself near the bench with his back to the window, at an angle that would block Ben's view of the installation.

Suddenly several sharp cracking noises rang out. In an instant the door was flung open and Fred Carter rolled into the office and onto his knees covering the room with his gun in swiping motions. Another WS guard, barely visible, covered the office from the door. At that moment the lights went out in the building and Ben could hear the security men running around and calling out to each other. Through the open door he could see red laser beams moving around the walls and ceiling.

He heard Victor call out and turned to see a red dot of light on Victor's forehead. As he turned back toward the door he looked straight into another red beam. Further explosions, like rapid fire followed.

Ben started to speak, but stopped as another loud shot rang out.

'What?' shouted Fred. 'Speak up'

Ben cleared his throat and said more loudly, 'It's just fireworks - the fireworks at the River Festival at Southbank, for the kids, you know.' He gestured towards the window where fireworks were reflected in the glass of the nearby buildings.

Jack Brown's voice came through the intercom: 'Fred, what's happening? Report now!'

Ben activated the intercom and said: 'The explosions are just fireworks ...'

Jack Brown interrupted. 'Fred, report now!'

Fred went to the intercom and shouldered Ben aside. 'The explosions are caused by fireworks, repeat fireworks, there is no apparent danger, repeat, no danger.'

'Understood! Switch the lights back on and return to your stations.'

Brian's urgent voice suddenly rang out over the intercom. 'Garry has been shot in the leg. He's bleeding badly.'

Ben jumped up and ran towards the door. Victor followed but the WS guards barred their way.

Ben swore. 'Garry is one of my staff. Let me through.' He pushed against the guards.

Fred shouldered him aside. 'You two stay where you are. Garry is one of ours.'

'What?'

'Garry is WorldSecure.' Fred smiled and pulled the door shut behind him

Ben was stunned. For a moment he couldn't speak. He banged on the door and shouted. 'I demand to know what's going on!'

He stumbled back as Fred opened the door again. 'OK. Come and have a look.'

Ben and Victor went out onto the balcony and saw Garry on a stretcher near the front door. One of the guards was bandaging his leg.

Brian looked up at them. 'It's not too bad, the bullet missed the bone; just a flesh wound.'

Fred motioned them to return back into the office. Two guards remained outside the door.

Ben started to speak but Victor put his finger over his lips and shook his head. 'Not now.'

As Ben stared in amazement, Victor took a set of playing cards from his desk and sat down at the bench overlooking the clean room. He shuffled the cards and dealt solitaire, his hands moving as quickly and precisely as a professional croupier.

Ben felt his temper rise and paced around the room. How come Victor was so cool about all this? Sometimes he felt that he knew Victor better than his own family. At other times the man seemed a real mystery to him. It was infuriating to think that Garry had been with them for three years and was really working for the WorldSecure. What about the rest of his staff? What about Victor?

He threw himself into a chair and stared out at the city skyline.

'They've finished.' Victor gathered the cards and replaced them on his desk. He glanced at Ben. 'You'd better calm down. We can't afford to offend these people.'

Ben took a deep breath and handed him the note counter. As Victor checked it and set it to Euro currency, Jack Brown and Fred Carter entered, followed by the two assistants.

Fred placed some bundles of notes on the desk. When the counting had finished Victor looked at Ben and said, 'Correct weight.'

Both Ben and Victor signed a receipt for the money. Jack Brown pocketed it, and ignoring Ben's angry expression said in a pleasant voice, 'On behalf of WorldSecure, we thank you for your cooperation. As usual, please insure that no records whatsoever are kept of this transaction' He looked away briefly. 'Also, that the incident with Garry is not mentioned again. I assure you - he will be well looked after.' He paused and added, 'I've already had a word with your other man. There will be no problem there.'

Ben and Victor accompanied them down to the lobby. A guard signaled them to stay inside and they watched in silence as the vehicles disappeared into the hazy night.

Victor ran back up the stairs to the office, but Ben waited until Brian had locked the door. 'Are you OK?' he asked.

'Yeah, I'm all right. And Garry seems OK. They gave me the number for the private hospital where they've taken him. I'll go see him in the morning.' Brian spoke quickly and did not look at him directly.

When Ben entered the office he saw Victor removing his watcher. He placed his right forefinger over his lips and gestured for Ben's watcher. He placed the two watchers in a wave shield box and removed a small oblong box from a cabinet. Ben recognized his company's latest bug detector. He placed the box on a stand in the middle of the room and pressed the start button. They waited in silence as the machine made quick sweeps of the office.

After a few revolutions it stopped and the small screen flashed green.

Victor said, 'OK. We can speak freely now'

'Good,' interrupted Ben. 'Now tell me this. When you handed Jack Brown the card for the strongbox you were going to say something to him, but you seemed to change your mind. What were you going to say?'

Victor looked puzzled. 'I don't know what you mean.'

Ben frowned. 'You started to say something. Then you stopped. You looked like you recognized him.'

Victor shook his head. 'I've never seen him before, and you know me, Ben, I can always put a name to a face.' When Ben did not reply, he continued. 'You have to believe me, especially in view of what I'm going to tell you now.'

Ben was starting to feel sick. He remembered the look on Victor's face as he had handed Jack Brown the swipe card. Why would he lie? He had always trusted Victor. He owed a great deal of his company's success to the man.

Victor didn't seem to notice Ben's hesitation. 'When I was playing cards I noticed that Brown and the others were having a discussion at the assembly desk. I used the override system on the intercom to switch the sound from the microphone down there to my watcher's earpiece. I couldn't hear much of what they said but one thing I'm certain of. It sounded like Hebrew.'

Ben was stunned. 'That's a hell of a thing to say. Are you sure?'

'Absolutely. You know what this means?'

'Of course I bloody know what it means. WorldSecure only uses English or Mandarin.' He paused. 'Have they changed the rules? Have you heard anything?'

Victor shook his head. 'It's a major breach of protocol.'

'Shit! How could they be bona fide WorldSecure and make a mistake like that?' Ben cursed again. 'Half our business is with WorldSecure. If there's been a security breach …' Ben realized he was shouting.

'For god's sake, calm down. We have to think this through.'

'Christ! They could be MOSSAD or anything.' Ben felt his head start to pound. He took a deep breath and tried to speak slowly. 'The eight watchers we handed over today are high security items. But even worse - those top four watchers can communicate now with all current WorldSecure watchers.' He banged his fist on the desk. 'God almighty. You realize don't you, that whoever gets these four watchers can now also access some of the current WorldSecure's scrambling codes?'

Victor did not reply. He went to the fridge and took out two cans of beer. He handed one to Ben, who pressed it against his head and slumped down in the chair.

Victor took a long drink. 'OK. OK. If Brown and any of the others are MOSSAD; well, either they've infiltrated WorldSecure, or they've been introduced on the quiet. Either way, that wouldn't surprise me. There have been rumors for years about a MOSSAD mole in the White House. In any case, for us the question is, what the hell do we do now? If we tell anyone about our suspicions, they could close us down.'

Victor fell silent. Ben rubbed his forehead and drank the rest of the beer. He looked up at Victor, and was surprised at the distress on the other man's face. 'What are we gonna do?'

Victor shook his head. 'Who knows what the hell any of them are up to? It's not really our concern is it? I suggest we do sweet F all. Let sleeping dogs lie.'

4

Alistair Stuart stood on the headland overlooking Moffat Beach. He held his left hand above his eyes to shield them from the sun and gazed out over the ocean. From where he stood there was a magnificent view of the beautiful Caloundra coastline and some of the best surf breaks in the Sunshine Coast. But Alistair's gaze was drawn to the small figures bobbing about in the big swell, some thirty meters from the beach. In his right hand he held a brightly colored patchwork flag on a short pole, and every few moments he raised it and waved it from side to side. His mother had used this flag to signal her children when she wanted them to come home; now he used it to try to attract his brother's attention.

Alistair waved the flag again. One of the distant figures broke away from the others and moved towards the shore. Alistair smiled and started to jog down the gently sloping path towards the beach. A few people he knew paused to exchange Christmas greetings. A very elderly man called out to him, 'Hello young Alistair. How're you going? I didn't think much of your brother's latest film.'

Alistair stopped and shook his hand. 'Well, you can't win them all.'

'Too true. Merry Christmas to you and your family.' The old man continued up the hill.

As he jogged along the beach, Alistair watched his brother's powerful arms driving the surfboard through the water. Jeremy reached the shallows, slipped off the board and waved to Alistair. A sort of sigh went up from the group of girls standing nearby, as Jeremy emerged from the water. Alistair couldn't help grinning as his brother blew a kiss to the girls, reducing them to fits of ecstatic giggles. Jeremy strode past them and throwing his arm around Alistair's shoulder urged him up the beach. They stopped at the cold water shower and Jeremy rinsed the sand and salt water off himself and his board. Alistair stood watching him, and not for the first time thought how amazing it was that they came from the same family.

'We didn't expect you till tomorrow,' commented Jeremy as Alistair handed him a towel.

'I managed to get on an earlier flight,' replied Alistair noncommittally. 'How've you been? I saw the reviews of "Not for Life". They weren't very good. I thought it was terrific.'

'An opinion not shared by our parents.' Jeremy smiled as he toweled himself dry. It was a relief to have a brother like Alistair. Their mother Fiona had only recently retired from an international opera career. Their father, Paul, was a renowned conductor, and their sister Claudia was one of the most popular musical stars in Australia. But Jeremy had eclipsed them all with his success in a string of action movies. His parents and sister were all very good looking but Jeremy was stunningly handsome.

Alistair's looks were at odds with the rest of the family; below average height and sturdy, with sandy receding hair. But his pleasant smile, sly sense of humor and good temper attracted almost as many women as did Jeremy's more spectacular charms. Alistair's career also took him in a completely different direction - the study of the geology of non-terrestrial bodies. In his own field he was almost as well known as Jeremy.

Jeremy chatted about the latest Hollywood gossip as they set off along the beachfront path. As they neared their parents' home he put his hand on his brother's shoulder. 'What's up? Is something wrong?'

Alistair smiled and shook his head. 'There's nothing wrong. I've got some rather spectacular news; really good. Or at least, that's how I hope you'll see it. But I'd like to tell you first.'

'OK. Let's keep walking for a while.' They continued on down the path.

'You know I've been in Geneva a lot over the last few months?' When Jeremy didn't reply, Alistair continued. 'Well, it wasn't really for the university. It was a sort of cover for the Earth 2 mission.'

Alistair glanced at his brother before continuing. 'Anyway, I got a call yesterday. I've been selected. They'll release the news when we are back in Geneva.'

'When are you going?' Jeremy sounded shaken

'Not for a while of course; lift off next November. But I have to go back to Geneva on Tuesday.'

'Is it absolutely certain?'

'Pretty much – they've selected the whole team now, plus backups in case anyone gets sick. There was a bit of a delay for me because they'd already decided on another Australian. You know, the team has to be international.'

'Let's sit down.' Jeremy walked a few feet off the path and dropped down onto the short grass leading to the beach. He leaned forward and stared out to sea.

'What do you think?' Alistair sat down and stared in the same direction.

'Hell! I don't know what to think. Can they keep you safe in Geneva?'

'Security is very tight. They might try to sabotage the mission but there hasn't been any more violence against us personally. I think David Liu's death gave everyone a shock; such a great guy. But you know the man who shot him is mentally ill. He couldn't even remember going to the airport.'

They were silent for a few moments and then Alistair gave Jeremy a nudge. 'Come on Jez. You gotta be happy for me. What a blast, eh?'

Jeremy pushed him back and laughed. 'Of course I am. It's just a helluva shock. So who's the other Australian?'

'She's a linguist – Sally Burns. You might know her. She's made some documentaries.'

Jeremy remembered Sally Burns very well. He had met her at several awards ceremonies. 'I have met her. She doesn't seem the type to get involved in something like this. What's she like; apart from being really stunning?'

Alistair suddenly had a clear memory of Sally Burns' face when Pierre Meyer's death was announced. She had looked shattered. 'The linguist who was first choice died suddenly – an aneurysm apparently. I don't think she really wants to go, but it's hard to tell what she's thinking. She comes over as very charming – but she makes me uneasy. She doesn't seem to take anything seriously. I can't understand why they haven't tried to find someone else.'

Jeremy looked at him and smiled. 'You don't like her, do you? Is it because she uses her looks, and sleeps around?'

'I don't dislike her.' Alistair's tone was defensive. 'It's just hard to work her out. She never talks about her family or any of the usual things women go on about.'

'Not everyone's got a family like ours. She's adopted you know. Her parents are nothing like her. I met them once; country people, quite plain and not super smart.'

Alistair was surprised. 'No, I didn't know that. She's never mentioned it.'

Jeremy got to his feet. 'Speaking of families, we'd better get back and face the music. There's no point putting it off.'

They walked back along the path and climbed the stairs to the verandah of the large wooden house.

The Stuart home had beautiful views of the ocean from the front verandah. Their parents were sitting there on the comfortable cane lounges, with their daughter Claudia and her husband Ben Sorensen. Their two small grandchildren - Emma and Sam - were playing on the floor around them.

Fiona jumped up when she saw her sons, and embraced them warmly. 'Come and have a drink.'

Alistair kissed Fiona and Claudia, waved to the others and sat down. He took a tall glass of sangria from his father and looked at the fruit floating in the pale liquid. The lively discussion of plans for Christmas continued, but he found it hard to join in.

'You're very quiet,' remarked his father.

'Perhaps he's in love,' joked Claudia. 'Again!'

Alistair smiled, but did not reply. He was steeling himself for his announcement. He waited for a pause in the conversation and said quietly, 'I have some news I have to tell you.'

His voice was so serious that everyone fell silent. Even Sam, playing with his toy cars in the corner of the verandah, looked up.

Fiona went quite pale. 'What is it?' she asked. 'Is something wrong?'

Alistair shook his head. 'No, not at all. In a way, it's good news.

Jeremy interrupted. 'It's fantastic news. Let me tell them.'

Alistair nodded. If anyone could persuade them it was ok, Jeremy could.

Finally his mother said, in a voice he had never heard before, 'If you do go, when will you leave? How long will you be away?'

'The departure's scheduled for next November. We take a direct route on the outward trip, stay on the planet for a few months, and then the longer trip back via Venus and Mercury. We'll be away about nine months, no more, if all goes to plan.'

There was a long silence, as this last phrase hung in the air. Finally, Fiona asked 'Are you quite certain you really want to do this?'

'Yes I am,' he replied. 'I still can hardly believe I've been picked.'

'But we'll see you again, won't we, before you leave?' Claudia sounded close to tears.

'I'll get a short break in March, and then we'll be locked up till departure time. Of course there will be the usual farewell functions, but we have to be isolated for the last few weeks - for health and other reasons.' Alistair looked at his family's downcast faces and tried to smile. 'I'll miss you all, but I couldn't bear not to go. You know how bad the funding for my area is now. This might be my last chance to do some real research.'

Ben changed the subject. 'Is that a new watcher?' he asked. His daughter Emma jumped up and exclaimed with delight. 'Look at Uncle Ali's new wotcha!'

Alistair took the watcher off and passed it to Emma. Sam tried to grab it but Ben reached down and took it from her. Claudia frowned at her children.

Ben's company owed its success to a breakthrough he had made several years earlier in the miniaturization of millimeter wave radar devices. The university where he worked had been slow to act on his behalf so he left his academic career in microelectronics to set up a company. A chance meeting with Victor Steiner, a Swiss investment consultant, at a trade fair had provided him with the necessary capital and Victor had stayed on as his business manager. Claudia was sorry he had left academia. As far as she was concerned he spent far too much time at work and she felt nervous of the tight security under which he worked.

Alistair was glad of the distraction. 'Is it one of yours, Ben?'

Ben turned the watcher over. 'It's probably got some of our stuff in it.' He returned the watcher to Alistair. 'So how many people are going?'

'Eight all up,' replied Alistair. 'Five scientists and three flight crew.' He paused. Ben was rubbing his hand across his forehead. 'Are you ok? You look a bit done for.'

Ben stood up. 'Just feeling the heat. I'll get some more ice.' As he returned from the kitchen, a musical chime sounded and Ben looked down at his own watcher. 'It's Victor. He's coming to dinner after all.'

* * *

After the children went to bed, the conversation turned back to Alistair's announcement. He wanted to reassure his family about the safety issues. He understood enough of the flight mechanics to feel very confident. Apart from that, they knew almost as much as him. The controversy over the two years of secrecy and the anonymous sponsors still dominated the headlines and details of the mission were discussed endlessly.

Paul interrupted. 'The question is where are the sponsors getting the money from and what's in it for them? Does anyone really believe we could live on Earth 2?'

As expenditure on global warming and the war on terror soared, government funding for space exploration had ceased. The international space station and the near earth telescopes relied almost entirely on funding from the tourism industry and private investors. The cost of the Earth 2 mission outraged a number of lobby groups who believed the sponsors could put the money to better use.

Alistair shook his head. 'Nothing's certain, Dad. But whatever we discover, it's bound to be worthwhile.'

'It's amazing no one's found out who the sponsors are. I thought you could hack into anything these days.' Claudia looked inquiringly at Ben, but he just shrugged.

Fiona looked uncomfortable and changed the topic again. 'What about the other seven?' she asked. 'What are they like?'

'I haven't met any of the flight crew, though we've had a few vidcons; two Americans and a Russian.'

Ben interrupted him by standing up. 'Victor and I want to go over a couple of things, so he'll be staying over,' he announced.

'Why don't you stay on for Christmas?' Fiona smiled at Victor. 'You look tired. You could do with a break.'

Victor glanced at Ben, who nodded slightly. 'Thank you. I will.' He leaned down and kissed Fiona on the cheek before following Ben.

Alistair noticed that Claudia was frowning as she watched Ben leave. 'Something wrong?'

Claudia shook her head. 'I just wish Ben would relax a bit more. I like Victor but he works Ben too hard. And it's getting worse. The last few months we've hardly seen him.' She paused and shrugged. 'Anyway, go on. Tell us about the others.'

'There's Vicki Law - a marine biologist from Hong Kong, a really nice woman.' Alistair smiled as he remembered the first time he had met Vicki. When she had stood up to make her short introduction, most of the people at the table instinctively glanced at Sally. Vicki was not beautiful, but she was very attractive and had a wonderful style. However, if anyone expected Sally to see Vicki as competition, they were soon disappointed. The two women had immediately become very friendly.

'Also another Australian - a linguist, Sally Burns. She can speak an unbelievable number of languages.'

'So two of the five scientists are women?' Paul sounded surprised.

'And one of the American astronauts,' Alistair added.

'You're so old fashioned.' Claudia smiled at her father. 'Why shouldn't they be?'

Alistair explained. 'The sponsors actually specified at least two men or two women; also different races, religions and so on, including at least one atheist.'

'That's weird! Why would they want that?' Claudia was interested. 'So perhaps one of the reasons you were selected is that you're a strong Roman Catholic.'

'Maybe. I don't know.' Alistair continued; 'They apparently want different aspects of humanity represented, in case we encounter intelligent life. Though that's really unlikely.' No one commented so he went on. 'So there's also a Zoologist - Mohun Patel. He's Indian but grew up in Trinidad: a real easygoing guy. The other guy, Thomas, is a psychologist. He's English but not one of those chatty English types; a bit aloof. He's done a lot of work in negotiation, hostage situations, emergencies and so on. All top secret stuff so none of us had heard of him.' He avoided mentioning that most of them would have preferred David Liu, whose death had cast a gloom over the first weeks of the meeting.

'Who's your medical back up?' Paul asked.

'Thomas, the psychologist, has a medical degree. Also the Russian astronaut was a field medic. We're all getting first aid training and we have unbelievable technology. It's probably not new to you, Ben, but ....' Alistair looked around and then remembered that Ben and Victor had left the room. His family looked back at him. They seemed different somehow, as though everything had changed.

He swallowed, hoping that his face did not reveal his feelings. 'Anyway,' he continued rapidly, 'We'll have these amazing body suits. They've got these tiny ultrasound devices - we call them MUDs - woven into the material. If anything happens to us - even a small change in body temperature – the MUDs alert the rest of the crew.' He could hear his voice speeding up as it did when he became emotional.

Fiona, always in tune with his feelings, got up and came over to where he was sitting. She perched on the arm of the chair and hugged him. 'We're so proud of you.'

Jeremy excused himself. As he passed the guestroom on his way to the toilet, he overheard Victor speaking. Something in the low, urgent voice made him pause.

'We can't tell anyone, especially not now.' There was a short pause. 'Three plus five; that's not the same configuration anyway. It's probably a coincidence. It's been three months and we haven't heard anything. We must be in the clear.'

He heard Ben reply. 'Shit! I hope you're right.'

5

'And this is where we've been living for the last month.' Alistair pulled open the heavy metal door.

His family crowded into the mockup of the Millennium airlock and followed him into the first junction area. His mother looked around and wondered how her son, who had been so hard to keep indoors as a child, could bear being cooped up in such a confined space. They peeped into several of the areas as they passed before Alistair ushered them into the sleeping quarters. Jeremy and Ben ducked their heads to enter the hatch.

Fiona looked at the photos and mementos that her son had displayed above his locker and bunk. She forced her face into a smile. 'Very cozy,' she said in a bright voice.

'It's a bit claustrophobic,' Claudia observed. 'Where are the view ports?'

Alistair smiled at his sister. 'Only in the control module. Would you like to see them?'

'I envy you that,' said Ben. 'A week on the space station, Venus and Mercury! I've always wanted to see the Earth from space.'

Vicki Law and her parents were approaching from the other end of the array of eight bunks so Alistair's family backed out into one of the junction areas. Alistair made a brief introduction and Vicki's parents stared at Jeremy's tall figure as the Stuart family retreated. 'Yes,' Vicki affirmed. 'That is Jeremy Stuart.'

'So handsome,' murmured her mother as Vicki pulled across the screen that separated the two sets of four bunks. 'Not like his brother at all.' She frowned as Vicki pointed out her bunk. 'And where do the men sleep? You don't all sleep together, I hope.' Vicki repressed a retort. Her mother was being hypercritical of everything she saw. Vicki knew that it was a cover for her mother's anxiety but it did not make it any easier for her father, who was starting to look quite morose.

'See how well everything is arranged.' She slid open the bottom drawer of her locker and pulled out the small shrine she had made to the family's ancestors. Her mother's face lit up and Vicki longed to embrace her, but she knew that it would probably provoke another flood of tears.

She was relieved to see Sharon Bright's curly blond head appear through the hatch. Vicki smiled warmly at the American astronaut and her large family, and edged past them towards the exit. Sharon nodded politely to Vicki's parents and gave Vicki a brief hug, raising her eyebrows, as if to say, 'I'll be glad when this is over.'

In the foyer, Alistair was talking to a young woman. As she turned Vicki realized that it was Loren Wellington, the young software engineer who had discovered Earth 2. Vicki looked around. The waiters were setting the tables for an informal lunch. Thomas Beecham, the English psychologist, was talking to a security guard at the door. None of his family or friends had come to this farewell function, and Vicki suddenly realized that she knew almost nothing about his personal life.

The second astronaut, Sima Vaschenko was chatting to Mohun Patel and his family. Sima had been given permission to return to Russia during his father's recent illness, so his own family had not made the trip over for this final farewell. His visit home had not been a happy occasion. The security was now so tight that armed guards had accompanied Sima everywhere he went. Sima smiled warmly at Vicki as she passed, and she felt a quiver of anticipation. He was her opposite in every way; tall, blonde, blue eyed and very reserved. But something about him, the shape of his hands, the economical way that he moved, appealed enormously to her.

Sally Burns was standing next to her adoptive parents - Hilda and David. They seemed to have run out of conversation and made a rather forlorn picture. Sally looked relieved as she saw Vicki and her parents approaching.

'You're looking a bit down,' Vicki whispered to Sally. 'Try to cheer up or you'll put our parents into even more of a spin.' She smiled at Hilda and introduced her parents. The two couples shook hands awkwardly while Vicki tried to think of something to talk about.

The flight commander John Armstrong was deep in conversation with a very tall thin man whom Vicki immediately recognized as Rick Jones. Several other people were also glancing at the American billionaire who had funded the development of the antigravity technology, but who was most famous for his purchase of the infamous Area 51, which he used as his company's headquarters. The amazing speed at which the antigravity drive had been developed had produced a flurry of speculations amongst UFO groups that Rick Jones had found the technology in Area 51, along with all the other alien relics that many people suspected were still hidden there.

Alistair's mother and sister were listening closely to the two men. John Armstrong's family had left the day before, and the farewells had been emotional, but now he looked as he always did – his dark handsome face calm and confident.

'I'm real glad you got the command. They couldn't have picked a better man.' Rick Jones shook his head. 'I still don't see why we couldn't have made it a joint mission.' He sounded wistful but then a smile lit up his long face. 'As soon as I get the word, I'll be hot on your tail.'

John Armstrong slapped Rick's arm. 'I look forward to that. You're lucky you don't have to handle the bureaucratic circus we went through.'

'It's gonna be great.' The two men smiled broadly at each other.

Fiona edged closer. They might feel confident, but every time she thought of Alistair's departure she shook with fear. She steadied her voice. 'Tell us again about the flyers. They look so fragile.'

John looked towards the main door where one of the small flyers stood. Rick Jones nodded politely at Fiona and turned away to speak to Alistair and Loren.

'Would you like me to show you how it works?' John volunteered.

Fiona and Claudia watched apprehensively as John mounted the flyer's square platform and switched on the anti gravity drive. They started back in alarm as the machine rose almost a meter above the floor. The low humming noise faded as the flyer descended gently back down to the floor.

'The AGD technology has really improved. It won't be long before you see these everywhere.' John smiled. 'But of course, they'll just be used for short range transport; we can't get small vehicles to go above 50k without losing maneuverability. We have two flyers - one in each of the shuttles. We've named them Snoopy and Lassie, because they do look a bit like dogs, don't you think?' He ran his hand over the flat solar panel which jutted out at the front of the flyer like a long sharp nose. Another longer panel at the back formed the 'tail', completing the image of a large dog.

The women stared at the flyer and then Claudia asked, 'Do you really believe that there will be no intelligent life on Earth 2?'

'The odds are very low. Of course, it might limit our ability to exploit the planet if we find more than rudimentary life.' John stepped off the flyer. 'I hope not. We haven't managed things very well on our own planet. I'm not sure we're up to managing another world.'

'But, they might be superior to us,' Claudia suggested. 'We might learn from them.'

'That's not likely,' said her husband Ben who had joined them. 'If they were much more advanced than us, they would have discovered us by now.'

'I meant, spiritually or morally superior,' Claudia retorted. John looked surprised but interested and Ben remembered that the commander was a devout member of the Baptist Church. As John started to reply, Ben frowned and turned away. Claudia's mouth tightened.

Alistair could see that an argument was about to develop. Claudia had never really come to terms with Ben's atheism. He took Ben's arm, and introduced him to Loren Wellington and Rick Jones.

'So what happened to that guy in Rome?' Alistair asked Loren

'Apparently he went into retreat. I haven't seen him since.' Loren looked thoughtful. She was still puzzled that Professor Belboa had never contacted her since the night she handed over her data.

'But did it get to court?'

'What?' Loren looked confused and then realized that Alistair was referring to the director of the supercomputer facility. 'I thought you meant my old supervisor, who seems to have disappeared off the face of the earth. But - Mackay - well, he got kicked out of his job of course, and he'll never get another job like that. He pissed off a lot of people besides me.' She grimaced and laughed shortly. 'But why should he care? The newspaper paid him a packet for the information. I've heard he's gone to some place where they can't grab him or his money - the Bahamas or somewhere. What an asshole.'

Alistair almost laughed. He found Loren's direct speech amusing. It was in such contrast to her strong religious beliefs.

'Actually, I've given him a job.'

Loren stared up at Rick Jones. 'Why the hell would you do that? You couldn't trust the guy in a pig's poke!'

Rick Jones smiled disarmingly. 'I know, but in his own way, he's quite brilliant; a pity to waste all that talent. Don't worry; I know how to keep him in order.'

'Well, that's a hell of a thing! The bastard tries to pinch my data and ends up in clover. And here I am scrabbling around for money just to do some simple programming.' Loren's pale face was flushed with anger.

'Simple solution! Come and work for me.' Rick looked down at Loren, his eyes bright. 'I know all about you and your opinions. If you can bear to work in the US, you can start tomorrow. You can do whatever you like.'

Loren's eyes widened. She was about to reply when a bell sounded and one of the waiters announced that lunch was ready.

As the group moved towards the buffet, Fiona Stuart looked around the room. Sharon Bright's younger brothers and sisters were laughing, teasing their sister. Her parents looked calm and unconcerned. Sally's mother was gazing in admiration at Jeremy Stuart as he shared a joke with his beautiful sister. Mohun Patel's large family talked excitedly; the women's bright saris glowed and their jewelry sparkled as they circled Mohun. The atmosphere was cheerful but there was a sharp edge to the scene as though they all knew they were playing out their last few lines and the next act was about to begin. She composed her face and moved towards Alistair.

6

The buzzer sounded the end of the thirty-minute session and Sima Vaschenko stepped off the vibrating platform. Vicki floated through the hatch and pushed her way awkwardly towards him. She handed Sima one of the drink tubes she was holding. He took it and grabbed the guide rail with his other hand. He sucked at the tube and watched as Vicki bent over to strap her feet into the platform's footrests. Vicki was a pretty sight in any position.

'You're not going to drink that, are you?' Sima asked as she raised the tube to her mouth.

The platform was in almost continuous use since nearly all the crew preferred it to the other forms of exercise. Three hours of exercise a day were needed to prevent loss of bone mass. However, only 30 minutes a day of high impact exercise was needed, so most of the crew opted to spend the remainder of the three hours in sessions on the platform. Sharon had put together a small bench top and attached it to the front bar of the platform, with straps to hold down books or small pieces of equipment. However, several bouts of nausea had proved that eating and drinking on the platform was not recommended.

'I've got the stomach of an ox,' replied Vicki and continued to suck from the tube. She rubbed her stomach and smiled provocatively at Sima. 'What are you doing now? Stay here and talk to me.'

'You talk and I'll listen,' replied Sima.

He was very pleased that Vicki had taken a liking to him. He realized that it was probably because Vicki loved to talk and he was a willing listener, but he hoped it was something more. It was hard to tell. Vicki's manner was naturally flirtatious.

Once a week, as their shifts crossed over, he and Vicki got together with Mohun, Alistair and Sally for coffee and a chat. The shift change was usually devoted to the exchange of technical information and a few pleasantries, but every 'Saturday' evening the five of them behaved as though they were sitting in a city café. They had even taken to wearing some item of personal clothing over their body suits. Vicki had brought a small collection of very expensive and beautiful scarves that she wore with great style. Sally had some unusual jewelry, which she had collected on her field trips. Mohun donned a beautiful emerald dhoti, which his mother had tearfully pressed on him at their last meeting and Alistair unfolded his crumpled bushman's hat.

One evening, when Vicki pulled her scarf over across the lower part of her face and shook her head in a girlish way at Mohun, Sima was astonished to feel something like jealousy. He felt stupidly relieved when Mohun grabbed the scarf and holding it in both hands above his head, sang out: 'When I marry, it will be a young girl, pale and beautiful. Let her know nothing, the better to appreciate me.' Sally and Vicki responded by ridiculing his marriage prospects, while Sima digested the idea that he was becoming very attached to Vicki.

Sharon laughed at their antics but Thomas and John looked on in amazement. Sima could understand John's aloofness as commander. Thomas was another matter. He rarely socialized, worked continuously; endlessly checking the crew's biorhythms, monitoring the complicated system of lighting and ambient sounds which mimicked the 24 hour earth day. He showed no insight into the crew's emotional states. Mohun and Sally had been severely disoriented for several days as they watched the Earth recede but Thomas had done nothing to help them. Sima wondered if Thomas was more suited to the emergency situations which he had dealt with on Earth. He seemed to expect trouble, to be surprised that the crew lived together so harmoniously despite the tedium of the uneventful days.

Anyway, Sima was very pleased that he and Vicki shared the same shift with Thomas and John. He had no competition there! He was her only source of entertainment and had her all to himself. While they were in space it would be awkward to take it any further, but once they were on the ground!

He smiled again and flipped open his data pad. Vicki didn't look offended. She knew that Sima could work and listen to her at the same time. He accessed the automatic translation program, which Sally had loaded onto his data pad and touched the screen to record what Vicki was saying. He touched an icon and the software translated Vicki's vivacious talk first into Cantonese and then into Russian. It was very fast and easy to use but he wondered how much help it would be if they encountered a completely new way of communicating. The important thing was to enter as much data as possible about what was going on at the same time. He input 'joke' as Vicki made a remark about the platform and was impressed when the pad displayed several alternative translations.

He had a talent for languages. In his undergraduate years he had studied several ancient languages, Greek, Latin and Norse, just for enjoyment and he was fluent in several modern languages. But he envied Sally's ability to pick up a new language almost overnight. When he asked her to describe her technique, she had replied that she didn't really know how she did it and couldn't relate it to anything she had studied. Her approach was to try to absorb as much as possible as quickly as possible and then try to relax and go on to a sort of 'automatic pilot.'

'You know,' Sally said, 'how some people speak a new language better when they are a bit drunk? Like it sort of breaks down your inhibitions and lets your mind work freely? Well, that's how it works for me. If I think too hard about it, I just slow down.'

Sima suddenly recalled a conference he had attended several years ago. A professor from New Zealand, a Maori linguist, had discussed that very topic. He scanned quickly through his data pad. He was sure that he had a copy of the conference papers.

Vicki was chatting about a conversation with Sharon, but for once, Sima did not pay attention. He was looking at a photo, taken almost ten years before, which he had forgotten about. It showed a large group of conference delegates and their partners, standing on a grassy lawn at the University of Auckland. He remembered the occasion well. The photo had been taken only three weeks before his wife had been killed in a traffic accident. He used the zoom button and saw his face in the front row. His wife's postgraduate supervisor was standing next to him, smiling widely, his arm flung around Sima's shoulders. However, his wife was nowhere nearby.

He scanned the photo; his heart beating faster again, he zoomed in on his wife's face in the back row. Sasha's image gave him a shock. In the year after her death he had looked at all of their photos and videos over and over again, until he felt he knew every detail by heart. But here was a new view of her, familiar yet strange; a young woman he had not seen for almost ten years. She was smiling, her head turned slightly to the left as though she were listening to the person next to her.

Sima gazed at the photo and bookmarked it so he could find it again. He moved the zoom away from his wife's face. He recognized the woman to Sasha's left as the author of the paper on language learning he had been looking for; a Maori woman with an intense, frowning expression on her handsome face. The tall blonde man next to her was looking away from the camera. Something about the couple's faces made Sima zoom in for a closer look.

'That's odd!' he exclaimed. He stared at the photo. After a few moments he released his harness and grabbed the handrail. Vicki was swaying to some music, her eyes closed. He touched her on the shoulder. 'Won't be long,' he said. 'I just want to talk to Thomas about something.'

'Are you all right?' she asked. 'You look a bit pale.'

'I'm fine, but I've just thought of something really strange. I want to check it with Thomas. Nothing to do with the mission,' he continued as she looked alarmed. 'Just something that happened a while ago, which I can't quite figure out. I'll be back soon.'

Vicki nodded and pulled her headphones on. She closed her eyes as she thought about the last time she had heard this song. She and Sally had danced for hours at the hotel nightclub on one of their few free evenings in Geneva. She smiled as she remembered Sima watching her dance.

Someone touched her shoulder and she opened her eyes again. John was frowning at her so she turned off the music.

'Sima's sick. I just found him in the toilet. Thomas has given him a shot to stop him vomiting.' He looked at the drink tube in Vicki's hand. 'You shouldn't eat or drink on that machine, you know,' he said sternly. 'Did Sima eat anything while he was on it?'

'No, he's a good boy,' joked Vicki. 'Anyway, it's never hurt me. I do it all the time.'

'It's not funny. He's really sick. Do you know what he was doing when he left here?'

Vicki remembered that Sima had looked pale and told John so.

'Well, just take extra care and if you feel unwell, call Thomas straight away. We don't want this thing spreading. Sima's MUDs didn't register anything, which is a matter of real concern. I want everyone to check their suits again.'

'Perhaps it was space sickness,' Vicki said. 'Those little guys never pick that up.'

'Yes, but Sima's never been space sick before; and anyway, he'd be sure to recognize the symptoms. Thomas thinks its food poisoning. He's doing some tests now. We should get the results soon. Have you tested your MUDs today?'

The crew were meant to check their body suits every morning to ensure that the little miniaturized optical and ultrasound devices were working OK. Even small changes to the crew's physical well being would be communicated to the ship's computer. In an emergency the MUDs would automatically seal a wound or ruptured artery.

Vicki was glad that she could answer yes. She could see that John was worried.

That evening during the shift changeover they crowded around Sima's bunk. He was feeling better and was puzzled about what had made him sick. Thomas had identified the guilty bacteria but was not sure how Sima had been exposed or why it had not shown up on the MUDs. Vicki and John had spent the 'afternoon' disinfecting, under Thomas's guidance. No one else had shown any of the same symptoms so they assumed that whatever had upset Sima had been eliminated.

'Did you find out what you were looking for?' When Sima looked puzzled, Vicki continued. 'You know, you were going to see Thomas about something. You looked a bit upset. Is everything OK?'

'I don't remember. What did I say?'

'Nothing really. You were looking at your data pad and you saw something you wanted to ask Thomas about. You said it was really strange.'

'I don't remember,' said Sima. He looked at Vicki and Sally and frowned.

He took his data pad off the shelf and fingered the reminder icon. He could not see anything on the list of items that he would need to discuss with Thomas. He touched the bookmark icon. He had not tagged anything during the last shift. He handed Vicki the pad and she replaced it on the shelf.

'I don't remember,' he repeated in a tired voice. 'I guess it was not important.' He closed his eyes and they left him to sleep.

7

Mohun clapped his hands over his ears as Sharon advanced towards him, singing loudly.

'Ding dong merrily on high,' she caroled and Mohun groaned loudly. Singing was not Sharon's greatest talent.

Sharon laughed, pulled his hands away from his ears and attempted a short twirling dance. Despite the low gravity in this area of the ship, it was not a success and they became tangled in Mohun's mesh hammock. He had installed it in the hydroponics bay and often preferred it to his bunk. He liked to swing gently in front of the array of greenery that he had been cultivating for the last two months.

As Sharon tried to free herself, Mohun decided to take the chance for a little romancing. He kissed her hard but briefly on the mouth and tipped her out of the hammock. 'Have no fear, fair maiden. I release you.'

Sharon laughed and bounced down to the floor and up again. She knew he was only joking but she wondered if he realized how darned attractive he was, even after weeks of very close contact.

The short-radius centrifuge mechanism in the hydroponics area produced only about twenty percent of the earth's gravity, but that would increase as they neared their destination. The crew were meant to spend at least one hour a day there but only Mohun could easily tolerate the change from weightlessness and back again. Mostly the others came to the bay for the sight of the bright green leaves poking their way up through the hydroponics material.

Mohun smiled and waited. He could see that Sharon had something on her mind and that she was trying to soften him up. She had acted this way a few times before – a couple of minutes of flirtation followed by a serious discussion. He was surprised that she was so interested in his opinion.

'Can I ask you something?'

Here it comes, thought Mohun. He nodded and settled back into the hammock.

'Do you think there's something wrong with the way I handle Sally?'

Mohun thought for a few seconds, although he could have answered straight away. He knew what Sharon was referring to. She had been trying to get Sally to take her technical training more seriously but Sally was acting stubborn. She did enough work to pass each test but then demonstrated clearly within a couple of days that she had forgotten most of what she had learned.

'I just can't understand her attitude.'

Mohun frowned. He really liked Sally, but Sharon was right. Sally was being unreasonable. 'I don't think it's anything to do with you. Perhaps you should discuss it with John.'

'I have. I've asked whether it would be better if we changed shifts so that he or Sima could take over Sally's training,' replied Sharon. 'John said he'd give me his decision by tomorrow. I just wondered what you thought. I've done this sort of thing a million times before.'

'But not with civilians.'

'I guess. Still, I don't think I've had any problems with the rest of you.'

'Not at all. You are always quite charming, as well you know,' said Mohun flirtatiously. 'I hope you don't change shifts with Sally. I'll miss you.'

Sharon tried to frown but failed.

Mohun changed the subject. Whenever Sharon looked even slightly angry he was reminded that she was an experienced combat officer. He had always found this combination of sweetness and ruthlessness quite irresistible in women. 'So have you decided what you're going to say tomorrow?'

'What?' Sharon was fascinated by the rapidly changing emotions passing over the handsome face. What on earth was he thinking about?

'What are you going to say in your Christmas message?' repeated Mohun.

In a few hours they would receive and send their final messages before they traveled out of communications range, behind the sun. They would then lose direct contact with home for at least three months, depending on how long they decided to stay on Earth 2.

'Oh. That was pretty much decided for us before we left. They got a speechwriter in and put together some inspirational stuff for us. You know - for the general public. And then, "love you, miss you, looking forward to the challenge, nothing to worry about," for our folks. That'll pretty much wrap it up for us.' Sharon looked at him. 'What are you going to say?'

'I don't have a clue,' admitted Mohun. 'I think I'll wait and see what my family says and just wing it.'

Sharon moved over to him and put her arm around his shoulders. She remembered his family very well from the farewell celebration, although there had been so many of them she could not now recall all their names. She bit her lip now, as she remembered her own mother squeezing her hand tightly at the farewell dinner. Her parents had never once complained to her about the anxiety she had caused them by her choice of career. Unlike John Armstrong, there was no military tradition in Sharon's family, and her family had been astonished when she had told them she was applying to join the US Air Force.

For a long time she had felt guilty for causing her parents so much anxiety. They had told her often how proud they were of her but she had not really believed them. Finally she realized it was true. They accepted that she was different. That was one advantage of coming from a large family, she thought. Her older brother and sister gave her parents support and the younger trio provided the usual distractions of teenage problems. It allowed her to make her own choices in a way that might be harder in a smaller family. She felt sorry for Vicki, being an only child of anxious parents. Mohun and she were both lucky in that way. She wondered if her family knew how much she appreciated them. She had a sudden idea.

'Just tell them how proud you are to be their son.'

Mohun looked at Sharon, surprised. She was right. That was all he needed to say. He hugged her gratefully but did not look at her again. He was experiencing a strong emotion that he could not quite identify.

'We probably should compare notes anyway,' continued Sharon. 'It would be a bit hard to go last and find that everyone has already said everything you wanted to say. Perhaps we could …'

She was interrupted by a loud wailing noise. The alarm broke into short bursts and increased in volume.

Mohun launched himself towards the hatch and hit the button to open it. Sharon was close behind and she took the lead, hauling herself along the guide rails. Mohun felt the sweat starting to drip down his face as he tried to keep up with the figure swinging ahead of him. As they wrestled into one of the junction areas they almost collided with Sally. She looked at them in alarm.

'First level emergency,' shouted Sharon. She disappeared down the ladder to the next level and Mohun ushered Sally ahead of him. When he reached the radiation cellar he saw the others pulling on their protective suits. John pushed Mohun and Sally inside, reached up to turn off the alarm. Mohun grabbed one of the suits. His heart was pounding.

'This is not a drill. I repeat this is not a drill. We are moving into a solar storm.' John's voice was urgent and Mohun's heart sank.

John pulled the heavily shielded door shut, secured it and pushed a large red button which would activate the magnetic field around the cellar. 'Well,' he said more lightly, 'at least we know the alarm works.' Everyone glanced at the radiation meter above the door, which showed the level of solar radiation outside the cellar. The needle was on zero. The early warning system had alerted them in good time.

Several small beeps sounded as the crew pressed the electronic panels on their suits. The suits were lined with the same polyethylene fiber that helped to shield the cellar. Whether they were really needed depended on the intensity of the solar flare, but they had no way of predicting that.

'Move it!' shouted John. The needle on the meter was starting to rise.

The soles on the boots of their protective suits were magnetized which made it easier to move around in zero gravity. But the cellar only just held eight people sitting and for a few moments the air was filled with heavy breathing and grunts, elbows and legs colliding as they struggled to put on the heavy suits. Sally fumbled as she checked the back of Alistair's helmet. He turned around and looked into her startled face. He tried to smile reassuringly as he pressed the electronic panel, first on her suit and then on his. Next to them, Sima was helping Vicki.

A loud, sharp buzzing noise sounded and they all looked around in alarm. Sally looked down at the small red light flashing on the front of her suit. The blood drained from her face. She couldn't move. Alistair pressed the reset button on her suit panel. The buzzer sounded again and the red light flashed back on. There was no mistake. Her suit was defective. She instinctively looked up at John.

'Sima! Sally!' shouted John through the helmet intercom. 'Unsuit, now! Sima, take Sally's suit!'

'What?' Sally couldn't understand what John meant but she saw Vicki staring at her, her mouth wide with horror. Sima gave a shrugging movement and slid the visor of his helmet up. Vicki did not move to help him and John reached out to release the back of Sima's helmet.

Sima looked away from Sally as he started to pull off his helmet. Behind him Sally saw the others, their expressions a mixture of dismay and disbelief. Only John and Thomas appeared calm. For a moment, Sally's mind went blank. Then she understood what was happening. Sima had been ordered to exchange suits with her. She heard John shouting but time seemed to slow down and she couldn't catch what he said. Everyone appeared to Sally as though they were moving at half speed. Sima's hand floated towards her. She looked down again. The red light was still flashing on her suit. It speeded up again, time returned to normal and she found herself not loosening her helmet, but securing it.

She heard herself say, 'I can't do that.'

'Unsuit now, Sally. That's an order!' John's voice was harsh.

'It's all right, Sally. I know the procedure.' Sima's voice sounded strange but steady as he reached out towards her, but Sally backed away. She looked up at the meter above the door. The needle was rising slowly but steadily. 'It's too late,' she said. 'There isn't time.'

'Shit!' John cursed. 'Sima, helmet on now!'

Sima gave Sally a steady look and pulled his helmet back on. Sally could hear Vicki gasping as Alistair pulled her back to one of the benches against the wall. She sat down. She could not look at any of the others. She watched the meter over the door as the needle rose from zero and slowly climbed. It suddenly flashed up to the red zone. The solar storm had hit with full force.

They sat in an eerie silence, broken only by their heavy breathing and the occasional clicking noise as someone moved slightly. Every few moments, someone seemed to catch their breath as though trying to keep from choking. It was strange to feel such a sense of danger with no visible sign of any threat, except for the needle on the meter. There was no noise, but they could imagine the cloud of protons racing through the Millennium like miniature bombs.

More like time bombs, Sally thought and suddenly felt sick with fear. She knew what would happen if any of them were exposed to high levels of radiation; a rapid decline in muscle coordination, memory and reasoning, or if you were lucky, months of medication and anxious waiting for signs of tumors. Sally felt something, and looking down saw that Alistair had placed his huge gloved hand over hers. She couldn't look at him.

'OK.' Sharon's voice came over the intercom. 'We don't know how long this will last. We can't leave this room until the radiation level outside drops back to zero. That may take only a few hours or it may take several days. As you know, you have some comfort facilities in your suit, sufficient for three days of normal use or up to a week if rationed.'

Alistair wondered if Sharon was going to mention the second meter that showed the radiation level inside the cellar. He noticed some of the crew looking in that direction but he couldn't bear to look.

'We need to continue exercising while we're in here. Cramped muscles are really unpleasant in these suits. I suggest you stand up and flex your muscles at least once every hour. I'll remind you.' Sharon's voice was level and unemotional.

Sally heard everything Sharon said as clearly as if it were written on the front of her helmet. She could not speak – she was still amazed at what she had just done. The image of Vicki's stricken face was fixed in her mind. Was that why she had backed away when Sima was prepared to take her defective suit? She didn't know. Images of people and places flashed though her mind. She thought this must be what it was like to die. The future was blank.

She suddenly thought of her parents. Until she had been assigned to the Earth 2 crew, she had lived as she pleased. Hilda and David were too reserved to make many demands on her. She had never bothered to think how they might really feel about her joining this mission. Like the rest of the crew, she was driven by the need to know, the need to excel. Unlike them, that was all there was to her life. She was constantly seeking new experiences, but nothing lasted. She was never satisfied.

She looked up, straight into Vicki's eyes, sitting opposite her. The usually cheerful face was distorted by crying. Sally smiled at her and Vicki tried to smile back. An idea entered Sally's mind like a beam of light. She could change. She was in the company of seven of the most interesting and brave people she had ever met. Until now she had never really thought of them as a team, committed to each other's survival as well as to the success of the expedition. She had seen them as individuals, some likable, some annoying. Vicki's distress and Sima's instant response to John's command, his willingness to risk his life, was astonishing to her. She felt that she had learned more in the last few minutes than all the years before. Even if she got no further, it had been worth it. She took a deep breath.

'Sorry for the dramatics, gang,' she said lightly. 'If something goes wrong, make sure I'm a good looking corpse.'

Several of the crew laughed, glad to hear her voice. Alistair touched her hand once more.

'We're not your gang and you'll wish you were a corpse if you ever disregard an order again.' John was trying to conceal his anger. 'Let's get something straight, all of you. What just happened could happen again. Next time I expect you to do as I order immediately. Is that understood?'

There was a chorus of agreement.

'I'm willing to overlook what Sally did, because most of you are inexperienced. That's why we have drills. Perhaps you'll all take them more seriously from now on. You must have figured out that we have plans for almost any contingency. And now you know. There's an attrition order on this ship. If someone has to be sacrificed, I know what has to be done and I will do it. Next time it might not be Sima. It will depend on the situation. I don't want to have to say this again and I don't need to explain myself to you. When you joined this crew, you accepted the line of command. The next person who disobeys a direct order from Sharon, Sima or me will spend the rest of the trip in the brig.'

There was a long silence. Sally felt ashamed. She decided she would apologize to Sharon and John and work as hard as she could. She could not stand to endanger another crew member. That is, she thought, if she got the chance. She felt a cold stab of fear again as the adrenaline ebbed away. She leaned forward and looked towards the smaller meter at the other end of the cellar. The reading was zero. She had to stay calm. She breathed deeply. But it was no use. The fear rose up and overwhelmed her and she had trouble staying seated.

She felt a sudden pressure in her bladder and the canister between her thighs became warm. Oh shit, she thought, I hope we're not in here long enough for me to have to drink that! She suddenly felt very tired. She closed her eyes and almost immediately fell asleep.

Sharon's voice woke her. She started, dazed for a moment, then looked with dread towards the internal meter. The needle had not moved. She felt sick with relief.

'So far, so good. I think we've been lucky this time. It must have been a small flare.' Sharon's voice was brittle with tension.

Most of the helmeted heads turned towards the door. The meter showed that the radiation level in the spacecraft had dropped below the danger level.

'Don't get your hopes up. It will take several hours for the radiation to drop back to normal.'

John had shifted to the other end of the room and was hunched over the small communications console. 'We should send our messages while we've got the chance. We may not get out of here before we lose contact. I'm afraid I can't give you much privacy.'

The two rows of helmeted heads made nodding movements.

'OK then. I'll play back the messages from the Consortium and the bits from Earth Control that aren't just technical stuff. There's a heap of data come through.

Basically there are no surprises except that they obviously missed this solar flare. That confirms that it was a quite minor event but it's comforting to know that our alarm system picked it up anyway. More importantly we have to work out how that suit became defective; it was checked last week.' John turned back to the console.

They listened as the voices of senior officials from ground control and the Earth 2 consortium each took turns to express their best wishes and confidence in the crew. It appeared that the United Nations had still not agreed on the name for the planet. The two moons had been officially named Selenis and Artemis but the crew were at liberty to name any of the other features from an approved list.

The first three personal messages were in English. As they spoke, the crew could imagine the families gathered together, trying to compress all they wanted to say in the three minutes allowed for each message. John's and Sharon's parents spoke of their pride, their voices trembling with repressed emotion. The sharp New York accent was followed by the Illinois drawl and then Thomas's mother's voice could be heard, her upper class English accent cold and clear.

Sally was surprised. Thomas never spoke about his family and she had sometimes wondered if his parents were still alive. Neither had appeared at any of the functions and she had not thought to ask where they were. Mrs. Beecham sounded stilted and unemotional as though she were having difficulty believing that she was talking to her son. She mentioned how proud his deceased father would have been, and finished by saying firmly, 'Good luck my boy. Whatever happens, I know you will do your duty.'

Sally looked towards Thomas but his face was turned away.

Mohun's family spoke to him in Konkani. He glanced at Sally and she signaled to him that she was turning her intercom down. It was natural for Mohun's family to assume that no one else would understand what they were saying and that they could speak accordingly.

Most of them recognized the next voice. It was Jeremy Stuart. The actor managed to convey more feeling in his summary of the family news than any of the other speakers. But that was his job, thought Sally. Each of the Stuart family spoke briefly, their emotions occasionally breaking through their well-modulated voices. Two small children spoke in excited voices and asked for bits of rocks to be brought home as souvenirs. The crew joined Alistair's laughter. Sally squeezed his hand and leaned forward to check the internal meter again. Still zero. The needle on the external meter had not shifted. It was just below the extreme danger level.

When Sally heard Vicki's father start to speak in Cantonese, she turned her intercom down again and noticed that Sima did too. A few minutes later, John signaled to her and she turned the dial up to hear her family being introduced. Her mother's first few words embarrassed her.

'It's Hilda and David Burns here. Hello Sally. Well, we hope that this finds you well, dear. We are all well here, though your father has had a bad flu.'

It was just as if she was speaking on the phone. Sally hoped violently that her mother would not continue like this for the rest of the message.

'Don't worry about us, my dear,' Hilda Burns continued. 'We couldn't be prouder.' She paused. 'And we know you'll be all right. You always know what to do. You always did. You were such a clever little thing; right from the word go. You just need to believe in yourself. Just follow your heart.'

Sally was astonished. Her mother had never spoken in this way before. She heard a rustling noise and then her father spoke. 'That's right, Sally. Don't let anyone tell you what to do. You just do what you think is best and we know you'll be fine.'

David fell silent and Sally thought that the transmission had been cut off; but he suddenly said, 'well, that's all right then. There doesn't seem much else to say. You take care of yourself and remember how much we love you. Goodbye for now.'

Hilda echoed her husband's farewell and a signal indicated that their message was finished.

'Well,' said Alistair, 'now we know where she gets it from.'

A few people laughed and Sharon said, 'what a sweetie your mother is, Sally.'

Sally was grateful and she tried to smile at both of them. She hardly noticed Sima's parents speaking. What an extraordinary message for her parents to send!

The crew made their replies in much the same order as they had received them. John started by mentioning in a light tone that they were all in the radiation cellar. He continued that this was nothing to be alarmed about but it might affect the quality of their transmission. Several of the crew were pleased that he had mentioned this. Despite their best efforts many of them sounded tense. Mohun's voice cracked several times and Vicki spoke as though she were having difficulty catching her breath.

Alistair finished his message by saying, 'Well, Jeremy, here we are at the Pillars of Hercules, at the boundary of human knowledge, heading towards the world behind the sun. But unlike Ulysses, it looks like it will all be plain sailing for us. I do believe we will find something wonderful out there. So have a beer for us all, down at the Irish pub. Here's to all explorers and here's to Loren and all of you for helping us to make this journey.'

He raised his arm awkwardly as though holding up a glass. There were a few laughs and some rousing cheers, before Alistair's transmission ended.

During the replies Sally had been wondering how to respond to her parents, but Alistair's message had given her an idea. When she was very young she had often sat with her adopted father after the evening meal while he read to her from his favorite 19th Century English poets – Tennyson and Stevenson. He had been immensely proud of the way she could memorize long passages with almost no effort. As she grew up she had decided that the poems were hackneyed and trite and had pleaded homework as an excuse to go to her room. David had never reproached her and had continued to read alone.

When John signaled her, she thanked her parents for their message. 'Perhaps you'll remember this, Dad. Maybe it was you who started me on all this.'

Her voice softened as she remembered how David would sit, his thumb marking the place in his much loved anthology, while she recited his favorite verses. "For always roaming with a hungry heart, much have I seen and known – cities of men, and manners, climates, councils, governments. I am part of all that I have met." For a moment she could not recall the next lines. "Yearning in desire, to follow knowledge like a sinking star, beyond the utmost bound of human thought. 'Tis not too late to seek a newer world. It may be we shall touch the Happy Isles. We are strong in will, to strive, to seek, to find and not to yield."

She could imagine David looking up the anthology and shaking his head at the liberties she had taken with the poem. But right now, it was all she could remember of Tennyson's "Ulysses". She hoped it would please them.

She echoed her parents' final words. 'I love you both. Goodbye for now.'

She was almost in tears as she heard John make some concluding remarks, finishing with 'That's all for now. I'm following this message with our final data transmission.'

The word 'final' hung in the air. John raised his hand to indicate that the transmission was completed and then turned back to the console. For a few moments no one spoke. Then Alistair said lightly, 'Well, this is a great way to spend Christmas Eve. What I wouldn't give for a beer!'

8

The descent was more frightening than Sally could have imagined. Taking off from Earth had been a slow, leisurely ascent and she had felt that if the shuttle should fail, they would fall gently and safely back to earth. She had known that it was an illusion but Sally had realized long ago, that when it came to fear, perception was everything.

Radon had shot out of the Millennium like a champagne cork. There had been a few moments of eerie silence and then the roar of the shuttle's AGD had risen to a shriek as they entered the planet's atmosphere. Now Radon pitched, yawed and plummeted, as Sima compensated for the unpredictable movements of the craft. Vicki's face was rigid with surprise. Sharon and Thomas looked unconcerned. Sally wished she had paid more attention to the simulations. Perhaps it was always like this.

The shuttle shuddered again after a long free fall, and rose sickeningly. Alistair turned from the porthole and made a triumphant sign – 'A OK.' His face was alight with excitement; he mouthed some words and gestured towards the porthole. Sally did not dare look. The planet's surface heaved in and out of view as the shuttle rose and fell like a ship in a tropical storm.

Just as Sally thought she might scream from nervous tension, the noise from the AGD died down slightly and the shuttle seemed to be floating rather than descending. The gyros suddenly cut out, replaced by a sinister silence. Then there were several small explosive noises from the maneuvering rockets and the shuttle started to fall again.

'Almost there,' Sima called. 'On course for a smooth, smooth landing.' The falling movement slowed to a drift; several small jolts, a loud whining noise followed by a series of gentle bumps. Sally gripped the arms of her seat and steeled herself but nothing happened.

'Congratulations Sima. That was wonderful.' Sharon's voice was steady.

Sally stared out the porthole. When they first sighted the planet, they could clearly see the equatorial ice belt and the vast ocean which separated it from the southern continent, but the Northern hemisphere had been blanketed by thick cloud and strong winds. Two probes had been sent beneath the cloud cover; both had malfunctioned. They had deployed three geostationary satellites and analysis of the imaging data showed that the northern and southern hemispheres were almost mirror images; a large landmass similar to the southern continent surrounded the north pole. Beyond that the northern sea stretched unbroken to the ice belt, apart from a scattering of islands near the main landmass.

The northern continent was much more interesting geologically; mountain ranges, canyons and most importantly rivers and lakes. But the turbulent weather persisted in the north so the southern continent was chosen for the first landing point. From their orbit around the planet, they had seen what appeared to be a featureless plain. Now it spread out before them - a flat, dark, dull surface, pitted with small holes and shallow depressions. To right and left, small sections of the rocky land formed shallow stairs before the land flattened off again. Sally gazed through the porthole. Something glinted in the distance, but there was no sign of water nearby. Nothing reflected off the surface of the rock.

'We thought we shouldn't land too near the ocean,' Alistair reminded them. 'With two moons, the tides will be quite different from what we're used to.' His face, like Vicki's was alight with expectation.

Thomas was making some entries in his data pad. 'Amazing.' He passed the pad to Sharon. 'I've checked the figures and you're right. 'The atmosphere is almost exactly the same. About point five percent more oxygen, fractionally less argon. It's extraordinary.'

'And no additional elements. Just as the probe showed. Looks like we're in the clear.'

'As far as we can see,' Thomas added. 'I think we should use the filters anyway.'

'Naturally,' said Sharon briskly as though annoyed that Thomas felt he needed to remind her. 'There may be wind borne elements, pollens, etcetera.'

'No sign of anything like that around here. Look at the sky. It's just like Sydney in the winter. Not a cloud in sight.' The sky was a perfect eggshell blue. It was difficult to believe they were on another planet except that the sky was so clear. Sally had never seen anything like it, even in remote areas of Australia or Africa.

Sima had finished his checks. He unbuckled himself and stood up. Like Alistair, he was grinning like a schoolboy. He reached below his seat and brought out a square black case. 'Will you do the honors, ma'am?'

Sharon took the case, her face reddened with excitement. She pulled her mask up so that it covered her face and ears and gestured to the others to do the same. Sally pulled on her mask and could feel the sweat dripping down the back of her neck. Her mind was clear but the scene still seemed unreal. She thought she should feel triumphant but instead she felt as though she might faint. She leant against the cabin wall to steady herself and breathed deeply. Sima pressed a number of switches next to the airlock hatch and Sally watched carefully, glad that she could remember clearly the function of each.

Sharon and Sima entered the airlock and the door slid shut behind them. A few moments later it opened again and the remainder of the crew joined them. The two shuttles had been originally designed for use on Mars and the large airlock had been built to accommodate the enormous space suits required for the Mars environment. Now the space was piled high with equipment leaving just enough room for the crew to exit. Some of the safety features had been disengaged although they could be operated manually if required. The crew could exit from the shuttle in a matter of moments.

A light flashed above the outer door. It opened automatically and the exit ramp slid into position. Sima stood to one side and Sharon disappeared through the opening. Sima followed but stopped at the top of the ramp so that Sharon clearly was the first person to put her foot on to the planet's surface. Then he too disappeared. Alistair and Thomas stood back for Sally and Vicki to go before them.

Sally was overwhelmed when it was her turn to exit. She checked that her video harness was steady and switched the camera on to record. Her knees felt weak and she stumbled forward, bumping into Vicki. She did not look around until she was standing on the ground; again she felt a fainting sensation. Vicki pulled her gently away from the bottom of the ramp.

The scene was much as it had been from the window of the cockpit, but Sally no longer felt disappointed. Selenis hung high in the sky; an astonishing large pale circle.

Further west the smaller darker disc of Artemis could be seen. They had seen the two moons clearly from the ship but seeing them here from the surface, Sally felt stunned. She had never quite believed it but now there could be no denying. They were the first humans to step onto this alien world. Her breath rose in her throat until she thought she would choke.

She wondered dazedly whether the others were feeling the same way. No one had spoken and the masks concealed their expressions, but their body language spoke volumes. Vicki lifted her hands to her face and then to her head. She turned around and around as though she could not believe what she was seeing. Thomas had wandered away and was staring out towards the ocean. Sharon was standing with her head bowed, as though in prayer. Sima was walking rapidly from one end of Radon to the other as though trying to take it all in. Alistair was on his knees fingering the dark rock. For some reason Sally started to laugh.

Her joyful voice seemed to break the tension. They all spontaneously rushed towards each other and embraced in an awkward hug. Even Thomas walked back over to them and stood at the edge of the group, murmuring congratulations.

'Damn!' said Sharon. 'How the hell do you blow your nose with these things on?' She sniffed noisily and bent down to the small black case.

Sally suddenly remembered one of the reasons why she had been selected for this mission. She walked back up the ramp to get a better view. The camera was still recording. She pointed it toward Sharon as she opened the black case and removed a small pyramid, about thirty centimeters high. Sharon lifted it up carefully as though it were much heavier than it looked. She glanced inquiringly at Sima. He nodded and she walked a few paces away from the ladder and put the pyramid down in a small shallow depression in the rocky surface. Sally checked the controls and followed Sharon with the camera.

'On behalf of the people of Earth, we come in peace and in the spirit of exploration, to seek new knowledge and to do no harm.' Sharon's voice shook with emotion but she spoke loudly and slowly and her words were clear to them all.

Each of them had seen the communications pyramid before it was placed into the case but most of them had forgotten about it. Alistair remembered it sitting on the conference table at their first training session, as John explained its composition and purpose; to store information and transmit it to the geostationary satellites. He had stared at the pyramid, wondering, as was his habit, under what circumstances he would see it again. Well, he thought, here we are, safe and well and the little pyramid will always be testimony to that. Long after they left Earth 2, it would remain and would probably outlast all of them. As well as the communications apparatus the pyramid contained descriptions of their planet and records of human achievements. They would place another pyramid on the northern continent and on each of the two moons, and would record details of their landing for future generations

Alistair looked around. He wondered if there were any other creatures here who might ever understand what it meant. Their current location did not look too promising but there was still the rest of the world to explore. He was filled with excitement. 'Amen to that,' he said. He shut his eyes and bent his head towards the ground. Sharon, Vicki and Sima did the same. Sally felt the usual awkwardness and stared around. Thomas was watching her. He turned away to look towards the ocean again.

9

Jeremy Stuart stared out the cabin window at the clouds. Now, whenever he flew, he wondered where Alistair was. Had they landed, or were they still orbiting Earth 2? He looked at his watcher again, even though he knew the time. Alistair, wherever he was, should be thinking of him in a few moments. Then he would carry out a small ritual he had performed every day since Alistair had left earth. They had arranged it on Christmas day, more than a year ago. The last Christmas Alistair had spent on earth. Funny, how a phrase like 'his last days on earth' had a completely new meaning to him now.

Jeremy noticed a flight attendant watching him. He gave her the smile he reserved for fans and was surprised when she did not respond, but walked on to the cockpit. He breathed deeply and tried to relax. He had felt bad leaving his family at this time. The nearer the Earth 2 arrival date had loomed, the more nervous his parents seemed to become. There had been no communication for more than six weeks, since the Millennium passed behind the sun, out of range. Until then, his mother had remained cheerful, endlessly telling anyone who would listen, every detail of her son's journey. In the last month, she seemed to have aged, and Jeremy had put off his departure to Los Angeles for as long as possible.

He checked his watcher again and turning back to the window he spoke Ulysses' words in a low undertone. "Brothers, that have come valiantly through hundred thousand jeopardies. You will not now deny to this last little vigil left to run, of feeling life, the new experience of the uninhabited world behind the sun."

He closed his eyes to fix his brother's image in his mind. He remembered Alistair as a small boy, asking his older brother what the poem was about, and who the 'brothers' were. Jeremy had explained that Dante's verses described Ulysses' journey through the Pillars of Hercules at the mouth of the Mediterranean, those ancient symbols of the limits of the known world.

Alistair's research had taken him to many remote places, and he had adopted the poem as a sort of talisman against danger. He told Jeremy that he had experienced a sort of thrill, when he realized that it would really come true for him, that he would be one of the small band of people to visit the world behind the sun.

Jeremy tried to imagine his brother reciting the same words, somewhere aboard the Millennium. Instead his mind painted a vivid picture of Ulysses' crew, calling out in terror as huge waves pounded their ship. Jeremy shook his head, to get rid of this depressing image.

"Think of your breed; for brutish ignorance your mettle was not made."

Usually these words steadied and inspired him - a manly call to courage and resolve. But today, he felt jumpy. He continued resolutely. "You were made men, to follow after knowledge and ..."

'May I have your attention please?'

Jeremy was startled at the urgency in the flight attendant's voice.

'Thank you,' she said. Her pleasant mid-western drawl had a sharp edge to it. 'You will notice in a few moments that the aircraft will be turning sharply. We have been instructed to divert to Papeete because of a technical failure at Los

Angeles airport. We will not continue to San Francisco or any mainland airport, as a large number of flights have had to be redirected. We will inform you as soon as we have news about the arrangements for travel to your US destinations.'

Jeremy beckoned to the young woman but she shook her head, and went back towards the cockpit. The other flight attendant who had been resting in one of the seats at the rear of the cabin followed her. Jeremy unbuckled his seat belt and started to stand up, but the aircraft began a steep turn and he fell back into his seat. He buckled his seat belt again and glanced at the monitor. Sure enough, the tiny plane on the screen was making a turn back towards the dot labeled Tahiti, a few centimeters to the south.

'Oh shit,' thought Jeremy. If this had happened earlier they could have returned to Australia or even New Zealand. This was just what his family needed right now, having their other son stuck on some island in the middle of the ocean.

To his surprise, the screen in front of him went blank. He stood up. The two other passengers in the first class cabin had their chairs in the recline position and sleep masks over their eyes, obviously resigned to the change in their plans. Their screens were also dead.

Jeremy picked up the in-flight magazine and turned to the international map. On the next page there was a table with the distances between the cities which the airline covered. He checked his watcher, did some quick calculations and sat back with a frown. Why were they going to Tahiti when they were much nearer to Hawaii? It must be a hell of a problem. Perhaps there had been a large-scale hack into the US airline systems, but it hadn't affected other countries. How could that be?

He pushed the call button for the flight attendant, but no one appeared. He pressed the monitor button. The screen was still blank, and when he tried the audio channels, he got the same result. He noticed the seat belt sign flashing and sat back with a sigh. He pulled down the blind and took up the script he had been reading.

He woke from a doze to hear the flight attendant announcing their arrival at Papeete. She explained that they would be in a wide holding pattern for at least two hours, because of the large number of diverted flights. Jeremy let the blind up and looked out. He could see several planes in the distance above and below. As the plane turned the sun dazzled him and he pulled the blind down again.

Almost three hours later he walked out of the connecting walkway into the total pandemonium of Papeete airport. After landing, they had been kept on the plane for nearly an hour and now he could see why. The airport was tightly packed with passengers from the diverted flights. He had expected that, but not the noise and frightening atmosphere. Children were wailing, men and women were shouting and crying. People pressed against the check-in desks. Others struggled towards the exits. The public address system continually broadcast instructions in French, English and Japanese, but they could not be heard above the racket. The large video screens were blacked out. Jeremy fought his way towards a wall and leaned up against it. He turned to the woman standing next to him, who was speaking in a frantic tone into her watcher, her hand over her other ear to block the noise.

'What's going on?' When she didn't answer, he tapped her on the shoulder and repeated the question. She looked at him as though he were mad. He thought she probably didn't understand English.

He activated his watcher, waited a few seconds and spoke into it. Because of the background noise, the watcher did not recognize what he said and repeated its request for input. Jeremy put his flight bag down and jammed it between his feet, and fast dialed his American agent, as people pushed past him.

He couldn't hear the phone ringing. He checked the screen. The call had been cut off. He tried twice more and then punched in the number for his Australian agent.

'Peter!' he yelled when he heard his agent's voice.

He pressed the control to increase the volume and just managed to hear Peter ask, 'Jerry is that you? Are you all right? Where the hell are you?'

'I can hardly hear you,' Jeremy shouted. 'I'm OK. Listen, we got diverted to Tahiti. I don't know why. There's about a million people here. I don't know when I'll get on another flight. Can you let the studio know?'

'Thank Christ you're all right. Listen Jerry; try to get on a flight back to Aussie.'

'Why? What's the matter?' He noticed a man nearby staring at him in amazement. The man looked haggard. He had his arms around a young girl who was sobbing violently.

'Haven't you heard?' Peter sounded as though he was crying. 'It's war, man, war! Five cities are out; New York, Chicago, Houston, Washington, San Fran, the whole Silicon Valley.' As Peter continued, Jeremy felt his legs give way and he slid to a sitting position against the wall. He almost lost his bag as someone was pushed violently against him. He grabbed it and pushed back as though his life depended on it.

A group calling themselves "Liberty Bell" had already claimed responsibility. No one seemed to know who they were. There were few casualties, as the bombs had exploded during the night. But almost everything relying on telecommunications – media, transport and power - had been knocked out across the US. There was widespread rioting. Martial law had been declared in several states.

'I'll ring your parents right away.' Peter was speaking more calmly now 'I've been on the phone most of the day. I can't get through to the states. No one can.' His voice broke slightly as he said good-bye.

Jeremy sat for a few moments in a daze. He switched his watcher to message mode and sent a brief text message to his parents. 'Diverted to Papeete. Am fine. Will ring later.' He shouted 'send' and waited until the icon flashed on to the screen.

A heavyset man tripped over his bag and cursed at him. Jeremy ignored him, but struggled to his feet and leaned back against the wall. For some strange reason, all he could think about was what Alistair might be doing. Good god! If Houston was hit, how would they make contact with the Millennium? He could feel the blood draining out of his face and he suddenly felt sick.

The woman next to him clutched at his arm. She looked up at him wildly. Jeremy shuddered and put his arm around her.

10

'I can't understand it.' Vicki looked woefully at Mohun's tray of seedlings. 'They were fine yesterday. Mohun's going to kill me.' John and Mohun were still aboard the Millennium, making the final checks on the three geostationary satellites, which they had launched on arrival at Earth 2.

The plants that had been left outside during the last four days had been growing strongly, but overnight they had withered. The remaining plants, kept on the shuttle under similar conditions to those on the ship were healthy.

'Perhaps you should start using your masks again. I still maintain there may be elements in the air we can't identify.'

Sima looked at Thomas. 'None of us have had any reactions. The daily blood tests are still negative. I'll do some skin scans. We'll check whether there is any variation between exposed and unexposed skin.'

'OK.' Sharon looked around. 'We'll use this morning to catch up. Sima, if you check Vicki and Alistair first, they can get on with the surveys.' Sharon picked up her mug and breakfast bowl. 'If nothing unusual happens today, we'll move camp again tomorrow.'

In the last four days they had all settled into their routines. The days were short but surprisingly mild and Alistair and Vicki had spent most of the daylight hours using Lassie – the small flyer - to survey the area nearby. 'Southland', as they now called the southern continent, consisted entirely of a rocky desert. Whatever forces had weathered the continent appeared to have ended eons ago. The land was almost flat with a few areas gently sloping up to around fifty meters.

They had moved Radon to one of the highest elevations further away from the coast. This gave them a better view, but there was nothing to be seen.

Vicki and Alistair had flown out to a random sample of the islands but they found nothing new there. They had taken soundings of the ocean as they returned and realized that the large number of islands was due to the fact that the continental shelf fell away very gradually. It was quite hard to see where the land began and the ocean ended. None of the islands rose more than a few meters above sea level and at high tide some of the islands further out disappeared for a few hours under the ocean. After high tide, the sea water remained in some of the coastal rock pools for several hours before draining off or evaporating. Vicki's tests on this sea water were equally disappointing. There was nothing in the water to inhibit the development of life but no sign of any of the building blocks from which organisms might develop.

Alistair and Vicki spent many hours discussing this puzzling phenomenon. Thomas was always aloof and Sima and Sharon were preoccupied with the endless technical checks. Sally was starting to feel isolated. She had run out of things to record and she now wished that she shared some of the others' expertise. She had wanted to join Alistair on the flyer but she knew that Vicki was more likely to spot something significant. So she helped process the data they brought back, hoping that this might in some way bridge the distance which seemed to have developed between her and Alistair. For a time on the ship they had become quite friendly, but after the radiation incident he became more reserved. She had often noticed him looking at her in a peculiar way and wondered if he had decided she was unreliable.

'Nothing interesting so far, I'm sorry.' Sally handed her data pad to Alistair and he flicked down the screen.

'Just as I thought; iron, some nickel. Like Thomas said, nothing worth mining here. I'm going to get some samples from the Western Hemisphere today but I don't expect to see much difference. Can you finish the rest of the tests today?'

'Of course,' Sally smiled. Alistair responded with a curt nod and called out to Vicki. She gave him the thumbs up. Lassie was checked and ready to fly.

Sharon emerged from the shuttle and called out. 'Wait up a minute. John's got some news.' She disappeared back inside. Sima started up the ramp but Sharon reappeared. She was pale but smiling broadly. 'Great news! The cloud has cleared over the north and the wind has died down. John says we can move as soon as we're ready.'

For a few moments everyone shouted and hugged each other, or danced around in excitement. Only Thomas appeared unmoved.

Sharon laughed at their reaction. 'I think we should dismantle everything as fast as possible and get moving. It will take about twelve hours flying time, if we don't stop. But it's summer up there of course so we'll make it before nightfall. All ok?'

No one disagreed. 'Let's have coffee and review what we have to do,' Sharon continued.

For a few moments they were silent. It was hard to digest the latest news. Vicki sipped her coffee. 'I can see this planet as a new start for mankind.' Her voice became animated. 'We could avoid all the mistakes we made on earth. It could be the new Eden.'

The others smiled at her but Thomas said abruptly. 'How can this be?'

'What do you mean?' Vicki asked.

'How can there be any life in the north if this hemisphere is sterile?'

Vicki flushed. 'It may be very primitive - mosses etc. Perhaps the ice belt inhibits the movement of organisms.' She turned to Alistair. 'It could, couldn't it?'

Alistair looked puzzled. 'We have to keep in mind that just because this place looks a lot like earth, doesn't mean that everything operates the same way. We've found some tectonic activity, enough to suggest life. What is more strange, is that there is nothing down here.'

'Well, we won't find out, just talking about it,' Sharon interrupted. 'Let's go find out.'

Thomas continued to frown. 'I think we should stay here for a while longer. The weather conditions might change again.'

Sally started to feel uneasy but the others chorused their disagreement.

'John believes we should take the opportunity and move now.'

'I hope at least that John and Mohun will stay where they are until we know it's safe?' Thomas turned to Sharon.

'That's right. Mohun is fuming but John won't come down until we've landed safely and checked everything out.'

'Poor old Mohun.' Vicki tried to sound sympathetic but gave a joyful shout.

They had moved camp twice already so decamping was becoming routine for them. But now they had a new motivation and worked faster than ever. The time dragged as Sharon insisted on checking everything twice, in case their impatience made them careless.

By ten o'clock local time, they were ready. Sharon looked around. Thomas was standing some distance away, staring towards the north. She called out to him but he did not turn around.

'What's with him?' asked Alistair.

'He doesn't show his feelings,' Vicki suggested. 'But I suppose like the rest of us he finds this all a bit overwhelming?'

Sima shrugged and set off towards the motionless figure. Sharon saw him speak to Thomas and then the two men started back towards the shuttle.

11

Sharon kept Radon as low as possible and Sally got her first good view of the southern continent and the surrounding islands. The scene reminded her of flying out of Helsinki. The coastline, like that of southern Finland, was sprinkled with hundreds of islands. She took out her camera and set it up to record through the porthole.

The number of islands dwindled as they headed north. They paused several times to take soundings of the ocean floor. The depth of the ocean gradually increased, until mid way between the southern continent and the ice belt it dropped off to nearly two thousand meters.

'We should take some more soundings every few hundred meters,' said Vicki. 'This might be the beginning of a deep trench.'

'Sorry Vicki, but we need to keep going so we can get to the northern landmass before nightfall. There's no large islands anywhere nearby for us to camp on and I don't want to be flying at night. We can come back later and have a closer look.'

Vicki protested. 'But Sharon, the best chance to find life here might be in the deep sea vents.'

'Two thousand meters is still pretty shallow water. It's not likely that it's going to suddenly plunge to ten k or something like the Mariana trench. If you look up ahead you'll see that there are more islands as we get nearer the ice belt. This might be as deep as it gets. I think most of us want to try our luck up north first.' Sharon looked around. Everyone nodded in agreement, except for Thomas who was still staring out the porthole.

Sharon waited for a moment. 'Do you agree, Thomas?'

Thomas turned around and they saw with dismay that he looked quite unwell. 'I'll go along with what the rest of you want to do. Sorry, I feel a bit queasy.' He reached under his seat for his medical kit. He swallowed some tablets, leaned back and closed his eyes.

The next two soundings showed that the ocean floor was gradually rising again and they could see small groups of islands, similar to those in the south. In the early afternoon they got their first glimpses of the ice belt. Sima took over from Sharon and veered westwards towards the wider areas of the belt. Small icebergs and islands gradually increased in size until they merged into an icy landmass. Thin ribbons of melt water laced a huge plain of ice producing a dazzling surface. Sally adjusted the camera for the glare.

Sima veered up and over some rocky crags piercing the white blanket. The descent made Sally gasp. Steep slopes shaded a wide valley, creating strange patterns of dark and light that made the crew call out in amazement. The view was crystal clear and the ice formations and shadows sometimes gave the illusion of large structures - gothic style buildings with piercing spires and ornate windows.

'We could be in Antarctica!' Vicki smiled around the cabin. None of them had ever visited the north or south poles but they had all seen recordings of landscapes similar to those below. Sally felt again a sense of unreality, as though they had never left Earth. She panned the camera across the cabin to record the crew's enthralled faces.

They soared over vast plains of tumbled ice, split by deep chasms. In some places the snow had been swept into huge dune like formations. The crew peered through their far range scanners. Nothing interrupted the white wilderness apart from the dark brown shadows cast by the rocky peaks.

Further north they reached an area where they estimated the ice belt was several hundred kilometers wide. As they neared the coast the ice started to give way to rocky valleys, and windswept hillsides.

'God, if only the northland is like this! We may find soil there.' Alistair's feelings were echoed by the others.

Sima followed the coastline east until the ice belt narrowed back down to a few kilometers. There were sighs as the shuttle turned north again and accelerated. Gradually the islands grew smaller until they disappeared altogether. For two hours they flew over empty northern ocean but the atmosphere of anticipation grew as two more soundings showed the ocean floor was rising again.

Sally craned around in her seat so that she could look at the distant view to the north. It was very similar to the one she had seen as they had left the Southland. The ocean lapped at the smaller islands and sometimes they were so close together that she thought that they had reached the coastline of the northern continent. She lifted the scanner slightly higher and called out to Sharon. 'I think there's a storm northeast. Can you see it?'

Sharon got up and leaned forward into the cockpit, her scanner raised to her eyes. 'It looks more like a dust cloud, but it appears to be at ground level and it doesn't seem to be getting any larger. Perhaps it's moving away. Well done, Sally.'

Sally smiled wryly to herself. Sharon still acted surprised every time she did anything halfway competent. She aimed the camera through the porthole and panned across the dark smudge on the horizon. The others were also now looking through the portholes trying to glimpse what Sally had seen.

'There's no doubt about it.' Sharon's voice was triumphant. 'That's no storm; it's a line of low hills.'

Vicki suddenly let out a piercing cry. 'Look! Below! Sima, slow down. Look at the island below us.'

Sima slowed down and brought the shuttle into a long descending arc. Vicki groaned in frustration as the island disappeared to the south but Alistair called out. 'I can see vegetation!'

They could all clearly see the three small islands below dotted with distinct areas of green. Vicki bumped against Thomas as she tried to get a better view. He put his hand to his mouth and reached under his seat again; then seeming to think better of it, he unclipped his harness and staggered towards the rear of the shuttle. Sally pulled herself reluctantly away from the view and followed him. He had shut the toilet door and she could not hear any noises. She banged on the door.

'Are you all right?' There was a muffled "yes" and the sounds of retching.

'Can't we land?' Vicki was almost beside herself with excitement.

Sharon was sympathetic but insisted; 'We'd better get to somewhere where we can put down for a time. Some of these islands might be flooded at high tide.'

Alistair gave a yell and Vicki saw that her question was irrelevant. As they flew north the amount of vegetation was increasing.

The tension grew as they approached the coastline. Sharon was talking to John. Sally imagined Mohun's frustration at not being with them. She tried to concentrate on capturing as many images as she could. The light was starting to fade and they were moving too fast to see what the green areas were.

Thomas emerged from the toilet, wiping his face. He looked very pale. Sally looked at him questioningly but he sat down and closed his eyes again. She forgot him a moment later as she looked out the porthole.

In the pale twilight they could see the dark line of hills several kilometers to the northeast. The land to the west of the hills looked flat and Sima headed in that direction. As they descended over the larger islands, the greenery was clearly visible. Small bushes gave way to larger plants, some as big as small trees. No one spoke. They looked at each other in disbelief. A curving bay lay ahead, sheltered by small hills. Beyond, a wide valley spread from the water to the line of hills. Sally stared as the motion of the shuttle's descent stirred up the long grass. Her heart pounded.

There was a series of gentle bumps and then the gyros cut out. The silence was eerie.

'We need to do some more tests before we leave the shuttle. We should all use our full body suits and masks again until we've made thorough tests.' Sharon's voice shook slightly. 'Also, since this is a quite different environment, we will take more security measures than we have in the last few days. No one is to go anywhere unaccompanied and without notifying Sima or me first. Keep a side arm with you at all times. We'll sleep on Radon tonight. One person will be on watch at the landing site at all times.'

They pulled on their masks while Sharon hunched over the console and Sima checked the view screens. The scene around the shuttle did not change. There was no sign of movement except for the vegetation stirring in a breeze.

'OK. Let's go.'

Vicki smiled self-consciously at Sally as she attached her handgun to her tool belt. Sally fumbled with the clasp and the weapon bumped strangely against her hip. She looked back at Thomas. His mouth was clenched into a thin line. He waved his hand at her and closed his eyes.

They exited from the shuttle in the same order as on the first landing. Sima had brought Radon down onto a small rise and they could see some distance in every direction. Most of the valley seemed to be covered in long grass, with occasional clumps of bushes and trees and rocky outcrops two or three meters high. To the east lay the line of hills; their distance and height were difficult to judge in the clear air. To the south they could glimpse the ocean through a scattering of trees. The valley extended northwards, terminating in a distant gray smudge which looked like a mountain range. To the west the trees thickened into a forest, blocking the view. The sun was low in the sky, casting a golden light over the ocean and the few wisps of cloud that were all that remained of the thick cloud cover.

Sally trembled as she lifted up her camera and panned around in a circle. The crew had spread out and as she moved the camera, first one and then another of them came into view. Sharon and Sima were scanning the landscape purposefully. Alistair looked around in wonderment and fingered a blade of the long grass. Vicki shook her head, picked up her specimen canister and squatted down. Sally walked slowly towards her, and zoomed in as Vicki snipped a small twig off the nearest bush. She looked at it and then dropped it into a specimen bag. She checked her data pad and carefully entered the exact location of the bush, and the time.

Vicki looked up at Sally who was earnestly following all her movements with the camera. She fell back on her haunches and suddenly started to laugh. 'One down and one million to go,' she said in a gleeful voice.

'Vicki! Quick over here!' Alistair was crouched over a bush, his two hands cupped together. 'Hold the canister just over my hands. When I open them, shut it as fast as you can. Sally - see if you can get this on film. Ready?'

He opened his hands and there was a blur of movement. Sally panned the camera quickly as the blur shot past Vicki's canister.

'Damn! What was it?' Vicki snapped the canister shut again.

'Some sort of large insect I think. It was moving too fast to see.'

'Let's have a look.' Sally hoped the camera had caught something as the tiny creature had whizzed past. She set the dial to slow motion and scanned back through the recording. 'Wow! Look at this.' She paused the image as Alistair and Vicki leaned over her shoulder to look at the display. They both gasped and called to the others. The perfectly clear picture showed a tiny bird, its wings outspread. It had a long curving dark beak and brilliant blue, yellow and emerald plumage. It was no more than five centimeters, from head to tail.

'Why couldn't we see it?' asked Alistair.

'The wings beat so fast – probably about a hundred times per second. It's amazingly like a hummingbird.' Vicki was almost jumping with excitement. 'You know what this means, don't you? There must be something here for it to eat. Probably insects. And of course predators. This means there is a complex food chain right here.'

They heard Sharon calling out. The sky was much darker now and Vicki's mention of predators made them look around nervously.

Sharon shouted again. 'Thomas isn't well. We'd better get back into Radon and decide what to do.'

Thomas had become very pale and his face was strained. Sima was examining him and Sharon was on the comms to John. Her voice was excited as she described their surroundings but became more serious as she described Thomas's condition.

'We're using the masks until we've done all the tests here, but I wonder if we should isolate Thomas. He's been a bit off all day.'

Sima interrupted her. 'I don't think that's necessary. See? He's looking better already. I think it was just a bout of travel sickness.' He turned to Thomas whose color was looking more normal.

'I just need some rest.' Thomas closed his eyes again.

* * *

Sally was dreaming. She floated high above a darkened land, carried by something which rustled loudly. She struggled as a face emerged from the darkness.

Vicki was leaning over her. 'Wake up. Thomas has disappeared.'

Sally sat up and shook her head to clear it. 'What do you mean?'

'Thomas has vanished,' Vicki repeated. 'Sima and Alistair have gone to look for him.'

Sharon was standing at the bottom of the ramp, talking continuously into her watcher.

'What happened?' Sally rubbed her eyes and looked at her watcher. It was just after midnight. She had been asleep for less than an hour.

Vicki shrugged. 'I don't know.'

Sally looked around nervously. The lamp spread a circle of light for several meters but beyond that it was very dark. She looked up but could not see either of the moons. Outside the circle of light, the sky was as bright with stars as it had been in the south. She wished she had paid more attention to the northern sky on earth. She felt quite disoriented.

Sharon ended the call. 'Sima was on watch. He heard Thomas moving around but he thought he was just getting up for the toilet again. He was inside the airlock before Sima could get to him. He operated the override and Sima had to open the door manually. I can't imagine what Thomas was doing. Sima said that he checked him only a few minutes before and his temperature and everything were fine.'

Sharon's watcher buzzed and she frowned as she listened to Sima. 'I don't think that's a good idea. I'm going to call John again. Why don't you get back here and we'll decide what to do next.'

She ended the call and said to Sally and Vicki, 'Sima wants to take Lassie up and do a more extensive search. I'm not keen on that. We don't know what's out there.'

Vicki grabbed Sally's arm and they looked at each other in alarm. Sally couldn't help putting her hand on her side gun, but the night was quite silent, apart from the rustling of the breeze through the trees. They heard the sound of Alistair and Sima returning and Vicki let go Sally's arm.

'There's no sign of him anywhere nearby. Unless we take Lassie up with a spotlight, we haven't a hope in hell of finding him.' Alistair looked angry as well as anxious.

'I can't understand it.' Sima sounded faintly apologetic. 'Whatever happened to him, it must have come on very fast. He had no signs of anything pathological.'

'John agrees with me; too dangerous in the dark. It'll be light in less than three hours. We'll take Lassie up then.'

Sharon and Sima kept watch at the top of the ramp while the others tried to sleep. At around two am Vicki stumbled sleepily out of the shuttle. She had been woken by some strange premonition. As she stood there, asking if they would like some coffee, the light breeze intensified and a soft rain began to fall. They sat in the airlock watching and listening.

'It's amazingly mild for mid-summer. What are we at – around 45 degrees latitude?'

'It must be the influence of the oceans,' said Vicki, still sleepy.

'Perhaps; but considering the more extreme tilt I would expect it to be much hotter. But the south was not as cold as we expected, either.' Sima didn't sound very interested and Vicki guessed he was too worried by Thomas's disappearance.

Sharon decided to try to get some rest and left Vicki and Sima alone. Vicki enjoyed the sensation of sitting close to Sima, staring out into the night. He had a way of making her feel protected, even though he knew she was quite capable of looking after herself. The rain fell gently but steadily for almost an hour. When the light cloud lifted, the sky was awash with the predawn light. One by one the few stars still visible faded out.

'We should wake the others. I want to start out straight away.' As Sima stood up his eye was caught by something dark amongst the green grass, about fifty meters away. He raised his scanner. 'Damn!'

'What is it?'

'I can see Thomas.' He spoke urgently into his watcher and moments later Sharon emerged from the shuttle, followed closely by Alistair and Sally.

'Stay here!' Sharon barked. 'Don't leave the shuttle.'

Sima and Sharon approached the dark figure cautiously. Thomas was lying prone, as though he were peacefully asleep. As they neared him they could see his chest rising and falling and Sharon felt a surge of relief.

Sima knelt and put his hand on Thomas's forehead. 'He has a high fever. Where's his mask?'

Sharon looked around. 'He must have pulled it off. Or not put it on.'

Sima cautiously examined Thomas for injuries. 'He seems ok otherwise. Damn! Alistair and I must have walked right past him last night.'

He shook Thomas gently and tried to rouse him. Thomas did not respond.

'Let's get him back inside.' Sima knelt down and lifted Thomas up over his shoulder. Sharon, for reasons she could not identify, kept her hand on her gun as Sima carried Thomas back to the shuttle.

12

'He's not well.' Sima sounded grave. The others looked at him in surprise. Thomas had recovered from the fever within a few hours and Sally had just seen him sitting up in his bunk, working with his data pad.

'I don't mean physically. He seems to be suffering from delusions. We'll have to watch him. He's quite convinced that we're all hallucinating. As far he is concerned, there's nothing here.'

Sima waved his arm around and they all looked back across the valley. They could see groves of trees and small streams glinting in the distance. Vicki had already collected several samples of small flowers from the long grasses in the valley and had heard the whirring noise of more of the humming birds or other winged species.

'According to Thomas, none of this is real,' repeated Sima.

'Well, it is amazing,' Sharon said thoughtfully. 'The landscape, the flora is so Earth-like. I don't know why, but I expected things to look completely different.'

'Not so surprising really,' Alistair cut in, 'once you get over the fact that this planet is here at all; same age, same distance to the sun.'

'Surely he understands that it's more likely that he's the one hallucinating, rather than all of us. Or is he not rational?'

Sima looked at Vicki. 'He has had a fever but he sounds lucid. According to him, part of the delusions would be to deny our experience. Right now he is trying to find some information about mass hallucinations, which he thinks he has on the system.'

'Suppose he's right?' Sally felt silly making the suggestion, but the others seemed to take the idea seriously.

'It is a possibility.' Sima shook his head. 'But it doesn't explain the data coming in from the satellites. And how could John and Mohun be affected as well, when they're not here? Considering that he was outside last night for several hours without a mask, it's much more likely that it is Thomas who is suffering from some sort of reaction. I will check for psychotropic elements and do blood tests on you all again.' Sima sighed and looked irritated. 'I'll stay here and start the tests. But I think it should be safe for some of you to go further afield. What do you think?' He looked at Sharon.

'I'll propose to John that Vicki and Alistair carry out some surveys of the nearby area. Sally and I can gather as many samples as possible from nearby and help you with the tests.'

'I'd rather stay here and take a closer look at the plant samples; if it's OK with you,' Vicki replied. 'Sally can go with Alistair and do some more filming?'

Sally arranged breakfast while Sharon called John. Thomas was hunched over his data pad and when she asked him what he wanted to eat she saw that his face had a strange rigid look. He glanced towards the cockpit and said in a low voice, 'Sit down for a moment.'

Sally perched on the edge of his bunk. She felt uncomfortable and looked towards Sharon, but she was talking intently into the comms unit.

'How are you?' Sally tried to sound neutral. 'Feeling better?'

'Listen, Sally. When you go outside again, try to focus. Try to empty your mind before you open your eyes. There's something very odd going on here.'

Sally had never heard him sound so agitated. She wanted to move away but she thought she should listen to what he said. 'I'll try. But what do you expect me to see?'

'Nothing! That's the point. Listen.' Thomas gripped her arm hard and she resisted the urge to push him away. 'You're all seeing things, I tell you. There's nothing here. It's just like the south, except for some hills.'

Sally pulled her arm away. 'Try not to worry. We'll check it out. I'll do as you ask, I promise.'

Thomas reached up and put his hand on the side of her face. His hand was very cold and she shuddered again. She tried to look away but he turned her face firmly towards him. He stared into her eyes and she started to feel nervous.

'You must empty your mind first before you try to look at anything. Otherwise you'll just see what everyone else is seeing.' Abruptly he took his hand away and looked back down at the data pad. 'I can't find the information I wanted.' He touched the screen and frowned. Sally stood up. He seemed to have forgotten she was there.

'I'll be out in a minute' called Sharon. 'Ask Sima to come in, would you?'

Sally picked up several breakfast packs and handed one to Thomas. He took it without looking at her. As she entered the airlock, she grimaced and tried to clear her mind. When the outer door opened, she stood for a moment with her eyes closed. She felt the light breeze across her face and smelt the fresh, slightly astringent air. She looked around; everything was as it had been before. Alistair was checking Lassie's controls. Vicki had erected a worktable and was laying out her sample canisters. Sima was sorting out some of the gear that they would need to reassemble the domes. Behind them the scenery spread out gloriously bright in the clear air.

When Sally told Sima about her conversation with Thomas, Sima frowned. 'I had hoped that he would forget this idea as the fever went down. Did he say why he left us last night?'

'No. Oh, also Sharon wants to talk to you inside.' Sima nodded and headed towards the shuttle. Sally took the other packs over to Vicki and Alistair.

'Thanks for offering to stay behind,' Sally said. Vicki smiled and nodded.

* * *

'It's not logical' John was telling Sharon. 'What we can see from up here confirms what you've told me. And how can the satellite data lie? And what about your recordings – plants, the bird, they look real to me and Mohun.'

Sharon explained that according to Thomas this was just part of the mass psychosis. 'He believes that we have fabricated this illusion because of our disappointment with what we found in the south.'

'That's ridiculous. None of us had any expectations about what we'd find here. Tell Sima to keep checking Thomas's blood. If he was exposed to something during the night, perhaps it will show up. I don't see any reason why Mohun and I shouldn't come down. We've loaded all the equipment into Xenon; the shuttle's cleared to go. We'll call you when we're ready to leave.'

Sharon ended the call and got up. She stood over Thomas for a few moments and then put her hand on his forehead. It was cool. He opened his eyes briefly, but seemed to fall asleep again.

'I don't think we should leave him alone. I'd like two people to stay here with him all the time. You and Vicki stay here and run the tests inside the shuttle, and I'll start putting the domes together. When Sally and Alistair come back they can help me.'

Sima nodded. 'That sounds fine to me.'

* * *

Alistair headed east towards the line of hills. They flew over grasslands interrupted only by groves of trees and small rocky outcrops. Sally panned across the horizon, zoomed in to take closer shots of the foliage. They stopped twice to take samples from two small streams. The trees growing on the banks were quite different from the ones near the landing site. They reminded Sally of bottlebrush trees but the flowers were much longer and a brilliant orange color.

As she stood in the shade of the trees she heard the whirring noise of small birds and insects, but she was not quick enough to get them on video. Alistair was looking around the banks of the small stream. 'No sign of animal tracks.'

He spoke in a matter of fact voice but Sally was struck by a sudden sense of unreality. She shivered as she remembered what Thomas had said. But the feeling was only momentary and she knew she had often felt this way. Overwhelming experiences often left her with a sense of disbelief. It was a perfectly normal reaction.

As they approached the hills the vegetation grew sparser and the ground became rockier. When they reached the tumbled rocks of the foothills Alistair gestured upwards. 'Shall we take a look?'

'You're the boss.' Sally paused. 'Doesn't it seem odd to you that the vegetation, the whole place looks so much like Earth?' The flyer wobbled as it ascended the hillside and she clutched the guardrail.

'I guess; but as I said before, it's more amazing that the planet is here at all.'

As the flyer rose slowly up the hillside she turned the camera back towards the west. Using the zoom she could just make out the shape of the shuttle and the tiny figure of Sharon moving around outside. She turned the camera on Alistair and said lightly, 'Now, Professor Stuart, tell me. What are your thoughts as you explore this brave new world?'

She was pleased when Alistair responded in a similar tone. 'Bloody bewdy, that's what.' Alistair laughed then blinked rapidly behind his mask, as though overcome with emotion. 'What a privilege for us to be here.' He waved his arm towards the valley. 'Look at it. It's unbelievable.'

Sally smiled at him and for a moment neither of them spoke. Then Alistair started to describe the geology of the area and following his lead, Sally trained the camera on the various rocks and landforms.

'This valley looks like a classic v-shaped valley as though there's been a massive glacier here millions of years ago. If we look at the rocks we passed, we can see that they appear to have been split open when the internal water froze and expanded. It's very similar to landscapes on earth that have been formed by glaciers. The planet must have been on a less extreme tilt back then. Interesting!'

'And do you have any idea yet why the southern hemisphere should be so different?

Alistair shook his head. 'Not a clue.' He laughed. 'Hey! You can edit that later. Just take some shots of me looking intelligent and when I've worked it out, you can dub in my voice over.'

As the flyer reached the top of the hill Sally's heart started to race. But there was not much to see. A huge flat plateau extended east and north to the horizon; the ground stony and dry, bare of vegetation. They headed south and Alistair stopped to pick up some small rocks. His eyes gleamed. 'Sedimentary!' he said triumphantly.

Sally panned the camera across the plateau from north to south and then across the ocean. 'Look at that!' She zoomed in. A small golden cloud hovered over the water. 'What do you think it is?'

Alistair scanned the area. 'Hard to say. It's too low to be a cloud; could be a swarm of insects or perhaps dust or pollen, although that would be a bit odd, so far out to sea.' He lowered the scanner. 'It's too far out to sea for us to go look, and it seems to be moving away.'

Sally watchered Sharon and described the cloud. As she closed the call Alistair called, 'what's that?' She looked to where he pointed, but the sky was clear and empty.

'Did you see that?'

'What?'

'Two black dots, moving very fast towards the south.' Alistair lowered his scanner. 'Damn! They were gone before I could focus on them.'

'Probably some more birds.'

As they moved south the plateau rose gradually and ended in an abrupt cliff that dropped sharply to the ocean below. Small islands glistened in the bright blue water. The flyer hovered over the edge before starting the descent. Sally scanned the cliffs. They stretched in an unbroken line for several hundred meters and then curved abruptly to the south.

'Do they remind you of anything?'

Sally lowered the scanner. 'They look just like the cliffs at the Gap, in Sydney.'

'That's what I thought.'

They turned east and headed back into the valley, pausing where the two small streams converged into a shallow creek. Sally panned the camera to the north and south, following the line of water. 'That's interesting!' She tapped Alistair on the shoulder and pointed.

Just before the creek entered a grove of trees it was bridged by several logs. They landed and Alistair jumped off. Sally followed more slowly. She looked towards the forest as Alistair knelt down at the water's edge and examined the branches.

'Hell's bells!'

Sally leaned over his shoulder. He didn't need to explain. It was clear that the small trees had been cut down using a very sharp tool, to form a rough bridge.

'If an animal did this, I'd hate to see its teeth.'

Sally looked around nervously. 'Perhaps we'd better be careful. Could it be something like an otter?'

Alistair pulled one of the trees free and examined the end. 'It would have to be enormous. I don't think so. There's no sign of any teeth marks. It looks like the tree was felled with just a few cuts.' He pushed the log back into the water and got up. 'We should call the others right away.'

He took the flyer up a few meters while Sally scanned the ground below. She kept feeling that something huge might spring out of the trees.

'Proceed with caution. That's the order.' Alistair turned Lassie west and they flew slowly along the edge of the wood.

The small forest gradually thinned out and they glimpsed water through the trees. When they reached the sea the view left them speechless. A narrow beach of brilliant white sand stretched for more than a hundred meters west, ending in a forested headland. Several islands were visible a few hundred meters off shore, floating like emeralds on the brilliant blue water. Sally looked back to the east where the deep green forest stretched down almost to the beach. She took a deep breath and panned the camera slowly to take in the whole view.

'I don't know what to say. It's unbelievable.' Alistair put his arm around Sally's shoulders.

She looked up at him, her face radiant. 'I feel so responsible. I never really thought what it would be like, to be the first person to see something like this and to be the one filming it for the first time.' She stopped the recording. 'I've got to check that this thing is working. I'd die if I got back and I'd mucked it all up.' She rewound the images and saw a miniature version of the scene around her.

'You silly thing.' Alistair hugged her affectionately. 'We'll be back. We've got all the time in the world.'

Sally laughed, feeling foolish at first and then found that she was laughing loudly with pure joy. Alistair smiled broadly as they swept west towards the headland. When they rounded the rocks they exclaimed again. The small bay in front of them was even more beautiful.

'It looks just like something out of a travel guide; your own tropical paradise.' Sally looked around. 'But isn't it amazing, the weather here is not subtropical, but the colors are so brilliant.'

Alistair shook his head. 'It's not what we expected. It'll be interesting to figure out how the climate works here.'

The small curved beach rose gently from the water, ending in several long dunes. Large flax like plants capped by tall stems of fluffy pale yellow flowers dotted the sandy slopes. Further back the land formed into several small hillocks. Small bushes with brightly colored flowers gave way to taller trees with the same long bottlebrush type blooms. Every single thing was delightful to the eye, but more than that, all of the elements combined in a way that produced an overwhelming sense of beauty. Sally had seen many breathtaking landscapes. She could not quite define why this place seemed so exceptional. Perhaps it was the clarity of the air.

Alistair landed the flyer on flat rock well away from the water. As in the Southland, there were many rock pools but these were teeming with life. The sides of the small pools were thick with mollusks, like large mussels with iridescent blue and green shells. Small crab like crustaceans scrambled across the bottom of the pools, burrowing into the sand as Sally put her hand into the water. 'Vicki will go mad when she hears about this.'

Alistair didn't reply. He was looking through the scanner along the beach to the west.

'What's up?'

He handed her the scanner. 'Look over there – near that large sand dune. Do you see those small piles?'

Sally scanned the beach and zoomed in. 'They look like heaps of gravel.'

'Let's take a look.' Alistair flew Lassie slowly over to the dunes and they landed on the fine sand. Now they could see that the small heaps were scattered along the beach, in the shelter of the dunes. Around and amongst the piles were small dark objects.

Alistair and Sally squatted down. 'Shells!' said Sally quietly. She shivered and looked around.

'And charcoal.'

They walked further along the beach, stopping briefly to look at the piles of charcoal and shells which were scattered a few meters apart.

Alistair spoke into his watcher. 'Sharon? We're coming back now. We've found something quite amazing. We're at a small cove about 3 k southwest of you. I'm pretty certain that what we've found is a midden. Combined with what we found at the creek it's pretty clear there's intelligent life here. The stuff looks as though it was left within the last few days. So we'd better decide what to do next.'

He paused as Sharon spoke.

'Yes. There's lots of small heaps of shellfish rubbish and charred wood, as though someone's been cooking and eating on the beach. There's also a few fish bones – quite large ones.'

He paused again. 'OK, see you soon.' He turned to Sally, who had started filming the middens. 'I think we should get out of here. If we're going to make first contact, we'd better get ready for it.'

As they rose up over the small hills behind the beach Sally kept the camera on and used the zoom to check for any movements. Her heart was beating strongly and she didn't protest when Alistair took the flyer up to its maximum speed. They flew over the flowery grasslands and then rose higher over the small groves of trees. As the trees cleared she looked towards the east and filmed the landing site. Sharon had started work on two of the domes. She and Vicki were now standing outside the shuttle, looking out for them.

Sharon ran over and secured the flyer. 'Sima's inside with Thomas. He's not any better. When we told him your news, first about the creek and then about the cove, he just seemed to shut off.' Her voice was serious but like Vicki, her face was alight with excitement.

'I've called John. They should be down before dark. We won't do anything till they get here.'

'I think that's wise.' Sharon looked surprised but Sally continued. 'We have to plan for this very carefully. If we mess it up, it might be very hard to undo the damage.'

'That's if these are sentient creatures?' Sharon looked at Alistair.

'It's incredible, but I don't think there's any doubt about it.'

Sally interrupted, annoyed. 'The middens show every sign of sophisticated behavior. The shells were carefully removed. And definitely, these creatures, whatever they are, know how to use fire.'

Alistair nodded in agreement and Sharon smiled at Sally. 'Could you put together some sort of agenda so we can get into action as soon as possible? We might not get to choose when we meet them. They might come looking for us.'

'Unlikely,' replied Sally, 'but possible. I'll get started.'

'I'm going to dismantle the domes.' Sharon looked at Vicki and Alistair. 'Can you two give me a hand? We might want to move quickly.'

Sima stood up as Sally entered the shuttle. 'Amazing news. Congratulations,' he said warmly.

'Poor you. Stuck here all day. How's Thomas?' She could not see Thomas's face. He was lying on his bunk with his face turned towards the cabin wall.

'It's hard to tell. Sometimes he seems quite rational. If it weren't for this fixation about the hallucinations and the occasional fevers I wouldn't be concerned. All of the tests are negative. Still, I wouldn't discuss what you've found. Not yet.'

'Did Sharon tell you about the cloud we saw? We thought it might be pollen.'

'That could be a problem – but nothing shows up in the tests here. I'll do some more if we see it again.'

* * *

Sally was still working on her agenda and briefing notes when Sima told her that John was about to land. She nodded. 'I'll keep an eye on Thomas, if you want to go out.'

Sima shut the inner door and Sally returned to her notes. When she looked up a few moments later she saw that Thomas was sitting up, watching her. She felt a twinge of alarm. His face was quite tranquil but something about his expression disturbed her. She was about to ask him how he was when he got up and went over to the airlock.

'Thomas! You have to stay here. You're not well.'

Thomas ignored her and pressed the button to open the door. Sally lifted her watcher and shouted 'Sima!'

Thomas leapt at her and grabbed her wrist. He pressed the 'call end' stud and tightened his grip on her watcher as the airlock door opened. Sally thought he was going to drag her in with him and she struggled frantically, but at the last moment he pushed her back into the cabin. As the door closed behind him Sally hit the open button again but the door stayed closed. She lifted her watcher up and shouted frantically into it, punching the airlock control again and again.

'Sally! What's the matter?' She felt sick with relief at the sound of John's voice.

'Thomas has gone mad. He's outside and I can't get out. He must have jammed the door.'

John didn't reply at once but she could hear him shouting to the others. When he spoke to her, his voice was gentle. 'Don't worry – sit tight. We'll get the door open.'

He ended the call. Sally realized he hadn't mentioned Thomas and shouted into the watcher again.

'Sharon! Did John hear me? Thomas has got out.'

'It's OK,' Sharon replied calmly. 'John and Sima have taken Lassie and gone after him. Are you all right?'

'I guess.' Sally still felt quite shaken. 'He didn't hurt me. Just gave me a hell of a fright.'

Sharon ended the call and Sally tried to calm herself down. It would be getting dark soon. If John had to use lights to find Thomas, it might scare off whatever or whoever it was that had made the middens. Damn Thomas. She shut her eyes and breathed deeply. It wasn't his fault. He was sick. Her watcher buzzed and she heard Sharon's voice.

'I'm going to try something. Put your mask on and don't touch any of the controls, OK?'

There was a grinding noise, the inner door slid open a crack and Sally saw gloved fingers slide through the gap. She grasped the door and pulled. The gap widened and Sharon squeezed through.

'You're stronger than you look.' Sharon pushed the airlock control and swore. 'What happened?'

When Sally explained how Thomas had grabbed her, Sharon swore again. 'Damn it! When we find him, we'll have to restrain him.'

'He took me by surprise, I'm sorry.'

'It's not your fault. No one could have expected this, or Sima wouldn't have left you on your own with him.' Sharon lifted her wrist. 'Vicki? I want you all to secure everything and then get back into Xenon. Tell Alistair or Mohun to keep guard outside. It'll take me a while to fix this door. Keep in contact, yeah?'

Sally sat in glum silence for a few minutes watching Sharon work on the door. Then she went back to her notes. The crew had trained for this occasion and knew the protocols for first contact by heart. Even so, she needed to think of all the practical details that she took for granted, but which the crew needed to know about. She checked the list carefully and then looked up. Sharon had dismantled the locking device. There was nothing she could do to help her.

She decided to review the translation software. To take advantage of all of the software's features, you needed to enter data about the surroundings and situation, adjust the variables, listen and observe. She had spent many hours practicing with the data pad so that she could enter contextual data fast and accurately, without having to look at the keypad.

It was difficult to concentrate. She got up and peered through the cockpit window. The landscape was washed grey in the deepening twilight and it was difficult to see anything clearly. Sally had never got used to the long twilit nights in northern Europe and she found the scene vaguely unsettling.

'What do you think about Thomas?'

Sharon looked around. 'Give me a moment. I think I've got it fixed.' She turned back to the door and Sally sat down again. The sound of Sharon's watcher woke her; she had dozed off and it was almost midnight. Sharon was in the cockpit, checking one of the consoles.

'They've got him. Sima's given him something to knock him out.

13

Mohun was so glad to be with them that he lifted all their spirits. He took Thomas's condition in his stride. 'Poor guy! What he's missing out on.' He looked at them all in turn, unable to contain his happiness.

John frowned. 'I spoke to Thomas when he woke up. He sounds quite rational but he can't give any proper explanation for the way he behaved towards Sally. He's arguing that he needs to get away, so that he's not contaminated by our delusions. He seems to think his training as a psychiatrist is helping him to resist them but that the rest of us are deluded and we should leave the planet.' He paused. 'Does anyone have any idea what he's talking about?'

Sima spoke slowly. 'Of course we've all heard of mass delusions. A crowd believing they have seen a vision, UFOs and so on. Jonestown is perhaps the worst example.'

Vicki and Mohun looked puzzled but Sima did not elaborate. 'But this is different. The sort of detail that we see, that we agree on – well, I have never heard of any sort of mass hallucinations like that. We've walked around independently. Everything we report fits together. And if we follow Thomas's logic, we were all affected before we left the Millennium. Pareidolia, mass psychosis or whatever; there's no record I know of for any delusion lasting this long or being this detailed.' He bent down and picked a small blue flower from the grass under his stool. 'What do you see?'

Sally felt uneasy as each person described the same flower in their own words while the others nodded in agreement.

John interrupted impatiently. 'Until we get evidence to the contrary, I suggest we carry on as usual. Thomas's objections have been noted in my record. I'm not letting him go back to the Millennium alone and I'm not going to order any of you to accompany him; unless of course someone wants to volunteer?'

No one replied.

'Of course not,' John continued. 'So the business of the day is to see if we can locate whoever, whatever left the rubbish on the beach. Sally will brief us all and then we'll use Lassie and Snoopy to look around. If you see anyone or anything that indicates someone is nearby, come straight back and we'll decide how to proceed. I'll stay here and keep an eye on Thomas.'

The flyers were unwieldy with more than two passengers, so Sharon and Mohun set off on foot towards the stream where the log bridge had been found. Vicki and Sima took Snoopy north to survey the valley. Alistair and Sally returned to the small cove that they now called Discovery Bay.

Later, it seemed almost too easy. They checked the middens but there were no signs of further activity. Alistair flew slowly along the edge of the forested headland, and then brought Lassie to an abrupt halt. Sally clutched the rail as he sped inland a short distance and landed with a bump between two trees.

'What's up?'

Alistair made a shushing gesture. 'I saw something,' he whispered.

Sally looked around, crouched down, as she glimpsed a flash of pale blue several meters away. As it emerged from the treed area she had to put her hand over her mouth to keep herself from screaming. The figure was tall, over two meters, and from behind, exactly resembled a young perfectly proportioned human male. Tight dark curls hung down towards his shoulders and his skin was a light golden brown. A short pale blue kilt was draped around his lower body. He was quite slender but he strode across the sand vigorously and waded into the calm water. He dived under, resurfaced, floated onto his back, and performed some rough somersaults, forwards and backwards. He leapt up, shook his head, tossing the water off his hair and then dived under again.

Alistair looked at Sally in amazement and dragged the flyer behind a larger tree. He whispered into the watcher. 'Sharon. We've seen something – looks like a man. Tell Vicki and Sima to get down.'

Sally peered through the branches as Alistair spoke. The alien man continued to splash around as though enjoying himself. After a few moments he stood up and started to wade back to the beach, trailing his hands in the water. Her heart began to race.

'He's coming our way. Call you back in a minute.' Alistair ended the connection and he and Sally crouched lower as the man approached. He stopped abruptly and gazed straight at them.

'Shit! He's seen us. What do we do now?' Alistair instinctively put his hand on his gun. They could now clearly see the young man's face. He was very handsome with regular symmetrical features and large dark eyes. His black hair clung to his head in small wet ringlets. Sally immediately thought of profiles she had seen on ancient Persian and Greek pottery. It was a very human face.

'We can't avoid it. I'm going to take my mask off.' Sally didn't wait for Alistair's reply. 'Follow my lead.' She stood up slowly and Alistair did the same.

The man stopped a few paces away. His face showed no fear or shock, standing calmly, his hands by his side. He waited a moment and then spoke softly. Sally stared in astonishment and then whispered 'record' to activate her data pad.

When they didn't reply, the young man spoke again. His voice was low and monotonous but Sally thought the sounds would not be difficult to imitate. She stepped forward, her hands in the classic greeting position. She could hardly believe what she was seeing. Her heart thumped so hard that she found it difficult to speak.

'Greetings,' she said.

The man spoke again and Sally thought he repeated what he had just said. She stepped forward again but the man stepped back so she stopped. They stayed like that for a few moments looking at each other. Sally felt her face trembling with emotion but the man gazed at her impassively then stepped sideways so that he could look at the flyer. His expression changed slightly and he spoke again.

Sally glanced down at the data pad and decided to take a chance. She repeated his words back to him. He responded immediately and talked for several moments. She waited until he had finished and made a gesture of helplessness to try to indicate that she did not understand. The man was silent for a moment. Then he said a few more words. His finely formed mouth moved very little as he spoke but Sally could glimpse regular white teeth.

'We don't understand your language.' Sally repeated the gesture. The man turned away and walked briskly into the forest.

Sally was stunned. In her wildest dreams she could not have imagined a first contact like this. She started after him but Alistair stopped her. 'What are you doing?'

'If he's alone, it could take us days to find him again. We can keep our distance and if there's any problem, take off in the flyer.' She ran off along the narrow path which wound between the trees. Alistair called out and she turned impatiently. 'Come on, we'll lose him!'

Alistair jumped on to Lassie and tried to steer the flyer through the trees. The flyer bumped from side to side as the path wound up the side of the hill. He called out to Sally again and cursed as Lassie slammed against a tree. He jumped off, secured the flyer and raced up the path. He glimpsed a flash of pale blue further up the hill but could not see Sally. The path rose steeply for several meters until it entered a small glade at the summit. Sally was standing a few meters ahead, looking down the far side of the hill. She made a beckoning motion and pointed downwards. As Alistair joined her, he could clearly see the young man walking across a grassy area towards a stone arch. They stared down from behind the trees but he did not look back. Through the arch they could clearly see buildings and several other people.

* * *

'Could Thomas be right? Are we seeing things? I mean, this doesn't make sense.' Vicki looked around the group. 'What are the chances of beings that look just like us developing here?'

'If the conditions have been very similar, I guess it's not impossible.' Mohun sounded doubtful. 'But it's highly unlikely.'

John turned to Sally. 'What do you think?'

'It's very strange. My best guess is that this planet has been settled from Earth.'

'What?'

'Think about it. Lots of people have speculated that there have been advanced civilizations on Earth before ours. Perhaps they developed space travel.'

'There's absolutely no evidence for that. We've been scanning for days now. There are no signs of any advanced technology on this planet.'

'Not that we've found so far,' Vicki interjected. 'And if the settlement happened millennia ago, they might have gradually lost their technology.'

'Yes. Any major incidents, natural disasters; that would account for it.' Alistair sounded doubtful; he still felt overwhelmed by the morning's events. 'And this planet's tilt should cause big differences in temperature between the seasons. Plus I'm still not sure about the effect of the moons – they might not keep the tilt as stable as our moon does. Any of these things could cause major setbacks for any kind of intelligent life.'

'Or another race could have abducted humans and just left them here.' Mohun looked defensive as John rolled his eyes up. 'Either of these ideas is more reasonable than humans developing here exactly as they have on earth.'

Vicki cut in again. 'Also, I haven't said this before because I'm still not sure; but most of the plants I've examined are remarkably similar to some on Earth. I have to do more tests but …' Her voice trailed off and then she continued more strongly. 'It is more probable that the plants were brought here from Earth; the similarities are highly improbable.'

'What the man said – the sounds indicate that their vocal equipment is very similar to ours; probably identical. And that would be hard to explain.' Sally continued. 'But it's not like any language I'm aware of, and I've studied every known language group, ancient and modern. If they came from Earth they've been here a very, very long time, millennia at least.'

John gave an exasperated sigh. 'This is all just speculation. We won't know until we get some more data, including some DNA. OK, here's the plan. The contact team will consist of Sally and Alistair, because they will recognize the one they have already seen. Sima will also go, to represent the command team. Sharon and I will stay here to maintain this site and keep a watch on Thomas. Vicki and Mohun will act as a half way team. Everyone keep their hand guns on ready at all times. Continuous voice contact. Any questions for Sally?'

Everyone shook their heads.

'As soon as we're more certain we'll send another communication capsule home.' As usual, John's voice showed little excitement. 'I guess we can abandon the masks meanwhile?'

Sima nodded. 'No problem with the tests.'

Although it was now late afternoon, no one could bear delaying the first contact. The crew separated in silence, still amazed by their discovery.

They approached the village from the north and found the path they had taken that morning. Vicki and Mohun watched enviously from the top of the hill as Sima, Sally and Alistair made their way down to the entrance to the village. Mohun checked their location. The village was about fifty meters inland from the beach of a small cove, sheltered to the west and east by the headlands of the cove and to the north by a short line of forested hillocks.

He trained the scanner on the village. The few houses which he could see through the trees were stained or painted in dull earth colored hues. The archway looked as though it were made from small blocks of stone, similar in color to sandstone. He could not see anyone in the village at all. He was aware of Sima's voice murmuring in his headset and as he looked, the figures of Sally, Alistair and Sima passed under the arch. His heart skipped a beat Vicki was gazing at the small figures on the screen of her data pad, her expression a mixture of anxiety and expectation.

Sally looked back up the hill and waved as she led the way through the arch. She always followed her instincts when she entered a new community and nothing suggested any danger to her.

She tripped slightly and looked down. Beyond the arch the path widened out into a broad paved lane. Alistair knelt to examine the stones and whistled in amazement. 'Looks like slate!'

Each side of the lane was lined with several single story dwellings. They appeared to be made of mud bricks, but the doors and window spaces were lined with dark wood. The roofs were irregular, with small wooden tiles around the edges and a sort of thatch work higher up. It was easy to see why they had flown by the day before without seeing the village. The colors blended in with the surrounding vegetation.

There was no one nearby but at the far end of the lane a number of people were standing. Sally checked that her data pad was on and then moved slowly towards them. A single figure stepped forwards and she thought she recognized the man she had seen that morning, although now he was dressed in a soft light brown tunic and loose trousers that fell to just below his knees. She stopped, and as he neared, she repeated her greeting. The man spoke and she felt certain that he was repeating what he said earlier.

When she did not reply at once, he turned away again, went past the people at the other end of the lane and out of sight. For a few moments the two groups looked at each other. When the crew did not move, the villagers slowly walked towards them, stopped a few feet away and stood silently. Sally, Sima and Alistair kept perfectly still, hardly daring to breathe. These people were dressed in similar clothes, but were clearly male and female. They were all dark haired and dark eyed, with light olive complexions. Their figures were slender and perfectly formed with no sign of disease or infirmity, their faces uniformly handsome and strangely alike, with fine, well shaped features.

Finally one of the women repeated the young man's words. Sally decided to say them back and got the same reaction; the woman spoke rapidly for a few moments, in a monotonous tone and waited for Sally's response. Sally looked down at her data pad. There was nothing new on the display.

Again, the woman's reaction was similar to the young man's. She spoke a few words to the others and they all turned away as though the crew were of no further interest and walked slowly away.

Sally turned to Sima. 'Let's try to offer them something.'

Sima reached into his backpack and took out one of the parcels. Sally picked out a beautiful piece of silk cloth, patterned with animals and birds. As they passed the houses, they noticed a few people looked out at them. Sally smiled but the faces remained expressionless. She counted what seemed to be about twelve separate dwellings and then the lane opened onto a small grassy area. Several people were reclining on the grass, some alone, some in pairs. Sally noticed for the first time that they all appeared to be around the same age. In Earth terms she reckoned them to be in their mid twenties to early thirties.

Alistair panned the video camera discreetly around the scene. No one paid any attention to him, which he thought was very odd. He zoomed in on several faces and each time he felt a strange constriction in his heart. He could hardly believe what he was seeing. He had always imagined a first contact to be accompanied by strong emotions on both sides. But these people, who looked so human, acted as though the newcomers were part of everyday life. That must be it, he thought. These people must get a lot of visitors and not all of them speak their language. It didn't explain their complete lack of curiosity about all the gadgets that they were carrying, but perhaps they didn't recognize them for what they were. To them, they might just be some strange forms of decoration. Whatever the reasons, their behavior was fascinating.

Sally cautiously made her way across the grass to where a small stream had been damned into a pool. Several pitchers and cups stood on a wide stone ledge around the pool. She examined them excitedly and called to Alistair and Sima. The cups and most of the pitchers were pottery but one of the pitchers was clearly bronze. A narrow relief with a leaf design was etched around the neck. She looked at Sima and Alistair. They were speechless.

While Alistair filmed the drinking vessels, the pool and its surroundings, Sally picked up the bronze pitcher and walked over to the nearest couple. Sima followed her closely. She gestured to the woman and held out the silk and the pitcher. The young woman took both from her and examined the silk. She spoke to her companion, gave the silk back to Sally and returned the pitcher to the stone ledge. Sally followed her and offered her the silk again. The woman said a few words but did not take the silk. When Sally did not reply she went back to her companion and sat down. Sally left the silk on the ledge and took the pitcher. As she walked away the woman got up again, picked up the silk and held it out to Sally. She did not try to take the pitcher from her.

'What was that all about?' Alistair had filmed the entire encounter.

'I've got a few ideas, but I'd like to think about it.'

Two broad paths led out of the grassy area. One to the south obviously led to the beach. They took the second path, which led towards the hill to the east of the village. No one followed them and when Sally looked back she saw that no one was watching them.

For a few meters the path wound through the same bushy flowering trees that covered the hills to the north. Sally stopped as the path forked; they could hear some voices in the distance.

Sima shrugged. 'Which way first?'

Sally turned left and the voices grew louder. The path widened out and suddenly they entered a large open area. A flat piece of land, about a hundred meters square had been cleared of trees and was planted out with vines, small bushes and rows of green and orange foliage. The area was a mass of color and the cultivation extended up the side of the hill. Several people were working in the gardens. Sally called out to them and they looked up. They did not speak and when she remained silent they returned to their work. She wondered whether the young man had warned them.

No one looked at them as they wandered through the gardens. Sally picked a large pod from one of the vines which was suspended from tall stakes. It was a greenish color, the shape of a mango, with pale reddish pink streaks radiating from each end. She took it over to one of the women who was stripping dead leaves off a tall plant and held it out to her. She repeated the phrase she had heard before, which she hoped might mean - "who are you?"

The woman looked at her calmly and took the fruit. She went back to where Sally had picked it and reached further up the vine. She was taller than Sally and could reach almost to the top of the stake. She pulled off another pod and gave it to Sally. This one was dark pink with only a few traces of green around the middle. It was obviously riper than the one Sally had picked.

'Thank you.' Sally offered the silk to the woman. She took it, looked at it and handed it back, without speaking. Then she went back to her work.

* * *

'Well, there's a million things I want to know, but two things at least are clear. There must be at least one other settlement quite nearby and there must be a very large population of them on the planet.' Sally had finished her summary of their visit and the others looked impressed at how much she had been able to glean from a two hour visit.

'Could you explain why you think that's so?' John was pleased that he had insisted they all stay aboard the shuttles in the meanwhile. For this meeting they were squeezed into Radon, Thomas still occupying one bunk and apparently oblivious to the proceedings.

Sally looked at Alistair and Sima. 'This is what I think so far. Please butt in if you disagree or think I've forgotten something.' She paused and looked down at her data pad. 'There's no sign of how they manufacture all the artifacts they use. Most of their gear is typical of a Bronze Age culture but there's nothing to suggest that this group work with metals or even turn pots or wood. And some of their items are much more sophisticated. We saw some box like objects which looked as though they were made of very light weight metal.'

She took a deep breath before continuing. 'Also they seem to eat a big variety of food. We saw evidence of bread, some stuff that looked and smelt like cheese and lots of different fruit and vegetables. These people obviously live by fishing. They have a small orchard and some gardens but not enough to supply them with that sort of variety. Certainly they are not cultivating grain anywhere nearby. Also, we didn't see any domesticated animals.'

Sima took up the argument. 'There were storerooms with dried fish and other containers which we didn't get a chance to look at. Our guess is that there is regular trading going on. And they do not seem to lack for anything. They obviously need not work very hard. Most of them were sitting around as though they were on holiday.'

'The strangest thing of all is that there were no children or elderly people there. We reckon that everyone we saw was aged between early twenties and late thirties.' Sally turned to Alistair and Sima and they nodded in agreement.

She went on. 'Perhaps they send their children away, for education or some other purpose. But it doesn't explain where the elderly are. They are all also remarkably good looking and appear to be in perfect health. I can't imagine they all just drop dead when they reach forty.' She paused. 'There are no ugly or deformed individuals in the group we saw.' She frowned. 'That may explain why there are no elderly people. Perhaps the old and infirm are kept elsewhere, or even eliminated.'

Mohun grimaced. 'They could have sent the children into hiding when they saw you earlier. But you would think that they would keep their older people around – you know, as sort of village elders, to meet you.'

'But they didn't show any interest in us at all. It's almost as though they meet strangers everyday – others who don't speak their language.' Alistair was still amazed by the encounter, mostly for what had not happened. He had expected fear, excitement or even revulsion, not the casual, off hand reaction to their appearance.

'Of course, we can't assume anything,' said Sally. 'These people look like humans and most of their artifacts are amazingly like humans'. But it's very difficult to work out what they are feeling. Their faces are quite expressionless, in comparison with ours and they have minimal non-verbal behavior when they speak. All of these must be much more subtle than ours, or they express emotion quite differently. The way they allowed me to take the fruit and the pitcher and would not accept anything in return suggests they have definite rules for things like hospitality.'

'How about the language?' asked Sharon.

'I managed to get a huge amount of data in, although not much in the way of non-verbal information. I found that by repeating back to them some things they said - that seemed to get them to say something further. The language is quite easy to pronounce. It sounds like a mixture of Italian and a Polynesian language, with a few words thrown in ending with softish consonants. They use very few gestures; very little facial expression and there's almost no tonal variation, so it's hard to get any meaning from it. I'm going to run the data through the translator and see what it comes up with.'

'Well, if we let you get on with that, I'm sure the others would like to look at the replays. Sima can check whatever DNA you picked up.' John looked over to Sharon. 'Is this door OK now?'

Sharon nodded and John turned to Sima. 'Any changes to Thomas?'

'Not really. I've given him something to help him sleep. We'll have to see what he's like tomorrow. If he wanders off again, he might injure himself this time. Also we don't know what these people are capable of. They may not be aggressive, but they have weapons, if you count their tools and knives. And if Thomas does something strange they make take it the wrong way.'

John stood up and picked up his pack. 'Sharon, Sima, you keep a watch on the perimeter. Everyone check their side arms. We'll meet again in a couple of hours to decide our strategy for tomorrow. Wherever these people came from, we need to find out if there are any more.'

14

'OK. Here's the plan for today.' John was sitting on Xenon's metal ramp, his data pad in his hand. 'There's no sign of any other settlement nearby, so we'll focus on these people. Hopefully the news will spread and others will turn up. None of the satellite data suggests any unusual electrical activity so they must be at a fairly primitive stage. Just as well for us I guess. Still we need to be on our guard.'

He and Mohun had spent most of the previous two days surveying the nearby area. There was no sign of any other settlement for a radius of more than 200 kilometers. In the north and east a flat barren plateau extended beyond the lines of hills. An unbroken line of cliffs to the east edged the coastline. To the west the grasslands alternated with small forests, bordered by beaches. Nothing suggested any recent habitation, cultivation or industry.

The rest of the crew had made several visits to the 'village'. The people allowed them to wander freely through the buildings and gardens and for the most part ignored them. Sally had introduced the crew and tried to get the people to give their own names. Each time they had spoken the same word – 'Anomee'. She assumed it was the tribal or family name. When she pointed to and named different objects, they did not respond, as though they did not understand that she was trying to learn their language. She had recorded many words but when she tried to use them, they just repeated what she had said.

John looked around at the crew's excited faces. Thomas was sitting slightly apart from the group, staring morosely at the ground. 'You OK Thomas?' he called. Thomas raised his head. His face was strained but he nodded. When the crew came back from the last visit to the village he had seemed to suffer from an enormous panic attack. Sima had sedated him but he looked as though he had hardly slept.

'I'll be all right.'

'Good, but in any case, you and I will stay here and work on the maintenance schedule. Sally and Alistair are heading for the hills. Sally can use the time to get more data into her translator.'

The previous day, Alistair had shown one of the Anomee women a picture of his niece and nephew standing next to Ben and Claudia, and Sally had made gestures as if to ask where the village children were. The woman did not speak but led them up to the top of a nearby hillock and pointed east towards the line of hills. She clearly gestured that she would take them there when the sun rose the next morning. Sally and Alistair were amazed. They were not sure that the woman understood what they were asking but finally they felt that they were starting to communicate.

'We don't know...' John paused. The crew referred to the Earth 2 people as though they were human but he still didn't feel comfortable with that. 'We don't know what this Anomee woman wants to show them, but they may as well go take a look. It's about a two-hour hike, perhaps three if the woman is in no hurry. That gives you a couple of hours to look around and then you start back. Understood?'

'Ok.' Sally nodded.

John checked his data pad. 'The DNA tests are still running. We can't speed that up, so Sima and Vicki are going back to the bay to collect marine samples. Just make sure that you aren't separated and if anyone seems to take offence at what you're doing, give it up and come back.'

Sima felt irritated. John was stating the obvious.

John continued. 'Thomas can help Sharon with the maintenance. It would be good if we could get Snoopy working again. We need to find out where the rest of these people are.'

Sharon frowned. 'I still don't understand what's wrong with the stabilization unit. It worked perfectly yesterday.'

John shrugged. 'Sorry Mohun, you get to stay here with us.'

Mohun nodded.

'Voice contact with me every thirty minutes for everyone out of sight of the camp. At all times you must be in visual contact with at least one other crewmember. Keep your side arms prepped.'

A few minutes later Sally and Alistair made off in the direction of the village. Sima and Vicki climbed up the small hillock to the west of the camp and disappeared from view. Mohun noticed that Sharon walked behind Thomas as they headed towards Snoopy.

John's watcher buzzed and he heard Sally's voice. 'Everything's OK. We're setting off now.' He could see them in the distance, the village woman walking ahead of them. He checked the sky. There was no sign of unusual weather and the barometer readings were steady.

Mohun sighed and followed John into Xenon. The next two hours passed monotonously; the tedious maintenance checks interrupted only by calls from Sima and Alistair. From time to time Mohun looked down the ramp and watched as Sharon and Thomas worked on the flyer. Thomas stood like a robot, passing pieces of equipment to Sharon.

John suggested they take a break. Mohun stretched his arms and legs as he walked back down the ramp.

'Coffee?' he called out. Sharon looked up and smiled. She finished the adjustment she was making and then walked over to the camp kitchen. Thomas followed slowly.

Mohun poured water into the heater and found the mugs. John sat down on one of the folding chairs and flexed his shoulders.

'Thanks Mohun. Sorry it was so boring.'

'It has to be done.' Mohun smiled and handed John a mug.

Thomas stood up abruptly. 'I need to pee,' he said and walked over to the small tent which housed the chemical toilet.

Mohun thought how Thomas always sounded strange when he used slang; after listening to Thomas's mother's cold voice on Christmas Eve, it wasn't hard to understand why. It was common knowledge that some people entered the medical professions because they had an almost pathological preoccupation with their own physical or mental health. Thomas was a real stitched up character, Mohun thought. None of the crew really felt they knew him. A pity about David Liu; everyone had liked the Chinese psychologist. He frowned as he remembered the scene at Geneva airport.

'Thomas. Are you all right?' John was standing in front of the small tent. There was no reply.

'Thomas!' repeated John more loudly. He waited a moment and then pulled back the flap. The tent was empty. He raced around to the other side of the tent. There was no sign of Thomas. The bottom of the canvas was furled up and it was clear how he had managed to get out without attracting their attention.

Mohun knocked his coffee over as he jumped up from his seat. John spoke loudly into his watcher. 'Thomas! Where are you?' He looked at the display and shook his head impatiently.

John cursed. 'Sharon! Is Snoopy fixed? Can you fly it?'

'I wouldn't like to take the chance. It's still unstable.'

'Shit! Sharon – you and Mohun take Lassie and look for Thomas. Keep in constant contact.'

'I could go faster if I'm alone,' Sharon interrupted.

'No! If you see Thomas, get him down and sedate him.' John didn't explain how they should do this and Mohun winced as Sharon checked her handgun.

John turned and raced up to the top of the hillock. He looked around quickly and then raised his scanner and surveyed the scene more thoroughly. He could see Sharon and Mohun flying steadily towards the east. They made a wide turn and headed south towards the bay. They were flying at maximum speed and Lassie wobbled slightly with the weight of the two passengers.

'Sima! Can you hear me?'

'I hear you John.'

'Thomas has gone again. He seemed OK, not like yesterday. Finish whatever you're doing and get back here pronto. Stay in contact. If you see Thomas, be careful.'

'Damn! OK. We'll be back soon.' John heard Sima shout something to Vicki before he ended the call.

John continued his scan, moving more slowly. There was not much chance he would spot Thomas if the man were trying to hide. The valley was dotted with clumps of trees and small rock formations. He saw Sharon and Mohun flying slowly over the village. They circled twice before landing. John cursed again. They had been trying not to over expose the Anomee to their technology.

'Making contact, John. We're almost at the foothills.' John heard Alistair's Australian accent with relief. He turned his scanner in the direction of the range of hills to the east but could not see them. A group of large boulders blocked his view.

'John! Are you there?' Alistair sounded alarmed.

'Sorry. We've got a problem. Thomas has disappeared again.'

'Do you want us to come back?' asked Alistair. John heard the irritation in his voice. He knew that the others were getting sick of this. They seemed to spend half their time looking for Thomas or discussing what to do about him.

'No. It's OK. Vicki and Sima are nearer and Snoopy still isn't operational. There's not much you could do.' He repeated his instructions to exercise caution if they saw Thomas.

'Understood. We'll stay in touch. We're heading for some caves but we won't go inside till we contact you again.'

John made another circular sweep with his scanner. He saw Vicki and Sima running towards him. They were about two k away and as he watched, he saw the flyer reach them. It hovered above them for a few seconds. Then it veered off to the north, as though Sima and Vicki had told Sharon that they had not seen Thomas further west.

John mounted a small rise and scanned the area systematically. It was hopeless. There were a million places Thomas could hide if he wanted to. The man's illness was seriously jeopardizing the mission. When they found him he would have to be restrained again.

The thought flashed through his mind that Thomas might be correct about the hallucinations and that he felt endangered by their behavior. John pushed the thought away. He was glad when Sima and Vicki came running up towards him. They leaned forward with their hands on their knees, breathing hard.

'Any news?' panted Sima.

John shook his head. 'I've told Alistair and Sally to keep going. There's no point all of us wasting the day on this.'

Vicki sat down, but Sima prowled around restlessly, frowning in thought. 'If only we could discover why Thomas is behaving like this, we could work out how to treat him. I think I'll have another look at all our blood tests. Unless, there's something else you want me to do?'

John shook his head. 'I can't think of anything. Vicki and I will go round the perimeter again just in case I missed something.'

'Where are Sally and Alistair now?' Vicki asked.

John looked at his watcher and swore. They were late calling in.

'Alistair! Where are you?' The watcher stayed silent. Vicki jumped up, dropping her water bottle. John frowned at her and gestured for her to sit down.

'Alistair?' He ended the call. 'Sally?' He took a deep breath and repeated the calls. There was no answer.

Vicki sat frozen, watching John check the GPS and the beacon and try twice more to make contact.

'This is too much of a coincidence,' he said finally. 'We have to consider that Thomas, in fact that all three of them may have been taken by force. There is no way that Alistair would have put himself and Sally out of contact with us.'

He stood up. 'I'm taking up Xenon to look for them. Sima - call Sharon and Mohun. I'll meet them at the foothills. Secure the site and take all the essential equipment into Radon. If anything unusual happens, take off. We'll rendezvous back here, or if that's not safe, back at our first landing site.'

He headed towards the shuttle, disappeared up the ramp and the outer door closed. A few minutes later some dust rose and a few papers blew off the table as Xenon rose vertically away from them.

Vicki felt paralyzed but Sima's voice snapped her out of her thoughts. For the next few minutes they raced around the campsite as Sima shouted orders. He circled the camp, his handgun held out at arm's length. Vicki felt as though she were in the middle of some ridiculous action movie. She tried not to think about why John and Sima were taking the situation so seriously. Surely Alistair and Sally had just gone out of range. She furtively dialed Sally again; no reply. She started to feel sick.

Finally, Sima holstered the gun and came over to help her push Snoopy up the ramp into Radon. They secured the flyer in the airlock.

'What now?' Vicki tried to control the panic in her voice.

'Stay here; any trouble, lock yourself inside.' Sima avoided looking at her and ran back to the small hillock to continue his surveillance.

Vicki sat tensely, clutching her gun. She kept pressing the call stud on her watcher, hoping against hope that Alistair or Sally would answer. When she heard Lassie approaching, she checked her watcher. It was less than an hour since John had raised the alarm. It had seemed like days.

Sharon went directly over to Sima but Mohun came to sit next to Vicki. He gave her a sympathetic hug. 'I'm sure that it's just a coincidence. They've probably gone out of range but have found something that they feel they have to follow up.'

Vicki shook her head. 'Sally might do that. But Alistair never would. They must have had an accident.'

Mohun rubbed his face and shut his eyes. He tried to focus on the problem. Something niggled at the back of his mind. He felt sure that if he thought about it hard enough he would recognize some clue as to what was going on.

A few moments later they heard Lassie's whining and saw Sharon flying alone back towards the hills.

Sima scanned the horizon. It was impossible to see the land at the bottom of the hills because of the large rocks scattered around the foothills. He looked over to the village. Everything seemed normal there. He descended the hillock in a few strides and started to circle back to the camp. A small rock hidden in the long grass sent him staggering to his knees and he sat for a moment cursing softly.

He looked around. This area had seemed like paradise when they had first glimpsed it. The long grass was lush dark green here, partly shaded from the sun by the small hill. He glimpsed something white near his boot, parted the grass and saw a small crop of white fungi. He picked one and looked at it more closely. It was like a miniature version of the wild mushrooms that grew in the forest near his parents' home. He crushed the small mushroom and smelled his fingers. The aroma was almost exactly the same and he was suddenly carried back to his last visit home. The family had spent several hours mushrooming and had carried back heavy baskets to share with families and friends. He closed his eyes. He felt as though something was squeezing his heart as he remembered watching his mother set the table for the evening meal, placing plates of his favorite sausage and dark brown bread on the table. She had added a dish of pickles and had turned to smile at him. 'To neutralize the vodka' she had laughed, referring to the fact that he and his father would inevitably drink more than she thought they ought.

After the meal he had helped to place the family samovar in the middle of the table. It looked just as grand and imposing to him as it had when he was young and had been told how many generations of Vaschenkos had taken tea from this ornate heirloom.

His heart contracted again as he remembered his father struggling to his feet to toast his famous son. Tears suddenly came to his eyes and he brushed them away impatiently and stood up. His mother had always encouraged him to let his feelings out, admiring her son's bright blue eyes, made more charming by the tears welling in them. But his father had told him to control himself. Better to be 'gloomy as doom than tearful as a stream' he had said, quoting the local saying.

He ran his hand over his short-cropped blond hair. He felt the same old frustration, the same tension between the desire to feel and the need to act. He ran back up the hill and saw that Mohun was slumped down, his face in his hands.

'Mohun!' Sima shouted. 'Stay alert.'

Mohun jumped up and paced backwards and forwards while Vicki watched him nervously. She felt drained of energy. She tried to concentrate on something else. She looked out over the valley. A small figure was approaching from the east. Her heart lifted and then sank when she realized that it was one of the village women. She called out to Sima and pointed. The woman was heading for the village but Sima ran out to intercept her. Vicki could see her standing passively as Sima gestured towards the hills. Sima seemed to be trying to persuade her to come back to the camp, but she pulled away from him and continued towards the village.

Sima walked slowly back to Radon and sat down on the ramp.

'Do you think that was the woman who went with Sally and Alistair?' asked Mohun.

'I don't know,' admitted Sima. 'I wish I had taken more notice of her. If we had known …' He frowned. 'It probably would not have helped. I still cannot see any difference between most of them; almost the same height, same age …' His voice trailed off.

'They are amazingly alike.' Vicki spoke quickly to fill the silence. 'Perhaps they are an extended family group; since they use the same name. It's so strange. They seem so perfect, so good looking.' She stopped abruptly. Neither Mohun nor Sima was listening.

Sima returned to his post at the top of the hillock. Each time he raised his watcher to his mouth Vicki's heart pounded. Mohun paced up and down, his face averted. The time passed drearily, interrupted by attempts to eat and calls from Sharon and John. As the twilight descended, Sima shouted out and they heard Xenon's low drone. Sharon landed Lassie a few moments later.

Vicki and Mohun set up the camp kitchen again and prepared some food. John and Sharon sat down without a word and they ate in silence. Finally they reported on their search. They had been unable to find the caves that Alistair had mentioned. They had landed and searched the area on foot for several hundred meters around the position of Alistair's last call. The upper slopes of the hills were quite bare of vegetation and revealed no sign of their friends. They had used the long-range scanners to scan the plateau and then flown along the cliffs.

John tried to speak calmly. 'There are two possibilities I can think of. The watchers can't be switched off and they are almost indestructible. So someone has either removed their watchers or is preventing them from using them. Or they have entered an area which somehow is blocking the watchers' signals.' He paused. 'Has anyone any other ideas?'

When no one replied he continued. 'In any case, we'll continue the search in shifts, using the spotlights.'

There was a long silence. When Sima's watcher buzzed Vicki started violently.

'The DNA tests should be finished by now. I may as well check them.' Sima entered the shuttle and a few moments later called out to John.

John found him staring at his medlab screen. 'The DNA software seems to have gone mad. None of the readings make any sense.'

John swore. 'What the hell? Can you fix it?'

'I don't know. I can download the software again from the Millennium system but I think all the data is corrupted.' Sima touched the screen. 'Someone else has rerun the program. He touched the screen again. 'Apart from you, me and Sharon, only Thomas can access medlab.'

'Why would he do that? He must be mad. Can you restore the data?'

'I can try.'

'For heaven's sake, don't say anything to Vicki or Mohun.'

Vicki and Sharon bunked down in Radon and tried to sleep. Sima watched as Xenon lifted off and then restarted the medlab program.

15

Sima stood for a moment studying Vicki, as she sat gazing out towards the hills. The sun was high in the sky but she was rubbing her hands together as though she felt cold.

Throughout the short night John and Mohun had continued the search. At dawn Sima and Sharon had taken over. For five hours, they had systematically searched every gully and crevice in the rocky landscape in a five hundred meter radius from Alistair's last call. Vicki had wanted to join them. She couldn't focus on any of her work. From time to time she dialed Alistair's or Sally's watchers. They remained unresponsive. She knew that the watchers were programmed to send out a signal if damaged or if their wearers' body suits malfunctioned and she tried to take some comfort from this.

Sima put his hand on Vicki's shoulder. 'Why don't we go back to Discovery Cove? The tide's out and we could collect some marine samples. We still haven't figured out how these people stay so healthy. I think their diet might provide a clue.'

Vicki shook her head. 'I want to look for Sally and Alistair.'

'Sharon and Mohun are taking the next shift. We can't do more until John fixes Snoopy.' Sima shook her gently. 'Come on. It will help us to think about something else for a while.'

Vicki felt drained of strength or energy. Sima took her hand and pulled her to her feet. She leaned against him for a moment and then turned away, heading for Xenon. She avoided looking at Sally's bunk and quickly loaded her gear into her backpack.

John looked around as they called goodbye and set off to the west. They passed several village people walking towards or from the beach. They glanced at Vicki and Sima, with no change of expression. Sima wondered again how they managed to have so much leisure time.

After a while Sima saw that Vicki was walking with more of her usual energy. They had been following a narrow track through the trees but now they emerged into open grasslands. He took her free hand and swung it. She tried to smile at him. This was one of the few times they had managed to be alone.

A mild breeze blew a fresh fragrance towards them. Some of the long grasses were flowering after last night's gentle rain. Tiny blue flowers bobbed as they pushed through the knee high grass. The weather was remarkable. The temperature varied only a few degrees from midnight to noon. Since the cloud cover had dispersed the sky was nearly always clear. The soft rain fell steadily almost every night, usually in the two or three hours before dawn, so that each morning they awoke to a scene of glistening freshness.

He glanced at Vicki. She looked disconsolate again. He put his arm around her waist but it was awkward trying to walk together through the grass, so he pulled her to a stop. He put his arms around her and kissed her. She responded warmly and they stood there for several minutes. They didn't speak but continued on their way, still holding hands.

As they reached the top of the hillock overlooking the bay, John called.

'Did you see that dark cloud? It appeared out of nowhere and now it's disappeared.'

Sima looked around. The sky as usual, was perfectly clear. 'Sorry. Didn't see a thing.'

'It didn't come up on the system. Very odd.'

'I'll watch out for it.'

Vicki walked ahead. She felt strangely moved by the beauty of the view. Perhaps it was because she knew she was not on Earth but something about the scene was quite magical. The bay was a perfect turquoise semicircle, lined with pure white sand. The receding tide had left hundreds of sparkling rock pools on the headland. She looked back. Sima was still speaking to John. She felt a sudden nervous energy and ran down the hill, over the sand dune and clambered over the dark rock. She knelt down and stared into a small pool. There were dozens of brightly colored mollusks clinging to the rocky sides, and small crustaceans busily swam around the sandy bottom of the small pool. She gazed in fascination for a few moments and then scooped some water and sand into one of her canisters. She used another jar to trap some of the sea creatures, tipped them into the first jar and closed the top.

Some of the water splashed onto her and she shivered slightly. She had the sudden feeling of being watched. She looked around but she could not see Sima. She stood up, almost dropping the canister as she did. She put it down and looked around again. 'Sima,' she shouted. 'Where are you?'

She heard a man's voice calling out. It seemed to be coming from the sea. She felt confused and disoriented.

'Sima!' she shouted again. She looked back towards the water and saw a figure sitting on a rock, looking towards her. It was not Sima. She backed away as the massive figure stood up. Vicki felt the blood pound in her ears and she tried to lift her watcher to her mouth. She felt her mouth open and close. She was trying to speak but the words would not come. A terrible weakness over came her and she could not move.

The man approached her with a slow, stately walk; his tall powerful figure was clothed in a long gown the color of seaweed, his face beautiful but strangely symmetrical and very pale. As he came nearer Vicki could see threads of what looked like silver and gold woven through his long tangled hair and golden brown beard.

He stopped a few meters away and beckoned to her. Her heart thumped in her chest. She shook her head and stepped back as he moved towards her. Unlike the Anomee, his face was full of expression – arrogance, amusement and then, as she continued to back away, anger. Her feet felt heavy and she could hardly lift them.

The man stopped and raised his arm. He spoke in a deep voice. Vicki sidled away, looking around frantically for Sima. The man spoke more loudly and she stumbled and sat down heavily on the sand.

He stooped down and took her arm. She felt a shock go through her as though she had been electrocuted. The man spoke again. The sounds were sharper and longer than the Anomee speech. When she did not respond, the man shook her arm angrily. He walked around her as though to examine her from every angle.

'Sima! Where are you?' Vicki tried to shout.

The man stopped and abruptly pulled her to her feet. He stared closely at her face. She could not look away.

'Who are you?' The man spoke harshly and shook her arm again.

Vicki's knees buckled at the shock of hearing the man speak English.

The man jerked her upright and with his other huge hand touched the corner of her eye. He looked puzzled and then smiled. 'Ah! Not Anomee. Mortal. Where are your friends?'

Vicki heard herself muttering, 'Sima, Sima' in a thin squeaky voice.

'What are you saying? Speak to me!' The man grasped her face and forced her to meet his eyes. They were a strange grey green color and very clear, like the eyes of a child.

Vicki gasped. 'Who are you?'

'You do not know me?' The man frowned and let her go. She fell backwards onto the sand and he smiled unpleasantly. 'You should know me. Have you forgotten so soon? I am Poseidon, brother to Zeus.'

Vicki trembled violently. She struggled to her feet and shouted Sima's name. The man swept out his arm and pushed her down. He walked several paces into the water and raised his arms. A loud sound like a trumpet call reverberated for several seconds. Vicki could hear herself screaming and suddenly Sima was kneeling beside her. She pressed her face against his shoulder.

'Vicki! Look!' Sima's voice was hoarse.

She followed his gaze and saw a large vessel approaching the shore. It was shaped like an ancient Greek warship. The sails were only half full but the trireme moved rapidly towards them. Several figures swam ahead of it, their green bodies glistening as they splashed through the bright water.

Sima pulled Vicki upright and they staggered back up the beach.

'Stay where you are!' The man's voice was thunderous.

Vicki stumbled and Sima looked back. The boat had halted a few meters from the shore. The sails remained inflated but the oars were drawn in and Sima could see no crew or what propelled the boat. His stomach lurched as three of the green figures swam rapidly towards the shore and sprang onto the rocks. Their green-scaled tails flipped and glistened in the sunlight. Three alien faces, surrounded by tangled green blond hair stared curiously at Sima and Vicki.

'It is a very long time since they have seen mortals.' The mermaids slid back into the water and one of them made a beckoning gesture. Sima started forward but Vicki pulled at his arm.

The man roared with laughter. 'You may go with them. I will take your woman.'

Vicki cried out but Sima was silent. The creatures' grey green gaze had an almost hypnotic effect. He could not turn away.

The man strode up to them and took Vicki's hand. He towered over them and smiled at their stunned expressions. He fingered the tips of Vicki's hair and stroked her face. 'You are very beautiful. Not like the Anomee.' When she pulled away, he smiled and grasped her arm. 'I will take you now.'

Vicki screamed and Sima shook his head. He felt dazed; he fumbled for his gun but the man reached out and pushed him away. Sima fell back, shook his head again and staggered to his feet. The man dragged Vicki towards the boat and as she resisted he picked her up. Sima lurched through the water and flung himself at them. The man dropped Vicki and slapped Sima down into the water. Something heavy pressed on Sima's back and he struggled violently. Darkness overwhelmed him, and he choked as water filled his nose and mouth. Then Vicki was shaking him. He gasped and coughed, his chest heaving.

'It's all right. He's gone.'

'What?'

'There was a noise; like thunder - strange flashing lights - over there.' She pointed to the east. He dropped me, and then I couldn't see him.' Vicki started to shake. 'I thought you were dead.' She wrapped her arms around him. Sima looked over her shoulder. There was no sign of the boat.

'Sima! Come in, Sima, can you hear me?'

Sima coughed violently and shook his head. 'Sorry John.' His voice was husky and he swallowed a few times before continuing. 'We've just had the strangest experience. We're going to start back right now.'

'I thought you were going to stay longer. Report, Sima. What are you talking about?

Sima briefly described what had happened, as Vicki leaned against him trembling violently. 'You'd better call Sharon and Mohun back,' he concluded.

Sima pulled Vicki to her feet. 'We have to get out of here.' He looked around on the sand and found his gun.

Vicki found it hard to stand upright. Her head spun. 'I need to talk about what happened. I can't believe it.'

Sima said grimly. 'It was real. That guy almost killed me.' He put his arm around her waist and they staggered up the small dunes. They stumbled on in silence for a few minutes, Sima surveying the horizon continuously.

'Where were you?' Vicki stopped. 'I was calling and calling for you. Where were you?'

Sima looked puzzled. 'I was talking to John. As soon as I heard you scream ...' His voice tailed off. 'It doesn't make sense. I didn't see anything until you screamed.'

Vicki dropped to her knees. 'What if Thomas is right? We must be hallucinating'

Sima knelt down beside her and stroked her hair. 'Be calm.' He took her hand. 'Look at your arm. Those finger marks are real. And my chest hurts like hell.' He let go her hand. He felt humiliated by his inability to protect Vicki. 'Don't say we just dreamed it up.'

'But he was speaking English. How could that be?' Vicki's voice shook. 'It can't be real.'

Sima leaned forward and kissed her hard. 'We're not hallucinating now are we?' His voice was rough and Vicki started to cry. He put his arms around her and kissed her again. She leaned against him for a few moments and then he shook her gently. 'We have to get back.'

Vicki nodded. She squeezed his hand and walked on determinedly.

It was a strange journey home. Everything looked different. The colors of the grass and flowers seemed exaggerated, too bright, too clear. Small clouds were gathering in the afternoon sky, as they always did. Vicki tried to think about what had happened. It was starting to seem unreal. Then the brutal man's face flashed before her eyes and her stomach heaved.

'Those damn birds.' Sima exclaimed and pointed to the south.

Vicki raised her scanner as the two black dots disappeared behind some trees. 'I can never get a fix on them. They look like ravens. It's strange that we never see them land.'

They called out as they approached the camp. Vicki felt a moment's terror when no one answered. The domes were empty. Then John emerged from Radon's airlock. 'We're in here. Mohun needs your help.'

16

Mohun was lying on a bunk shivering uncontrollably, his teeth chattering. John looked at him with real distress. 'We've given him a mild tranquilizer but we didn't want to do anything else until you'd examined him.'

Sharon was sitting next to the bunk, her face set and strained. They watched silently as Sima pulled Mohun's body suit off. He started back in shock. Mohun's chest and arms were dotted with small dark punctures. Sima pulled on some gloves and examined the marks closely. Mohun did not react when he touched them.

'They don't hurt at all,' Mohun stuttered and clenched his teeth. He took a deep breath and spoke slowly. 'My whole body feels numb. I thought I was going to pass out.

'I'm going to take a sample. Stay still.' Sima swabbed one of the larger punctures with some local anesthetic and prepared a syringe. 'I don't want to put anything on these things until I find out what they are.' He took a small sample and then swabbed Mohun's skin again. He inserted the capsule into the medlab and tapped in the readings he wanted.

'They don't look as though they're getting worse. There's no swelling.' He helped Mohun pull on his suit.

Sharon had heated up some soup. Sima gripped his warm mug. In the familiar surroundings of the shuttle, the attack at Discovery Bay seemed like a bizarre nightmare. 'Vicki and I had a very unpleasant experience today, but I think we should let Mohun tell us what happened to him first. He needs to rest.'

Mohun still had difficulty speaking. 'We were heading back, when we saw something dark moving in a clump of trees. We thought it might be Thomas. We took Lassie down and I went in to have a look. Don't worry,' Mohun added as he saw John frown, 'Sharon could see me the whole time. That is until, something hit the flyer.'

Sharon interrupted. 'I was watching Mohun, and looking around with the scanner. This brilliant flash of light appeared – it looked about a mile away, and a few hundred feet up, but hard to tell. I couldn't look at it directly – too bright. It sort of hovered for a few seconds. Then it headed straight for me. I thought it might be some electrical charge that was attracted to the metal on the flyer so I went to jump off, but it was too fast. It was like being hit by a bolt of lightning. I heard a crashing noise – like thunder and then I was on the ground - a clear ten meters from Lassie.' She frowned. 'But I wasn't hurt. I wasn't even winded. I couldn't believe it. I was lucky to be alive.'

She hesitated and her face reddened. 'The peculiar thing is, my body suit was unzipped right down the front. I suppose I must have done it when I was semi conscious. It's stupid I know but I feel like there was someone there with me.'

Sima said gently 'I'd better check you too, especially after what happened to us.'

John interrupted. 'There was no sign of any electrical activity or any other unusual phenomena on the system. I checked when Sharon called me. And Lassie's not damaged apart from a bent handrail.'

'I wanted to get Mohun back here so I didn't look closely. But I couldn't see any burnt material, grass or anything around the flyer.' No one spoke so Sharon continued.

'When I found Mohun, he was in a really bad way. He was delirious, thrashing around all over the place and shouting and cursing. When I tried to help him, he almost knocked me out. I gave him a stun shot. It was the only thing I could do.' She looked at Mohun apologetically. 'I don't know how long I was out cold, or how long he was like that.'

'You couldn't have been unconscious for long – only five minutes between your calls.'

'It was like a bad dream,' Mohun said. His voice was shaking. 'I thought I saw someone ahead of me. I thought it might be Thomas, so I didn't call out. Then I realized it was just the very dark bark of a tree. Well, I turned round to go back and straight away I saw this streak of light come from nowhere out of the sky. I ran towards the flyer and then suddenly they were all around me. I lost sight of Sharon. I couldn't see what was happening to her.' His voice rose and he took a deep breath.

'I don't know how to say this, but the bolt of light that hit the flyer, when it stopped, it looked like a man. A man in a sort of silvery body suit; or with silver skin.' Mohun rolled his eyes up and Sharon leaned forward and took his hand. 'He was just a blur of light, as though he was travelling at enormous speed but when he reached the flyer he just stopped dead. I've never seen anything like it. He knocked the flyer sideways. I saw Sharon flying through the air and then they were all over me.' Mohun's mouth trembled. 'You must think I'm mad,' he said. 'I can't explain it any other way. That's what I saw.'

'Don't feel bad,' said Vicki. 'After today, I'd believe anything.'

Mohun and Sharon looked at her in alarm.

'It's all right,' Sima touched Vicki's arm. 'We weren't hurt. Let Mohun finish.'

Mohun shook his head. 'It's unbelievable I know. This man, this thing, he turned to me and smiled. Just before I lost sight of him, he smiled! An evil smile. Good god! I couldn't see Sharon. I couldn't do anything. They just appeared from all over the place. Small flying creatures. Shining, like huge insects, but with faces, awful faces, like the man. They covered me. I could feel them stinging me, all over me. I tried to pull them off but I must have passed out.' Mohun clasped his arms around his chest and shuddered.

'I'm going to give you another shot.' Sima tapped the syringe. 'In case of delayed shock.'

Mohun closed his eyes. There was a long silence. Sharon was thinking about the trip back, trying to keep Lassie steady, watching out frantically for the silver light and looking at Mohun's pale face as he lay slumped at her feet on the flyer's platform.

Sima stood up. 'I'll check the medlab. Vicki, will you tell them what happened to us?'

Vicki tried to remain calm as she recalled the man. Sima interrupted as Vicki was describing the mermaids swimming back to the boat. 'I was quite mesmerized by those creatures. I don't know how I would have reacted if one of them had seriously tried to get me into the water.'

A chime sounded and he looked at the medlab screen. 'I'm not sure if you'll be pleased or sorry to hear this Mohun. Your wounds are consistent with being punctured by some semi noxious plant.'

'I know what I saw,' said Mohun in a stubborn voice. He closed his eyes and turned his head to the wall.

'And we know what happened to us.' Vicki pulled up her sleeve and showed the bruises on her forearm. 'Sally was right. This planet must have been settled by humans a long time ago.'

'If what we all saw today was real, their technology is far in advance of ours.' Sharon looked at John.

'Or Thomas is right, and we are hallucinating.' John spoke reluctantly.

'True,' said Sima. 'We haven't identified any psychotropic elements but there could be stuff our system can't identify.'

Vicki stared at Sima. 'That's not what you said before. What about these bruises? Look at Mohun.'

Sima hesitated. 'Let's get some coffee. We need to think clearly about this.'

He got up but Vicki pulled at his arm. Her voice was angry. 'I heard that man. I saw him pushing you under the water like some worthless piece of shit. Why would I dream that up?'

'I don't know. But I feel as though something was affecting me in the cove. I lost almost five minutes. Remember? One minute I was talking to John and then I heard you screaming.' He looked at Vicki quickly. 'Even our injuries could be psychosomatic. That's what Thomas was trying to establish.'

'Are you mad?' Vicki realized she was shouting. She looked at Mohun. He appeared to have fallen asleep but she lowered her voice. 'He would have killed you. What would have happened to me, then? The only reason he let you go, was that noise.'

'But I wasn't killed, was I?' Sima spoke steadily. 'Think about it, Vicki. If we were acting out some kind of delusion, we could have injured ourselves.'

Vicki was so furious she could not speak.

John looked at Sharon. 'What do you think?'

'I can understand what Sima is saying, but it doesn't seem right to me. What we all see, our stories, are so consistent.

Sharon paused and took a deep breath. 'And besides, if Thomas is right, then we're trapped. Even this discussion could be an illusion.' She paused again. 'But I can't believe it, no.'

'So what's your theory then?'

Sharon thought for a moment. 'I agree with Vicki. I think that there are other beings here. I think it's most likely that other humans got here first and that they are trying to make us leave. But why? And if I take this idea to its logical conclusion, it becomes more and more absurd. It means that these people are much more advanced than us and have access to knowledge about us. Otherwise, how could they know about Poseidon and Zeus?'

Vicki interrupted. 'That man at the cove, whatever he is; he said *was* Poseidon!'

A long silence.

'You have no memory of what happened in the time between finishing our call and seeing the stranger?' John spoke calmly.

Sima shook his head. 'None. I could see Vicki clearly all the time I was speaking to you. She was next to the rock pools.' Sima paused. 'I might have turned away for a few seconds, but no more. Just as I exited the call, I heard her screaming.'

'And there was no one else there during that time?'

'I didn't see anyone.'

'None of the Anomee? Did you see anyone on the way there?'

Sima looked annoyed. 'I've told you. There was no one; nothing suspicious.'

'But when I looked for you, you weren't there.' Vicki trembled as she remembered her panic. Sharon leaned over and patted her hand.

'I can't explain it.' Sima looked around. 'But none of this makes any sense. That's why I think that something is affecting us.'

'Ok then.' John's voice was still neutral. 'I think Vicki and Sharon are partly right.' Sima started to speak but John continued. 'But I have a different opinion about who these other beings might be,' John went on. 'Just think about the way this expedition was planned. There was a long gap between when Loren made the discovery and when the news was leaked to the press. I know for a fact that Loren's supervisor disappeared almost immediately after she showed him her results. No one really tried to find out what had happened to him.'

'Loren mentioned it at the farewell party. She thought Belboa went into retreat.' Vicki recalled Loren's animated face and Rick Jones' laconic replies.

John continued. 'Well, I know that there were a couple of weeks when only Loren and this Belboa guy had the data and then there was a period of time when all the data was in the hands of some scientists at EARN. They said they found the whole idea so unbelievable they wanted to check the data. ESA did the same. So NASA didn't get its hands on the data till much later. Also there's the business of our mystery sponsor and two more years of secrecy. Who's to say Mackay didn't sell the data to someone else as well, that another group didn't send an earlier expedition?'

'Why the hell would they do that?' asked Sima. 'Why bother to spend the money? After all, this is an international venture. The sponsors, whoever they are, set it up that way, so everyone could share in the benefits.'

'Exactly! So whoever got in first, doesn't want that.'

'But who on earth could manage to fund something like that?' Sharon interrupted. 'And how could they carry it off it without anyone else hearing about it? How could they even have left earth without NASA or ESA knowing; or the Chinese, for that matter?'

'There are a lot of very powerful groups that operate outside the government, especially in Eurasia.' John glanced at Sima. 'And it's still not clear who might have biological weapons. We don't know what half these guys have been up to in the last twenty years'

'And why play all these stupid games? There are easier ways to scare us off.'

John shrugged. 'I don't know. We need to look for answers. We'll do a complete survey of the planet. We have to find out who's doing this.'

'We have to find the Sally and Alistair first!'

'Of course, Vicki. I'm not suggesting otherwise. We'll move everything nearer the foothills tomorrow and carry out an intensive search. We must find out what happened. The fact that the GPS on their watchers are not responding supports my theory. They've been abducted.'

Vicki thought of Thomas. They had hardly mentioned him.

John must have been thinking the same thing. 'Not forgetting Thomas, of course. He's one of the reasons why I've come to this conclusion. His behavior has been downright peculiar ever since we got here. Why should he be the only one not affected? We have to consider the idea that he might represent some other interest.'

Vicki looked at Sima. He stared at his feet, his face set in a deep frown. He seemed about to say something then he clenched his jaw and his frown darkened. Vicki found it hard to believe he was the same man who had kissed her.

John continued. 'So, my preferred action would be to spend as much time as we think necessary to find the others and then do a close survey of the rest of the planet.' Neither Sima nor Sharon spoke. 'We should wait till we have further data before we report home. It's too fantastic; no one would believe us.' He grimaced and continued. 'But I also think that at least two of us should get off the planet as soon as possible, to see whether there is any change in our behavior.'

'And who do you think that should be, John?' Sima asked harshly.

Vicki felt cold as the two men eyed each other. She glanced towards Sharon. The blonde woman shook her head as though asking Vicki not to say anything. John hadn't specifically referred to the situation in Russia but Sima might think that John was attacking him personally. Sharon was familiar with John's combative style. She wasn't sure how Sima would react.

'It doesn't really matter; of course at least one of us – you, me or Sharon.'

Vicki saw Sima's shoulders relax slightly.

17

'Stay there!' shouted Sima. He clambered back up to the top of the ravine. As he pulled himself over the ledge he looked down at his watcher. The reception was OK here. It was almost noon, local time. He called out again and waved, and Mohun and Vicki started to run towards him.

'John! Can you hear me?'

'I can hear you. What's up?'

'We've found Thomas; about half a k from the camp. He's about ten meters down into a ravine. He's unconscious, looks comatose. Sharon has stayed with him. I had to climb back up. There was no reception down there.'

'What? Are you sure?'

'Absolutely!'

Vicki and Mohun peered down into the jagged rift in the rocks. Sharon was wedged between two rocks, supporting Thomas's head. He was lying precariously close to a sheer drop to the bottom of the ravine.

'John! Are you there?

'Yes. Any sign of the others?'

'No, not that I can see. Where are you?'

'About ten minutes away. I'm turning now.'

'OK. We'll keep you posted.' Sima turned to Mohun. 'Stay in contact with John and keep watch up here. I'm going back down. Vicki! You come with me.'

Mohun set up the winch; Sima attached the ropes and threw the medical kit over his shoulders. He started to lower himself down and signaled for Vicki to follow. A small shower of dirt hit him as Vicki slipped on the mossy rock.

Mohun steadied the winch and then raised his scanner to the west. John had left very early that morning to start his survey, determined to find some evidence of what was affecting them. Mohun swept the horizon with the scanner and zoomed in on the village. They had made several attempts to question the people about their friends' disappearance. They had shown them group photographs of the crew and tried to communicate that their friends were missing. It had been hopeless. None of the Anomee showed interest in anything they did. Mohun had to suppress the desire to do something violent, just to get some reaction from them.

He sighed. John was right. They could not go home with so many questions unanswered. But the thought that they would spend many more weeks here without Sally and Alistair was very depressing. Mohun gave himself a mental shake. There was still hope. Thomas might know what had happened to the others. He looked down into the ravine. Vicki and Sharon had unfolded the stretcher and were securing it to the ropes. Sima was examining Thomas. Mohun checked the winch again and then looked back to the west. As he turned the scanner towards the bay he saw a large cloud of golden dust over the ocean to the east of the village. He pressed the record button. He watched for a few moments to see if it was moving in their direction but it seemed to be stationary, except for a few wisps drifting to the west in the slight breeze.

A movement caught his eye. A large black bird swooped downwards and disappeared behind the hills. Then he saw Xenon descending, blowing up a gust of small stones.

'What's the status?' John looked down at the small group below.

'They're out of contact down there. I think they're almost ready to bring him up.'

John paced up and down. Mohun watched him silently.

'How are you feeling?' John asked suddenly.

'Slightly better. I still feel as though I've been poisoned. It's very odd since Sima found almost no residue from those plants, or whatever they were.' Mohun tried not to think about the experience. The faces of the creatures that he still believed had stung him were vividly real to him. If they were delusions he had no idea why he had dreamed up such horrible images. 'Did you see anything interesting this morning?'

'What?' John peered impatiently down into the ravine. 'Oh. No, not really. I went down as far as the equator and then towards the larger islands. But a dust cloud blocked the view most of the way back. I was going to head east when I got your call.'

'I saw the cloud. I didn't realize it was so large.'

'I took some readings, but I haven't checked them yet. I thought it might be a very thick cloud of that pollen we've been seeing.'

'Possibly,' said Mohun. He raised his scanner and looked back towards the ocean. 'It seems darker but it could just be denser.'

They heard Sima call out and the rope on the winch tightened. Sima was unable to activate the winch from below and Mohun went over to turn it on manually. He watched as the stretcher rose slowly. Sima followed behind supporting it from below, while Sharon and Vicki scrambled up on either side. Mohun could see that Thomas's face was very pale and he was not moving. He leaned forwards and grasped one end of the stretcher as it reached the jagged rim of the ravine. He stared at the still figure and wished violently that Sally or Alistair were lying there instead.

John bent over and lifted Thomas's wrist. 'Where's his watcher? Why would he take it off?' He dropped Thomas's hand. 'I'll give Sima a hand with Thomas. The rest of you - continue the search. Go back to where you found Thomas and search below. One person to remain at the top at all times. Keep in voice contact. Check for anything that may be blocking our signals.' John turned towards the bay. The thick yellow haze still hung in the air. 'We'll keep an eye on that pollen, or whatever it is.'

Sharon looked around. They had set up camp at the point where Alistair had last called in and had worked their way systematically south. It had taken almost four hours to cover a few hundred meters. The lower slopes of the hills were littered with huge boulders and rocks, and riven by dozens of deep gullies. It would take days for a full search. By then it would be too late, if Alistair and Sally were in the same condition as Thomas.

'If they were together and something happened to make them fall, they should be quite nearby.' Mohun sounded almost cheerful.

Vicki couldn't speak. Her heart was thumping in her chest and she had a terrible feeling of dread. It took Mohun and Sharon almost half an hour to lower themselves to the bottom of the ravine and search it thoroughly. When they climbed back up they didn't speak. For the next two hours they searched in a widening circle. At each moment they hoped and feared to find some sign of their missing friends. At last Sharon called a halt.

'We'd better rest and eat. The last thing we want is another accident.'

They sat glumly on a group of small rocks. The air was warm and a light breeze stirred the short grasses and tiny wildflowers strewn amongst the rocks. Selenis was a large pale crescent near the horizon. Artemis was invisible in the still bright sky. Looking to the west, Sharon saw that the pollen cloud was dispersing. The haze had thinned to a golden mist.

'Come in Sharon!'

Sharon stood up and walked a few paces away. She did not look at Vicki and Mohun.

'You haven't found anything?'

When Sharon replied in the negative, John continued. 'Thomas is conscious. Finish what you're doing and then get back here.'

By the time they reached the shuttle they could hear Thomas's voice. They crowded inside and saw Thomas struggling to sit up. A portable drip dangled from his arm. Sima was trying to calm him down.

'Take your time, Thomas. You're safe now.'

'Where are we?' asked Thomas in an urgent voice.

In a few words John described their search and their present location.

'You must move away from here. The land here is unstable. There was a landslide.'

They assured him that they were not close enough to the hills to be in any danger and he told them his story in a slow, breathless voice.

'I had to get away from you. I couldn't believe that none of you realized that these things we were seeing weren't real. I'm sorry'

Sharon didn't think Thomas looked very sorry. He didn't look anything at all. His face was even more blank than usual. 'Where's your watcher? Do you remember taking if off?'

Thomas grasped his left wrist and shook his head. 'I don't know.'

'All right. Go on.'

'I caught up with Alistair and Sally but I kept out of sight because they were behaving so strangely. Sally looked as though she was talking to someone, but there was no one else there.'

'Where did the woman, the Anomee go?'

Thomas looked quickly at John and then away. 'What woman? There was no woman.' His voice rose slightly. 'There never have been any people here. I keep telling you that.' He closed his eyes for a few moments. 'They walked right up to the rock face and then started scrabbling at it as though it wasn't there. I don't know if they dislodged something because suddenly the whole side of the hill started to slide. I yelled out to them. I ran towards them, but they didn't seem to notice me. I saw Sally fall. Alistair tried to pull her out and then a whole load of rocks and earth came down on top of them.'

Vicki started to make a low moaning noise and Thomas closed his eyes again. 'It happened so fast. There was nothing I could do. The slide continued for several minutes. I started back to get help but I must have tripped and fallen. I don't remember.'

John was furious. 'Why didn't you call us?' He couldn't believe that Thomas after all their training, and with his years of experience, would react this way.

'I couldn't get through. I'm sorry. I'm very tired.' Thomas closed his eyes again.

Sima took Thomas's pulse and then checked his blood pressure. 'I think we'd better leave it for now. I gave him a mild sedative and it's starting to work.'

John gave a disgusted snort. 'We won't get anything more from him this way. He's obviously lying or deluded. We got no signals from their MUDs or their watchers.'

'Agreed.' Sharon said grimly. 'There's no problem with reception on the surface near any of the foothills. Reception cuts out about five meters below the surface. And why the hell did he take his watcher off?'

'Sima, you stay here with Thomas. If he makes a move, stun him. Mohun, you come with me. We'll take the flyer along the top. Sharon, you and Vicki can search the area at the bottom. Bring the light explosives pack.'

Vicki's face was deathly white. Sharon took her by the shoulders and stared into her face. 'Pull yourself together. Otherwise you should stay here.'

Vicki nodded. 'I'll be ok.'

Sharon and Vicki worked their way back along the lower slopes of the hills, close to where they had found Thomas. Vicki looked higher up and saw some small bushes with their roots exposed. They clambered up over the rocks and found that the bushes were surrounded by a mixture of dark earth and pebbles, as though someone had been digging them up. Moments later, the flyer descended and hovered above the bushes.

'Looks like Thomas was right,' John said. 'There are signs of a recent slide just up there at the edge of the plateau.' He sounded disbelieving. 'I don't know why I didn't notice it the other day.'

Vicki pulled angrily at the bushes, her heart racing. The rock she was standing on started to move and Sharon grabbed her arm. Together they slid and slipped down the pile of rocks. John and Mohun followed.

'We'll bring one of the small earth movers back here,' said John finally. Sharon nodded but Vicki couldn't speak. She was having difficulty breathing.

Sima was waiting outside the shuttle, watching out for them. His face was white. He held out the scanner to John.

'Look over towards the village,' he said. John took the scanner and looked down to the west. He moved the scanner back and forth and then gave a gasp.

'The pollen cloud's gone,' commented Sharon. 'I can see that from here.'

'So has the village,' said Sima. John handed the scanner silently to Sharon. He looked sick.

'Thomas settled down OK so I came out here to keep an eye on things.' Sima's voice was flat, as though he couldn't believe what he was saying. 'I was watching the pollen cloud drift away and I didn't realize for a while what had happened.'

'What can you see?' Vicki asked. She looked around for another scanner, but Sharon handed hers over and Vicki put the glasses to her eyes. For a few moments she couldn't see anything; then she recognized the small hill behind their campsite. Where the village had once stood was a group of sand dunes and small grassy hummocks. There was no sign of any buildings or people. The fishing boats, storage sheds, gardens, had all gone.

Vicki lowered the scanner and passed it to Mohun. Lights flashed before her eyes and she felt herself fall. As her mind went dark she heard John say, 'Lift her up. Sima, get a stimulant!'

She was drifting away, something cold slid across her cheek and then a vile smell made her choke and sit up. Sima put his arms around her and squeezed her gently. 'Sorry, sorry.'

Vicki shook her head and started to cry. She tried to stop but couldn't. She shook violently. She felt as though she was about to become hysterical. In between convulsive sobs she glimpsed John pacing up and down and Sharon standing, her arms rigid by her side, her fists clenched and her head bent.

Sima was still holding her and Vicki made an enormous effort to gain control of herself.

'Take some deep breaths.' Sima hugged her again. Gradually she felt the panic leaving her. She tried to think of something else but Sally's face flashed through her mind and she started to sob again.

'Give her something, Sima.' John's voice was harsh. 'We can't afford to have anyone else down.'

John's words had a galvanizing effect on Vicki. She leant on Sima and Mohun and staggered up. 'John's right. You'd better give me something. I don't think I can keep this up, otherwise.'

Sima shook his head but went for his medlab kit. Vicki stood unsteadily. She could feel Mohun straining to support her.

'We're going to find them,' said John, 'even if we have to pull that hill apart to do it. Something's going on here; I know it.'

18

The woman walked ahead rapidly and Sally broke into a run to catch up with her and Alistair. She had been fiddling with her data pad, trying to improve the range at which it recorded.

'Anomee?' she called out. The woman stopped and turned around. Sally mimed that she was trying to catch her breath. Alistair looked at her inquiringly.

'I want to ask her where we're going' Sally explained. 'At this rate, we're not going to learn any new words.' She pointed towards the hills and asked 'Over there?' The woman did not reply and her expression did not change.

The woman waited a moment longer and then walked off even more quickly. It was the first time that Sally had seen any one of the Anomee in a hurry. She wondered why the woman was so eager to reach the hills.

Alistair stopped from time to time to take samples of the soil and vegetation and to record their surroundings. The flat grasslands that surrounded their camp were giving way to gently rising land with rocky outcrops and sparse bushes, with the occasional clump of taller trees. Many of the bushes had very small flowers that looked similar to some Australian wildflowers. The leaves gave off a sharp aroma when crushed, different from the light perfume of the grassland flowers.

The weather remained mild and the breeze blew gently but steadily. Perfect weather for walking thought Alistair. He watchered John and then called out to Sally, 'How about a short break?' They had been walking for almost two hours and he could see that the terrain ahead would be more difficult. The land climbed steadily towards the foothills.

Sally lifted her data pad and said 'wait!' She called out 'Pettari!' and was very pleased to see the woman stop. Alistair pulled off his back pack and took out the food containers and water flasks. He offered a cup of water to the woman but she shook her head. She remained standing while they drank and ate, and kept turning her head towards the hills and then back to the village.

'I think she's on a tight schedule. Perhaps she has to return to the village by a certain time.'

Alistair shrugged. It was impossible to tell, but they felt uncomfortable keeping her waiting. They gulped down some water and both stood up again.

'I need a toilet break' said Sally and went behind one of the rocks. The woman started to follow her. Alistair put out his hand to stop her, but pulled back at the sudden look of alarm on her face. She shrank away from him as though she thought he was going to strike her. Alistair tried to look apologetic and put his hands down by his sides, palms outwards in a mollifying gesture.

'What was that all about?' Sally was adjusting the leggings of her suit.

'No idea. It's the first time I've seen one of them look worried.'

The woman had started along a narrow path between the rocks and she looked back at them from time to time, as though wondering what they might do. She seemed keen to keep her distance from them. The rocky outcrops were becoming larger and closer together. Soon they had to use their hands to balance themselves as they made their way over rougher ground. It became harder to keep up with her but they glimpsed her from time to time, scrambling agilely between the rocks. Sometimes they lost sight of her altogether for several minutes only to find her waiting for them. Each time she moved away rapidly as soon as she saw that they were following her.

Just as Sally thought that she could go no further without a rest, they rounded a large boulder and almost bumped into the woman. She put out her arm to prevent them from moving forward and Sally noticed again the smoothness and even color of the woman's skin.

They were standing at the edge of a gully, partly hidden by some small bushes. If the woman had not stopped them, they might have fallen into it. Alistair leaned forward to peer down. 'That's interesting.' He held the data pad over the opening and moved it around slowly. He looked at what he had recorded. 'It's pretty deep.'

Sally interrupted him. 'She's gone again.' The woman had disappeared.

They edged their way carefully around the gully, leaning back against the large rocks. There was a small rift in the rock face a few yards away, but after that there was no room to walk. They pushed their way into the rift and Alistair helped Sally scramble up to the top. She could see the woman a little further on, waiting for them. As soon as she saw Sally she turned and continued along the top of the boulders and then dropped down out of sight.

Sally yelled 'Pettari' again, and the woman's head reappeared.

'She'd do well in a bloody marathon,' grumbled Sally as she teetered over the top of the rocks. She slid down the side and stood next to the woman, rubbing her hands where she had grazed them slightly.

The woman moved away slightly and pointed. The foothills rose up about fifty meters away and Sally could see a dark shadow on the side of the nearest slope. It looked like a cave. She turned to Alistair but he was still standing on top of the rock, using his watcher. She called out. He looked in the direction of her outstretched hand and waved.

The woman glanced back at Alistair and then gazed towards the foothills. Sally got a strong impression that the woman was worried about something although nothing showed on her face. Sally moved around making visual recordings on her data pad and took the chance to zoom in and record the woman's face in close up. She wondered again about the unvarying physical beauty of these people.

Alistair slid down the rock beside her. He looked annoyed. 'Thomas has taken off again.'

'Does John want us to go back?'

'No, he'll probably turn up again as soon as we do. We'll check out the cave and then call again. John sounds pretty fed up.'

The woman had already moved away. It took only a few minutes to reach the foothills. The land was not so rocky and within a few meters they came to a path. It had been cleared of stones and they could see drag marks and heavy indentations in the sandy soil. The path led directly from the cave and continued a few meters to the south to a wide gap between two high rocks. Sally and Alistair looked at each other in excitement. This seemed to indicate that some type of transport was in use.

'I wonder why she didn't use the path.'

Sally shrugged. 'Do you want to go back down it and see where it leads?'

'Perhaps later. Let's look at the cave first.'

They took the path up to the cave entrance. It was much larger than they had thought – about five meters wide and several meters high. Alistair gestured to Sally to stay where she was and walked just inside the entrance. He sniffed. 'The air smells OK. No sign of anything in there.' He turned on the high beam of his light and shone it into the cave. 'It looks man made. The roof is quite smooth.'

He lifted his watcher to his mouth. 'John!' He moved a couple of meters away from the cave and tried again.

There was no reply. Alistair looked at the watcher. 'That's odd. There's no signal here.'

Sally noticed the woman looking at them. Again she had the impression that the woman was nervous about something.

'We'd better go back down and see if the reception is better there.' He moved away, looking down at his watcher and Sally started to follow him.

'Alistair!' Sally grabbed his arm. The woman was entering the cave. A moment later she had disappeared from view.

Sally called out 'Pettari! Pettari!' and ran back up towards the cave. She heard Alistair shout her name and then she suddenly felt a strong force like a gust of wind against her back. She tried to turn around but the wind pushed her forward. She twisted her head around and saw Alistair looking at her in astonishment. There was a roaring noise as the wind echoed through the cave. His mouth was moving but she could not hear what he said. He staggered against the wind, gesturing frantically and she tried desperately to move towards him. She felt him grab her arm and thought for a moment she was safe but she was swept back. Alistair was pulling so hard at her arm she thought he would wrench it from its socket, and she screamed in pain. She lost her balance and was lifted into the air. She felt Alistair's hand lose its grip on her arm and then she tumbled and hurtled through the cave as though she was falling down a steep hill. She glimpsed rock face just inches away and she tried to cover her face with her hands. The wind was so strong she couldn't move her arms. The roaring noise rose to a thunderous crashing and then stopped as abruptly as though it had been switched off. She fell on to the sandy floor of the cave, landing heavily on her backpack.

She lay stunned for a few moments and then struggled to sit up. She could not tell how far inside the cave she had fallen, but the light was dim and she could not see the entrance. She was paralyzed with fear.

'Sally!' She turned in the direction of Alistair's voice and saw a narrow beam of light from his torch. She fumbled at her belt and turned her torch on. Alistair's face shone whitely in the light. He crawled over to her and probed the darkness with the torch light. The cave was as high and wide as at the entrance.

'Anomee!' Sally called out several times but heard nothing. The silence was total apart from the whisper of the breeze. The air smelt fresh and Alistair put up his hand to feel from which way the breeze was coming. He made a deep cross in the sandy soil with his foot and then pulled Sally to her feet.

'Where the hell did that wind come from?' Sally was glad that her voice was steady.

'I don't know. It was like some huge vacuum sucked us into the cave. I can't tell which way is the entrance. We'll go in the direction of the breeze, and if it's a dead end, we'll come back.'

Sally was relieved that Alistair sounded so calm. She looked down at her watcher and shook her wrist to illuminate the screen. It showed local time, but no signal

They walked for about twenty meters and then came to a bend in the cave. A few meters further on the cave ended abruptly in a pile of rocks. Alistair examined them and his heart sank. He remembered the crashing noise but did not mention it to Sally.

'No luck this way, we had better go back.'

Sally shone her torch around and called out to him. In one corner of the cave, several large crates were piled up. Another two were lying on their sides as though they had been knocked over.

They looked at each other in amazement as they examined the boxes. They were finely made, with iron pegs securing the lids. Sally pulled at the pegs and they slid out easily. She lifted the lid. The crate was packed with metal and pottery bowls.

'It looks like this is a storage depot.'

Alistair nodded. 'Well, this is a good sign. Whoever brought these things here will be coming back.'

'We'd better look for the woman. She might be injured.'

They retraced their steps until they came to the cross in the sand. Ten meters further on the cave narrowed and the roof became lower until it resembled a tunnel about three meters wide and high. Alistair flashed his torch at the walls and roof. They were quite smooth.

Sally touched Alistair's arm and pointed to the tunnel floor. There were footprints in the sand. He put his finger to his mouth and lowered his torch so that it illuminated only the ground ahead of them. They walked for several minutes in silence, the tunnel winding in long curves and gradually climbing. A faint noise ahead of them became gradually louder until they recognized the sound of falling water. The light also became slightly brighter and the tunnel widened out until they entered a large cavern. At one end they could see the glisten of a small waterfall, as it tumbled down the wall into a small round pool. The woman sat on some rocks next to the pool, dipping her hand into the water and drinking. The cavern was brighter than the tunnel but they could not see the source of the light.

'Anomee!' Sally tried to sound calm. The woman jumped up and ran into the left of two tunnels behind the pool. Alistair sprang across the cavern and disappeared into the tunnel.

'Pettari! Pettari!'

Sally could see the flashing light of Alistair's torch just ahead. She called out again but could hear nothing except the sound of running footsteps. She yelled Alistair's name and when he did not reply she ran after him. She tried not to panic, running almost blindly in the darkness. She panted with fear as she bumped against the wall, grazing her hands, relieved when she heard Alistair cursing just ahead of her.

Abruptly the tunnel widened into another cavern, smaller than the last and less brightly lit. The Anomee woman was sitting on a rock, her hands on her knees, her chest heaving, but as soon as she saw them she leapt up and staggered across the sand. Alistair made a frantic leap forward and caught her just as she passed into the narrow exit. He pulled at her tunic and wrestled her back into the cavern. She screamed and thrashed around, then suddenly collapsed onto the ground, her hands over her head as though she expected to be hit. When neither Sally nor Alistair moved, she looked up at them.

'Pettari!' Sally said once again, breathlessly but firmly. 'Settu ri? Where are you going?' The woman stared at them, her face rigid.

Sally repeated herself. She pointed to the passageway and tried to look puzzled.

'Er harne,' said the woman. Sally checked her data pad.

'What did she say?'

'I think she said – "the village", or "our village". I'm sure it's the same word they use to refer to where they live.' Sally felt an overwhelming relief. 'She must be leading us to another exit.' She paused as she saw Alistair frown. 'What's the matter?'

'I don't know. I've got a pretty good sense of direction and we're definitely travelling east, south east away from the village.' He shrugged. 'Perhaps she comes from another village. We'll just have to wait and see.'

The woman was stirring restlessly. Sally smiled at her but she looked away. Sally wondered again how the Anomee expressed emotion.

* * *

'Wait up a minute.' Sally's hunger pangs were becoming so strong she could not ignore them. They had just entered yet another of the small caverns and she stopped to look at her watcher. It had been almost three hours since they were swept into the caves. She tapped the screen; still no signal. She pulled off her pack and sat down.

The woman waited at the far end of the cavern while they ate. Alistair moved his flashlight from side to side, and brushed his hand along the wall. 'This is an amazing feat of engineering. I wonder who built these tunnels.'

Sally swallowed the last of her food and stood up. The woman looked back at them and then slipped into the tunnel. They threw on their packs and followed. She was walking more slowly now, and they glimpsed her face in the torchlight as she turned to look back at them.

'How does she see without any light?' Sally wondered aloud.

Alistair shrugged. 'This whole place is a puzzle.' He was glad when Sally didn't reply. He had a strong sense they were walking into a trap. His sense of direction told him they were still traveling east. At the rate they were walking, they were at least 10 kilometers from the foothills. Their surveys had shown that the plateau was edged by sheer cliffs which extended south east for at least fifty kilometers. He couldn't understand why these tunnels had been built and or where they might lead.

'What's the matter?' Sally noticed him shiver. He had been so calm and matter of fact. She hoped he wasn't losing his nerve now.

'Nothing.' He smiled. 'I'd just like to get out of here.'

As though his words were a signal, the tunnel ahead brightened suddenly. Alistair stopped and Sally bumped into him. He put his hand back to stop her moving forward and she could hear him breathing heavily. The woman had disappeared around a bend in the tunnel. They moved forward cautiously and followed. The light increased as they turned the corner. The tunnel ran straight for a few meters and then turned sharply again. There was no sign of the woman.

They stood still for a few minutes in the silent tunnel but the woman did not return. Suddenly they heard her voice, louder than they were accustomed to and it was joined by several other voices. Alistair gestured to his handgun and Sally fumbled for her holster. Her hand was shaking and she had trouble finding the safety catch. Alistair moved ahead slowly to the turn in the tunnel and peered around it. He stepped back and gestured for Sally to take a look. The tunnel widened out into another larger cavern, similar to the one at the entrance to the caves. Behind it they could see bright water and a sandy beach. The woman was standing in the center of the cave, surrounded by several men. They were all similar in appearance to the Anomee, but they wore short dark kilts and carried spears.

'What shall we do?' Alistair didn't answer. He was looking down at his watcher; still no signal.

Sally replaced her gun in its holster. 'There's no other way out. We don't have much choice.'

Alistair stretched out his hand but she walked slowly towards the group of people. As she approached they stepped aside and she hesitated. Alistair checked his gun. A few moments of uneasy silence passed. Then one of the men gestured to the cave opening and spoke loudly. Sally looked at Alistair and he shook his head. The man spoke more loudly and gave Sally a small push towards the exit. Alistair reluctantly moved through the cavern and out into the bright sunlight.

19

Alistair sat down on the bed and pressed his fingers to his temples. 'The fact is, this place should not be here! We've flown over this area at least twice.' He rubbed his forehead and glanced at Sally. 'There's no way we could have missed seeing it.'

'I don't know what to say.' Sally shook her head. 'Perhaps Thomas is right; maybe we are hallucinating.'

After they had left the cavern Sally and Alistair had tried to look around to get their bearings but the men with the spears had urged them onwards. They could hardly see in the bright sunlight. They stumbled along the small stretch of sand, and then were pushed up a shallow stone stairway. Alistair realized there was no point using his gun. They were outnumbered.

As she mounted the stairs Sally shaded her eyes and looked around. Several small piers extended out into the water, crowded with boats. A few of these resembled the fishing canoes they had seen at the village, but most of them were much larger, like huge gondolas. She paused at the top of the stairs and looked out over the water. Several other vessels were approaching.

Sally's stomached tightened and she turned away. For a moment she felt faint. A wide square faced the water. It was tiled in a complicated multicolored pattern and lined on three sides with tall stone buildings. Massive columns supported verandahs off the second and third floors, and she could see figures in bright clothes behind what looked like trellised shutters. She clutched Alistair's arm and he gave her a dazed look.

As the armed men urged them forward, a stream of Anomee emerged from the buildings, carrying chairs and long tables. One of the guards pushed them towards a table and pressed Sally to sit down. Sally tried to pull away but he thrust her firmly down.

Alistair sat down next to her and put his hand over hers. 'We'd better cooperate.' His voice was husky.

They stared at the scene around them. More than twenty tables had been erected and the Anomee were now setting out large covered dishes and tall pitchers. Sally watched in disbelief as a woman placed ornate plate and goblets before them. When the woman turned away Sally said quickly 'Anomee, pettari!' The woman hesitated but the guard took her arm and led her away.

Alistair picked up a metal goblet and tapped it. 'Silver!' he exclaimed.

Sally stared at the goblet in front of her. It was etched with a fine pattern; angular lines crisscrossing small circles. Something about the markings seemed familiar.

Alistair was examining his chair. 'Look at this!' The arms of the chair were inlaid with a fine tracery of metal and colored shell. 'This is something!'

'For god's sake Alistair! Look!'

The doors of the building to their right were flung open. Several very tall people in long brilliantly colored robes emerged and strolled towards the table opposite. They stood for a few moments, looking towards Sally and Alistair and then slowly seated themselves, their robes draping gracefully around their chairs. A strange scent drifted across the plaza and Sally felt disoriented and slightly sick. The scent became almost overpowering as more groups emerged from the stone buildings and took their places at the tables. Sally felt a growing sense of alarm. She tried to stand up but the guard pushed her down again. One of the men seated at the table opposite laughed loudly. Sally caught his eye. He gazed back at her and she shivered.

These people were quite different from the Anomee. Some were dark but there were blondes, redheads and a few with bright chestnut hair. They were taller too, ten or twenty centimeters taller than the Anomee. And their handsome faces were lively with emotion; staring at Alistair and Sally, whispering, laughing, grimacing, and pointing.

Alistair's voice was strained. 'It looks like a B grade movie.' As he spoke, most of the people stopped talking and stared at him. When he fell silent they laughed and spoke in excited voices.

Sally could not reply. She looked around in a daze. Alistair was right. The long flowing robes, the elaborately dressed hair, the ornate tables and chairs, all looked like something from a sword and sandals movie – the Hollywood version of ancient Rome or Greece. The man still staring at Sally shouted sharply and the guard leaned forward and poured something into her silver cup. Sally picked it up and sniffed the liquid. It had a fruity, alcoholic aroma.

'Don't drink that!' Alistair snatched it away from her and stood up. He pushed the guard aside. The crowd became silent. Dozens of faces watched them with cool amusement.

Alistair looked back towards the beach. He could see that where they had exited from the cavern, the beach ended abruptly in a steep rocky headland. To the east the large buildings extended down to the water.

A loud trumpeting noise rang out and everyone rose to their feet, and looked towards the esplanade. Sally climbed up on to her chair, to see what was happening. As the guard pulled at her, she glimpsed several people stepping out of a huge gondola. She slipped and sat down with a thump. The tall people had risen to their feet, shouting loudly and punching the air with their fists, their expressions a mixture of jubilation and pride.

As the new arrivals approached, the Anomee scattered and the tall people became silent and drew aside to clear the way. Alistair put his arm around Sally; she could hear his quick breathing and his muscles tense. A very tall, massively built man in a dark purple robe walked past them and stopped at the head of their table. Two Anomee ran forward with a huge, elaborately carved chair and backed away hurriedly as he seated himself. A woman of similar appearance, with shoulder length curly black hair seated herself on his right. They both had magnificent figures and perfectly formed faces, with dark eyes and very pale olive complexions. The man looked briefly at Alistair and then stared at Sally with real interest. The woman gazed at them with no attempt to conceal her hostility.

The other two women were fair with blue eyes. One had a calm serene face, with plainly dressed pale blonde hair. The other was stunningly beautiful with a glowing complexion and a profusion of golden curls falling almost to her waist. The shortest of the group, a man with curly chestnut hair gave Sally an insolent stare as he sat down. She felt a strong desire to look away but was mesmerized. She glanced from face to face with an increasing sense of unreality.

The silence was broken as the crowd reseated themselves and resumed their meals. Several Anomee approached, placed platters and flasks on the table and withdrew hastily. The movement broke the spell and Sally tore her gaze away. She clutched at Alistair's arm. 'Do you see what I see? What's happening?'

Alistair shook his head. He was trying not to look at the radiant blonde who was staring at him intently. He fingered his gun and released the safety catch. 'Put your gun on stun. We might have to make a run for it.'

Sally fumbled with her gun. She forced herself to look at the five people sitting at the head of the table. Both the men smiled leeringly at her and the dark haired woman half rose in her chair, her face contorted with fury. Her companion put his hand on her arm and she sat down again. He gestured to Sally, as if to say 'eat, drink.' Sally turned away with an effort and saw that the two blonde women were looking at her in alarm.

Alistair cursed softly. 'I think we should try to leave.' He pushed his chair back and picked up their packs.

The plaza fell silent again. Everyone stared at Sally as she slowly stood up. She tried to smile as she backed away from the table but her heart thumped and she was almost transfixed by the five faces. The tall dark man looked amused, while his companion glared at Sally, her brilliant dark eyes narrowed in anger. The woman with pale blonde hair frowned and shook her head. The beautiful woman now looked quite terrified.

Sally cleared her throat and said huskily, 'We must leave now and return to our friends. We thank you for your hospitality.' To her dismay, the tall dark man burst out laughing. He spoke loudly and two of the men carrying spears came forward.

'What now?' Sally whispered.

Alistair glanced at the armed guards. As well as the spears they wore long swords and daggers tucked into their belts. Their faces showed no expression and as Alistair stepped away they kept their distance. 'Let's see if they try to stop us.'

'Which way?' Sally croaked. She clutched the holster of her side arm.

'There's no point going back to the caves. We could try taking a boat.' Alistair looked up to where the hills rose behind the town. 'No. I think we should try to reach the plateau.'

The group of five did not move as Sally and Alistair changed away from the table. The plaza was silent as they walked slowly past the tables towards a gap between the buildings on the north side. The guards walked on either side but made no attempt to stop them. Sally kept her eyes fixed on Alistair's back. She did not dare look around. As they reached a high stone arch Sally glanced back. Every eye was fixed on them.

'If we go a bit higher we might be able to get a signal,' Alistair said quietly.

Sally nodded and took a deep breath. As she went under the arch, the oppression she had felt under the dark man's gaze lifted slightly.

On the other side of the arch a wide paved lane rose gently for a few meters and then more steeply in a series of shallow steps. They walked quickly for a few moments. When Sally turned to looked down the lane the guards stopped too, their faces impassive as usual. No one else followed them. Beyond the arch the tables were still full. They seemed to have been forgotten.

Sally realized that she was still shaking, but she felt a great sense of relief. Alistair was already engrossed in examining their surroundings. Every few meters alleys led off the central lane and they could see similar buildings to the right and left. They were constructed from what looked like sandstone, contrasting with the dark wood of the windows and doors. Some of the stone lintels were carved with images of leaves and flowers, or more abstract designs. Window boxes on the upper stories overflowed with bright flowers and foliage.

Sally stared around. 'This place reminds me of Venice. Look at the watermarks on the buildings. It must have been flooded a few times.' Her voice shook slightly but she felt calmer.

'The whole thing is bizarre,' said Alistair. He looked back at the guards. They were still following a few paces behind.

They walked for several minutes, the lane rising steadily before them and peered cautiously into the alleys as they passed.

'No one here,' commented Alistair. 'They must all be down there.'

'No sign of any children here either.'

Higher up the houses were smaller and humbler, as though the beautiful view over the town was not important. Suddenly the paving ended and the lane widened out into a dusty square. Mud brick houses, similar to those in the village, spread out in all directions. Alistair turned and looked back down the hill. They could now see over most of the town. To the east, the tall stone buildings lined the coast for two or three hundred meters right up to another spur of hills that descended steeply to the water's edge. There were several rows of smaller buildings behind them, some of them appearing to be built into the side of the hill. Alistair used his scanner to look down to the plaza. Most of the tables were still occupied but the tall man and his party were gone. He scanned across the water. Directly south was a small island a few hundred meters from the shore. Smaller islands could be seen in the distance. The two headlands blocked his view to the east and west.

Sally was using the video camera to record as much as she could. She zoomed in on several buildings and then panned out across the water. How could they have missed seeing this place? She thought again of Thomas and his theory that they were hallucinating; she thrust the idea away. She turned the camera towards the mud houses. They were packed together with narrow walkways between them. A short distance away, a sheer cliff rose more than a hundred meters up to what she assumed was the plateau.

Alistair was checking his watcher again. He looked up at the sky and started across the square. 'We're still out of range.'

Sally and the guards followed and they entered one of the narrow lanes. After a few meters they reached a t-junction and Alistair stopped. He turned left and then right again a few meters further on. They continued on like this for some minutes, with Alistair continually glancing up at the sky and checking his watcher. Finally he stopped.

'It's no good. We're just going around in circles. Look, if I give you a leg up, do you think you could get on to the roof and see where we are?'

When the guards realized what Sally was doing they leapt forward and tried to take hold of her. Alistair managed to ward them off while Sally pulled herself over the rough tiles and clambered onto the thatched roof. One of the guards ran around to the other side of the building but returned a moment later when it was clear that Sally was not trying to escape. The two men stared at Alistair and he took out his gun. Their expressions did not change.

Sally looked towards the cliff and traced a path between the huts. She checked her watcher again. They were still out of range.

She called out and Alistair helped her down. 'I think I've got it. Follow me.'

The guards stayed close behind as they wove their way towards the cliff. Sally's heart dropped as they came to a dead end. To left and right, the huts butted up against the rock.

Alistair sighed impatiently. 'It'll take us days to search this. I guess we'd better go back down to the waterfront and see if we can borrow a boat.' he said.

'I don't know. Could we wait till those people have gone?' Sally paused. 'I hate to be a nuisance, but I really need to pee. Can you stand guard? I'll just go around the corner.'

Alistair tried to stop the guards from following her but they pushed him aside. Sally said 'pettari!' several times and tried every gesture she could think. Finally in desperation, she started to pull down the bottom half of her body suit. The reaction was immediate. One of the guards pushed open the door of the nearest house and gestured that Sally and Alistair should enter it. As they looked inside, the guards pushed them in and slammed the door behind them. Alistair tried to open it but it would not budge. The wooden shutters of the window were also locked.

'Damn!' He felt stupid. He wondered what John or Sima might have done in the same situation.

Sally looked around. The room contained two beds, a rough table and chairs and an archway to another smaller room. It was very similar to the houses they had seen in the village, where all the bathing and cooking was carried out in a communal area. She knew that the smaller room would contain water for washing and a bucket for night dirt.

* * *

'Are we hallucinating?' Sally repeated. She sat down next to Alistair. The bed was quite comfortable and, like the rest of the hut, it was clean. She pulled one of the pillows behind her and rested her head against the wall. 'Perhaps Thomas was right. We are suffering from delusions.' she said slowly. 'This place is too fantastic to be real. We could be in ancient Greece or Rome. How is that possible?'

'There's too much logic to what's going on. And if we were hallucinating we would have other symptoms.' Alistair ran his hand across the bed. The coverlet was coarsely woven in dull earthy colors. 'I have to believe what I can see and touch.' He stood up and looked around. 'I have a real bad feeling about this. These people look too much like us. And way they dress ... It's as if they're putting on an act, like they know our history.'

He pulled the table against the door and then took the food and drink packages out of his pack and spread them on the bed. 'You look pale. We'd better eat something and try to get some rest.' He checked his gun and slid it into the recharger. 'Then we have to get out of here one way or another. We have to warn the others.'

Sally put her hands to her head. She wondered what the crew were doing.

20

A loud banging noise woke Sally from a fitful sleep. For a moment she did not know where she was; then she sat up abruptly. Pale beams shone through the shutters, dimly lighting the small room and she saw Alistair pulling the table away from the door. He gestured to her and drew out his gun. Sally glanced at her watcher. She had slept for almost an hour.

The banging noise was repeated and the door to the hut was pushed open. The woman who had brought them from the village looked inside, said 'pettari', withdrew quickly and slammed the door again. Alistair pulled on the handle but he could not move it. It had been bolted again from the outside. He swore and shook the handle in frustration.

'She said we should wait. Perhaps they're going to let us out.'

'I don't think so. We'd better be prepared to defend ourselves. And we should hide our other stuff.'

They stowed their data pads and other equipment into one of the backpacks. Alistair flicked the dials on the lock and pushed the pack under one of the beds. They piled the remainder of their supplies and their first aid kit into the other pack and Alistair flung it over his shoulders. He set his handgun to stun, released the safety catch and positioned himself beside the door.

'When the door opens, get behind me.'

For several minutes they heard loud voices and what sounded like a bell ringing in the distance. The bolt scraped against the door. Alistair pushed Sally further away and raised his gun as the door opened. The same woman entered and looked around the apparently empty room. She started back as she saw Alistair and the weapon. He pushed her into the room and slammed the door shut, then opened it again cautiously and looked out. There was nobody else nearby. He turned to the woman, smiled as pleasantly as he could and put the gun back into its holster.

Sally put out her hands in an appealing manner. 'Sorry' she said. 'We were frightened.'

The woman's expression retained a faint expression of alarm. She backed out through the door and beckoned for them to follow her. When they hesitated, she spoke rapidly and made several gestures.

'What do you think?' Sally asked. 'Should we go with her?'

'We can't stay here. Finding a boat may be the only way out.'

The Anomee looked back at them frequently, as she wound her way through the maze of small houses. Alistair looked around him, trying to memorize their route. When they reached the dusty square they could see some of the Anomee walking down the lane ahead of them. Further down, some of the taller people emerged from the houses and also headed down the hill. They looked curiously at Sally and Alistair, their faces alive with interest but no one spoke to them. Sally noticed that the Anomee stopped and turned their faces away as the taller people passed.

Alistair paused to survey the scene. Several boats were moving swiftly across the bay towards the small island. The plaza was still crowded with people but the tables were gone.

The woman made gestures that they should hurry and Alistair walked on. Sally glanced behind her. No one followed them.

'Thomas!' Alistair grabbed Sally's arm and pulled her into one of the side alleys. 'Did you see him?'

'What?'

'It was Thomas – I'm certain of it.' Alistair ran to the end of the alley. He looked to the left and right and then swore loudly.

'Did he see you?'

'He sure did. He was talking to a woman, one of the Anomee. He was standing only a few meters away. As soon as I shouted, they both took off.'

'What! Are you sure? How could he? He doesn't speak any of the language.'

'Oh yes! Damn!'

They walked slowly back to the lane where their guide was waiting. Her face was without expression but her eyes darted left and right as though she was watching out for someone.

'But how could he have got through the rock fall? Did he look all right?'

Alistair's face had a white tinge to it and he slumped back against the wall. 'He looked perfectly all right to me; the picture of bloody health in fact. I don't know what's going on.' He looked at Sally. 'He was dressed like an Anomee, but I'm sure it was him.'

Sally hesitated. 'Perhaps one of them brought him to find us?'

'Then, why did he take off when he saw me? No one made him!'

Alistair was interrupted by some rapid words from the village woman. She pointed down to the square, making gestures to usher them onwards.

Sally's heart thumped. 'I don't want to go down there.'

'I know, but if we don't, they'll probably just come and get us.' Alistair took Sally's arm. 'No one's tried to harm us.'

They continued slowly down towards the square, this time looking carefully into each alley as they passed. As they went under the stone arch, two guards fell in on either side of them, and the woman turned away.

They paused as they entered the plaza. The buzz of conversation stopped and hundreds of faces turned to look at them. A group of the tall people moved towards them, halting a few feet away. A woman with flowing red hair and pale skin moved closer. Sally's chest tightened as she looked into her eyes. They were pale green with long dark gold lashes. She looked too perfect to be human. She stretched out her hand and touched Sally's black clad arm. Sally jumped back in alarm and the woman laughed. She said something to her companions, her voice loud and tuneful. She gestured and one of the male Anomee came forward with a goblet and offered it to Sally.

'Wetakari – thank you,' said Sally tentatively. The Anomee's expression changed slightly. The woman said something in a sharp angry voice and he disappeared into the crowd.

Alistair took the goblet from Sally. 'I don't think that was a good idea. Let's move on and see what happens.'

They walked forward and the people moved slowly back to let them through. Several of the women reached out as though to touch them. They called out to each other, smiling and laughing, but Alistair angrily pulled Sally away. 'I don't like this. They're making fun of us!' He started to push more quickly through the crowd, holding tightly to Sally's hand. She tried to keep up but started to stumble. Strange images and odors overwhelmed her - smooth, tanned arms with brightly enameled bangles, turquoise embroidery edging a fine white material, a pale, perfect foot with brilliantly polished nails in a jeweled sandal. And all the time, sharp tuneful voices rising and falling in an alien language. Sally lowered her face and focused on Alistair's hand, pulling her forward.

As they reached the esplanade, a loud bell sang out. The Anomee immediately turned their faces aside, but the other people started to shout and wave their arms as they had done earlier.

Near the stone stairs, a large platform had been raised, although Alistair could have sworn it was not there when they entered the plaza. A marquee had been erected above it, covered with swathes of material in white, saffron, rose and purple. The colors glowed and shimmered unnaturally.

In the middle of the platform, the tall dark haired man and woman were seating themselves on a pair of large, high-backed chairs. They were dressed even more elaborately than before, in heavily embroidered robes, gold, silver and jewels glistening on the arms and hair. The man stood up and waved to the crowd. The chanting and shouting stopped abruptly. He spoke in a loud voice, looking directly at Sally. He gestured to several smaller chairs on the platform and Sally felt someone push her from behind.

'We can't get away,' Alistair said quietly. 'We'd better cooperate.'

Sally clung to Alistair's hand as they were thrust towards the platform.

They mounted the steps and the man gestured grandly for them to sit down. Sally seated herself next to the stairs and Alistair sat next to her. He took her hand in his, kissed it and stared defiantly at the man. To Sally's horror the tall man threw back his head and burst into thunderous laughter. He called out something and the woman leapt out of her seat and looked at Sally with loathing. The huge man pulled her back, smiled at Sally and laughed again. She heard Alistair cursing. With difficulty she looked away from the man and down at the crowd. Some looked amused but as the laughter ceased, most of the faces became apprehensive. There was a long ominous silence.

Alistair's grip on her hand suddenly tightened. 'Over there!' he whispered 'Its Thomas. It's definitely him.'

Sally looked in the same direction. Thomas was standing on the edge of the crowd. He looked back at Alistair and Sally, with no sign of emotion, as though he didn't know them, and made no effort to conceal himself. After a few seconds the Anomee woman standing next to him spoke and they moved out of sight.

Sally felt faint. She wanted to close her eyes, to make it all go away. Suddenly the floor vibrated as the man strode to the front of the platform. The crowd cheered wildly as he waved to them. He shouted a short phrase in a huge voice and turned to Sally and Alistair, his face triumphant.

'My people.' He paused. 'For you too are my people and always have been. And now it is time for you to see us as we really are.'

Alistair stared at the man in amazement. He had spoken first in the alien tongue and then in English. The accent was strange but perfectly clear. He felt Sally leaning against him. Her eyes were wide with terror.

The man turned to the crowd again and waved his arms in a grandiose gesture, like a boxer at the end of a match. 'The old times have returned and we will take our rightful place once again.' The crowd roared in reply. He swung around and held out his hand to the tall dark woman. She rose from her seat and went to stand next to him, facing the water.

The man's voice boomed out in a ringing chant, and the people cheered even more loudly. The platform rocked and Alistair jumped up, pulling Sally with him. The chant grew louder and louder until Sally clapped her hand over her ears. The man made violent movements with his arms, as though thrusting back some unseen force. The noise of his voice and the cheers of the crowd increased until everything seemed to be vibrating from the sound.

The platform shifted again and Sally clutched at the chair for support. Alistair turned towards the lake to see what Zeus was doing.

At first he thought it was an earthquake. The water near them was quite calm but further out a mass of turbulent waves rose, higher and higher until they threatened to engulf the island. As the waves spread, the boats by the esplanade started to rock wildly. Alistair heard Sally gasp and she clutched his arm painfully. The island was moving and the air around it shimmered as though in a heat wave. It suddenly disappeared, as though it had been a mirage and the shimmering air lifted like a theatre curtain, revealing a cone shaped mountain. The slopes shone brilliantly as though covered in snow. As the air cleared, great white marble buildings became visible, covering the lower slopes and the surrounding hillsides. More land heaved into view; rows of columns, arches and walls spread across the landscape.

Alistair staggered back. 'What the shit!' He shook his head as though to clear it but the scene remained, dazzling in the afternoon sunlight.

'My god!' Sally screamed.

The tall dark man turned towards them. 'Yes, my children. I am your god - the great and true god; the god of your ancestors.'

'What the hell is going on? Did you hear that? What are you seeing?' Alistair shook Sally's arm.

Sally did not answer. She was staring at the man. He was still in human form but suddenly looked completely alien. He seemed even taller, and his skin and hair had a metallic sheen in the afternoon sunlight.

He smiled. 'You may pay homage to the great Zeus.' He put out his hand to her and Sally recoiled in fright. A frown passed over the brilliant face and then it reddened violently. Beads of perspiration sprang up on his forehead and he exuded a powerful animal scent.

Sally cowered behind Alistair and Zeus's frown deepened. Alistair could hardly stand upright. He could not take his eyes off the enormous man in front of him, but Zeus ignored him and moved around him to look at Sally.

'It would be wise of you not to anger me,' Zeus continued as Sally shrank away from him.

'Let me make sport of them.' The woman had been silent but now she stepped forward. Alistair saw that she was even more beautiful than before, with long, glistening dark curls and a flawless complexion. But there was something sinister beneath the beauty. Her face was both youthful and ancient at the same time. He could not quite understand why, but he felt that she might at any moment be transformed into something appalling.

He felt a movement and Sally stumbled past him. She fell to her knees and pressed her face to the floor. Then she raised her head. In a strong voice she called out, 'Oh mighty Juno, protect me. Deliver us from this peril.'

The tall woman's face darkened. She leaned down to Sally and raised her hand as though to strike her. Zeus laughed and pushed her hand aside. 'You should address your supreme goddess as Hera.' The woman looked furious but Zeus laughed again. He took Sally by the hand and pulled her to his side. Alistair started forward, but Zeus pushed him away. Alistair crashed back into one of the chairs and for a few moments lay dazed.

Zeus released Sally's hand and waved to the crowd. Hera grabbed Sally around the neck and pulled her away. She took Sally's place and raised her arms. The crowd roared.

'Behold my people, your gods,' Zeus thundered. He took Hera's hand and ignoring Alistair and Sally he descended the stairs. The crowd called out to him and parted as he led Hera down to the waterfront.

Alistair staggered to his feet, still winded by Zeus's blow. Sally was gasping for breath, and he could see the angry red marks on her throat where Hera had grasped her. He pulled Sally against him as Zeus glanced back at them and gestured to the guards. Alistair looked around wildly. The crowd still pressed against the platform. There was no escape.

The woman with pale blonde hair whom they had seen earlier spoke to one of the guards who were urging Sally and Alistair down the stairs. She put her hand across Sally's neck and when she removed it a few seconds later, the red welts had disappeared. Alistair looked at her in wonder. A slight smile crossed the woman's serene face, and then she moved back into the crowd.

The crowd jostled Sally and Alistair as they were pushed towards the esplanade. Zeus was standing with Hera next to one of the long gondolas. He beckoned to them but Alistair grasped Sally's arm and stood his ground. He tapped his gun and muttered, 'No more!'

When they did not move, Hera shrugged and stepped into the gondola. Zeus called out and the beautiful woman with the mane of golden curls walked slowly towards them. She ignored Sally, but stood close to Alistair and looked into his eyes. She raised her hand and touched his cheek. 'You are my honored guest. Please come with me.' Her voice was soft and alluring. 'Do you not know me? One of my names is Venus.'

Alistair's head spun. He stepped back. The woman smiled brilliantly and put out her hand, but he pushed it away. The woman's expression changed and became almost pitiful. 'Please don't anger Zeus.' Her voice trembled and tears appeared in her huge blue eyes. Her scent overwhelmed him and for a moment he could not move.

He heard Sally cry out and with enormous effort he turned away. A guard was dragging Sally towards the large gondolas. As she struggled wildly to free herself the man pulled her head back and slapped his hand across her mouth. Her eyes stared into Alistair's for a moment. Then the guard pushed her down into the boat.

Alistair fired without thinking. The shot missed the guard but another Anomee toppled from the pier. He heard shouts and a dark haired woman pushed past him and leapt towards the boat. Venus gasped and clutched Alistair's arm. He threw her off and ran forward. The dark haired woman had felled the guard with a swipe of her arm and was stamping in rage as the boat receded from the quay. Alistair could see Zeus standing at the prow of the boat looking towards the island. He screamed Sally's name but there was no sign of her.

Someone touched his arm and Alistair looked around frantically.

'I am Ceres. We will help you.' The same blonde woman who had healed Sally's neck looked at him calmly. Venus stood next to her, her eyes wide with alarm. Alistair felt the power of her beauty again and backed away. 'Not her! Get her away from me.'

The woman calling herself Ceres nodded at Venus and she moved back and looked down. Alistair felt a huge sense of release.

Ceres urged Alistair towards a gondola. She called out 'Diana!' The dark haired woman's face was livid with anger but she seemed to calm down as Ceres spoke. She nodded, gave Alistair an indifferent look and darted away into the crowd of interested onlookers. Ceres beckoned to Alistair. 'Be quick, if you want to save your friend.'

Within a few seconds the boat was traveling very fast. Ahead Alistair could see the other vessel was nearing the island and as if Ceres had read his mind the boat increased its speed again. He looked towards the island and shouted. Zeus was stepping onto the quay. A guard followed him, with Sally slung over his shoulder. She was not moving and Alistair's heart sank. He watched in horrid fascination as they moved across a wide courtyard and disappeared behind a row of tall white columns.

Before he could speak, the boat shot forward and he fell back. There was a loud rushing noise and Ceres called out in alarm. Alistair could not understand what he was seeing; a huge pale green wall was sweeping across the water towards them. Bright objects flashed across it and lines of silver and white curved over its surface in giant loops. As Alistair looked towards the top of the wall, he realized with horror that it was a giant wave. The water rushed towards them and the boat rocked wildly. Alistair clung to the side but Ceres rose to her feet. She raised her arm and put out her hand. To Alistair's amazement, the wave turned slightly and veered westwards. Several dark shapes emerged from the wave and sped towards the island. Ceres shouted and Alistair saw the silhouette of a huge man turn and pause. Ceres called out again but the figure resumed its course and swept on through the water.

The rush of water carried their boat over the quay and across the courtyard. The dark figures were nowhere to be seen. Ceres leapt out the boat. 'Stay here!' she commanded and raced across the white tiled courtyard, in the same direction as Zeus.

Alistair almost fell out of the boat. He lay still for a moment recovering his breath, the water gushing around his feet. Then a huge smashing noise made him start up. He looked around. The water was receding but the courtyard was empty. There was no sign of the wave.

He stumbled towards the row of pillars and up three broad steps. A wide hall led to an internal courtyard. He could hear more crashing noises as though huge rocks were being flung down from a great height. The ground trembled and he ran frantically through one passageway after another. They all led to large empty rooms and he lost all sense of direction. Panic overwhelmed him. He leant against a wall, his chest heaving. There was a long silence followed by several more crashes, each one fainter, like a giant storm moving away. The cold marble chilled him and he felt despair. He sank down onto the tiles. He thought suddenly of Jeremy and felt sick with longing for his family.

The sound of footsteps made him look up. A tall, slender young man was crossing the room towards him. His heart leapt in his chest as he recognized the silvery hair and high cheekbones. He burst into tears and staggered to his feet.

'Jeremy!' As he called the name, he stopped. Every detail – the shape of the man's head, the way he walked, mimicked his brother. But this man was huge – at least seven feet. His stomach jerked.

The man looked at Alistair's tearful face with disdain. 'I am Heracles. Ceres sent me to find you.' He spoke perfect English in a rough, cold voice 'For some reason she regards you kindly. Follow me, if you wish to see your woman again.'

Alistair followed him mutely for several minutes. He felt sick. Someone was playing a sadistic game with them; it was the only explanation. Finally the man stopped and gestured for him to go ahead. He stared at Alistair for a moment and then strode away. Alistair shuddered. He had to force himself to look into the room.

Sally was lying sprawled on the floor. Her cheeks were scarlet as though she had been slapped, her eyes were closed. Ceres knelt beside her, her hand on Sally's forehead. Alistair sank down on to the floor next to her. When he took her hand, Sally opened her eyes. She gave a faint smile and closed her eyes again, her face peaceful as though asleep.

'She will be well. Poseidon came before Zeus could take her.' Ceres paused and listened but there was nothing to hear. She gave him a quick smile. 'I think that we will not see them again today.'

Alistair started to speak but she stopped him. 'We should take Sally back to the Anomee. It will be safer there. Zeus will be very angry when he returns.'

Alistair looked at her serene face. 'Who are you?'

'As I have told you, I am Ceres. Or perhaps you know me as Demeter, but I do not like that name.'

'But who are you really? Where are we?'

Ceres looked puzzled, and then her face cleared. 'I understand. You know nothing. I will explain everything to you when you have rested.'

Alistair felt as if he would choke. 'Tell me now. That man; he called himself Heracles. But he looks just like my brother…'

Ceres exclaimed loudly and stared at him. 'Do not tell this to anyone.' She frowned. 'Zeus must not know.' She shook her head as he tried to interrupt her. 'Hurry!' She picked Sally up as though she were a small child and carried her out of the room. Alistair followed, feeling completely helpless.

As they approached the boat, Ceres looked up. A silver light streaked across the sky above them and passed behind the mountain. 'We must hurry.'

Alistair stared down at Sally as they sped away from the island. She looked unharmed; the red marks were gone and her breathing was relaxed, her face peaceful. Ceres did not speak. She stood at the prow, looking from side to side. The sky was starting to darken. Alistair could hardly believe that less than twelve hours had passed since they left the camp.

Several Anomee women waited on the quayside. Next to Venus stood the lithe, dark haired woman, Ceres had called Diana. While Venus gestured to the other women and they lifted Sally from the boat, Diana spoke to Ceres in short sharp phrases. Ceres answered briefly and turned to Alistair. 'Venus and Diana will help you. I will return tomorrow and answer any questions you have for me.'

Before Alistair could protest, she pushed the boat off from the shore and it moved quickly away. The women were already carrying Sally into one of the tall buildings that faced the plaza, and Alistair hurried in after them.

Diana looked inquisitively at Alistair but she did not speak. Venus touched his arm and he felt his blood start to race again. She looked down at Sally's still figure and smiled sympathetically. 'She will be well. If you need anything, call one of the Anomee. They will bring you whatever you want. But you must not try to leave.' She smiled again as she followed Diana out of the room.

Alistair checked Sally but she seemed to be sleeping peacefully. He could feel the symptoms of shock setting in. To distract himself he made a quick inspection of the room. It was large and high ceilinged. The air was fresh although the shutters were closed. There was no sign of any staircase leading to the upper floors. He went around the room carefully. All the shutters were bolted on the outside.

The walls and ceiling appeared to be whitewashed but they had a faint silvery shine. One wall was almost covered by a large mural in pale hues, depicting a group of the 'gods', seated at tables similar to the ones in this room. The room was furnished simply but luxuriously as a living and dining area. Long low couches, raised at one end and covered by a finely woven blue cloth faced several small tables, set with dishes and vessels. Alistair lifted one of the lids but the smell of food made him feel sick.

Two doors led into sleeping rooms. Alistair looked into one of the rooms and saw an archway opening into what looked like a bathing area. The second room was similar except for subtle differences in the decoration. A third door led into a small chamber whose purpose was not clear. A table seemed designed for reading and writing. Some square shapes might be some types of equipment.

He heard Sally call out. She was gazing around, her face puzzled. She looked as she always did to him, radiantly beautiful, as though she had just woken from a long, restful sleep. 'Where are we? How did we get here?'

Alistair sat down beside her and took her hand. 'Do you remember what happened?' he asked anxiously.

She shook her head and swallowed several times. 'I remember that man - Zeus. I tried to push him away but he just laughed at me. He hurt me.' She shuddered and then looked puzzled. 'Then... then there was water everywhere. I saw fish; enormous fish. They looked like people.' Her face twisted. 'Zeus – he started fighting – with this other huge man. It was terrible.' She ran her hands through her hair. 'Have I been asleep? Did you give me something to make me sleep? Was I dreaming?'

'I'll try to explain. I can't believe it myself.' As he described the events of the last few hours he became agitated. He felt suddenly humiliated as he remembered his helplessness and the contemptuous way his brother's image had spoken to him. He was about to mention the man who resembled Jeremy but he remembered Ceres' warning and stopped short. He walked around the room to distract himself, checking the door and the windows again. The door opened inwards, but he could see no way to lock it. He dragged a small cabinet across the room and pushed it up against the door.

'What are you doing?' Sally asked.

'Just trying to take some precautions,' he replied. He felt like smashing something. He prowled around the room, checking the windows again. He stopped and breathed deeply, trying to regain his self control. He had to stay calm. He turned to Sally. Her face was white and shocked.

'You should try to rest.' He helped her to stand and led her into one of the sleeping rooms. She stretched out on the bed and reached out to him. 'Don't leave me,' she said faintly. 'I can't bear to be alone.'

He sat down beside her, and rather awkwardly took her hand.

'Please don't leave me,' she repeated. She half sat up and leaning over, pressed against him. Her mouth tasted strange but alluring. He recoiled, as though she were offering herself to him in return for his protection. 'You don't need to do that.' Her kiss had aroused him.

'Don't let's talk any more. None of it makes any sense.' She started to cry and pressed herself against him. 'I've wanted to do this for ages,' she said 'and I know you want it too. This might be our last chance. Who knows what might happen tomorrow.'

Alistair felt infuriated that something he had longed for so much could happen in such circumstances. If they were hallucinating, they could be lying in a squalid mess. Or even worse, someone could be watching them. He sat up and looked around but Sally clung to him.

He groaned and gave in to his feelings. They made love frantically like two condemned people, counting the moments until they would perish. He tried to control himself and show her consideration but everything Sally did seemed aimed to make him forget any inhibitions he might have about their awful situation.

Afterwards, he fell asleep almost immediately. When he awoke, he heard a noise in the next room. Sally was sitting at one of the tables, making a meal from the assortment of food that had been laid out for them.

Alistair couldn't bear to remind her that the food might not be safe. He had no idea where his pack was and they needed to eat. When he sat down beside her, she threw her arms around his neck and hugged him hard. He felt annoyed that his body responded at once, but when he looked at her face, he was surprised to see that she was quite radiant.

'I've never felt like this before,' she said. 'Don't laugh at me Alistair, please. I think I'm in love with you.'

Alistair was astounded and then immediately wondered if this was just another aspect of the hallucinations. He knew how he felt, but how could Sally have fallen for him so suddenly?

Sally held him by the shoulders and looked at him. 'You don't believe me, do you? You think I'm just scared. Don't you think I'm capable of loving someone?' She spoke in a sad but defiant tone.

Alistair felt ashamed. 'I've had strong feelings for you for months,' he admitted. 'I just never thought you felt anything for me at all.'

'I'm pretty good at hiding my feelings,' she said in the light tone she had used before. 'But there's no point now, is there?'

She moved slightly away from him and for a few moments they stared at each other. Alistair felt a sudden enormous thirst. He looked doubtfully at the table, shrugged and poured himself a drink. He took a round white bread roll and started to eat. The soft dough was delicious but he had trouble swallowing.

Sally was talking again. She told him of her childhood, her futile search for her real parents and how she had tried not to become too attached to anyone. The words came out in a gush and not all of it made sense to Alistair. But he realized, as he should have known all along, that Sally's attitudes were deeply rooted in the mystery about her parents; growing up in an environment in which she had always felt an outsider. He felt foolish and petty to have been so resentful of his growing attraction to her. She fell silent and he reached out and stroked her cheek. That seemed to be enough. They sat in silence for a few minutes and then she smiled at him and took another drink.

The water was scented with something fragrant, which cleared the head but also made him feel as though all his senses were heightened. He remembered the flavor as the one he had tasted on Sally's mouth a few hours earlier. He turned towards her again. She looked back at him, her eyes shining and he took her in his arms.

21

Alistair awoke before Sally. He sat up quietly and looked down at her. She had rolled away from him during the night and was now lying hunched near the edge of the sleeping platform, clutching her pillow. Her forehead was rumpled in a frown, her mouth clenched.

He pulled on his body suit and cautiously entered the living area. He could not hear anything outside, so he pulled the cabinet back and slowly opened the door. The light was still quite dim and the plaza was quiet and empty. He pushed the cabinet back against the door and looked at the table. The dishes were as they had left them last night. He uncorked one of the unopened bottles and sniffed its contents. It had a lighter fragrance than the liquor they had drunk the night before. He filled two goblets, went back into the sleeping room, shook Sally's shoulder gently and sat down beside her on the bed.

They didn't speak as they drank from the goblets. Alistair felt an immediate benefit from the liquid but Sally looked listless and tired. He stroked her cheek and said quietly 'I love you. Whatever happens, I will never forget last night.'

Sally kissed his hand and squeezed it. 'I had a terrible nightmare.' She tried to smile. 'You weren't in it. I was on my own. I was floating out to sea; very cold. I could see people only a few meters away, but they couldn't see me.'

Alistair put his arms around her. He had slept well and could not remember if he had dreamed. He hoped she would say something about what had happened between them.

'I do love you Alistair,' she said, as though reading his mind. She kissed his hand again. 'We'd better get up and decide what to do.' She sounded depressed.

He went back to the living room and laid out some food on the plates. He was very hungry again. Although the room was quite warm, all the food looked fresh. When Sally joined him he was eating a bread roll spread with a magnificent cheese. He handed her a plate and she ate without much interest.

Alistair went into the bathing area and splashed water on his face. He looked in the mirror above the bowl and then peered closer. He turned his face from side to side. Considering what he had experienced, he appeared surprisingly well. He wondered if he was just dreaming.

He shook his head and looked around. A small square of the floor was tiled in a different pattern and when he stepped on to it, a heavy spray of warm water drenched him. He pulled off his body suit and stood for a few moments lulled by the familiar sensation of the shower. When he stepped back the water ceased abruptly. He moved forwards and the water streamed down again. He could not see anything which resembled soap but when he finally stepped away he felt as though he had been thoroughly cleaned. He picked up a blue cloth from a pile on one of the benches and dried himself.

Sally was pacing up and down the room. Her apathy had disappeared, her face agitated. 'We have to get out of here.' She looked at Alistair as if he might disagree.

'I don't know,' he said doubtfully. I think we should wait until Ceres, or whoever she is, comes back. She said she would explain everything.'

'And then what?' Sally looked as though she might explode. 'I came this close to being raped yesterday. I might not survive the next attempt.'

Alistair's reply was interrupted by a loud banging at the door. The door was pushed open and the cabinet tipped over. Sally gasped and ran back into the sleeping room. The cabinet was flung aside and four of the tall Anomee entered the room and stood with their arms folded. Alistair could see several more outside. They were dressed like Roman centurions in short leather tunics which showed off their heavily muscled bodies. For a moment Alistair stood in amazement, then leapt for his gun. As one of the men advanced on him, he fired a warning shot. The soldier ignored him. Alistair fired again and the man collapsed on the floor. Two more rushed at Alistair and overwhelmed him. His gun was seized and flung across the room. He struggled violently and glimpsed Sally clutching at the bedroom door as another man tried to drag her out. She let go suddenly, the soldier stumbled and she rushed towards the exit. Two more men grabbed her, she screamed and struggled for a moment and then went limp. There was no use resisting.

Alistair tried to catch her eye as they were pushed across the plaza but Sally stared ahead. Several of the large vessels were moored at the piers and more boats arrived as they watched. Further out a stream of vessels was traveling at high speed towards the quay. Sally yelled in alarm when she saw Zeus. Hera stood next to him and when the two gods turned to look at them, Alistair was astonished to see fear on their faces. Zeus turned back to the people disembarking from the boats and spoke to them in a loud commanding voice, but Hera stared at Sally and Alistair, her face contorted with anger. The soldiers halted but they did not release them. When Alistair tried to pull free, one of the men tightened his grip painfully.

The atmosphere was quite different to the day before. Several people seemed to be arguing with Zeus. They gestured at Sally and Alistair, and Zeus responded in a loud harsh voice. Alistair saw Ceres and Venus at the edge of the crowd. They both looked distressed. When Ceres met his eyes, she looked away in an almost guilty manner.

The piers were soon crowded with boats and hurrying figures. Most of them went straight past Sally and Alistair and headed towards the archway. A few stopped to listen to Zeus. Many of them stared at Alistair and Sally with a mixture of contempt and hostility.

As if to reflect this change of mood, the air became heavy and oppressive. Sally looked up and called out to Alistair. A large, roiling cloud was moving swiftly across the sky. He had never seen anything like it. It seemed huge but also unimaginably high, as though outside the very atmosphere. The rest of the sky was clear but the cloud grew rapidly. Alistair could not tell if it was expanding or if it was descending rapidly towards them. He felt dizzy from this loss of perspective.

'What do you see Sally?' he asked urgently. It bore no resemblance to any weather he had ever seen, here or on Earth.

'It looks like locusts,' she whispered. Alistair saw that the cloud was indeed moving with purpose and direction. He felt the soldier's grip loosen. The Anomee was staring at the cloud, his face full of fear.

The cloud covered the sun and the light dropped dramatically. A strong breeze grew into a wind. A few of the people cried out and started to back away from the water, looking up at the cloud with dread. Zeus was shouting and gesturing as though ordering them to stay where they were, but several ran towards the nearest building. Zeus shouted to the soldiers and they turned and pursued them. A faint metallic scraping noise grew suddenly louder. It was like the rustling of millions of insect wings. A cold blue light grew around the edge of the cloud, which now filled most of the sky overhead. Sally felt her hair lift away from her ears and flatten against her head. She turned around. Beyond the cliffs, the sky was still clear.

The soldiers were transfixed by the cloud. Alistair wrenched his arm away and grabbed Sally's hand. 'Quick! We've got to find cover.'

He tried to pull Sally away, but Zeus shouted again and the solders dragged them back. Alistair clung onto Sally's arm with one hand and fought mightily to free himself. The people whom Zeus had been haranguing fled in all directions.

The rustling noise was becoming louder and Alistair looked desperately up to the sky. The cloud was much lower now and he could see flashes of color spreading across it in rhythmic patterns. The cloud swirled furiously, forming into a huge inverted triangle.

'Jesus!' he shrieked. He struggled violently. 'Let us go. It's a tornado.'

He pulled frantically at Sally but the soldiers continued to haul them back towards Zeus, who was still gazing heavenwards. The wind from the cloud was now making the boats rock violently in the water. The rustling noise became so loud that Alistair wanted to cover his ears but he gripped Sally's hand harder and tried to pull her away. Something rough hit him and he stumbled. Sally's hand was wrenched out of his grasp and he heard her cry out. As he turned, the wind lifted him off his feet and he collided with Sally. He pushed her down trying to protect her from the force of the wind.

Just as the noise became unbearable, it dropped abruptly to a loud rustling drone and the wind fell. Zeus shouted something and a strange voice replied in the same tongue. Sally felt a terrible reluctance to look up. 'What's happening?' she whispered.

When Alistair did not reply she looked across at him. He was gazing up with an expression of awe. Colored lights were playing across his face, like spotlights at a theatre.

'We're saved,' he whispered. He rose to his feet and stepped forward. Zeus stretched out his arm and pulled him back but Alistair ignored him. He stared towards the water, his face shining.

Sally looked up at the cloud and fell forward. She buried her face in her hands. Her head felt like a drum with rocks banging around inside it and she shook with fear.

Alistair reached down, took her hand and pulled her up. She kept her eyes closed.

'It's all right.' His voice was calm. 'Everything will be all right now. We have found what we were meant to find. It all makes sense.'

Zeus laughed and said something in his own language. Then, as if remembering that Sally and Alistair could not understand him, he said in English, 'You fools! Say nothing and follow what I do.' His voice hardened. 'You are in the greatest danger of your lives. Make one wrong move and you will perish.'

Sally clung to Alistair. She still could not open her eyes. Alistair was breathing heavily as though in the grip of some great excitement. He did not reply to Zeus, but instead stepped forward one small pace. She felt him bow his body at the waist and heard him say in an unsteady but joyful voice.

'Michael! Tell me what we must do.'

There was a loud crashing noise and the ground vibrated under Sally's feet. With a great effort, she made herself look up, instinctively shielding her eyes with her hand.

The angel stood no more than a few paces away, although he was so tall that she could not feel sure of anything she was seeing. As her eyes moved upwards, she took in the loose gown of gold, cream and red and the arms clad in what looked like chain mail. She looked quickly at the brilliant but grim face with the mane of shining gold red hair streaming out behind, and then dropped her eyes again. She saw a bright flash, heard the same crashing noise and felt the ground tremble again. Out of the corner of her eye she saw Hera recoiling, her face pale with fear.

An alien voice roared out. 'Stop! You worthless gourds. Stay where you are.'

Sally forced her eyes open again. Michael was brandishing a long metal staff. She looked up past the terrible figure. Three great angels hovered slightly above and behind Michael. They were of a lesser height but their appearance was almost as awe inspiring. Above and beyond these three, countless ranks of the winged creatures hovered. They hung almost motionless in the air, their great wings moving gently, their feet pointed sharply down. The sun shone through their ranks, producing the bands of flashing lights which had dazzled her. The rustling noise swelled and faded into patterns of sound.

All the angels she could see clearly were human in appearance, saving their strange wings, and their hair, standing out from their heads like fine strands of wire. Their faces were grave and still. They could have been sleeping but that their eyes were wide open. She glanced fearfully at Alistair. He was still gazing at Michael with the same rapt expression. She pulled his arm but he ignored her. She shielded her eyes again and looked towards Michael. When he moved his eyes towards her she felt their full force. They were a bright, cold blue and they shone with an alien light. She looked down.

Michael spoke and it was as though the earth opened up and a great wind rushed out.

'Stand, Alistair. Do not move.'

Sally felt Alistair tremble and his knees buckle. She put her arms around his waist and supported him.

Zeus spoke. His voice was calm but Sally thought she heard an undertone of fear. She could not understand what he said until he suddenly spoke in English, as though he wanted them to hear him.

'I am no gourd. I am Zeus, supreme in Olympus, as we agreed. And see how I have protected our guests. Here they stand unharmed. Why do you arrive in this manner in my country, armed as though for war?'

The ground shook again and Sally felt Alistair jerk with alarm. She smelt smoke and felt a blast of hot air on her face. A terrified shout behind her made her turn. The bushes at the edge of the esplanade were burning and she saw two bolts of fire hit the square and set alight the podium where they had been sitting the day before. The few remaining gods who had lingered to see what would happen, now screamed and ran for their lives. Only Hera remained, defiant and upright but her eyes cast down to the ground.

'Silence!' roared Michael.

Alistair sank to the ground and Sally knelt down beside him. Zeus had stepped back and was slapping at his purple cloak, which was smoldering with orange sparks. His face was red and contorted with rage, and Sally instinctively cowered away. She looked towards Michael and saw that he was observing her and Alistair without expression. He turned back to Zeus and his face hardened. He raised the shining staff and pointed it at Zeus again. A brilliant gold light flashed from the shaft. A small explosion in front of Zeus made him leap back again and his face became even more enraged. Michael lowered the staff and then raised it again. Before he could release its energy, one of the three angels behind him moved swiftly down and laid his hand on Michael's arm. He spoke quietly to Michael, who shook off his hand and raised the staff again. The angel put out his hand and pushed the staff down.

Without taking his eyes off Zeus, Michael spoke to the other angel. In contrast to his violent actions, his voice was now even and revealed no anger. 'Gabriel' he said. He spoke some words that seemed strangely familiar to Sally. She caught a phrase that she knew meant 'this must end.' She tried to identify the language but her head spun.

The angel Michael had addressed as Gabriel replied, but too quietly for Sally to hear. Michael spoke more loudly and she heard another phrase which she understood. 'There is no other way.'

Zeus reacted violently. He spoke in the same language as the angels but Sally could not make out what he said.

Michael hit the earth again with his staff and the ground vibrated. 'Do not use our words, you mischievous and heedless being. You and your people will pay for your wickedness.'

Gabriel again placed a restraining hand on Michael's arm and the huge archangel turned his head aside and lowered the staff. Gabriel now faced them and spoke to Zeus. Sally suddenly saw him as a tall handsome young man, his pale brown hair curling softly over his shoulders. His gown was blue with flowing sleeves of shining white and all at once he appeared as a medieval knight, his long sword shining at his waist. Images of him which she had seen on

Earth flashed through her mind: stained glass windows, illuminated manuscripts, children's story books.

Like Michael, Gabriel spoke in clear but strangely accented English and Sally saw once again an alien creature framed by huge wings. 'We have returned from the Earth where we have witnessed the havoc you have wreaked. And you have done this all for your own amusement so that you could play with these mortals without our knowledge. Did you think that we would not recognize your handiwork?'

Zeus started to speak but Gabriel gestured for him to be silent. 'You have wrought terrible and useless destruction. We have left half our force on Earth to contend with the forces of ungoodliness. If any of our company is destroyed in this war, you will pay a double penalty. What have you to say for yourself?'

Gabriel's words stunned Sally. She shook Alistair urgently. 'What does he mean?' Alistair did not hear her. He was still gazing at Michael, his face rigid with awe.

Zeus was now shouting in his own language. Gabriel answered in a calm voice which seemed to enrage Zeus further. Finally Zeus screamed in English, 'It's your fault!' Hera seized his arm, as though to restrain him but he pushed her away. She staggered back.

Sally tried to pull Alistair to his feet, but he was a dead weight, transfixed by the sight of the angels.

Zeus made an explosive, inhuman snorting noise and drew himself up. His face was red and contorted. 'It is you,' he repeated in a voice vibrating with anger. 'You have brought catastrophe on the mortals. You don't understand them. Not as we do. You have never lived there as we have,' he said with an air of great consequence. 'It is your fault and it will all be for nothing. You were wrong then and you are wrong now. You have learned nothing.'

Gabriel had listened closely to everything Zeus said, but without showing any anger. Behind him, the other two great angels were talking quietly to Michael as though to keep his attention away from Zeus. The ranks of angels above remained unmoved, maintaining their original positions with short, precise movements of their wings. To Sally, their unconcerned expressions were almost as frightening as Michael's anger.

When Zeus finished speaking, Gabriel hesitated and turned his head to one side, as though thinking over what Zeus had said. After a few moments he said quite gently, 'You are correct. You are not the only cause of the war. But you are wrong in everything else that you say.'

'Wrong! Right!' Zeus shrieked. 'Because you are sure, does not make you right.'

Gabriel did not seem surprised at this reaction and said, 'We are the messengers of the good. We are always right.'

Zeus stepped forward as though to strike Gabriel, but at that moment Michael turned back to face him and Zeus faltered mid stride.

'Leave us!' Michael ordered. His voice was less angry, as though the other angels had been successful in their efforts to calm him. 'Return to your homes. We will think on this and tell you our decision tomorrow.' He spoke as though to a badly behaved child and turned away with a dismissive wave of his hand.

Zeus shook with rage. 'You cannot tell me what to do. This is my country. You can take the mortals back to your domain. You should have sent them there when they arrived.'

Gabriel turned his head to one side again. 'You knew what our intentions were, but you interfered,' he said. 'And now we must decide what to do.'

Hera was pulling at Zeus, as if trying to make him leave. Zeus thrust her away and stood firm. 'Take the mortals,' he repeated. 'Take all the mortals and leave our country. We want nothing more to do with you. You will discover soon enough how wrong you are.'

This last remark seemed to provoke Michael beyond restraint. He leapt away from the other angels and shot like an arrow into the air, one arm straight up above his head, holding the shining staff. As he soared up, the ranks of angels jostled each other to get out of his way. Their wing strokes increasing in speed, they rapidly cleared a path for him. Suddenly the huge archangel spun around. His great wings stiffened out, with a noise like a giant whip cracking through the air and he sped back down towards the ground at enormous speed. As he flew, a blue light radiating from his wings spread out until it surrounded him. The metallic crackling noise grew so loud that Sally clapped her hands over her ears. She gazed in horror as Michael sped toward Zeus, who was now running across the square. Hera fled after him. As the two gods reached the far side of the square Michael caught up with them. He turned sharply, came to a halt in mid air and swept one great wing across the top of the archway. The wing sliced through the arch with a thunderous hissing noise and large chunks of stone crashed to the ground, narrowly missing the two gods.

Michael leapt onto the top of the ruined arch and leant down towards the cowering figures below him. His voice roared out. 'We have left you in peace for more than two thousand years, despite your meddling and your malice. You are heedless and dangerous. If you continue in this course of action we will annihilate you. We are the army of the good as well as its messengers. Do not forget it.'

Zeus did not reply. He stood quite still for a few moments and then turned back towards the water. Hera followed him. Michael folded his wings back, rose up into the air and watched as Zeus and Hera boarded their vessel. Sally could hear Zeus shouting as the boat moved rapidly out into the water. 'Mortals beware! I have warned you.'

Sally closed her eyes and wrapped her arms around Alistair.

'It's all right, Sally' she heard him say. 'We must trust them and do as they say.'

Sally did not know how to reply. She leaned her head on his shoulder and tried not to think. She had a great desire to never open her eyes again. Images of Vicki and Sharon flashed through her mind, but their faces seemed strange. She felt that she ought to be terrified but she was too tired. She felt herself drifting away but Alistair moved slightly and she was suddenly aware of his skin against her cheek. Her eyes flew open. He stared back as though he could not see her.

She felt a cold sensation on her shoulder and looked up to see an angel gazing down at her. Over his shoulder she saw that other angels had flown down and settled like statues on the tops of the buildings and the trees near the foreshore. The remainder kept to their positions in the sky. She shuddered and tried to move away.

The angel spoke quietly. 'I am called Uriel. Take no heed of Zeus. You need not fear for your friends on earth. No one you know has been hurt. We will tell you more of this tomorrow.'

As soon as he ceased speaking, the angel's voice seemed to fade from Sally's mind so that she was not sure that he had really spoken. Uriel stood silently for a moment, looking towards the great mass of angels above the water. As if he had signaled, several angels moved out of the throng and soared across the plaza. They hovered for a moment, folded their wings and descended into a circle around Alistair and Sally. They stood very still, their faces without expression, their eyes slightly elevated. Sally shivered as she stared at them. They were similar in size and build, with regular, beautifully formed features. Their pale faces were almost identical but each was clothed in different colors and styles. Apart from the astonishing wings, the only distinctively alien thing about them was their hair; the colors varied from silver, through blonde and pale red and brown to deep copper, but they shone brilliantly, each individual hair seeming to stand slightly apart from the others. Sally had the strong impression that they were all male but somehow that word did not seem to fit these creatures.

Alistair started to stir and look around. He still had the same dazed and radiant expression. He made signs of respect to the angels but they ignored him. Sally shook him. He turned towards her and she took his face between her hands. 'Listen to me; something very strange. I understood some of what these creatures said. I think they were speaking some form of Hebrew.'

Alistair nodded. 'You're right. Tradition says that the angels' language is very similar to Hebrew. Thank god. We're safe now.'

Sally stared at him. 'What are you talking about?'

'I can hardly believe it myself, but what else can it be? It's amazing, but everything we were taught, it's true.'

Sally's teeth started to chatter with shock. 'What do you mean?' She shook him again but he took no notice.

'It will all become clear. They will tell us.' Alistair gazed around, his face still full of awe.

For a few moments Sally felt numb and then was seized by an awful dread. She pulled away from Alistair and stood up. The circle of angels did not react. Their faces remained impassive. Trembling with the effort to overcome her fear she walked towards one. The angel put out his hand to stop her but she dodged sideways. The next angel moved his arm to form a barrier. She stood there for a moment before the nearest one slowly turned his head and looked directly into her face. She felt a wave of nausea as the great face peered at her. The eyes were light hazel, luminous and perfectly shaped but they held no expression. It was like being examined by a large intelligent insect. She saw that the face was unnaturally symmetrical. The skin was taut and elastic but it somehow seemed unimaginably old. He was both amazingly beautiful and repulsively alien to her.

'Where are our friends? What have you done to them?' She could hardly hear her own voice.

The angel looked at her for a moment and then turned away to where Michael and the other archangels stood. Sally's heart was pounding and her knees shook. After a few moments, the angel said slowly in a stilted voice as though it was a long time since he had last spoken, 'Your friends are safe. They are where you left them. Sit down now.'

Sally was aware again that she could not remember how the angel sounded as soon as he stopped speaking. His mouth had moved and she had understood what he said but she could not recall his voice.

When she did not move, the angel moved slightly towards her and she felt a sudden sense of danger. She stared at the huge wings. Close up, she could see that each feather seemed to be made of fine hairs, which stiffened and relaxed, as the angel moved.

She backed away hastily. She felt dizzy and exhausted. Alistair tried to take her hand but she pushed him away. She put her hands over her ears and tried to reason with herself.

As a child, she had attended church with her adoptive parents; she had enjoyed the ceremonies and the music. But when Hilda and David realized that she thought of church services in much the same way as the local amateur theatre's performances, they had asked the Rector to speak to her. She still remembered the way he had looked at her as she argued with him. After that, her parents allowed her to stay home. She had been an atheist for as long as she could remember. Angels! Her mind reeled. Surely Alistair couldn't be right? She shook her head. No! If these were really angels, what were the other beings, who called themselves gods?

As she thought of Zeus she shuddered. She had only a dim memory of his attack. She wondered what Ceres had done, not only to heal her wounds but also to wipe out the revolting memories. The image of Ceres' serene face calmed her and the quiet rustling of the angels' wings lulled her strangely. She was not sure how much time she passed in this state, before Alistair roused her.

'Sally! Look. It's Thomas!'

She staggered to her feet and peered through a gap in the angels' wings. Thomas was in earnest conversation with the angel called Gabriel. He was still dressed like an Anomee, and the woman who had been with him the day before stood off to one side. She noticed Alistair and Sally staring at them and stepped forward to touch Thomas on the arm. Thomas and Gabriel turned towards Sally and Alistair. Their eyes locked for a few seconds and Sally felt as she had before, that she could not meet the angel's eyes. When she looked up again, she saw Thomas approaching them. The angels moved aside to let him through and then closed the confining circle again. Thomas gazed steadily at them both. He looked quite different. Sally had always thought that he appeared young for his age, but now he could pass for a man in his early twenties.

'Where have you been?' she asked roughly. 'We saw you yesterday and you ignored us. What are you doing here?'

'I came to see if you were all right.' Thomas spoke as though it was the most ordinary thing in the world.

Sally could feel panic overwhelming her again. She stared at him. Why didn't he say something about the angels, about the city? She swallowed hard. 'It looks as though you were right. We've been hallucinating, just like you said. Where's John? Where are the others?'

Thomas smiled gently. 'Everyone is fine, although they must be worried about you. I haven't seen them since I followed you to the mountains.'

'How do you know they're ok? Why haven't you called them?' Sally grabbed at Thomas's watcher, but he stepped back quickly and evaded her grasp.

'It's no use,' he said. 'There's no point calling them until we've decided what to do.'

'What do you mean?' demanded Sally. 'There's nothing to decide. We must go back. How did you get here?'

'No!' repeated Thomas. 'We can't go back yet. Not like this. Michael will decide what to do.'

Sally felt sick but she made one more effort. 'Thomas,' she said slowly. 'Do you remember when we first landed, how you told us we were all having hallucinations? Do you remember the people in the village? You said they didn't exist. That they were just in our heads, that we were sharing our delusions. Do you remember that? I know now that you were right.'

Thomas looked briefly aside and shook his head. 'No, Sally. I was trying to protect you. When we arrived here I knew what we should have found, but the gourds disobeyed us and allowed you to see the Anomee.' He grimaced slightly as though something disgusted him. 'It was essential to get you all away from here before something worse happened, but I could not find Michael or any of my company, and I was instructed not to reveal my identity to you.'

Sally stared at him and he met her eyes without changing his expression.

'And you really believe all this?' Her voice shook.

'I have never lied to you. The gourds can change the appearance of what you see, but that does not affect us. What you saw in the valley is not what I saw.'

'Us? What do you mean – us?' Sally felt numb but she grabbed Alistair's arm and shook him. 'Alistair! Come on!'

Alistair was gazing at Thomas in awe. She shook his arm again. 'We have to get out of here. It's dangerous. Come on.'

Alistair shook his head. 'No. We must stay here. We must wait.' He took her hand and tried to put his arms around her.'

She tried to push him off but he tightened his embrace. 'Don't worry. Everything will be all right now.'

Sally felt something snap. She pushed Alistair away and flung herself against the angels. She punched and kicked and screamed in terror. Her hands and feet rebounded slightly as though she was punching a sponge and then they jarred painfully against stony surfaces. She leapt back and stared. The angels were unmoved. Alistair called out but she dropped to her knees and thrust her head and shoulders between the long robes. A sudden glimpse of a thin white foot with perfectly formed nails made her gag.

Gabriel waved his hand and one of the angels reached down and picked her up as though she were a small toy. She flailed her arms and kicked out but the angel held her at arm's length. She felt frenzied, as though fighting for her life but some cool part of her mind told her that something must have an effect on this mad delusion. In desperation she raised her fist and smashed it as hard as she could into her own face. She felt an awful pain in her nose and tasted blood.

Alistair cried out in alarm and the angel put her down at his feet. He ignored Alistair and rejoined the circle. Sally sobbed with pain, clutched her nose and stared at the scene. It was no use. Nothing had changed. Everything was as before.

Thomas pushed Alistair aside and despite Sally's resistance, he laid his hand over her face. His hand was so cold that she flinched away but he held her firmly and after a few seconds she felt the pain grow less. Thomas kept his hand there and gradually the pain disappeared. When he removed his hand, she jerked upright and touched her nose. There was no sign of her blow except for some traces of blood on her fingers. Thomas stood aside, breathing on his palm as if to cool it. Tiny red grains like scarlet sand floated off his hand and drifted to the ground. Alistair crouched down and put his arm around Sally but she pushed him away.

'None of this is your fault but we cannot return you to your friends until we have decided what to do.' Thomas turned his head to one side, as though in thought and Sally suddenly recognized him for what he was, despite his human guise. 'You should rest now,' he said.

The circle of angels ushered them across the plaza. Sally followed Thomas numbly as he led them back to the apartment they had occupied the previous night. Two of the angels guarded the door and the remainder flew slowly upwards to the roof above them.

'You should rest now,' Thomas repeated. 'I will have some food and drink brought.' He spoke to the angel at the door and then went back across the square. Immediately an angel entered with a tray of dishes, placed it on the table and retreated without speaking.

'How do you feel?' Alistair's voice was gentle but it galvanized Sally into action. She felt the numbness disappear and her anger returned. She leapt off the couch and ran over to shut the door behind the angel.

'You should sit down. You've had a shock. We both have. But we're safe now.'

'Safe? Are you mad? Shut up!' In a sudden fury Sally swept the dishes off the table. They clanged as they hit the floor and she saw a movement. Ceres was standing in the doorway of the sleeping chamber.

Alistair exclaimed and went towards the door as if to raise the alarm, but Sally stopped him. 'Don't!' she shouted. 'Let's hear what she has to say.' Behind Ceres she could see Venus and a dark haired woman.

'Don't listen to them.' Alistair's voice wavered and he shook his head as if confused.

Ceres hesitated and then entered the room. The dark haired woman followed, looking around suspiciously. Venus hovered in the doorway, her eyes fixed on Alistair.

Ceres glanced at the dark haired woman. 'You remember; this is Diana. She helped you before.' When no on spoke, she continued quietly. 'Nothing is as it seems. We came here to warn you.'

Venus rushed forwards. 'You must help us. Michael will punish us all for what Zeus has done. But it is not our fault. We cannot oppose Zeus.' As Alistair backed away, she sank back down onto the couch, her face in her hands. 'They will destroy us.'

Ceres laid her hand on Venus's arm and continued. 'Remember what we did for you. You should speak on our behalf. The Diptera must understand who is at fault. Else we are all lost.'

'Diptera?'

'The ones you call angels.' Ceres walked slowly over to Sally and touched her neck. She smiled and Sally suddenly remembered Ceres leaning over her.

'Why should we believe you?' Why would the angels want to harm any of us?' Alistair's voice shook slightly and Sally saw his face contort. The serene expression which had so infuriated her was gone.

Venus gave a choking sob and Ceres looked at Sally appealingly. 'If you believe that, you are fools. Zeus spoke one truth today. The Diptera do not care for you two anymore than they do for us. They are guided by some strange spirit, which only they comprehend.'

Alistair rubbed the back of his neck and closed his eyes. 'I need to think.' He turned to Sally. 'We should rest.' When she shook her head, he stared around, his face confused and walked heavily towards the second sleeping room. Sally felt alarmed and followed him but he sat down on the bed, his face turned away.

She jumped as Ceres touched her arm. 'You must talk to him. Make him understand.'

Sally looked at the three women. They seemed so real, each of them individual, reminding her of other people she knew. Ceres stood erect, alert but calm. Diana lounged back as though bored. Venus was looking nervously at Sally. She constantly touched her hair and her face and fingered the neck of her robe.

Sally had difficulty speaking. 'How is it that you know English?'

Venus replied eagerly. 'We lived for a very long time on Earth. We have been everywhere.'

Ceres spoke sharply in her own language but Diana interrupted her. 'We may as well tell her. She and her friends will not be returning to reveal any of this to their people.'

Ceres shook her head and looked down.

Diana continued in a sharp, almost amused voice. 'It is easy for us to travel to earth.' She laughed. 'You must have heard of such events. Many of you have seen our vessels.'

Venus interrupted. 'And we need to bring back mortals.'

Sally could not respond. In one part of her mind she was sure they must be talking nonsense or playing with her. But she also had the sickening feeling that it might be the truth.

There was a pause as the three women stared at Sally. Ceres' expression remained gentle and sympathetic. Venus was still agitated, but Diana looked almost contemptuous.

'If you can visit earth so easily, why do you bring people back here? Where are these people?' The questions sounded ridiculous as she spoke them, but again she felt as though some awful truth was about to be revealed.

'You don't understand' said Venus. 'You are so …' She made a graceful movement. 'And we have been forbidden to live on the earth since …'

She broke off as Diana seized her arm and shook her. 'That's enough,' Diana said harshly. 'We need servants. We only brought back sufficient for our needs. We have rarely visited you in the last millennium.'

Sally had a sudden sickening thought. The Anomee all looked so alike. 'Do these humans live as long as we do?'

'Oh! Much longer,' said Venus, 'although it does not seem to bring the Anomee the same pleasure as it does us.

Of course, they cannot have children, which may be why they are sad.'

Diana gave her a warning look and Venus said no more. Sally thought of the Anomees' passive faces and shivered.

'We have only done what is necessary.' Ceres' pale face was calm and she spoke in a measured, rational tone, but her words made Sally feel dizzy. 'It is Zeus and the others who have angered the Diptera, not us. I and many of the Olympians have done a great deal for you mortals.'

Sally cut in. 'Wait a minute. You said "Olympians". What do you mean?'

Diana laughed. 'Zeus likes to play the god. I know what that word means for mortals. We are immortal but we are not gods.'

Ceres frowned. 'No one is indestructible, except the Diptera. That is why they are feared. They say they are here for the good of all but they don't understand you. We are the ones who know you, who know what you want, what you need. It is not right that we have been forbidden to live with you.'

Sally felt as though she might collapse at any moment but she forced herself to speak. 'What do you mean?'

'You mortals are very imaginative. But you have often needed our help. Consider the great catastrophes. How do you think your kind survived?'

Sally shook her head and closed her eyes. Her legs felt heavy and she had difficult staying upright.

'You need time to recover.' Ceres was looking at her sympathetically.

Venus interrupted. 'And you must help us. You must explain to the Diptera.'

'You can stay here,' Sally said. 'I will help you if I can.' She clutched at the arm of the couch to support herself. 'Are you hungry? Please take whatever you need.'

Diana laughed. 'Your food is not necessary to us.'

'I have to think. I can't …I'm too tired.' Sally backed away and closed the door on the three staring faces.

Alistair appeared to be sleeping but as she sat on the side of the bed, he turned over.

She could not look at him. She leaned down and put her face on his chest. 'I can't understand anything,' she whispered.

She felt his arms tighten around her. 'Try not to worry, Sally. I know it's hard to believe, but everything will be all right now. It's wonderful.'

Her heart sank but she did not resist when he kissed her.

22

Sally lay in a stupor. She tried to think but could not focus on anything for more than a few seconds. Tight bands of pain pressed across her head and neck. Images of the last day flashed before her; a startling vision of two huge figures wrestling across a vast white room. She sat up abruptly.

Alistair stirred and she stared down at him. He had fallen asleep, and his face was still tranquil. She felt the anger returning. How could he sleep at a time like this? She tried to control herself. It was not his fault. She pulled her hand away from his and stood up.

'What's the matter?' Alistair's voice was sleepy and unperturbed.

Sally could think of no reply. She opened the door and then backed away. Thomas stood there, his hand raised as though about to knock.

'Gabriel wishes you to go with him,' said Thomas. 'You cannot stay here with the gourds.'

Sally stared at him. He looked the same as usual. 'Who are you really?'

'You know who I am. I am Thomas.' Thomas held out his hand to her and she recalled the feeling she had when she first met him at Geneva airport. She recoiled.

'So where are your wings?' Sally laughed sharply. She couldn't believe what she had just said.

Thomas smiled slightly. 'I can show them to you if you wish; but not now. Now we must leave.'

'We should go get our packs first.' Alistair came to stand beside her. 'The gourds might find them.'

'That is not necessary. We can get them later.'

Sally could not bear it. She tried frantically to think of something that might change the situation. 'Why can't we go back to our crew?'

'Gabriel will tell you, when the time is right,' Thomas replied serenely.

'If we can't go back, I'm not going anywhere.' Sally sat down on the bed. 'I can't take anymore.'

'This will require no effort, on your part,' insisted Thomas. 'Please make yourselves ready.' He turned towards the door.

'Thomas, wait,' said Alistair. 'Why do you call those people 'gourds'? What does that mean?'

Thomas looked sideways for a moment. 'It is the English word for their real name. You called them gods, immortals on Earth and they came to like the name. It is true that they are as near immortal as any living being can be.' He walked to the door and then turned again. 'Do not worry. You are in no danger.' It was as if he had suddenly remembered that he had once had some responsibility for their welfare.

When he had gone, Sally pushed past Alistair and headed towards the other sleeping room. Ceres, Diana and Venus had gone. She stood for a moment, breathing deeply and trying not to panic. She went into the bathing area and slowly splashed water onto her face. She could hear Alistair calling to her but she ignored him. She looked down at the basin. As if from a great distance, she saw that the rim was carved with tiny characters. They looked familiar and she remembered the goblet she had seen the day before.

'Come on. We have to go.' Alistair looked nervously over his shoulder. Behind him Sally could see Thomas and two angels.

'I'm not going anywhere. I'd rather trust Ceres than these ...' She glimpsed Thomas's face and felt rage rising in her again. 'You can go if you want.'

Alistair walked over and put his hands on her shoulders. 'Don't be ridiculous, Sally. What if Zeus comes back? And this is our chance to find out what's really happening.'

Sally pulled herself out his grasp. 'You're the one being ridiculous,' she said angrily. 'What the hell do you think is going on? Let's see what they're prepared to do, to make us go with them.'

Alistair stretched out his hand but she dodged away and clutched at the basin.

'You must come,' said Thomas in the same calm voice. 'It will do no good to delay.'

Alistair muttered a protest as one of the angels brushed past him. The angel picked Sally up in a cold vice like grip and holding her out in front of him carried her into the living area. Behind him she saw Alistair speaking to Thomas. Thomas shook his head and Alistair looked at Sally, his expression a mixture of fear and embarrassment.

Sally's resistance collapsed. As if sensing her mood, the angel let her go and she walked through the door. The square was empty apart from the charred remains of the podium and the angels standing like sentinels on the rooftops. She looked up the hill towards the cliff, and then across the water. There was no movement. The gourds and the Anomee were hiding or gone. The island and the cone shaped mountain were shrouded in mist.

As they went towards the waterfront, several angels drifted down from the rooftops and joined them. The sky was clear again now, with only a few small puffy white clouds in the south. The air was fresh and warm. Sally's eyes filled with tears as she thought of the crew. Where were they? Why weren't they searching for them?

They reached the water's edge and the one called Gabriel held up his arms. The fresh breeze grew suddenly stronger, but as she looked around, she realized that it was caused by the beating of the angels' wings. Thomas stepped back and raised his arm in farewell.

'Give me your hands.' Gabriel reached out. Sally clenched her teeth as he circled her wrists with his huge hand. The skin was cool and felt smooth and soft, but she felt a tremor like a mild electric shock spread up her arms. She shuddered and glanced at Alistair. His face was pale but full of excitement.

The wind of the angels' wings increased rapidly and they closed in around the two humans. A strong smell like ozone made her gasp. She tried to move her hand to cover her nose but she was pressed in at all sides. Suddenly her feet left the ground; she kicked helplessly and screamed as they started to move upwards. Their speed increased rapidly until they shot up like an out of control elevator. Her stomach heaved and she retched. The ascent lasted only a few seconds; the movement ceased abruptly and she felt a floating sensation. She fought against a violent wave of nausea, twisted her head up and caught a glimpse of blue sky above Gabriel's hair. She called out to Alistair and thought she heard his voice. Until then she had not been so aware of the noise – the same loud rustling noise she had heard when the storm of angels arrived.

For a few minutes nothing seemed to happen although she sensed that they were moving horizontally. Then just as abruptly they started to descend. Her stomach dropped and she gagged, her face jammed up against the white cloth of Gabriel's robe. The smell of ozone became stronger again and the rustling noise became a series of loud abrupt hissing sounds. She felt cold air on her feet.

As their descent slowed the band of angels loosened slightly and Sally bent her head to look down. She gasped and retched again. They were hundreds of meters above a blinding expanse of white. Her legs shook and Gabriel tightened his grasp. As they descended she realized that they were above the equatorial ice belt. What appeared to be cliffs and valleys gradually became a finely etched landscape, and finally the outlines of what looked like a great white city became visible. The scale was impossible to judge but it seemed to cover hundreds of kilometers. Tall buildings topped with elaborate domes and spires were linked by a tracery of walkways and bridges. Wide stairways disappeared though elaborate arches. Flashes of colored lights appeared at what looked like huge windows. She heard Alistair gasp and looked up at him. He was gazing down, his face rapt.

She clutched Gabriel's gown and was aware of the cool hard surface beneath it. She snatched her hand away and closed her eyes again. Moments later she felt her feet touching a cold soft surface. Gabriel released her and she stumbled forwards and sat down heavily, panting with fright.

They had landed in a large empty expanse, surrounded by tall white structures. The strangeness overwhelmed her and before she could move another angel caught hold of her. He lifted her up, holding her out before him, and swept across the ice. As they approached one of the icy edifices she heard a slow, deep, almost hypnotic chanting, which gradually faded away.

The angel put her down at the foot of a huge stairway and a moment later Alistair was standing just above her on one of the wide shallow steps. Gabriel went ahead towards the great doorway and as if signaled, a large group of angels emerged all at once at the top of stairs. He turned and beckoned to them. Alistair started to climb the stairs and then, as if suddenly remembering, looked back. Sally couldn't move. She could hardly stand. She was only aware that she ought to feel very cold. She looked down and stamped her feet. The snow was soft and cool but her feet were warm. She bent down for a closer look but Alistair called out to her.

She thought that she would never forget this scene. The small group who had flown with Gabriel were standing like statues. Behind them, huge white shapes loomed, lit here and there by lights – golden, blue, green and rose. Beyond Alistair's excited face, Gabriel and the other angels stood gazing at her. She looked up. The icy wall glinted in the midday sun, marked with intricate patterns like wrought iron railings, and with darker squares, which might be small windows or balconies. The reflected sunlight made strange brilliant images on the dazzling surface.

The cooler air had cleared her head but nothing made sense. She stepped forward and the patterns disappeared.

At the top of the stairs the enormous entrance opened onto an immense empty area resembling an atrium. Narrower stairs led off left and right and when she looked up she could see other stairways and galleries, as far as the eye could see, like a huge honeycomb. The walls were undecorated, but punctuated at regular intervals by wide openings. The uninterrupted whiteness distorted her sense of perspective. From the outside, this building had seemed four or five stories high. Now they were inside it seemed vastly bigger.

Alistair was staring around in fascination. 'Look!' He pointed up. High upon the walls, they could see window like apertures. Suddenly they were illuminated, as if by the sun. The light threw golden patterns onto the pure white floor below. They stood transfixed by the images until an angel urged them towards another staircase.

The chanting began again and as they passed the openings, they saw groups of angels within, standing in small circles, their wings folded close behind them. They were swaying slightly, their eyes closed. The scene was repeated over and over as Sally and Alistair climbed the next staircase and two more.

Gabriel finally stopped and the angels made a path for Alistair and Sally to walk through as if they were expected to join him. The chanting faded to a low hum and Sally looked behind her. Hundreds of angels were gathering at the foot of the stairs, looking up at them.

Gabriel swept his arm sideways and the angels dispersed. 'It is here that we keep all records of happenings on earth. All natural events and deeds of individuals and nations can be found here. We study these records and when we need to act, we do. Here you will find a good record of your history and of how the gourds have treated your people. When you have consulted them, you will be better prepared to make your decision.'

Sally started as if from a dream. Her heart thumped. 'What decision?'

'We will speak of that later. You may enter here and learn whatever you wish. I will show you the way.'

Gabriel went up the last few steps and turned into one of the galleries. Sally started to follow him but Alistair did not move.

'Are you saying that we can see anything we wish?' he asked, his voice shaking.

Gabriel turned. 'If it is recorded here, you can see it. There are some mysteries that cannot be revealed. Only

Michael may see those. No one is permitted to enter his abode.'

'There are more places like this?' Alistair sounded agitated. 'What is this place called?'

'It is not important, so we call our abodes by numbers. This is the sixth abode. Michael's is the seventh. Only these two abodes contain the words. There are no other words on this planet.'

Alistair looked shocked. He was silent for a moment as though trying to take in what he had just heard. Gabriel waited patiently. Finally Alistair asked, 'words? Why do you call these places, "words"?'

Gabriel said gravely, 'All things start from words. At the start of all things were words.'

Alistair now looked as though he were going to faint. Sally sprang over to him and put her arm around his waist.

Gabriel watched without expression until Alistair stood upright again, and then continued along the gallery. There was a small entrance at the end and he walked through. Sally and Alistair followed him and stopped, in shock. The doorway was only a few meters from the staircase on one side and from the wall of the building on the other side. Despite this, the room was vast – at least a hundred meters square. As far they could see it was completely empty. There were no windows. The illumination came from the walls, which appeared to be made of ice, but which shimmered strangely.

'I don't understand.' Alistair stared around.

'Surely you know by now, that many things here are not as they are on your planet. Consider what the gourds have shown you.' Gabriel turned to the left and walked along until he was a few meters from the door. He glanced back at

Sally and Alistair for a few seconds. 'I will show you why you should not trust the gourds.' He closed his eyes, placed one hand on the wall at shoulder height, and leaned slightly towards the wall

Next to Gabriel's hand, a large section of the adjacent wall slowly brightened. The light became more intense and gradually they could see different colored shapes, which quickly resolved into a clear picture of an icy landscape. The sky was dim and the sun was just above the horizon. The perspective narrowed and a small figure appeared. Sally moved closer to the wall. As if reacting to her approach the wall showed the figure in close up. It was Ceres. She was dressed in similar robes to those she had worn when Sally last saw her. In place of her usual serene expression, rage and some terrible strain contorted her face. She raised her hands high above her head and mouthed some words but there was no sound to accompany the image.

The scene changed and now they saw a huge dark object rushing towards them. Its surface started to glow red and fiery sparks shot out from it. Suddenly it seemed to rush past them and again, they could not help their reaction. Gabriel did not move, but Alistair and Sally both instinctively leapt away and turned their heads to follow the object's path. When they looked back at the wall, they could see that the object was a meteoroid. It was headed directly for a planet that they immediately recognized as Earth. The image showed it smashing into the North Pole with frightful force, sending huge plumes of ice and water towards them. The scene changed to a long shot and they could see a dark cloud covering the Arctic.

Gabriel pressed on the wall again. Ice gradually spread down from the pole, enveloping northern Europe. The picture tightened and they saw what seemed to be a swarm of ants moving south, but as the picture enlarged they realized that it was huge numbers of people fleeing before the encroaching ice. Occasionally the face of a terrified person showed on the screen. They clearly saw Zeus, his face like thunder. There were scenes of chaos and war as people tried to find safety, only to be driven out by the people already living there. Avalanches destroyed small villages. As the ice melted, the rivers flooded and washed away whole settlements. Endless lines of refugees trekked south. Children scrabbled for food by the roadsides.

Gabriel looked at their shocked faces. 'Ceres wanted revenge on Zeus, but she involved all your people in her tragedy. Such would be the fate of earth to this day, if we had not forbidden the gourds to visit your planet. I could show you many such events; times when we have averted disaster, but there is no need to distress you,' he said.

Alistair shook his head, but Sally asked 'Are you saying that the woman really is Ceres; that she lived on Earth; that it's all true?'

'Ceres was greatly loved by your people because she helped increase the earth's capability. But when Zeus gave her daughter away in marriage to strengthen his alliance with Hades, Ceres took her revenge. She brought winter to a world that had never known it, ruined Zeus's kingdom in Europe and forced him to move south. It took him thousands of years to regain his prestige and power. He has never forgiven her. He would destroy her if he could.' Gabriel paused and looked away for a moment. 'I know this is difficult for you to believe. It is against everything you have been taught, but many of your myths have a basis in historical fact.' He paused again. 'You cannot go back to the gourds. We are instruments of the good. We cannot allow the gourds to use you to regain what they once possessed on your planet. We will make you comfortable until we decide what is to be done.'

'Is this heaven?' asked Alistair, his voice shaking.

Gabriel immediately lifted his hands up, palms facing outwards and towards Alistair. He turned his head away, as if he was warding off the question. 'Michael holds the mysteries in his domain, but he will not answer your questions. We cannot deceive you but there are many things we may not tell you.'

Alistair nodded as though he had expected this reply. Sally wondered what he was thinking. She touched her face. There was no trace of her injury. There was no point trying to understand. It made no difference. She could not believe this was happening but she had to pretend it was.

She took a deep breath. 'Could we use the wall to find out what is happening to our friends?

'Certainly,' replied Gabriel. 'We have a little time before I must join the others.'

Sally walked up to the wall and tentatively pressed it with the palm of her hand. The wall remained blank. She pressed harder but nothing happened. It was as though she could not actually touch the wall.

'What do you want to see?' Gabriel asked.

'I want to know what is happening to our friends. They must be worried about us. I want to know they are safe.'

'The word shows only events on earth,' said Gabriel. 'It cannot show events elsewhere.'

'May I?'

Gabriel nodded and Alistair put his hand on the wall. After a few seconds the white surface started to shimmer and he felt a throbbing sensation. It grew stronger and he automatically removed his hand. The light faded. He replaced his hand and tried to think hard about his family. Where were they now? What were they doing?

He suddenly saw his mother's face, so close to his own that he cried out. Her mouth moved as though she was shouting and he turned to see what she was looking at. The perspective moved so that the whole scene was laid out before him. Small children were playing cricket. He recognized the color of Sam's sports uniform and spied him near one of the wickets. His nephew was hopping from one leg to the other as he always did when he was bored. He turned his head back to his mother's face and now saw that the whole family was watching Sam's match. Jeremy and Paul sat on either side of his mother.

As Alistair watched, Claudia leant against Ben and he put his arm around her. Victor, who was standing next to Ben, looked at them anxiously. Alistair gazed at each of the faces in turn. Only little Emma was smiling. The adults all looked as though they had just received very bad news. 'What are they worried about? What has happened?' he asked himself. The scene did not change.

'Alistair! What is it?'

He removed his hand. Sally touched his shoulder sympathetically, but he could not speak. She looked at Gabriel and he nodded so she took her place next to the wall.

'Show me my father and mother,' she said as she placed her hand on the wall. The blurred colors became a room, which she immediately recognized. David was watching TV while Hilda was cutting out a dress pattern on the dining table. She looked up and said something and David turned around and smiled at her.

Sally didn't know how to feel. 'Show me where I was born.' The scene faded and a new room appeared. The walls were painted pale green and a light floral curtain covered the foreground. A nurse entered and pulled the curtain back. A very young, dark haired woman was sitting up in a hospital bed. She looked very angry and seemed to be arguing with the man sitting in the chair by her bed. As the nurse moved around to take her temperature, Sally expected to see the man's face, but he remained with his back to her. He had crisp, dark curly hair and broad shoulders. The young woman held out her arms and thrust a small white bundle at the nurse. The man rose halfway from his chair and then sat down again. The nurse looked surprised. As she walked back towards Sally, she saw that the nurse carried a very small baby. The nurse carried the baby out of view.

The young woman in the bed moved into close up as Sally stared at the image. Something about her seemed familiar. 'Show me my real parents as they are now.' Her heart thumped. The scene changed again and she saw a tall slim woman seated at a desk, using a computer. As the woman turned away from the screen to consult a book, Sally felt a terrible shock. She had actually met this woman several times. It was Erina Pomare, the famous Maori linguist.

Sally was stunned. If this was the truth, her mother was a woman she heartily disliked. Each time she had met her, they had argued violently. Erina had written several damning criticisms of the research behind Sally's books and documentaries. In turn, Sally had told Professor Pomare she was arrogant and narrow-minded.

'Show me my father, as he is now,' asked Sally miserably. The scene faded and the wall became blank.

'Show me my father, the day after I was born.' Sally felt desperate. The wall remained blank. Sally turned to Gabriel. 'Why can't I see my father?'

The angel looked back at her without emotion 'He must have died. The word does not show people after they die. How could it?'

Sally stared at him aghast, but Gabriel turned away. Sally touched his arm and recoiled at the strange sensation. 'How far back does the word go?'

'From the time we arrived here; many millennia.' Gabriel held up his hand against further questions. 'We must leave now. You may consult the word again, if you decide to stay.'

'If we decide to stay? What do you mean?' Alistair started after Gabriel but the angel either did not hear him, or chose not to answer, and passed through the doorway.

Sally put her hand against the wall again and thought of Steven and Lifescape, but the wall remained blank. It seemed that Gabriel's presence was needed. Alistair put his arm around her as they left the room and followed Gabriel back along the gallery. Neither of them spoke. Sally felt as though she might vomit.

A crowd of angels were gathered on the wide landing at the top of the stairs and as Sally and Alistair approached, the chanting started again. Sally had hardly noticed it before but now she found it unnerving. She heard a single voice rise above the rest for several beats.

'What are they chanting?' she asked Gabriel as they went back down the stairway.

Gabriel stopped and looked back up at them. He turned his head to one side, as all the angels did when asked a question. 'It is our way of sharing what we know, of making sure we are in unison. There are many things that need to be communicated and decided. There are changes here and on Earth which must be attended to.'

Sally looked at Alistair. He looked distressed and she remembered the tension on his family's faces.

'Can you tell us what is happening on earth?' Alistair asked. 'Why Michael threatened Zeus?'

Once again Gabriel looked aside. His silence seemed endless. 'I lack the time now. But you should not worry about your families and friends. They are not in any danger.' He hesitated again and then continued. 'We concluded that Zeus had started the trouble on your planet to distract us from our task of attending to you here, but we were wrong. He merely took advantage of our absence. He broke his contract with us as he has done many times in the last three millennia. For that reason we must find a way to restrain him further.'

Gabriel turned away again and was now descending the staircase at greater speed. The angels dispersed back into their rooms and took up their previous positions; the chanting grew louder. Gabriel beckoned to one of the angels guarding the entrance and spoke to him. He gestured at Alistair and Sally.

'Zadkiel will take you to where you can rest. I will speak to you again.' He did not wait for their reply but ran towards the huge door. His wings spread out behind him and as he reached the doorway his feet left the ground and he sailed gracefully into the air and through the huge doorway. They could see him soaring like a great bird towards the sun and then he turned northwards and out of sight.

The angel to whom Gabriel had spoken walked towards them, his garments flashing in bands of violet, purple and royal blue. His hair was the color of corn and he looked younger than the other angels. He nodded courteously and said in a rather stilted voice. 'Close your eyes. It will only be for a moment.'

Sally hesitated and then quickly closed her eyes as the angel's wing swept towards her. There was a rush of air for a few seconds, Alistair made a startled noise and she opened her eyes reluctantly. They were standing in the middle of a large, white, featureless room. The walls and ceiling were seamless. There were no doors or windows.

'This is where you are to stay. Gabriel invites you to make yourself comfortable.' The angel walked towards one of the walls and his foot passed through it as if it was not there.

'Wait!' called Alistair. 'We can't stay here. We need food, somewhere to sleep.'

The angel turned. 'You will be given whatever you ask.' He disappeared through the wall. Alistair ran across to where he had exited and pushed against the wall. It did not budge. He spent a few frantic moments trying to find a way out and then sank down slowly with his back against the wall. He saw Sally's frightened face and closed his eyes, feeling completely useless.

'Oh God!' he said, 'how do they expect us to survive?' He thought of the anxious expression on his mother's face. Would he die here and never see his family again? 'If only I could get home,' he muttered, 'I'd never leave again.'

Sally shouted and he opened his eyes. The icy chamber was transformed. They were sitting in the middle of the living room in Alistair's Brisbane apartment. The table was set with plates of food and the door to his bar fridge was open showing several cans of beer.

Sally's face was a sick white and her chest heaved. She gasped. 'I don't think I can stand much more. I think I'm going mad. We both are.'

'No!' Alistair jumped up and strode around the room. It was a perfect replica of his own – right down to the crockery he had left on the draining board. He ran to the hallway and grabbed the door handle. The front door opened on to a wall of ice. He slammed it shut and leaned against it, panting hard.

Sally remained slumped on the floor, her face in her hands as though she could not bear to look around her. Alistair took her by the shoulders. 'Sally. Listen. We're not going mad. You saw how they have records of everything on earth. They must have some way of replicating things.'

Sally stared at him. 'What?'

'Think about what Zeus did; the way that mountain appeared out of nowhere.' Alistair looked around. 'This is my flat; just as I left it.'

Sally shook her head and closed her eyes again.

'Remember what Arthur C Clarke said? Advanced technology is just like magic to people who don't understand it.' Alistair paced around the room and whistled. 'They must have some huge energy matter conversion technology. Bloody hell! What we can learn here.'

He was interrupted by the sound of Sally's gasping breath. He leaned down and took her face in his hands. 'We need to rest. There's nothing we can do for a while. There's no point worrying. And we must be safer here than with that maniac, Zeus.' He looked at the barbecue and the small bar fridge. 'Well at least we won't starve. I guess that's what he meant when he said we would get what we asked for. Do you want to have a go?'

Sally's eyes were wide and staring. Alistair pulled her upright and led her to his old cane couch. He pushed her onto it and sat down next to her. He pulled her hand across the cushion. 'Feel that! It's real. We're not going mad. They're just way ahead of us, in every way. You can understand that, can't you?'

Sally took some deep breaths. 'It's ok. I know what you're saying. I just need some time to get used to it.'

Alistair gave a short laugh. 'Pot plant!' he said loudly and watched in amazement as the air shimmered for a moment and the plant from his verandah appeared before him.

'Don't do that!' Sally closed her eyes.

'This is proof we're not hallucinating. It's logical. It all fits together. The angels have advanced technology and Zeus, the others, they use it too.' For a moment Alistair felt disoriented again. What did this mean for Earth? All the stories about the appearances of angels and gods; could they really be true?

He shook his head impatiently. No need to worry about that now. He kissed Sally on the cheek. 'If we can get what we want we might as well do it in style.' When she did not reply, he kissed her again. 'Go ahead; whatever you want '

Sally gave him a weak smile but sat upright and said loudly. 'Hilton Harbourside! Room service.' Then she closed her eyes tightly.

Alistair watched as his apartment was rapidly replaced by the anonymous luxury of a first class hotel. The air shimmered and there was a faint whooshing sound as each of the items appeared. It was like watching a holofilm but the elements quickly took on solidity, intact and complete.

'It's ok. Open your eyes.'

Sally gasped. She jumped up and touched the room service trolley, then jerked back as though it might burn her.

Alistair pressed his hand into the carpet, touched the leg of an upholstered chair, wandered around the room. One door opened onto a large bedroom, another led to an opulent bathroom. Everything was just right - weight, color, touch. They were in a luxury suite in an international hotel. He shuddered. What sort of power could produce this? How would such a power deal with them?

He walked towards a curtain that covered one whole wall, raised his hand and then hesitated. In his mind he saw a clear picture of the Sydney Harbour Bridge and the Opera House, shining in the moonlight. He pulled open the curtain and looked through the pane glass windows. The scene was as he imagined, but the sunlight glittered on the water. He felt a terrible homesickness and closed the curtains with a jerk.

He heard the sound of water and went back to the bathroom. Sally's silhouette was bathed in mist behind the shower screen. He pulled back the sliding door and she tried to smile. She was rinsing off her hair. 'God knows what I really look like,' she said, 'but at least I feel clean now.'

'You look fine to me,' he said. She gave a muffled cry and pulled him into the shower.

23

The room was dim and silent. Alistair looked around startled and saw Sally lying on the floor next to him. He started up. The room was as before, bare and featureless, a faint light emanating from the high ceiling. He could feel his pulse accelerating as he pressed against the walls, searching for a flaw in the seamless white. Again he had the same impression as when he had been circled by the angels. As he touched each surface it seemed to give slightly and then become rock hard. It looked like ice and felt cold to the touch, but the sensation did not last. He felt a sudden shock and paced quickly across the room, counting his steps. When he walked back his heart thumped. It was as he had suspected. It was impossible to judge exactly the size of the area. He felt panic rising and thought of his family's anxious faces. He had to stay calm.

Sally sighed heavily and Alistair saw her turn onto her side. He quickly lay down next to her and closed his eyes. 'Let it be as Sally requested,' he said softly. A few moments his body shifted slightly. He opened his eyes. Everything was as he remembered it from the night before. Sally sighed again but did not stir.

He pushed the blanket back and quietly left the bedroom. The luxurious living area looked the same except that the room service trolley was gone. He felt slightly dizzy. He walked over to the sliding doors, hesitated and drew back the curtains. The water shone faintly in the early morning light. The sun was just below the horizon. Or at least, in this world it was. He wondered whether it really was morning. According to his watcher almost 48 hours had passed since they left the Millennium crew. 'Sydney time,' he said loudly, but the screen did not change. He spoke again, tried the manual override. The signal icon was still blinking red. None of the other functions worked.

A bitter taste rose in his throat and he closed the curtains. He pushed his feelings down. He could never think straight when he was hungry. He had fallen into a deep sleep last night; his arms wrapped around Sally, and had not woken for more than ten hours.

'Breakfast!' He smelt coffee and turned around. Another trolley stood in the center of the room. He lifted the lid on a metal serving dish. It looked identical to that of an American hotel chain where he often stayed. A large English style breakfast, fruit juice, pots of coffee and tea – the trolley's shelves were stacked with food. He poked one of the eggs and tasted it cautiously. Like all the food he had eaten in the last two days, it tasted absolutely authentic.

As he ate he tried to remember everything that had happened, from the day when they had landed on the southern continent. Images flashed through his mind; the half assembled domes, Sharon leaning over the small communications pyramid, the white sand at Discovery Cove. As he remembered the angels' arrival, he felt panic rising again and a sense that he had forgotten something important.

Last night Sally had refused to discuss their situation. His attitude to the angels obviously disturbed her and she was angry that he accepted what they had told him. When he had tried to reason with her, she had pulled him towards the bed and told him to forget about it. He could not resist her.

He tried to see the angels from her point of view but every time he thought about them he felt a sense of shock.

He shivered as he recalled Gabriel soaring into the sky. He wondered how Thomas concealed his wings. And why was he so much smaller than the others? They must be able to change their appearance as easily as they could conjure up everything in this room. And why did the gods call the angels "Diptera"? He had heard that name before.

Suddenly he remembered what had been eluding him. Coffee spluttered out of his mouth. He jumped up and started pacing the room, adrenaline flooding through him. Gabriel had told them that they could not return to the gourds and he had accepted that. In his relief at being rescued from Zeus, he had forgotten what Thomas had said – that they could not return to their friends until some decision had been made. His heart began to pound. Why could they not return to their crew?

He sat down panting. He had to remain calm. He took some deep breaths. He tried to fix an image of Thomas's face in his mind but each time, the picture wavered. Alistair's heart started to race again. He had to face this.

Like many scientists who were Christians he had thought of angels and other symbols of the supernatural as elaborate symbols to help the ignorant understand fundamental concepts such as good and evil. But yesterday everything had made sense to him. He had witnessed a confrontation between two mighty forces, and he had felt a wonderful vindication. His faith was solid. He had seen the physical, visible proof. His exhilaration had carried him through all the events that followed; until now.

Sally called out to him and he went quickly into the bedroom. She was half sitting up, looking around with a dazed expression. She looked tired and drawn but she started to smile at him. She stopped when she saw the fear on Alistair's face. 'What is it? What's happened?'

'My god, Sally. I've just remembered. Thomas said we could not go back to the others. Not until some decision was made.'

Sally slipped out of the bed and started to pull on her body suit. Alistair realized he was still naked and looked for his.

'What can we do?' Sally shrugged. 'Let's get some breakfast.'

Alistair fastened his suit and sat down. 'You seem to be taking this very well.'

For a moment Sally looked furious and then her face took on the closed, withdrawn look that he had seen before. 'I've hardly slept and I'm sick of thinking about it. I spent most of last night trying to work out what was happening. While you were sleeping, I went over the walls, inch by inch. I imagined every situation and place I could think of, to try and find a way out of here. I even called up a fire, to try and melt the ice. It's useless. There's nothing we can do.'

Alistair realized why the illusion of the hotel was gone when he had first woken up. 'I'm sorry.'

As he leaned down to kiss her, she stood up abruptly. 'If this is a hallucination, either it will wear off or we'll die here. If it's real, we're in the same boat. If it's some elaborate game that someone is playing with us, we had better go along with it until we figure out what to do. It doesn't matter how either of us feel and I've run out of ideas. I'm going to get some breakfast. This food may not be real. It may not keep me alive, but it tastes good.'

Alistair followed Sally into the living room.

'You can't help what you believe anymore than I can,' she continued. 'I've never understood religion or why people need it. Now I think there must be something to all those myths and legends, but it's not what you believe.

I don't trust these angels. I think their idea of good is quite different to ours.'

'I don't feel so sure myself anymore,' admitted Alistair.

'I mean, Alistair, where do you think we really are? My best hope is that we're really lying in one of the domes and that they're all racking their brains trying to work out how to wake us up.' Sally looked at the trolley, closed her eyes and said 'breakfast!' When a bowl of fruit appeared on the table, she pushed it aside and said loudly 'English breakfast.' She sat down and flung herself at the bacon and eggs as though it was the last meal she would ever eat.

Alistair picked at the fruit. It tasted like paper in his mouth. Sally ate silently and they both started when they heard a sharp rapping noise. It was repeated and an angel appeared through the wall. He looked around for a few moments.

'You were able to make yourselves comfortable?'

Alistair nodded. Sally ignored the angel and continued eating.

'Gabriel sent me to announce him. If it will not disturb you, I will arrange the room for him.'

Alistair nodded again. The angel looked around again and some of the furniture disappeared. There was flash of pale blue light, and Alistair felt a sudden movement of air, as though a vacuum had been created. Gabriel appeared in the middle of the room. The angel bowed slightly to Gabriel and left the way he had entered.

Instinctively, Alistair rose to his feet but Sally remained seated. She toyed with her food, avoiding Gabriel's gaze.

'We have decided what good may be done in this situation.' When neither of them spoke, Gabriel continued. 'You understand that you cannot return to your friends or to Earth knowing what you do?'

'Why not? Are you going to keep us here by force?' Sally's voice was steady. She pushed her plate away.

Gabriel looked sideways for a moment. 'But the consensus has been made. It does not accord with our plans. Your people must not learn about the gourds or us.'

'That doesn't make sense. A lot of people on Earth believe they have seen angels. I recognized Michael from pictures I got when I was a child.'

'Only a minority believes in our existence and they are generally derided. Moreover, they do not know where we reside. They must not know.'

Alistair started to reply but Sally cut in. 'Then why the hell did you let us come here? Why didn't you stop us?'

A very long pause as Gabriel turned his head away. 'We took appropriate actions; they did not have the desired effect. We are taking action now to achieve the same purpose.'

As Sally sighed in exasperation, Alistair asked. 'You could at least tell us something about your plans. What are they? What have they got to do with us?'

'Our plans are to promote the good. But I cannot explain further. My nature requires me to be accurate but I am not required to tell you everything.'

Alistair felt like a small child, facing an intractable parent. Fear rose in his mouth. 'What will you do with us?' he asked.

'If you decide to return to your friends, we will cause you to forget what you have seen here. They will find you and Thomas near the rock fall. If you decide to stay here, they will find only Thomas. He will persuade your friends that you have died. We will find a way to make them leave as quickly as possible and not be eager to return. We will not harm them. Thomas will leave with them to prevent any further expeditions.'

Alistair could hardly breathe. He felt giddy with relief. He glanced at Sally but she still wore the same closed expression.

'You have seen a great deal of our world now. You have sufficient information to make a choice,' continued Gabriel. 'You could enjoy a good life here. You are scientists. We have more knowledge here than you could ever obtain on earth. If you decide to stay, you will be kept safe, as long as we remain here.' He paused and looked sideways. 'But we think it is advisable for you to leave. You will become discontented, if you are isolated from your own people.'

'What about the other people here - the other humans?' Alistair could not take in so much information all at once.

'There are no other humans here; only gourds and Anomee.'

'You mean the Anomee are not human?'

'The Anomee are nothing. Do not concern yourselves with them.'

Sally spoke angrily. 'You talk as though you came from somewhere else. Where did you all come from? Why are you here?

Gabriel looked down and hesitated, 'Is there any point my answering your questions, when you have not yet decided whether you will stay or return to earth? If you leave here, you will have no memory of what I tell you. What will you do with what I tell you?'

Sally was startled. She looked fleetingly at Alistair and saw that he too was puzzled. She leaned forward, her arms held tightly by her side, as though she was trying to control her feelings. 'Don't you know anything about us?' she asked intently. 'Of course, it matters to us. We're human.' She spoke slowly, as though Gabriel might not understand. 'When I die everything I have learned will be lost to me.

I know that. What difference does it make, how long we know things? The point is, to find out, while we're still alive.'

Gabriel stared at her intently and Sally's heart raced. She felt as though she were on the edge of a precipice. 'So', she asked impatiently, 'Where do you come from? Why are you here?'

Gabriel looked aside. 'I cannot explain to you where we came from.' His face tightened. 'You brought us here. Your lack of progress, your nature, your incessant, idle curiosity made it necessary. You waste your time and resources seeking knowledge you have no use for, which you cannot act upon.' The angel drew himself up and his wings stiffened and rose behind him. He leaned forward, looking closely into their faces. An eerie blue light filled the room. Alistair exclaimed in alarm.

Gabriel's wings slowly rustled down. He stared at the wall for a few moments. When he looked up, he was as before, calm and serene. 'I will return in two hours. When you have made your decision, you may ask other questions.' He turned away.

'Two hours!' Alistair was horrified. 'We can't. We need more time'

Gabriel looked over his shoulder. 'If you and Thomas are not returned to your crew today it will be hard to disguise what has happened to you. We wish to minimize the untruths that will result from our actions. You must decide now.'

'Wait! I must know this. I cannot decide unless I do.'

Gabriel turned and looked at Alistair.

Alistair hesitated. He was not sure how to express himself. 'You seem to know everything about us so you must know that I am a Christian and I believe in God. I need to know ...'

He stopped as Gabriel backed away from him. He used a gesture that Alistair remembered seeing before. He brought his hands up in front of his face, palms outwards, closed his eyes and turned his head and body away, as if to avert his gaze from something he should not see.

Gabriel lowered his hands and opened his eyes again. 'I cannot speak of your beliefs.' He looked sideways and continued. 'Do not think that if you stay here that we are able to answer all your questions.'

Alistair received such a forceful impression of being warned that for a moment he could not speak. He took a deep breath. 'May I then ask you, what do you mean by the "good"?'

Gabriel repeated his head movement and was silent for longer than usual. 'It is difficult to understand what explanation would help you.' He paused. 'The good is harmonious; the way everything should run, if it expands and moves onwards. Ungoodliness occurs when something prevents this progress. There is the danger of discord, of falling apart. We wait and we watch. When something occurs that may lead to this undesirable state, then we must reach accord and take action.'

Alistair had no idea what Gabriel meant. He tried another approach. 'And the gourds, what part do they play in all this?'

'They have not carried out their assigned roles. Their behavior has been defective and counterproductive. You destroyed the others so that interactions have been faulty and incomplete. Some of the gourds are now malevolent. You have made them so.'

Alistair's fear must have shown on his face, for Gabriel said. 'This does not concern you as individuals. It happened a very long time ago. We act when it is necessary and there is no reason to take action against you two.' He turned away. 'I must leave now' he said. 'I will return in two hours.'

'What?' Sally interrupted. 'What do you mean? Who did we destroy?'

Gabriel did not reply. He stepped back two paces, closed his eyes and disappeared through the white ceiling in an upward moving blur. The wind caused them to rock back on their heels and all the small objects in the room crashed to the floor.

24

Alistair reached out for a chair and collapsed on to it. 'There's no point going over and over it. It doesn't matter what we do. Whatever we decide, we're bound to regret it.' He put his head in his hands. 'I can't talk anymore. Nothing makes sense.'

Sally had pulled back the curtain and was staring down at the simulacrum of Sydney Harbour. 'I'm staying' she said. 'I want to find out who my father was, even if he is dead. That woman – I've met her and I ... She obviously didn't want me. I don't even look like her. I've wondered all my life where I came from. I need to know.'

Alistair couldn't speak.

Sally continued: 'I can't make the decision to lose these memories And I want to know what the angels are planning. Something important, some disaster has obviously happened on earth. Perhaps they won't hurt humans, us, if they don't think it's necessary, but I don't believe we're important to them. They don't know everything about us. I could find out what they're doing here and get out, warn everybody else.'

Alistair shook his head. 'No! If this is real, and I think it is, we don't have a hope of getting away from them. We could die here.'

'I don't know that. I have to try.'

'No!' Alistair repeated. He felt suddenly angry. He remembered Sally backing away from Sima in the radiation cellar, pushing up her mask as she went after the young man, running into the cave. 'You're always rushing into things. You can't decide just like that.'

Sally's face paled and then hardened. 'If this is real, we have to make up our minds now. But we don't both have to stay.' She turned her head away. 'You should go back with the rest of them. You'd be unhappy here if you could never see your family again.'

'That's not what I mean. We need to think this through.'

'You just said it. It doesn't make sense so there's no point going over and over it. We have to choose.'

'I can't leave you here.' Alistair's voice shook. 'I couldn't bear to leave you here.'

Sally's voice softened. 'You wouldn't have to bear it. You wouldn't remember anything that had happened to us here. You'd just feel sorry that I had died. That's what they'll put in to your memory. But I couldn't bear to do that. If I stay, I'll lose you, but if I go, I'll lose you anyway. I'd rather lose you than lose these memories of you.' She tried to smile. 'You know what they say – better to have loved and lost, and all that.'

'But, it will happen to us again,' said Alistair desperately. 'If it was meant to happen, it will happen again.'

'I don't believe all that destiny crap.' Sally sounded bitter. 'I might never have realized how I felt about you if all this hadn't happened. I want to keep that.'

Alistair regretted his suspicion that she was just using him. He tried to put his arms around her, but she pushed him away. 'Don't do that' she said. 'I know you can't stay. It would hurt your family too much.'

Alistair sat down. He felt as though an icy hand was squeezing his heart. 'Why should we believe anything Gabriel says?' he asked. 'Why should we believe they can change our memories?'

'I've thought about that. Do you remember that night when Sima was sick? You remember – we couldn't work out what had made him ill? Vicki told me that he went to talk to Thomas about something. She was really upset about it. She said that Sima was looking at his data pad and he wanted to check something important with Thomas. But afterwards he couldn't remember anything about it. I think he found out something Thomas didn't want him to know.'

Alistair recalled Vicki's puzzled face as Sima fell asleep. She had asked Thomas if Sima was worried about something, but Thomas told her it was not important.

'If I stay here perhaps I can influence them. I don't know what I could do, but they don't know us as well as they think they do.' Sally suddenly felt very tired. 'Knowing what I do, I just can't make the decision to go. I can't lose my memories. But I understand why you can't stay. You might never see your family again. It's easier for me. There's no one else I care so much for.' She had a sudden memory of being in Hilda's kitchen; she could smell the aroma of banana cake. She turned her face away so Alistair would not see her cry.

Alistair stood up abruptly and started to pace up and down. 'You can't stay here. You would lose everything. And for what? The whole thing might be some huge delusion.' He grasped Sally's shoulders and shook her.

Sally spoke slowly. 'I feel as though nothing that happened in my life before this trip was any use. I never felt as though I belonged anywhere, or to anyone.' She looked up at him. 'Don't you understand? I've never known where I came from. I never felt anything so strongly until I met you and the others. I don't think I ever loved anyone before.'

'But none of this may be real! We don't know why any of this is happening.'

'I know that. How can we decide? But if we have to choose, I choose this; my memories of everything that's happened, of you – if I don't have those, I don't have anything.' She put her head in her hands. 'I'm sorry. I have to stay.'

Alistair couldn't bring himself to argue any longer with her. He felt emotionally exhausted. He could not imagine making a decision that would mean never seeing his family or friends, his world, again.

'I will find a way to come back,' he said. 'Can you give me something of yours? Something that will make me wonder why I have it; that might make me remember?' He looked bitterly at his watcher and wondered what John, who had such faith in technology, must be thinking. He fingered his ID bracelet and thought of the day in Geneva when John had handed them out. He had felt such great anticipation, mixed with apprehension, just as he did when he opened a new diary and wondered about the year ahead. Years that he had expected to be happy had been wrecked by unexpected tragedy. Other years that he had braced himself to endure had turned out surprisingly well.

But nothing he had experienced could help him now. He thought of the images of his family and the awful anxiety on his mother's face. He fiddled with the catch of his bracelet, and took it off for the first time in almost a year. He handed it to Sally. She shook her head sadly but she took her own bracelet off and replaced it with his. Her bracelet felt warm and instinctively he raised it to his face. It seemed to retain a faint aroma from her skin.

Without saying a word, they went into the bedroom, lay down and wrapped their arms around each other. Despite their closeness Alistair felt no sexual desire. He concentrated on remaining calm and trying to imprint every sensation onto his memory. He remembered some times when he was a child, usually around Christmas, when he had looked around at his family and realized that this particular, special moment would never be repeated. He would close his eyes and try to form a mental photograph of the scene. He had such clear memories of those times. Could he somehow keep the memory of this time with Sally?

* * *

Sally awoke feeling refreshed and for a few moments, completely happy. Then she remembered where she was and her heart went cold. She sat up with a jerk; Thomas was sitting on a chair on the other side of the room. Her movement roused Alistair and he put out his hand. She looked down at his wrist and saw that he no longer wore her ID bracelet. Her own wrist was also bare. She looked at Thomas with hatred.

Thomas's expression did not change. 'Did you think that Gabriel wouldn't notice what you'd done?'

Sally couldn't speak. She could feel Alistair sleepily moving against her, reaching for her, unaware that they were not alone.

Thomas ignored her hostility. 'Have you decided what to do?' he asked.

'I'm staying. Alistair will return with you.'

'Is that wise? Think of how Alistair and the crew will feel if they believe you have died. You should come with me, back to the Millennium crew.'

'Don't talk to me about feelings.' Sally shouted. 'What do you know about feelings?' She felt as though she would explode. 'You're the reason I can't go back! The idea of being oblivious to everything that's happened, while you smugly shepherd us all back to earth. I couldn't bear that.'

Thomas started to speak but broke off as Alistair sat upright. He took Sally's hand but she pulled away. She slipped off the bed onto her knees and threw herself at Thomas. He tried to push her away but she clutched his arm.

'Thomas, I'm begging you. Please try to remember. Remember what it was like on earth, how we came here. We were a team. You were meant to protect us.' She was sobbing now with no pretence at all and when she looked up she saw a strange expression on Thomas's face. For one wonderful moment he looked almost human, and then it passed.

'I will protect you. Believe me Sally. No harm will come to you if you return with me.'

'That's not what I mean. That's not what I want.' Sally screamed in rage and despair. 'Look what you've done to us. You've destroyed my life. I hate you. You're evil.'

She tried to hit him but Alistair rushed forwards and pulled her back. She fought against him but he took her face in his hands. 'I'm staying too.'

Sally shook her head violently but Alistair persisted. 'I know that if I leave, I'll forget everything; none of this will matter. But while I know what I know, while I can still remember everything, I can't make the decision to leave you here alone. I just can't do it.'

Sally could not speak. She put her hands over her face and her shoulders heaved.

Alistair looked at Thomas. 'I hope you're happy.'

Sally pulled away from Alistair and went over to the window. She drew the curtains and looked out over the image of the harbor. 'I don't want you to stay. You'd end up hating me. If things go wrong here, you couldn't help me anyway.'

Alistair looked at Thomas. 'Would you mind giving us some privacy,' he said resentfully.

Thomas turned to look aside briefly and rose to his feet. 'You must decide now. Gabriel will return soon.' He left the bedroom and Alistair caught a glimpse of white as he passed through the wall.

* * *

When Gabriel entered, he looked intently at them both for several moments. Alistair stared back defiantly. Sally kept her face turned away.

'Very well,' Gabriel finally said. 'Thomas will return to your crew. He will convince them that you have died and that he only escaped death narrowly himself.' He thought for a moment and said: 'As a special dispensation I can show you your friends before they leave for your earth. Do you wish that or not?'

Sally answered 'no' and Alistair 'yes' at the same moment. Then Sally said 'yes' in a quiet voice.

'It will not be for some little time. I will tell you when it will happen.'

Alistair thought of something. 'Can we consult the wall again?'

'When your friends have left this planet, you may use it whenever you please; that is to say, when it is not required for our use. Until then you must stay here.'

Gabriel prepared to leave, as he had before. 'Is there anything I can do for you?'

When they both shook their heads, he said, 'I will send Thomas to you. He will know better what should be done.'

25

They stood in a semi circle around the cairn of stones, while Sima read from a small book. "Fear no more the heat of the sun or the furious winters' rages. Thou thy worldly task hath done, home art gone and taken thy wages."

John pressed a key on his data pad and the notes of the Last Post rang out, strangely clear in the alien air. Vicki felt her legs tremble and she leaned against Mohun. He put his arm around her waist and they walked forward. She pushed a stick of incense into the loose earth at the top of the small cairn. Her hands shook and Mohun took her flint and lit it for her. The scented smoke drifted into the air. Underneath the stones they had placed some mementos – photoprints of the crew, one of Vicki's scarves that Sally admired, and a diskette of Alistair's favorite music. Sharon had retrieved the second pyramid from where she had placed it the night they landed on the northern continent. Now it stood next to the cairn.

Sharon bent her head in prayer and Vicki wished that she could join her but her mind was a blank. The sedative had calmed her but she felt distracted and feeble. Her head was throbbing and she needed all her will to stay upright.

Sharon clenched her fists. She could not accept it. She had attended many military funerals where no remains could be retrieved for burial and the families of the dead remained unconvinced that their sons or daughters had really died. For the first time in her life she could not come to terms with what had happened. She turned and looked at the group. John's face was rigid. He was preparing himself to speak. Vicki and Mohun looked dazed. Sima was clutching Sally's little book of Shakespeare's sonnets, his head bent and his eyes closed. Thomas was staring at the ground, his arms hanging by his side, his face blank. He showed no reaction as John started to speak.

None of them remembered much of what John said. Sima was thinking of John's reaction when they found Alistair's ID bracelet. John was convinced that Alistair had left the bracelet as a clue. He did not believe Thomas's story. He thought he was lying or confused. Sima didn't know what to believe. He had questioned Thomas about the medlab and the DNA data. Thomas had denied accessing the system. He had watched silently as they searched for Alistair's and Sally's bodies. Their efforts had caused another landslide and it would take months to search through the debris.

Sharon watched John as he spoke and wondered at his calm. When they returned to the village and found nothing there John had gone almost berserk. He had ordered Sharon and Sima to set the explosives and had excavated an area several hundred meters square. Vicki and Mohun had looked on in horror. Sima had not spoken. He had followed John's orders as though they were perfectly reasonable. They had found nothing. There was no trace of buildings, clothes, tools; no bodies or anything at all to suggest that people had once lived there.

Vicki thought of the intense joy she had experienced when they had landed in the grasslands. She looked back now at the valley. It seemed so serene; the plants and streams still evidence that this planet could support life. Were the Anomee really an illusion as Thomas continued to argue or had someone, something, violently demolished their village and taken them away? She thought of Poseidon's strange pale face and shuddered.

'When we return, we will build a memorial to you. I swear to that.' John turned and surveyed the group. Thomas was looking south towards the gully where they had found him. The others looked back at him.

They stood silently for a few moments and then John continued. 'We can't change what has happened but we can make sure that we do not dishonor their memories by abandoning hope and reason. We will find out what has been happening here and we will finish the mission. We started our journey with the hope that we would find a planet that humans could explore and occupy. That is still our goal. Thousands of people have worked to send us here. Billions of dollars have been spent that could have been used for other purposes. If we give up now we cannot go home with any pride. We have made our plans. Now is the time to put them into action.'

He wheeled around towards the cairn and saluted sharply.

'Thomas!'

Thomas turned his head slowly and looked at John. He turned away again to stare at the foothills.

John beckoned to Sima. 'You'd better give Thomas some more stuff and get him into Radon. I don't want him left alone.'

26

As the images disappeared, Sally wiped her eyes with the back of her hand. Alistair's face was turned away. She thought bitterly that the angels had probably chosen to show them the memorial service to persuade them to change their minds, or at least to convince them that their friends thought they were dead and there was no possibility of rescue. She felt her thoughts slip sideways. Was any of this real? Did it matter what they chose to do? She had a sudden awful feeling that she and Alistair were abandoning their friends.

Thomas interrupted her thoughts. 'There is still time. We could devise a way that all of this has been a mistake - that you survived the landslide.'

For a few moments they did not understand what he was saying.

'You mean we could still go back?' Alistair felt his heart leap in his throat.

'You must decide now. It would be completely implausible if you were to return any later. We have considered all this.'

Sally took a deep breath and tried to speak calmly. 'Thomas, think about this very hard. You've spent so much time on earth. Why can't we keep our memories and go back to the others? Can't you convince Gabriel to let us go?' As soon as she spoke, she felt stupid and futile. Still she had to try.

Thomas hesitated as usual and then shook his head: 'The situation on earth is so complicated that it would be dangerous to introduce any new factors. No one must know we are here, otherwise we may lose our ability to influence the outcome.' He paused and then went on, 'In any case that is not the way we think or work. No one of us can change anything. We are of one mind, perfectly clear in all things.'

Alistair cursed softly. 'There are many people on earth, for whom everything is perfectly clear as well. We think of them as dangerous. There is an old Roman saying – "Beware the man with one book".'

Thomas did not respond.

'I have to stay,' Alistair continued. 'It would be a betrayal of the others, to go back to them ignorant of everything we've experienced.'

Sally felt an overwhelming sense of relief as Alistair spoke, followed by a crippling feeling of grief. It would have been kinder, she thought, if Thomas had not given them a second chance. Thomas looked at her and she shook her head.

'So, I will make my farewells to you both.'

Astonishingly, he held out his hand to Alistair. He took it reluctantly as though Thomas might even now try to effect some change on him. Thomas shook it briefly and turned to Sally. He looked directly in to her eyes. She couldn't bear to look at him. She tried to think of something else.

Thomas put his hands on her shoulders. She felt again the brief shock like a weak electrical current. He gazed at her for a moment. 'Now is the hour for us to say goodbye.'

Sally stared at him. For those brief seconds he had looked human again. He turned as he reached the wall and gestured farewell. There was a glimpse of white as he disappeared. She ran to the wall and pressed against it. As usual it reziled slightly and then became solid and immovable. She turned back into the room and sat down. She felt numb.

'What did he say to you?'
'What?'
'He wasn't speaking English. What did he say?'

Sally stared at Alistair. 'Didn't you hear him? He said, "Now is the hour for us to say goodbye." I don't know why.'

Alistair was insistent. 'He wasn't speaking English.'

Sally had to think for a minute until she recalled that Thomas had spoken in Maori. She suddenly remembered. When Thomas had looked at her, the image of her birth mother had flashed through her mind.

'Oh god!'

'What is it?' Alistair sat beside her.

'Shit! I think they can read our minds!' Sally explained what she meant. 'It's the first line of a famous Maori farewell. I was trying not to look at him and I suddenly thought of my real mother - that woman. She's Maori; I've met her. How could he have known that?'

Alistair was silent for a moment. 'Are you absolutely sure?'

'Yes, it was definitely Maori. I don't speak it fluently but I remember those words. It's a famous song.'

Alistair thought for a moment, his heart sinking. 'I guess they know everything about us. Perhaps Gabriel told him about you seeing her on the wall.' He paused. 'All that chanting; Gabriel said that's how they share their knowledge. Like some great super computer. It all fits, when you think about it.'

Sally interrupted. 'But why would he do that, even so? Why now? He must have known what I was thinking about.' She sighed in exasperation. 'I feel there's something important. Something I can't remember.'

Alistair groaned. 'We'd better try to find out. If they know everything we're thinking we haven't a hope. Shit! This is beyond belief.'

27

John brought Xenon down in almost exactly the same spot from which the shuttle had taken off the day before. He turned to Mohun. 'How do you feel?'

'Fine!' In truth, Mohun wished that John had asked someone else to accompany him. Day after day he had sat in the shuttle with his silent commander while they scoured the northern hemisphere for signs of anything unusual. But he understood John's reasons. He had left Sharon in command of the camp. Sima was busy trying to restore the medlab as well as monitoring Thomas, who had managed to leave the camp several times despite being sedated. Vicki was not fit; she was still distressed and had made several important errors in the last few days.

'So what's the schedule for today?' John had finished the tedious review of their security arrangements and Mohun was desperate for distraction.

'We're going to test for unusual magnetic activity,' John replied.

Mohun sighed and John looked at him sharply. 'You know that radioactivity can cause hallucinations. Do you have any better ideas?'

'We've focused on the continents. Shouldn't we take a closer look at the ice belt and the islands?'

'I agree, and if we don't find anything unusual here or in Southland, we'll widen the search. Alistair told me that several things about this planet puzzled him. For example, why aren't there any northern lights? The magnetic field is very similar to Earth's.'

Mohun frowned. 'It's still midsummer. The aurora wouldn't appear for another couple of months.'

'Not according to Alistair. Because of the more extreme tilt we should see them now.'

Mohun shrugged. 'He could be right. It's not really my field.'

John nodded and continued: 'While we're checking those out, we're more likely to pick up any unusual signs of electrical activity or some other artificial source of power.'

They trudged across the rock littered landscape until they reached the cairn they had built for Sally and Alistair. John did not speak and showed no emotion as he checked the small pyramid and uploaded the latest data. The records of the crew's work would be transmitted to the satellites, and relayed to Earth in the next communications capsule.

Mohun shivered as he looked at the small cairn of stones, and glanced up at the rocky slopes of the hills. He still found it hard to accept that Sally and Alistair were buried there somewhere.

John spoke briefly to Sharon and told her they were heading towards the northern polar region. Mohun tried to remain objective as they flew over the stony plateau, but he felt little interest in the day's schedule. He often wondered what he would do when he returned to earth. Sometimes he had the dreadful premonition that the happy, useful part of his life was over and that he would be haunted by this mission forever. He thought of his family. He longed to see them but he could also imagine their disappointment. He had always been the lucky one, the blessed son for whom everything turned out right. Now his resilience and cheerfulness seemed to have deserted him.

'Give it time,' he muttered to himself. He was expecting too much. He would recover from this. He had to. He remembered what John had said about honoring Alistair's and Sally's memories and immediately felt stronger.

As if John could read his thoughts, he said, 'I'm glad to have you along, Mohun. Thanks for all your help.'

Mohun was astonished. John rarely spoke in such a personal way. He glanced at the other man's face but he wore his usual calm expression.

'When we reach the Pole we'll take some drill samples, so we can compare them with the results from the ones that Alistair took down south. We'll see if there's anything unusual about the rate of radioactive decay.'

'You mean, compare it with the probable rate of decay?'

'Yes. I've got all the data and gear to do that. We haven't discovered any elements here that don't occur on earth. It should be quite easy to see if something strange is going on.'

'It's a bit hit and miss, isn't it?'

John frowned. 'We have plenty of time.'

Mohun felt his spirits drop again. When Vicki had asked John again how long he was prepared to spend on the surveys, he had replied tersely, 'As long as it takes.'

They had adequate supplies for at least four months. And if Rick arrived before their supplies ran out, they could be here much longer. Mohun felt so despondent at the prospect of such a long stay that he decided not to raise the topic again. He didn't want to hear John's reply.

The day developed into a pattern; mapping, measurements and landings every thirty minutes to extract ore samples. They arrived at the magnetic north pole around the time they would expect to see the northern lights. The sky darkened gradually but remained clear and the brilliant canopy of stars emerged. Mohun filmed the shuttle and John against the magnificent backdrop of the night sky.

Before eating, Mohun did thirty minutes of vigorous exercise. He feared that he would not sleep unless he tired himself. In the last few nights he had had unpleasant dreams and had woken sweating in the middle of the night, unable to go back to sleep.

John held his data pad in one hand and ate with the other. Occasionally he mentioned something they should follow up but otherwise they did not speak. As he cleared away the remains of their meal, Mohun asked John what he should do next and then continued with the work until he felt exhausted. When he finally stretched out on his bunk he could see John sitting in the cockpit, checking the instrumentation. When his watcher woke him the next morning, John was already up.

* * *

Mohun lugged the rest of the equipment into the shuttle and secured it. John was satisfied that there was nothing of interest in this area and they were preparing to head south. The mystery of the auroras would have to wait.

'If he makes any more trouble, restrain him!' John gestured impatiently. 'What does Sima say?' He listened intently, his dark face creased into a frown.' Ok then. We're heading south.'

Mohun took the copilot's seat. 'What's going on?'

'Thomas has been stirring Vicki up.'

Xenon lifted gently off the ground. The sky was clear and Mohun felt overwhelmed by the view as they climbed steadily to two hundred meters. The landscape was so familiar. He could have been in a hundred places on Earth. At the same time, it somehow seemed strange. The light, some quality of the air was different, giving the colors and shapes an exotic appearance.

'Phew! Look at that.' John sounded excited.

Without any warning the rocky plateau had terminated abruptly and they now soared over a wide canyon. The sides of the canyon were scarred by giant landslides, which had created huge funnel shaped formations, some several hundred meters across. Mohun peered out. As the canyon stretched west it split into a complex system of deep winding rifts. He winced as Xenon suddenly plunged downwards and wove between two huge pillars of rock.

'It's more exciting in real life, hey?' John sounded exhilarated.

Mohun remembered looking at the canyon on the satellite images. It seemed a lifetime ago. He looked back as they rose above the canyon again. It extended west as far as he could see but on the southern side the landscape reverted to the same pattern; a rocky, gently sloping plain interrupted by the occasional small rise.

Mohun was surprised when the shuttle took a hard turn to the west.

'Looks like some heavy weather developing ahead.' John observed. 'We'll go around it.'

Mohun looked up and saw a dark cloud on the horizon. 'Whoa! Where did that come from?'

'Don't know. But it must be moving fast. The sky was clear a minute ago. Keep an eye on it would you?'

Mohun checked the instrument panel and view screens. Elsewhere the sky was clear. 'That's odd. The barometric pressure hasn't changed.' He looked at the cloud again. It was no larger but he could have sworn that it was closer and it seemed to have changed direction. 'There's something wrong here. The cloud is moving faster than the wind and it's not changing shape at all.'

John accelerated and Mohun picked up his scanner. 'I don't think it's water vapor. It might be a darker version of those pollen clouds, but that doesn't explain why it's moving so fast.'

Mohun stared through the scanner and felt a rising sense of panic. The surface of the cloud was impenetrable and roiled with movement. He lowered the scanner and saw with a shock that the cloud was much larger. It was hard to get a sense of perspective but he didn't think it had grown; it was just much closer.

'John! I think we should get down. I think it's moving towards us.'

John responded by accelerating again and Xenon's nose lifted steeply. 'We can outrun it easily.'

Mohun was pressed back in his seat and the cloud disappeared from view. There was an enormous roaring noise, like a huge waterfall, which made him clap his hands over his ears, then a few seconds later a loud bang. The retort propelled him forwards against his safety harness.

'What the hell?' John sounded incredulous. 'We've been hit.'

The shuttle lurched and went into a steep descent. John hit the stabilization key, they leveled off and the terrible whining noise faded.

'Sharon! We're in trouble. Something's hit us and we'll have to make repairs.' John swore briefly. 'Sharon! Have you got a fix on us?'

Mohun leaned forward and surveyed the sky. He could see the black cloud in the distance. 'I can't see anything that could do that to us. Could it have been that cloud?'

'No idea,' replied John curtly. He was wrestling with the manual joystick and as he spoke the shuttle lurched sickeningly. Instead of the usual background hum of the AGD, there was a series of loud popping noises followed by a sinister hissing sound.

Mohun saw that the cloud was moving towards them again and lifted the scanner to his eyes. The surface of the cloud was now spotted with bright luminescent red dots arching out from the surface. Suddenly a bolt like lightening shot out of the cloud, accompanied by the same deafening roar.

'John! Watch out!'

John pulled back hard on the joy stick. The shuttle wobbled frighteningly and then went into a sharp climb. Mohun saw a flash of light pass below them. John turned the shuttle again. 'I'm heading for the sea. If we get hit again, we'll be better off coming down in the water. What the hell is it?'

Mohun reached up and pulled the rear view screen down on its cantilevered arm. He could see the cloud clearly. It was definitely following them. He saw a bolt of light shoot out and shouted a warning to John. This time John ascended and turned hard to port. The light flashed past them and hit a small hill a few hundred meters ahead. Geysers of flame erupted and shot several meters into the sky. To Mohun's horror a red liquid started to pour down the hillside.

'I think something about the shuttle must be attracting it – something electrical.'

'Sharon! We're gonna need help. But don't approach until it's clear.' He paused as Sharon spoke. 'I haven't tried that yet; don't think we've got anything that would do it. I've never seen anything like it. Just get over here.'

Several more bolts of light shot past them and crashed into the ground. The earth exploded and rocks shot up into the air. Mohun could see that where the lights hit the surface of the plain, it was turning to molten lava.

He was pressed back into his seat again as John put the shuttle back into a steep ascent. Mohun looked into the rear view screen and saw the cloud receding into the distance. His profound sense of relief was cut short by a loud wrenching noise. The shuttle plummeted.

'It's no good. We're going down. We should make it to the water. Get ready to take up crash position.'

The next few minutes were a nightmare. The cloud gained rapidly on them and at every moment Mohun expected the shuttle would be hit. The sight of the blue water was the most wonderful thing he had ever seen. John swore and cursed between clenched teeth as he worked the joystick. About fifty meters from the water he pushed the joystick forward.

'That's it. We'll have to land. You ready?'

Mohun braced himself but they came down with a surprisingly gentle thump.

'Let's get out of here.' John grabbed his pack and slammed the override button on the airlock door. The inner door opened but the outer door remained closed. John hit the override button again. The door opened a crack, held fast. Mohun touched the metal and flinched. It was very hot and the heat in the airlock was increasing. John looked around, wrenched a metal bar from one of the storage racks and inserted it into the small crack. The door was forced open a fraction and hot air rushed in through the narrow gap. Mohun grabbed some thick gloves from a storage locker and threw a pair to John. They braced themselves and hauled back on the door with all their might. The door inched back and then slid aside so suddenly that John almost fell through the opening. Mohun grabbed him and looked down in horror at the flow of lava less than a meter below.

John straightened up and reached above the door. 'I'll give you a leg up,' he shouted over the roaring noise. 'There's a small ladder on the roof. Push it back down for me.'

For a moment Mohun could not move. He looked down at the lava and saw that it had risen slightly in the last few seconds. Everywhere he looked the ground was heaving and he suddenly felt the floor tilting beneath his feet. With a revolting sucking noise the shuttle lifted slightly out of the molten rock and Mohun almost lost his footing.

'Go! That's an order.' John's voice snapped at him. Mohun put his foot into John's cupped hands and strained upwards. He reached for and grabbed the end of the ladder but it did not move.

'It's stuck,' he gasped. He rose slightly higher as John heaved him up.

'Get up there and unlock it.'

Mohun scrambled onto the roof and then ducked as another flash of light shot overhead. He fumbled with the release mechanism, the ladder slid free and he pushed it down over the side. A few moments later John's head appeared over the side of the vehicle's roof. He slung Mohun's pack to him and pulled himself up onto the roof, slapping at the sparks on his body suit.

The shuttle was now jerking in an alarming way. Lava poured down the hill to the east but on the western side of the shuttle the ground was clear as far as the rocky headland. They ducked down again as another light came dangerously close and exploded into the ground several meters away.

John pushed the ladder across and they clambered down the other side. The smell of sulfur was so strong that both men retched as they ran towards the water. The roaring noise was getting louder and bolts of light hit the ground all around them. The land rose slightly terminating in a small cliff several feet above the water and John clutched at Mohun to stop him toppling over. They both looked back. The shuttle had not been hit but it was now surrounded by lava. John groaned. If the lava rose any further the machine would be beyond repair.

'We should get down into the water. There's an island not far out.'

'Wait a minute.' John was calling Sharon.

Mohun forced himself to look up. The cloud was hovering about thirty meters above the shuttle as though something in the vehicle attracted it. But the roaring noise had died away and no further bolts of light appeared. The lava was lapping around the rocks only ten meters away at the bottom of the small rise. Mohun sat down heavily and started to shake.

'What the shit!'

Mohun sprang up. John was staring towards the water and Mohun almost fell over again. A very tall young man was standing at the edge of the rocks, balancing lightly on the balls of his bare feet. He stared at them angrily. 'What fools you mortals are. Stay where you are and do not move.' His voice was cold, with a strange but clear accent.

The figure leaned forward as though he expected a response, and Mohun realized that he was exceptionally tall. He was naked except for an animal skin drawn casually around his waist, revealing a slender but deeply muscled figure. He was nothing like the village people. His face was beautifully symmetrical, with large brilliant sapphire blue eyes beneath arched silvery blonde eyebrows. His hair was of the same color, cut short and worn in tousled curls. Despite its beauty, the face terrified Mohun and he felt a terrible chill of déjà vu. He had seen this man before.

Mohun glanced at John. His face had paled to an ashy gray. Mohun watched in awful fascination as the alien man frowned and stepped down to the water. He seemed to drift across it. Mohun put his hand over his mouth to stifle a hysterical laugh.

John still didn't speak. He looked as though he might collapse and Mohun pressed him down towards the ground. He glanced behind. The line of lava was gradually creeping up towards them. The cloud still hung over the shuttle, a sinister splotch of black and red against the clear blue sky.

'Mohun! Can you hear me?'

For a moment Mohun couldn't understand where Sharon's voice was coming from. Then he raised his watcher to his mouth. 'Where are you?'

'About thirty minutes away. Can you hold out? Where's John? Can you check that I've got your location right?'

Mohun answered as quickly as possible. John was leaning heavily against him. His eyes were open but they had the glazed appearance of a person in shock. Mohun pulled off his pack and scrabbled inside for the medical kit. He looked up. The strange man had halted some thirty meters away and now turned towards the shore. He lifted up his arms towards the cloud and made threatening gestures. Incredibly a long booming noise came from the direction of the cloud. The alien's gestures became more violently angry.

Mohun couldn't look away. He fumbled in the kit and found the smelling salts. John responded immediately, gasping and jerking upright. Mohun took a sniff before replacing the tube in the kit. He gagged but immediately felt more alert.

John staggered to his feet. 'What's happened? Report!'

Again Mohun felt a terrible desire to laugh 'I don't know. We must be hallucinating. Look at that man, that thing out there.'

The confrontation continued. As the booming noise grew louder the alien's gestures became more violent. Suddenly the alien whirled around, sweeping his arms in a wide circle. As though in response, the water started to rise into steep waves, encircling the tall figure. Mohun looked back up at the cloud. It was shrinking and had become more intense in color. The streaks of sulfurous light had disappeared but now the cloud was striped with brilliant bands of purple and saffron light. For a few seconds a huge figure could be seen. Then the cloud receded rapidly. In only a few seconds it was merely a black speck in the sky.

The smell of sulfur alerted Mohun. He looked down and saw that the lava was only meters away. 'Come on, we have to get down to the water.' He pulled at John's arm.

The alien roared out 'Do not move!' The waves heaved around him but he stepped through them as though they were mere ripples. When he reached the shore, he plucked a huge boulder from the rocky headland, lifted it above his head and threw it with terrifying force onto the ground. Rock hit rock with a deafening smashing noise and the ground split open. The earth shook and Mohun and John tottered on the edge of the small piece of safe ground. The water below them was sucked out as the waves piled up behind the alien.

They watched transfixed as he threw another boulder and it hit the ground with tremendous force. With an enormous cracking sound a channel appeared in the small headland. The waves poured in and swept across the plain in a massive flood. Jets of fire sprang up and the water hissed deafeningly. Huge rocks shot into the air with ear splitting explosions. Mohun thought that this must be what hell looked like. They stood frozen as the water surged toward them, covered the shuttle and swept it away like a small toy. A wall of water and rocks rushed towards them and then, amazingly, it seemed to run out of power. Only a meter from their feet it swept back and within moments the water had subsided and was calm again.

John was still leaning heavily against him, shaking violently. Mohun looked around. A dense mist shrouded the plateau and the shoreline. There was no sign of the dark cloud or the shuttle. Suddenly Mohun felt a hand on his shoulder. He turned, stumbled back and John slumped to the ground.

The alien loomed over him, his expression grim. 'I have protected you from my father this time. I will not attempt it again.'

Mohun glanced at John, but his face was still rigid, his eyes wide in a fixed stare.

'Who are you?' he whispered.

'I am Heracles. This is the second time I have broken the earth and left my mark to warn you. I tell you for the last time. Go no further. Remember Ulysses!' He closed his eyes as though he could not bear to look at them, raised his arms above his head and shot up into the sky. Within seconds his figure disappeared into the mist and they could see no trace of him.

When Sharon brought Radon down, she saw them sitting on a small island of rock surrounded by water. The mist had dispersed and the water was calm.

28

'We have to go back down and try to salvage Xenon.' John's voice was calm; he seemed to have recovered completely from their ordeal. But Mohun was suffering from delayed shock and still shivered from time to time. He looked at John in amazement. Neither of them had spoken about John's collapse when confronted by the alien. By the time Sharon had landed, John had recovered his usual composure. He had looked at Mohun challengingly when Sharon had asked them what had happened, and Mohun had returned his gaze steadily. He had no intention of undermining John's authority.

Sima shook his head. 'We need to secure the Millennium as a top priority. In my view we should break orbit while we analyze what happened.'

John had opposed the idea that the crew should return to the Millennium but in this instance Sharon had supported Sima. Mohun and Vicki could scarcely conceal their relief as they lifted off from Earth 2.

'What analysis? Are you still convinced these are hallucinations?' John asked. 'How can you think that? Look at these burns! They're real. Mohun and I were almost killed today. Someone put on a very convincing performance to get us off this planet and we're not leaving until I know who.'

Thomas interrupted. 'I have to state my disagreement. It doesn't matter that you don't believe me, but you should stop endangering the crew. We should leave before everyone becomes ill.'

'Why is he still here?' John asked angrily. 'Take him back to sick bay.'

Sharon gestured to Thomas and he slowly undid his harness.

'And tell me this - why don't you share any of our delusions?' Vicki demanded.

'I've told you before. I've had years of training and experience as a psychiatrist.' Thomas spoke slowly as if to a child. 'I'm better able to resist the effects of any psychotropic elements.'

'That's ridiculous,' interrupted Sharon angrily. 'John and I have had intensive training on every technique under the sun; and Sima too. You don't suppose our government lets us loose in war zones without making sure of that, do you?' She had vivid and very unpleasant memories of some of the sessions she had been put through.

'There's no point arguing with him.' John looked at Thomas with contempt. 'I'm not interested in your opinions.'

Thomas shrugged and pushed off towards the hatch. Sharon followed him. 'I'm going to take a break. Do you need me for anything?' When John shook his head she pushed through the hatch.

Mohun turned to John. 'Couldn't we leave it another day before we go back down? I can't get my head around all this.'

John shook his head. 'We'll make a start first thing tomorrow. If we're to have any chance of locating Xenon, we should get down there as soon as possible. Why don't you try to get some rest before dinner?' His voice was sympathetic.

Mohun didn't move.

'Is there something else you're worried about? If they meant to kill us, they could have blown us out of the sky when we first got here.'

Mohun shook his head. 'It's not that. I'm still trying to understand what happened to us.' He paused. 'For example, what did that creature mean when he mentioned Ulysses?'

Vicki spoke tentatively. 'If this is a conspiracy, whoever is doing it wants to undermine our self-confidence, make us think we're losing it.'

There was a long silence as they thought about the idea. Mohun still felt uneasy but it took him several moments to work out why. He exclaimed loudly. 'I've just remembered who he reminded me of. That creature, that hologram or whatever of Hercules was the mirror image of Alistair's brother – Jeremy Stuart.'

Vicki and Sima looked shocked but John seemed undisturbed by this piece of information. 'I realized that too. It only goes to support my theory. They've probably grabbed images from films and other stuff to build these simulations.'

'I still think it's possible that this planet was settled a long time ago.' Vicki wriggled in her chair. 'But, then how come these people, Hercules, Poseidon, speak English? No! It doesn't fit.' She reddened and looked away. 'I've thought of something else. What if we never left Earth at all? What if this is just some big show to keep some group on Earth happy?'

'You mean some giant simulation? Why?' Mohun looked incredulous.

Vicki moved uncomfortably. 'Perhaps to test us; to see how we would all react.'

There was a long silence.

'It's just an idea,' said Vicki.

To her surprise John leaned forward and put his hand on her arm. 'All ideas are good. We can think about it, but we can't test it. In the meantime we have to work with what we know.'

29

Sharon woke with a start and sat up abruptly. The cabin's interior was brighter than usual and she felt confused and slightly giddy. Her reading light was still burning and she stared at it for a few moments before reaching up to switch it off. She released her harness and slowly swung her legs over the side of the bunk, waiting until the vertigo passed.

Vicki and Mohun were still asleep. A sharp beep from her watcher made her shoot upwards. She grabbed the ladder to the top bunk to steady herself and looked down at her watcher. The alarm was flashing but it was not her wake up call. It was one of the regular alarms she set to remind her to carry out routine jobs. The watcher showed 9 am, two hours past the beginning of her shift.

She pulled the sliding screen back between the two sets of bunks. John's and Sima's were empty. Why had they let her and the others sleep in? She raised her watcher to her mouth and called John. There was no reply. Her heart started to race. She tried Sima; no response.

She twisted around, grabbed Mohun's arm and shook him violently. She pulled herself down to the bottom bunk and did the same to Vicki. 'Wake up!' she yelled. 'Mohun, Vicki, wake up! There's something wrong.'

Mohun sat up almost straight away, rubbing his eyes. He stared at her. 'What is it?'

'Get up! It's nine am and I can't raise John or Sima.'

Mohun slid down from the bunk and they both tried to rouse Vicki. She was still deeply asleep. Mohun pulled her out of her bunk and patted her face. Her eyes opened but she looked dazed.

'What's the matter?' she asked in a weak voice.

'I don't know. Stay behind me. Something's happened. Mohun, bring your gun.'

Vicki rubbed her face hard to wake herself up. She felt dizzy and she banged several times against the walls as she followed Sharon and Mohun towards the control module.

Sharon pulled herself through the control room hatch and grabbed a stanchion. Vicki bumped into her and then reeled over in shock. John was floating just above them, his arm extended over his head as though he had been trying to reach for something. Near the control panel Sima's foot had caught in his harness and his body swung gently to and fro.

Vicki pushed off against the wall, and dived past John towards Sima. 'He's breathing.' She looked back at Mohun. 'I can't see anything wrong with him.' She shook Sima gently and to her immense relief he started to stir.

'John's OK, too, but I can't raise Thomas. I'd better get down there.' Sharon looked around incredulously, propelled herself back towards the hatch.

Mohun pulled John down onto one of the bunks. He closed the harness over John's shoulders and then crouched down beside him. As John shook his head in confusion he told him briefly what had happened.

John looked at his watcher and made an agitated gesture. 'Damn it! I've been out to it all night.' He unclasped the harness and pushed himself back over to the bridge. Sima was already in the other chair. Several lights were flashing on the console. As John touched a panel a series of beeps rang out.

'Our orbit hasn't decayed.' John's voice was terse as his fingers flew across the panels.

'Beep! Unauthorized access to main computer! Beep! Main airlock compromised! Beep! Unauthorized access to port A! Beep! Shuttle locking clamps insecure!' The computer droned on.

'Radon's gone!' Sima stared in disbelief at the screen.

'What?'

'Mohun?' Sharon's voice was loud and sharp. 'Thomas is not in the sickbay.'

'The shuttle! It's gone!'

'Sharon?' Mohun repeated her name when she did not reply immediately.

'Where the hell is Sharon?' John turned around, his face angry.

'She went to check on Thomas. She says that the sick bay is empty.' Mohun called her name into his watcher again and then started towards the hatch.

'Sima! Have you located Radon?' As John turned back to the console Sharon pulled herself back into the control area. She was holding a data module under one arm and her face was pale and set.

'It's silent.' Sima was hunched over the screen. 'Either Radon's comms are out of action or someone has turned them off.'

'Beep. Check air pressure in main airlock. Beep. Auto open disabled.' The computer beeped several times and then continued in the same droning voice, 'Unauthorized access to main computer. Main airlock compromised ...'

'Turn that damn thing off!' shouted John. 'Find out when all this happened.'

Sima silenced the computer audio and John shouted again, this time into his watcher, 'Sharon! Where the hell are you?'

'Here.' Sharon spoke quietly and they all turned to look at her. She had flipped up the module's screen. 'He's deleted everything,' she continued. She touched the screen. The message was written large enough for them all to read. 'SORRY. ALL MY FAULT.'

No one spoke until Sima said, 'According to the computer, someone disengaged Radon at 1.45 am. The computer was accessed using a code I've never seen before.'

'Let me see that!' John pushed Sima aside and ran his fingers over the console. A series of numbers flashed onto the screen and John swore. He touched the screen and it went blank.

'What the hell?' Sima reached forwards but John pushed his hand away.

'What are you doing?' Sima's voice was angry. 'Are you deleting the code?'

John ignored him and continued to key commands into the console. Sima pushed himself around to face the others. 'Sharon? What's going on?'

John's voice was unemotional again. 'Sharon. Detain Sima and take him to the brig.'

Vicki gasped. 'You're mad!'

Sharon had pulled out her sidearm. It was aimed directly at Sima's chest. Her face was pale and her mouth was pressed into a thin hard line.

'Sharon!' Mohun's voice shook. 'Think what you're doing!'

'I know what I'm doing. Get up Sima!'

Sima released his harness and pushed himself up out of the chair. He nodded briefly at Mohun and Vicki, his face grim as he pushed away from the flight area. Sharon followed him and they disappeared through the hatch.

'I'll explain in a minute. You two stay where you are. Do you understand?' John turned back to the instrument panel. A heavy silence followed until Sharon reappeared.

'I've checked all three satellites. There is no data on Radon's flight path.'

Mohun opened his mouth to speak but Sharon put up her hand in a gesture of warning. She strapped herself into the other seat and for a few minutes she and John carried out a series of checks. Mohun looked at Vicki. Her face was pale with shock.

John leaned over and whispered something to Sharon. She nodded and they both turned their seats around to face the other two.

'Let me explain something.' John's voice was as calm as usual. 'Every day, the command crew – the three of us – change our emergency codes in a very complicated way. It's done as a security precaution, for obvious reasons. The latest code is held by one officer on duty and one officer off duty. Sharon and I were the only ones who should have known the emergency code last night.'

'So why arrest Sima? Why not Sharon?' Vicki turned to Sharon. 'Or why not John?'

'The code was used by an unauthorized person. If John or I had been the one to help Thomas to get out of sick bay, to access the shuttle, it would not have shown up as an unauthorized use.'

Vicki shook her head in confusion.

Mohun interrupted. 'But if the code is secure, how could Sima have got it?'

'There is an emergency override. But Thomas couldn't have got it without Sima's help. As you know, Sima, Sharon and I have access to each other's watchers and to yours as well. But none of the rest of you can access ours.'

Mohun knew that, but he was distracted by a sudden memory of the watchers being given out in Geneva. He remembered the others groaning as they tried to figure out all the new features on the upgraded watchers and data pads. The scene was clear in his mind and he put his hand over his eyes as he saw Sally waving her data pad around and laughing.

'When the emergency override is activated, the computer initiates a warning – you just heard it. For some reason, none of us were woken by it. We have to reconstruct exactly the events of last night.' Sharon's voice was gentle. 'As soon as we know for sure, we'll decide what to do.'

'What happened to you and Sima last night?' Mohun asked John. 'Do you remember anything?'

'I'm not sure. I seem to remember seeing Sima trying to get up from his seat and then I felt real strange. I called you, Sharon. When you didn't answer I tried to sound the general alarm. After that, nothing.' He looked inquiringly at Sharon.

'I don't even remember falling asleep. I was lying in my bunk reading. That's all I remember. My light was still on when I woke up.'

'Same for me,' said Mohun quietly and Vicki nodded.

'Right. It's pretty certain we've been drugged. Vicki! I want you to take blood tests from everyone and find out what knocked us out. Sharon's going to extract data from the watchers and data pads to find out where everybody was and when. Mohun, you help her and also record anything else that anybody thinks is helpful. When you've finished, Sharon and I will interrogate Sima. In the meantime, I'll try to locate Radon. Until then, we're marooned up here.'

He paused. 'Any questions?' He looked at Vicki. 'Are you all right? Ok then. Sharon, take Vicki down to Sima first.'

When Vicki looked back on the following two hours, it felt like an out of body experience. She could see herself clearly, extracting the blood samples and putting them into the centrifuge, but the actions seemed to belong to another person. She had never felt so lonely in her life.

Sima had smiled reassuringly at her as she swabbed his arm. 'Don't worry. John will sort it out. He's not stupid.'

She had tried to smile back but her eyes had filled with tears and she had difficulty pressing the automatic syringe to the right place. When she fumbled, Sima took it off her and did it himself.

As she waited for the results, she tried to remember everything that had happened the previous evening. At dinnertime, Thomas had started on about the hallucinations again and John had told Sima to take Thomas back to the sick bay area. She was certain that Sima had returned immediately to the flight control area, because she had remained there, listening to the dispute between John and Mohun. They had spent two days scanning for Xenon without success. Mohun argued that it was too risky to take the remaining shuttle planet side until they had worked out what was going on. John disagreed. He was determined to get evidence of the conspiracy.

Sima had pulled her aside to kiss her goodnight. When she had reached her bunk Sharon had been reading. She tried to recall how she had felt before she fell asleep but she couldn't even remember getting into her bunk. Where had Mohun been? He had followed her but she had no memory of him entering the sleeping quarters.

The centrifuge beeped and she looked at the readings. She recognized the description and accessed the inventory. There was no record of anyone using the medication since take off. She pulled herself up and across to the medical cabinet. Nearly all the sleeping tablets were gone. She checked the computer again and then watchered Sharon.

'We were all given strong doses of a sleeping tablet, around eight pm last night. Thomas must have introduced it into the evening meal. He's taken most of our supply, which means he could do himself serious harm, if wanted to.'

She heard Sharon speak to John. There was a short silence. 'Ok. As soon as you're done, get back here. We need to discuss this.'

30

'No need to apologize.' Sima stretched out his legs. 'I would have done the same.'

They sat in a gloomy circle in the command module. Vicki had felt weak with relief that Sima was cleared of all suspicion. All data sources indicated that he had spent the night in the control area, in much the same position they had found him in. Sharon had been able to track everyone's movements and no one had spent any time alone with Thomas.

Now Vicki's joy had evaporated. They could not locate Radon and were stranded on the Millennium. The small Emergency Crew Rescue Vehicle was limited to one-way trips. If Thomas truly was involved in a conspiracy, Sally and Alistair might still be alive, but they had no way of finding them.

Sima believed that Thomas was completely paranoid and had taken the shuttle to prevent the crew from returning to the planet's surface and endangering themselves. John refused to consider the idea; Thomas was involved in the conspiracy to keep them off the planet. 'He probably has expertise in a whole range of areas that we don't know about. One thing's for certain, the guy's an expert in subterfuge.'

'I still don't understand how Thomas got access to the code. I tried a deep recovery on his data module but it didn't bring anything up.' Sharon shook her head in frustration. 'I've never seen anything like it.'

'Definite proof of sabotage,' John replied curtly. 'Someone must have enabled his equipment to access the command watchers; probably before he left Earth.'

'Perhaps he's landed safely and will contact us.' Vicki felt as she spoke that it was a silly suggestion.

But John nodded. 'If I'm right about him, he's had flight training too. But my guess is we're not going to hear from him. He's probably reporting to his superiors right now that his mission has been successful.'

'So what's next?' Mohun couldn't stand this endless discussion.

'I propose that we spend the next few days extracting as much information as we can from the satellite data.' He looked around but no one spoke. 'We have to set up the early warning system too. Also we should take a closer look at the moons, even though we can't get down to them. Then, when we're satisfied we have all possible intelligence, we launch the comm capsule and wait for Rick.'

'How long?' asked Mohun. 'What if someone's got to him too?'

John looked around the circle of downcast faces. 'We left Earth without incident. There's no reason why he … If he's coming we should hear something within the next three weeks. If not …' he shrugged. 'But I'd bet heaven and earth he'll be here.' He gave a grim smile. 'And if so, I'll be staying on. Sharon will command the mission home.'

'What do you mean?' asked Mohun. He glanced at Sharon but she showed no surprise.

'I'm not leaving till I find out what's being going on here. As far as I'm concerned this is clear proof of sabotage.'

Mohun felt a sudden anger. 'Was it always your intention to wait for Rick, to stay on here with him?'

John did not reply.

'What about us? Shouldn't we have been told?' Mohun turned to Sharon. 'Not that I don't have every confidence in you and Sima, but still …'

'My plans were always flexible,' John said coolly. 'But it makes no difference now. Someone has as good as declared war on us. Whoever these people are, whatever their motives, we can't let them take control of this planet.'

'I agree with John. We have to stick together on this.' Sima looked at Vicki. She was running her hands through her hair; her face was frantic. 'What is it?'

'I don't know. Sometimes I think you must be right and then I think Thomas is. Nothing seems real. I feel as though I've been in a dream; as though I never went down to the planet at all. And some of the things Thomas said seem to make sense now. I mean, how could they have set the planet up to look so much like earth – the people, the plants, everything? And why would they do that? I feel as though things might have happened that I can't remember. Was anything we did, normal?'

'What exactly are you saying?' John's voice was harsh.

'I don't know. I can't work it out.' Vicki rubbed her forehead. 'I feel as though something else is going on here.' She blinked as tears sprang into her eyes. 'What if Sally and Alistair are still down there somewhere?'

There was a long silence and Sharon said quietly, 'John and I have discussed the idea of using the ECRV; if we locate one of the shuttles. I would volunteer to go down.'

Mohun made a loud exclamation. 'It's too risky. If something went wrong you'd be stranded down there with no way of getting back.' He knew he was stating the obvious but he couldn't believe what he was hearing.

'I agree!' Sima looked alarmed.

'We'd only do it if we were certain that the shuttle could be brought back up. We haven't located either of them yet, so this is just hypothetical.' John looked at their shocked faces.

Sharon wished she had not raised the subject. 'Let's wait and see.'

31

Mohun pulled himself through to the bridge and handed Sharon the coffee mug. 'Are you sure you want this? You really should get some rest.'

Sharon took the mug. 'I'd rather keep working. I find it hard to sleep.'

As Mohun pushed back from the seat Sharon said, 'Don't go. Keep me company for a while, if there's nothing else you have to do.'

Mohun smiled warmly at her and maneuvered himself into the other seat. He could see the northern continent of the planet clearly from this position, and on the port side Artemis was rising. He wished that he could feel the same thrill that he had experienced when he first glimpsed the planet. Now he just wanted to leave. He remembered the days on the space station when they had spent all their spare time staring down at Earth. A wave of homesickness gripped him. Time passed slowly; the astronauts had plenty to keep them busy there was very little for him or Vicki to do. They were living in limbo, waiting for Rick's message.

'Can I help you?'

Sharon handed Mohun her data pad. 'You could read the figures out. It'd be quicker that way.' She had no real reason to want to speed up the work. The software for the asteroid early warning systems had been bedded down on the three satellites and when her current project was finished she would have to find something else to occupy her. But she always found comfort in the sound of Mohun's warm voice.

She sighed. They had not located either of the shuttles. Sharon thought it was a vain hope. Xenon was probably damaged beyond repair, at the bottom of the ocean, while no one had the slightest clue what had happened to Thomas and Radon. There had been no message from him, and the comms on both shuttles remained dead. Still, John continued to scan the planet in ever increasing detail for some sign of them. In the last two days he had hardly spoken, except to issue instructions. In his summary of events for the capsule which would relay their news to back to Earth he had focused on Thomas's sabotage and had downplayed the idea of hallucinations.

'Are you all right?' Mohun leaned forward and then exclaimed 'Look at that!'

Sharon could see clearly what Mohun was referring to. An immensely long line of white cloud was moving across the northern continent. As they watched, it spread quickly and within a few moments most of the northern hemisphere was blanketed in the same thick cloud that the planet had displayed when they first arrived.

'My god! That was fast! Call the others!'

Mohun raised his watcher, his eyes fixed on the cloud. Sharon was checking the instrument panel. She touched a number of icons and rows of figures appeared. Mohun leaned forward to look at them as John came through the hatch.

'What's up?'

'The cloud cover is back. I didn't see where it came from but it moved at an unbelievable speed.'

Vicki and Sima had joined them and were peering through the viewports. But now there was nothing to see. The edge of the cloud remained steady with no further movement.

'Do you mind if I check something?' Mohun turned to Sharon. When she nodded, he touched the screen and rows of figures scrolled rapidly down. A few seconds later he paused the display. 'I thought that was odd. Look John, here are the figures from when we first arrived. See – they're typical of altostratus. There are these wave type formations in the layers of cloud here. Just as you said - typical of high turbulence and cold fronts moving through.'

'And so?' John sounded impatient.

'Well, now look at the current readings. The temperature at ground level is only a couple of degrees lower than when we were down there, and there's no sign of turbulence. But it must be altostratus. It looks exactly the same from up here – same altitude range, everything.'

'Let me see that.' John leaned forward and peered at the screen. He frowned. 'That's really odd. Nothing's changed in the Southern hemisphere; keep an eye on it would you?'

John pushed off, back in the direction of the hatch but Sima caught hold of the harness on one of the couches and secured it. 'Vicki and I have finished for the moment. Why don't we take a break?'

Vicki smiled and pulled herself down to sit close to him. They had not resolved their disagreement about what had happened on Earth 2 but it made no difference to their feelings.

Sharon did not reply. She was staring out the main viewport, her face tense.

As John entered the hatch Mohun called out. 'Good heavens! Look!'

The thick blanket was shifting. Great wedges of cloud lifted up at enormous speed, slid back down and rose again. It was like watching the violent break up of ice in a river during a spring thaw. As the sections of white cloud moved they could see long pale ribbons which seemed to flash at regular intervals. Streams of blue and yellow, then violet, pink and green flowed along the top of the cloud, disappeared, only to be replaced by new streams of different colors.

John pushed back from the hatch. 'Turn everything on,' he shouted. 'We've got to get all of this.'

Sharon leaned forward and pressed the panels on the console, hardly able to take her eyes off the scene below her.

Vicki clutched Sima's arm and they watched transfixed as the streams of lights moved even more rapidly across the clouds.

'What the hell is doing that?' John prodded Mohun to move aside and he took his seat. He checked the screen and shook his head in frustration.

'Sharon! Play back some of the data. We need to know what we are seeing.'

Sharon complied. 'There's nothing there. There's nothing to show anything's happening down there.'

John swore. He poked his screen savagely and when he saw the display he swore again.

'Ai, yai!' Sima let out a yell followed swiftly by exclamations from Mohun and Vicki.

A black cloud had appeared on the edge of the white blanket. A red tongue snaked out from it and parted the nearest section of white cloud, like a knife cutting through a sponge cake. The white cloud split so cleanly that they could see the outline of the land below. Then within seconds the cloud closed up, surrounding the smaller black cloud. Streaks of fire continued to shoot out of the black cloud and the white mist fell back and advanced as if in response.

'John!' When John didn't reply, Mohun grasped his shoulder. 'John! It's just like the cloud we saw. Look at the flames. But it's much larger. It's enormous.'

John remained silent. He was alternately staring out the viewport and gazing desperately at the console as if one of the screens would reveal what was happening.

The activity below became even more violent. The dark cloud increased in size and raced away from the white cloud. A thin spearhead branched out from the white cloud and followed as though pursuing the darker form.

'What is it? What is it?' Vicki was yelling.

'We should break orbit.' Sima said sharply and released his harness.

'I agree. John?' Sharon's voice rose rapidly as John did not reply. 'We should leave. We don't know what it is, what it might do.'

'We can't leave now. This is amazing. We have to see what happens.'

'But nothing's showing on the screen. Look!' Sharon pulled at John's arm. When he shrugged her off she looked urgently at Sima.

'John! Listen! We have to leave. Sharon, prepare to break orbit.'

Sharon leaned forward but John shouldered her aside. 'We can't leave. This might be our only chance to find out what's really going on.'

Vicki was still clutching Sima's arm, but he pushed away from her and grabbed the back of John's seat.

Sharon had pushed past John and was punching the controls. As John grabbed at her again Sima seized his arm.

John looked around, his face furious. 'Get to your stations; harnesses on, now!'

Sima hesitated and then as the AGD turbos revved up, he moved back to the couch and refastened his harness.

The view of the planet shifted slightly as the Millennium started to turn. The black cloud had disappeared over the North Pole and the large blanket of white was receding towards the equator. As it moved it seemed to separate into long streamers, striped with pale bands of light. Vicki couldn't believe what she was seeing. As the streamers diverged and moved south each was illuminated by a single color; green, blue, violet and pink. When they reached the thick belt of ice, they thinned out and disappeared.

'Did you see that? Vicki touched Sima's arm but he didn't answer. He stared through the starboard viewport.

The black cloud had reappeared, much larger now, and it sped south. Behind it streams of white cloud emerged over the rim of the planet and raced after it. As they converged around it great flashes of flame shot out, answered by pulsing lights in every color of the rainbow. Vicki realized that the ship had slowed in its movement away from the planet. Sharon sat like stone, her hand on the joystick. Vicki wanted to tell her to move. She felt a terrible premonition of danger, but she couldn't speak.

As she watched, the dark cloud intensified in color and red lights flashed over its surface. With horrid fascination she saw that it was changing shape, rising above the white layer which surrounded it. For a moment she did not understand what she was seeing; then she shrieked in terror. The cockpit was full of shouting voices and finally Sharon moved as though released from a spell. She pushed the joystick hard forward and the ship lurched. There was a terrible grinding noise and the image of the planet disappeared.

'Incoming missile! Brace for impact,' yelled John. He grabbed Sharon's hand and they both pulled back on the joystick. The ship lurched again and a huge dark shape shot past the viewport.

There was a moment's silence, then several horrible thudding noises. The Millennium rocked violently, started to roll and the planet slid past the viewport again and disappeared. A loud wailing noise rapidly increased in volume.

As John leaned forward to switch off the alarm, several objects zoomed past the port followed by what looked like a pale mist.

'The hull is breached!' Sima shouted. 'We're venting oxygen!' He unfastened his harness and pushed towards the hatch.

'Everyone listen. Suit up now! We've been hit.' John's mouth moved as though in slow motion and Vicki felt Mohun pulling her away from the console.

Part Two

Pandora's Box

PROLOGUE
373 BCE

The final stage of the journey from the academy at Corinth had been tiring. The landslides had damaged long stretches of the coastal roads, and they were now crowded with angry travelers. For Althamas, impatient to be home, the delays were intolerable, and the sight of Spartan warships patrolling the coast made him nervous.

He had finally decided to take the longer route across the hills, clambering for hours over piles of rocks until at last he reached the older but still intact hilltop road. When he realized where he was he smiled wryly. Perhaps fate had brought him here, but he was glad of any excuse to take a rest. He hesitated for a few moments, but heard only the sound of the light breeze stirring the trees and the faint calls of the sea birds; so he turned off the road and took the few steps down the well-worn path toward the huge triangular rock. The glade in front of the shrine was empty. He hitched up his chiton, knelt down at the mouth of the small cave and made a sign of respect. A few votive tablets were scattered across the sandy soil but there were no other signs of any recent visitors to the shrine. Althamas was not surprised. Although this site was popular with Hercules' devotees in Bura, the constant tremors would make people wary of the climb. And according to rumor, the great statue of Hercules in Bura had just been refurbished. Althamas yearned to see it but he did not dare enter that city.

The dark entrance to the cave was quiet. He wondered if he had time to cast his dice. He longed for a sign but if the omens were not clear it would take too long, and he would not reach Helike before night fell. He looked up at the great rock looming above him and muttered a prayer but Hercules did not reveal himself.

His heart sank and he felt a sudden chill. He rose to his feet and gazed out across the valley. The blessed river Serinis glinted in the distance, capturing the sunbeams, as it made its way east to the sea. To the south of the river the shining city of Helike spread out in all its splendor, evidence of the grace and favor of the great Poseidon. The temple to the god of the sea dominated the city. Set on a small rise, the enormous statue of Poseidon could look over the city and across the gulf, all the way to the fabled oracle at Delphi. Althamas shivered. Even though the huge figure's eyes were fixed to the north, many believed that when Poseidon inhabited the statue, it became all seeing. Perhaps even now its gaze might fall on Althamas and discover his heresy.

The air was still and he could see small plumes of smoke rising skyward as hundreds of families made preparations for the evening meal. The sight calmed Althamas and he smiled at the prospect of the celebration dinner. He had not seen his home for several months and his mother and sisters would have spent the day preparing for his return. Then he thought of his father and his face fell. His father must not find out that Althamas had visited Hercules' shrine. Admiration for Hercules was tolerated in children but it was unwise for any citizen of Helike to express devotion to the hero in the current political climate. It signified at the very least sympathy with the fanatics in Bura, who claimed Hercules as their own; or worse, it might be taken as evidence of treason against Poseidon and Helike.

Now the earth was stirring again for the first time in living memory. His father and other orators at the agora blamed the people of Bura and the other gulf cities who had abandoned Poseidon, to worship Hercules or Athena. They spoke of Poseidon's generosity, the gifts of the sea which sustained them all, and warned of the god's vengeful rage against those who failed to demonstrate their continuing faith and devotion.

Althamas gazed up at the rock above the cave, willing Hercules to appear, as he had done so often, but there was no change. He stood for a few moments downcast and pondered again what he had learned in Corinth. He wondered how he would break the news to his father. As if to reflect his mood, the sky suddenly darkened; storm clouds were gathering across the gulf. He shook his head abruptly and turned back to the shrine. It was getting late. He must decide what to do. He must consult the oracle. He broke a small branch off a nearby bush and swept the area in front of the cave opening, clearing it of debris. He smoothed the sandy soil with his hands. A small jar of honey and a flask of wine were all that remained of his provisions and he placed them carefully at the mouth of the cave.

He felt inside his bag for the four wooden dice and held them tightly in his hand. Glancing up, he saw with relief that Hercules stood astride the summit of the rock. But the hero's expression was enigmatic. Althamas closed his eyes and muttered the familiar words. As he straightened his arm to cast the dice, the earth trembled and the small pieces of wood shot out of his hand. He groaned in dismay, scrambled forward and searched through the small bushes that framed the cave opening. He finally spied one of the bright tokens, but as he reached for it the earth shifted again and he fell backwards. A loud cracking noise issued from the cave and then a voice like roaring water called out, 'Remember Ulysses.'

Althamas looked up but Hercules had withdrawn. Behind the sharp crest of the rock the trees were trembling and as Althamas stared in amazement they started to wave violently. A sinister rumbling noise grew into a thunderous roar. He backed away, broke into a run as large boulders slid down the hillside towards him. The rocks smashed into the crest of Hercules' shrine and lethal shards shot across the glade. The earth was shaking violently now and Althamas stumbled down the steep slope, slipping from tree to tree to break his descent. He glimpsed one of the paths down to the valley and thrust through the dense foliage to reach it.

For long minutes he raced down the path dodging between the shaking trees, ignoring the branches that tore at his shoulders and arms, and the rain of earth and small stones stinging his face. His heart lifted as he glimpsed the southern walls of Helike below him and then a violent tremor made him stumble. His left leg was jarred painfully and he felt the ground fall away beneath his feet. A river of trees and earth plummeted down the hillside carrying him with it. He slid downwards for a few terrible moments grabbing frantically for something to break his fall until he landed with a painful thud on a rocky outcrop. He pressed against the rock as a torrent of debris poured overhead.

When he had the courage to uncover his eyes he saw that the hillside around him was now almost bare of vegetation. The rocky ledge on which he stood was the only stationary object in a massive landslide. On both sides the earth raced down like a dark waterfall. He turned to face the valley and stared aghast, unable to understand what he was seeing. The whole of Helike was moving, first gently as though shaken by a small child and then so violently that buildings slid sideways and collapsed. Althamas could hear a high-pitched whining noise, which he suddenly recognized as the sound of several thousand people screaming, as they fled through the streets, trying to find a way out of the city. But some dire curse had been laid upon the land. The ground shimmered like water and the people slipped and fell into the mire. The paved square fronting Poseidon's temple split in two and the halves tipped sideways and were upended as they sank into the mud. The surrounding columns toppled like a child's blocks until only the massive statue remained upright.

The rock beneath Althamas suddenly heaved and slanted. It seemed as though the slab was being thrust up but he realized that the valley was sinking. Heart thumping, he tried to catch sight of his parents' house but several fires had broken out and the city was now blurred by smoke. A stream of people rushed through the southern gates heading for the coast, but suddenly the crowd halted.

Althamas clambered to his feet to get a better view and fell back against the rock in terror. What he had thought were storm clouds was a huge wall of water, racing across the gulf towards Helike. The coastline was exposed, the warships and fishing boats stranded on the dry seabed as the water was sucked out towards the enormous wave. The crowd remained motionless. There was no escape. Althamas watched in horrid fascination as the wave swept in, closer and closer to the helpless city. Poseidon finally revealed himself as the water crashed onto the shore. He rode the wall of foam, his trident held high in his right hand, the burnished tines glinting in the light of the setting sun. With his left hand he flung out his net over the crowd and dragged them behind him as the wave carried him over the city. Althamas shrank back against the rock to avoid the god's angry gaze. The huge green eyes swept past him as Poseidon sped towards the hills. Althamas gagged as he saw the struggling figures crushed within the net and then the water surged over the rock and took him.

For an endless time he was swept along, bodies and furniture, objects familiar and strange surging around him. A young woman stared desperately at him. A pale green fish woman had wound the girl's long hair in her fist but when she saw Althamas she released the girl and undulated towards him. Althamas turned his head away, terrified of meeting the Nereid's fascinating gaze. Something hard struck his neck and water filled his mouth. He clutched the branch and dragged himself up it, until he saw the darkening sky above him. He lay across the tree trunk, gasping for air and vomited a stream of water into the pungent leaves. A hand grasped his foot but he kicked it away and clutched the fallen tree. For several moments he lay unable to move. Then he pulled himself further up the tree until he reached its exposed roots and the dark earth of the bare hillside.

He lifted his head and forced himself to look around. The wave was nearing the steep slopes of the western end of the valley. Green fountains soared into the air and collapsed into mountains of froth where the water sought an outlet. Then the sea poured back and Althamas frantically scrambled up the steep slope. The sun had fled but the full moon had risen and the great white goddess stared down at the scene. In her silver light Althamas could see Poseidon clearly. The angry god stood further up the range surveying the wreckage of the city. The giant net writhed as the people struggled to free themselves. Dozens of other still figures lay nearby. The god slowly looked from side to side and Althamas pressed himself against the earth, fearing he would be seen.

Poseidon raised his trident, silver now in the bright moonlight. The sky was clear and Althamas saw that the gods of the night had appeared. Poseidon gesticulated angrily with the trident and suddenly the world turned dark. Althamas looked desperately for the moon but she had covered her face. The distant homes of the gods shone more brilliantly in the darkened sky, and as Althamas watched, one of the bright points of light, the red star, grew larger. It was as he had been warned in Corinth. The war god was approaching. He felt a fatalistic calm overcome him. There was nothing he could do.

The dreadful red world approached, until it was as big as the moon. Blinding lights suddenly streaked from its surface, raced across the sky and stuck the prongs of Poseidon's trident. The lights flashed around the trident, expanding outwards into a giant circle, illuminating the surrounding hills in a ghastly red light. Poseidon gestured again with the trident, the lights stilled, shimmered for a moment, and then the god and his victims vanished.

The moon uncovered her face and Althamas watched numbly as the water subsided. But the land had sunk so deep that not all the water could escape. Finally the ocean became still, and Helike was lost beneath a shining lagoon.

1
More than 2000 years later

'I need to talk to you. Meet me on the roof in ten minutes.' Rick Jones' slanting smile flashed for a second on the screen of Loren's watcher.

Loren Wellington sighed. She was in the middle of a long and tricky software test, which she really shouldn't interrupt, but she longed to see Rick again. She tapped a key to rerun the program and the screen filled with figures again, scrolling rapidly downwards.

'Hey Jenny! The chief is back. Keep an eye on that would you?' She smiled at the young woman seated opposite. 'Shut it down if there are any problems and send me the logs.' She picked up two small black boxes. 'I'll take these with me.'

Several faces looked up inquiringly as Loren made her way through the maze of desks. She still found it hard to believe that she had more than twenty top rate people at her command. Funding for her kind of research had evaporated in most countries and many of her former colleagues were now working as glorified programmers, trying to fix the American telecommunications grid.

She had made a flying trip home to Australia for her mother's birthday and her parents had begged her not to return to Nevada. She was sorry that they worried about her, but there was no way she was giving up this job.

'It's the chance of a lifetime. Anyway, I'm probably in the safest place in the world,' she had tried to explain during one of their frequent arguments. Two of her brothers who had been working in the US had returned home after the high tech bombings, and her parents had expected her to follow. The Liberty movement had not spread to any other country but sabotage of government buildings and telecommunications and IT companies continued in mainland USA. Transport, power grids and water supply were now chaotic in most of the larger cities. The wealthy had barricaded themselves into their high-rise buildings or gated villages and hired guards to protect them. The ordinary people were still pouring out of the cities, away from the looting and violence.

'How can you say that?' Her father sounded infuriated. Before she could reply, her father had continued. 'You're virtually a prisoner! When did you last walk on grass, or swim in real water?'

'I can leave any time I like! Anywhere we want to go, we go. But I'm in the middle of this really exciting project. I'll come home for another visit when it's finished. You have to believe me. I'm not in any danger.' When she thought of her real reason for staying, Loren suffered twinges of guilt. But her feelings were too strong. The arguments of her parents and five older siblings could have no effect.

Loren made a mental note to call her family again as she waved her key card at the elevator door. It slid open immediately. When she first started work at Rick's headquarters, the AGD elevator had made her nauseous. Now, some four months later, she stepped out onto one of the floating platforms without giving it a thought. A few meters to her right she saw the short stout figure of Jason Blackburn, Rick's chief of staff. He raised his eyebrows at her. 'Any idea what this is about?' he called out.

Loren shook her head. 'Not a clue. Perhaps he wants to talk about the latest message from the Millennium. I heard that it came through a couple of days ago. But they seem to be keeping it under wraps.'

Jason shook his head. 'The whole scheme is mad.'

Loren smiled slightly. The contrast between the ever optimistic Rick and his cautious chief of staff always amused her. She reached for the rail as the door slid open, and stepped onto the artificial lawn. Most of the rooftop was taken up with a large exercise circuit which circled the landing pad. At the eastern end, a pavilion, swimming pool and barbeque had been built for staff gatherings. Nearby a square structure housed communication and meeting rooms. Loren looked around. Some fifty meters away two figures were jogging slowly towards them but there was no sign of Rick.

She strolled over to the railing and looked out over the desert. Jason stood silently beside her for a moment and then said 'Unbelievable, isn't it?'

To the northeast Loren could glimpse the shining surface of Lake Groom. The long runways stretched south and east and beyond them huge tents and rectangular demountables spread out across the barren land. The silvery security fences twinkled in the cool sunlight. They crisscrossed the landscape like discarded tinsel, circling the glass tower which Rick had built to house more than two thousand personnel, and fencing off the old buildings of the Area 51 site.

Loren peered downwards. Thirty stories below several trucks were waiting to enter the safety zone which surrounded the tower. Beyond the zone small figures like colored ants milled around or formed into long lines, waiting in the endless queues for accommodation, food vouchers or medical attention. In the distance, she knew that an even larger number of people were camped outside the perimeter fences, hoping to be allowed in to the relative comfort of the refugee city. Loren turned away from the depressing view.

As if he read her thoughts, Jason said, 'There's no way we can take any more people. And I guess we won't have to for a while at least. I've just heard that the ET is blocked all the way to Alamo. Someone bombed a truck and the road is cut. God knows what those poor bastards are going through.' He pointed up to where a convoy of helicopters headed north.

'Gone to drop supplies, I guess; a drop in the fucking ocean.' His watcher beeped and he bent his head to take the call.

Long-range scanners were installed every few meters around the roof garden. Loren adjusted one to her height and zoomed in on the area west of Lake Groom. A large area was littered with buildings and oddly shaped installations. Her heart beat faster as a shuttle emerged from one of the hangars and moved towards the launch pad. She watched in fascination as it ascended slowly into the sky. She knew that the containers strung out behind it carried the final components of the Phoenix. Somewhere up there, nestled against the space station, the Phoenix was ablaze with lights as the technicians raced to finish their work. Another week of testing and the spacecraft would be ready.

'Better you than me.'

Loren stepped back and Jason took her place at the scanner. He moved it to focus on the northwest entrance. He frowned. 'The road's blocked. Nothing's moving. We'll have to fly everything in now. I just hope Rick knows what he's doing. If this lot get violent we'll be in deep shit.'

Loren shivered and wished she had brought a jacket. 'They should be grateful.'

'People are rarely grateful.' Jason sighed loudly. 'This place was such a bargain. The government was happy to get rid of it. Now half the nutcases in America are probably camped on our doorstep.'

'You must have known that would always be a problem. Didn't you have any trouble when you moved here? What about tourists?' Loren didn't like to admit that she had always been fascinated by the stories about Area 51. So far the reality had been much less interesting. All of the old buildings were now in use as warehouses or research labs, connected to the glass tower by underground passages. But she often wondered if Rick had been completely honest about what he had found when he moved in. Or whether there were areas which remained hidden.

Jason gave a short laugh. 'Would you believe it? We actually ran guided tours. Just to let people know nothing spooky was going on. Not that everyone was convinced. People still believe we have aliens in the basement.' He paused. 'I just worry sometimes about how many of those people down there are genuine refugees and how many of them are conspiracy freaks.'

'Well, there's no way they can get past the fences, even if they wanted to.'

'I guess you have greater faith in technology than I do.'

As Loren started to explain the building's security system, Jason raised his hand. 'I've heard it all before. I just don't quite believe it. Anyway, here comes the man.' He pointed to a silvery flash hovering over Lake Groom.

Loren couldn't help laughing. Rick was approaching in one of his new flyers. As he descended towards the rooftop he performed a steep loop, clutching at the flyer's safety rail.

Jason gasped and swore but Loren laughed again. 'He's such a boy!'

'He thinks he's Flash Gordon,' Jason muttered. 'One day he'll go too far.'

Loren ran towards the landing pad as Rick stripped off his silver flying suit and helmet. He checked the controls and then greeted Loren warmly. 'Hi cutie! How's things?'

Loren tried to look serious. 'You big oaf; you might have hurt Rex.'

'Nice to know you care.' Rick patted the flyer's control panel. 'Rex is just fine, aren't you boy?'

As the flyer responded in a voice uncannily like its inventor, Jason gave an exasperated sigh. 'You didn't fly all the way on that thing did you?'

'Yup!' Rick grinned and ruffled his bright hair. Just as quickly his expression changed. 'There's a lot to discuss,' he said in a serious voice. 'But let's hear your news first. How's our project going?'

'Great! I think we've solved the power problem. I can give you a small demo right now if you like.' Loren had been expecting this and looked forward to seeing Rick's reaction. She glanced around. The joggers had left the roof. She handed one of the small black boxes to Jason. 'Would you mind standing over there? Just a few feet away.'

Jason moved away. 'What now?'

'Hold the box around waist level and point the red side towards the wall.' Loren imitated Jason's position. 'Look Rick – over there.'

The pale blue wall of the elevator shaft shimmered for an instant, disappeared in a burst of flame. Loren heard Jason gasp. The image persisted for a few seconds before the blue wall reappeared.

'Cool!' Rick looked at her admiringly. 'What's the scope and range?'

'It's stable for around 50 meters, up to 5k. And the control pads only need to be a few feet apart. Pretty soon we should have that fixed; it's not really a problem.'

'Impressive.'

'There's something else I've been working on. Watch this.'

Rick put his arm around her waist but she wriggled away. 'Don't distract me. Jason! Could you take the box over to the wall?'

'Is this ok?' Jason stood awkwardly as though wondering what might happen.

'Closer to the wall and just a bit to the right. Then, if you could not move too much for a couple of minutes. Thanks.' Loren waited until Jason was in position and then pointed the small black control box at him. She was gratified to hear Rick exclaim as Jason disappeared. A few seconds later the wall seemed to shimmer and Jason gradually reappeared.

'Hot damn it, woman. You're amazing. I didn't realize you'd got so far.'

Loren shook her head. 'It needs a bit more work. The subject needs to be pretty close to the background, and not moving. It's not so convincing in open spaces. But we think we have the solution to that.'

Rick squeezed her hand. 'What would I do without you?' He smiled lovingly at her and then his face fell.

'What's the matter?'

'Bad news!'

Loren's heart froze and she couldn't speak.

Rick shook his head. 'No, not your family. It's the Millennium. Come on, let's go inside.' He called out to Jason and they entered the communications block. A young man greeted them enthusiastically and ushered them into a large room. Three of the walls were bare. The fourth was lined with small couches and comfortable armchairs.

Jason sank down onto one of the couches. He waited until the young man was out of earshot. 'So you're sticking to the date?'

Rick perched on the arm of the couch. 'Why, what's the problem?'

Jason frowned. 'When word gets out about where you're going and how much this is costing, you'll be very unpopular. Have you thought about moving the shuttle site?'

Rick shrugged, then grinned and slapped the shorter man on the back. 'You worry too much.'

'You pay me to worry. You should have set up a management team months ago. You've been running this place like it's your own private playground. You can't expect people just to take over at a minute's notice.' Jason frowned, scuffing his expensive loafer across the thick carpet. 'And what's the hurry? Wouldn't it be safer to wait till you get more detailed information?'

'As you well know, if we miss this window, the trip will take weeks longer. Anyway, we've just got news from the Millennium and now it's urgent.'

Loren's heart thumped again. 'What is it? Tell us.'

Rick sat down next to Loren. 'In a nutshell. Sabotage! They've lost both shuttles and three of the crew have disappeared. Sounds like the whole thing has been a disaster. John is planning to wait it out until we get there.'

Jason's face was white. 'What! I don't understand.'

Loren had a clear image of the farewell party and Fiona Stuart's strained expression. Her throat felt dry. 'Which crew? Who?'

Rick looked away. 'Thomas, Sally, Alistair.' Loren could see him swallowing hard. When he turned back his face was tight. He put his hand on her head as she covered her eyes.

'I don't understand,' Jason repeated. 'Everything was fine. They landed ok and all. How could anyone do that? Plant something that only takes effect months later?'

'No, it's not like that. John believes that another group got there first. He believes Thomas is their agent.'

'What?' Loren wiped her eyes and looked up. 'That's impossible. No one has that sort of capability, do they?'

'I know it doesn't make sense. Why not sabotage the Millennium before it took off?' Rick paused. 'Some of the crew apparently have different opinions but John didn't say much about those. He doesn't take them seriously.'

'Shit!' Jason stood up. 'Well, you can't go now.' He paced up and down. 'You'll have to get the military involved. What does the ESA say?'

'The usual. They're all running round like chickens with their heads cut off. The UN's the same. But it sure has cut the red tape for me. Not that I was gonna let that stop me.' He looked hard at Loren. 'If I don't go, no one else will. Anyway, we have time to do some refitting. I'll take some firepower with me.'

Jason swore loudly and sat down with a thump. 'What did you say the rest of the crew thought?'

'Hallucinations, aliens. It's hard to get the whole picture. John thinks some of them are cracking up.' Rick squeezed Loren's shoulder. 'You can change your mind. I wouldn't blame you. It's not gonna be the fun trip we imagined.'

'Mr. Jones. We're ready!' The young technician had been working at a podium and now the three bare walls started to brighten.

'Give us a minute, would you?' Rick replied. 'I've arranged a vidcon with Alistair's family,' he explained. 'They've heard the news and want to talk to me. We can talk to your family too if you want.'

'Oh hell! What am I going to tell my parents?' Loren rubbed her eyes.

'Tell them you're coming home.'

'No! If something's going on up there, you'll need all the tech support you can get.' Loren's heart was racing but she tried to speak calmly. 'You can't leave me behind.'

'We'll talk about it later.' Rick nodded to the technician and the walls brightened again.

Loren shook her head but didn't reply. The technician handed each of them a thin silver headpiece and left the room. Loren noticed her hands were shaking as she secured the microphone.

A cheerful comfortable room appeared brightly on the three walls. It was strewn with well worn furniture, and photos and souvenirs of the family and their careers. But the air was tense. The Stuart family gazed back at them silently. Then

Claudia stepped forward and spoke. 'It was good of you to make time to talk to us. Thank you.'

These kind words from Alistair's only sister broke Loren's calm. 'I'm so sorry,' she stuttered and burst into tears. She felt Rick's arm around her shoulders and some paper tissues pushed into her hand. As she wiped her eyes she saw Fiona's face.

Alistair's mother looked drawn and tired but showed no sign of distress. She said firmly, 'There's nothing to be sorry about. If any harm had come to Alistair I would know it.'

Loren looked up at Rick and he shook his head slightly as though warning her to keep quiet.

Claudia had seated herself next to her brother Jeremy. Loren looked briefly at Alistair's brother. He was so stunning that it was difficult to look away from him. Two men stood behind; Loren recognized them as Claudia's husband, Ben Sorensen and his business partner, Victor Steiner. Like the Stuart family, Ben was tall, fair and very handsome. In contrast, Victor was much shorter, with crisp dark hair and bright intelligent eyes. Both men's faces were tense and nervous.

Fiona glanced around at her family and then sat down by her husband. Alistair's father appeared ill and seemed to have shrunk in some indefinable way.

Rick perched on the arm of Loren's chair. 'Let's start by telling you our plans. I know you've been given a full transcript of latest message from the Millennium, so you probably know as much as we do.' He paused and when no one spoke, he continued. 'You may be aware that I had hoped to join the Millennium mission, but there was strong opposition to any commercial interest being involved.' He looked down briefly. 'I had discussed with Major Armstrong, that I would fund the next mission. The UN now considers it urgent to find out what is happening on Earth 2 and to retrieve the crew. They've given us clearance to leave as soon as feasible, which I estimate to be within the next ten days.'

Loren was surprised to see Claudia's face light up with joy. She realized that Claudia, like her mother, was convinced that Alistair was still alive.

Jeremy spoke slowly. 'And there is no opposition from your own government?'

Rick frowned. 'They're not in any position to interfere. I don't know how much news you get over there but the situation here is truly appalling. I've done what I can. I've spent a fortune on getting some of the infrastructure back up. But it's never enough. Of course a lot of people think this trip is a waste of money. We've had some trouble.' He shook his head in disbelief. 'It's hard to understand how the situation could deteriorate so fast. The government has completely lost control.'

There was a moment's silence. Loren looked at Jeremy. The handsome face was downcast and she remembered hearing that he had lost a friend in the San Francisco riots.

'But,' Rick continued slowly, 'this has made me even more determined to get to Earth 2. The situation here could get even worse. We have to find out whether the planet is habitable. And if John Armstrong is right ...' He looked around at each of the Stuarts in turn, his face suddenly grim. 'We can't risk leaving Earth 2 to people who are our enemies.'

'I can't understand what it all means.' Paul's voice quavered and Fiona stroked her husband's hand. 'How could this man, Thomas Beecham or whatever his real name is – how could he have done this? Who is he working for? Why would anyone want to do this?' His voice faded and he turned his head away, his mouth trembling.

Rick spoke slowly. 'There's a lot we don't know. Some of John's message didn't make much sense. I guess because he had to send it in a hurry. But we've started a search into Beecham's background and so far none of the records check out. We can't find his mother and everyone we've talked to finds it hard to remember the guy at all. It's a mystery.' He frowned. 'As you know, the Consortium which sponsored the mission has been disbanded; another mystery.'

Jeremy spoke for the first time. 'Do you think it could be the same group who carried out the US bombings?'

Rick started to reply, but Victor interrupted. 'There's something Ben and I need to tell you.' Ben coughed nervously and his fair skin flushed. Victor seemed to brace himself and then said, 'We've been going through Armstrong's message, trying to figure out what might have happened.' He cleared his throat. 'I'm sure you know the business that Ben and I are in?' He looked at Rick, who nodded. 'About fifteen months before the Millennium took off, we filled an order from WorldSecure for eight watchers. When Alistair came home for Christmas to tell us that he would be on the Millennium, Ben and I recognized his watcher as one of the eight we supplied to WorldSecure.'

Rick cut in impatiently. 'And so? Why is that important?'

Ben started to speak but he could not continue. Claudia turned to him, her face questioning, but he looked away.

Victor cleared his throat. 'Two things; four of the eight watchers were configured for a very high level of security. The other four were for low security – Alistair had one of those. There's nothing strange about that. We've often supplied orders with that sort of configuration. But now...' Victor closed his eyes for a moment. 'When we heard what Thomas Beecham had done – how Armstrong described it - we realized that Beecham must have had one of the four watchers with the top-level security codes. From what Armstrong said, that's the only way he could have wiped the data and accessed the shuttle.'

'What!' Claudia leapt up and her glass crashed to the floor. 'Why didn't you tell us this before?' She stared accusingly at her husband and when he did not reply she pulled on his arm.

'For heaven's sake Claudia, calm down.' Jeremy reached out to her but Claudia pushed him away. 'Answer me, Ben. What's going on?'

'Please Claudia, let me finish.' Victor spoke quietly.

Ben tried to take Claudia's hand but she jerked away. Her face was blazing with anger. 'I remember. One of the last days we were all together. I can't forget anything about that day. You looked at Alistair's watcher and you asked him how many people were going. When he told you, you went pale, you looked sick. You said you weren't well. But you went off and called Victor.' Claudia stared at Victor. 'He did, didn't he? And you came over right away. You knew! You knew something was wrong and you didn't say a thing.'

'What is she talking about?' Fiona looked pleadingly at Ben.

Rick interrupted. 'We need to hear what they have to say.' He looked coldly at Victor. 'This had better be good.'

'I need to explain properly.' Victor rubbed his forehead. 'If we had thought it was important to the mission, we would have said something then. But we had other problems.' He described briefly the events at MWA and concluded; 'so, you see, we thought that we might lose the whole business. What could we do if Mossad or some other group had spies in WorldSecure?'

'Are you saying this is some sort of Jewish conspiracy?' Rick snorted. 'That's impossible. The Jewish state has enough problems without engaging in something like this.'

'I'm not saying that,' Victor replied. 'All I know is that the WorldSecure team were speaking what sounded like Hebrew, down in the clean room. I'm not saying that those guys have any connections with any Jewish organizations. They could work for a company or some other group who have designs on Earth 2. But what we had to face was this. If we had gone to WorldSecure and told them that some of their operatives had broken protocols …' He wiped his hand across his face. 'For certain, one of two things would have happened. MWA would have been shut down for allowing a breach of security. At the very least we would have lost ninety percent of our business. Or worse, WorldSecure is corrupt. And then Ben and I would have just disappeared. And the rest of you could have been in danger.'

'We really did think it through.' Ben's voice was steadier now. 'When Alistair told me there were only three astronauts going, I assumed that one of the scientists had top level security clearance for the fourth watcher.'

'Or you wanted to believe it! All to save your wretched company!' Claudia was pacing up and down, wringing her hands.

There was a long silence. Loren looked around and thought she would never forget this scene. Claudia was staring at Ben as though she hated him. The big blonde man's face was flushed with distress. The rest of the Stuart family sat like stones, their faces frozen in surprise.

Rick looked angry. 'Well! Better late than never I guess. We can at least check our own equipment.' Ben started to speak but Rick ignored him. 'And I'll contact WorldSecure. Whoever Thomas is working for might still have access to the codes. We need to warn them.' He turned to Jeremy. 'But you obviously didn't know this when you contacted me? What did you want to talk about?'

Jeremy roused himself. He squeezed his sister's hand and stood up. His family watched him as he paced across the room. Loren was annoyed at her instinctive reaction to the man's beauty.

Jeremy stopped and turned to face them. 'As soon as I heard that Alistair was missing, I decided that I had to go with you.'

Rick shook his head. 'No! I can't risk it. If Ben and Victor are right the situation could be dangerous. We have no idea what we'll be facing. But whoever they are, it's clear that they have advanced technology. All my scientists are flight crew. And I'll be taking a company of experienced men – ex military. We'll be armed to the teeth.' He smiled slightly. 'I have some tricks that perhaps even Thomas and his friends won't know about. But it looks like we can expect a fight. I can't afford any dead weight.'

'I won't be dead weight. If anyone can find Alistair, it'll be me.'

Alistair's father interrupted. 'This is madness! Are you saying that you expect to be fighting a war? You'll all be killed.'

'I have to do this.' Jeremy's face convulsed with emotion. 'I will not leave my brother to rot on some god forsaken rock.'

'You'll have to show you're fit to go.' Rick's expression was calculating and Loren wondered what he was thinking.

'I'm fitter than most of you.' Jeremy spoke slowly, his voice full of emotion and Loren wondered again at the man's power to captivate. 'Alistair is alive. I speak to him every day.'

Fiona stretched out her hand. Her face was calm. Jeremy took her hand and they smiled at each other. 'I know he's in trouble. Twice I lost contact, but that was weeks ago. He is still alive.'

2

Sally awoke in Iceland as she did every day. She would drift out of sleep, peaceful for a few moments until she suddenly recalled where she was. Then grief and fear would cut through her heart like a jagged knife and she would spring up as though someone had struck her. If Alistair was still beside her she would turn to him for comfort, but more often he would be gone and she would find him staring down at the simulacrum of Sydney Harbour.

She sat panting for a few moments before turning her head. Alistair's pillow was smooth, the coverlet pulled neatly into place. She lay back and pulled the sheet over her face, unable to find the will to move, unwilling to face another day. Her chest tightened and her heart started to race until she felt physically uncomfortable. She gradually steadied her breathing until her pulse slowed, thrust the sheet back and stared around the room. If she wanted to, she could change it to anything she wanted, create any scenario she pleased. But she had never been interested in fiction or fantasy, and after a few half-hearted attempts she had left it as she had first imagined it – a luxurious but anonymous hotel room.

There was nothing here to distract her and she groaned as the familiar cycle of bitter thoughts started to run through her mind. When she made the decision to stay she had no idea it would come to this. She had imagined hardship, even danger, but not these long days of nothingness. They could not consult the word wall until the Millennium crew had left Earth 2. They knew that John had intended to stay as long as possible, even until Rick's mission arrived and Thomas would have a hard time convincing him otherwise. Every few days her longing for news would become intolerable. They could summon an angel just by calling out, but each time the response was the same. The Millennium crew were still on Earth 2. Questions about the situation on Earth were met with brief replies. The United States was in turmoil but the rest of the world was largely unaffected. Their families were safe. Until the Millennium crew departed, the angels would give them no further information.

Sally counted the times the sun rose and set over Sydney Harbour, but they could not be certain how much time had really passed. Nor could they record what was happening to them. One day they spent several hours writing down everything that had happened but when they woke the next morning, their papers were blank. Sally had become frantic. She had conjured up an assortment of beads and used the Quipa system to record the events of the day. She had felt relief and a strange satisfaction when the bracelet remained untouched the next morning. For weeks she kept up the habit even though most days were the same. Now the bracelet lay neglected on her dressing table. She had given up everything to retain her memory and now she could hardly remember one day from the next.

Alistair wondered why she bothered. She had tried to explain that she was living in a linguist's hell. For the first time in her life she had no way of learning anything new. For a while she had hoped she might learn the angels' language and perhaps the origins of Aramaic, since she was quite fluent in modern Hebrew. But the angels would not answer her questions about their language and spoke only in English when with them.

It was easier for Alistair. The angels allowed them to take regular tours of Iceland, and he searched for clues to the planet's geology and the source of the angels' amazing powers. She always accompanied him but the meticulous way he approached the task bored her. And she realized that her impatience irritated him. After reviewing their situation several times they didn't seem to have much to say to each other. The nights brought them comfort but in the morning they went their separate ways.

The area in which they were confined seemed to be endlessly expandable. Alistair created a gym and spent much of his time there, as though fearful of losing his physical strength. Sally had never needed to take regular exercise to remain fit. She returned to eating as her main source of amusement. At least that brought her immediate comfort and it didn't matter what or how much she ate, her figure was unaffected. When she looked at herself in the mirror she was angry to see how well she appeared. Then she would wonder if it was all an illusion. It was at such times that she felt weakest.

She felt the energy draining out of her, and sat up abruptly to clear her head. She pulled on a light tracksuit and some slippers and drew back the bedroom curtain. The sun was well above the horizon. She knew where Alistair would be and she knew not to disturb him.

She looked down at the glittering blue water and the arch of the Harbour Bridge. Early morning traffic streamed across it; below, the commuter ferries emerged from its dark shadow, thin trails of foam marking their passage. A few times she had the strange feeling that the tourists on the pleasure craft were waving to her. She pressed her face sideways against the window. As far as she could see, the façade of the building and those next door were identical to the high-rise hotels west of Circular Quay. She looked down. Tiny figures scurried in and out of buildings, traffic lights changed, cars moved slowly through the crowded streets, just as they did every day. She knew the scene by heart.

She banged her fist against the glass, tried to calm herself. If the day started like this, it was going to get much worse. She went into the bathroom and splashed some water on her face.

Alistair was where she expected to find him, staring out towards the shining sails of the Sydney Opera House. She heard him speaking softly the familiar words; "You were made men, to follow after knowledge."

This ritual which Alistair performed faithfully at the same time every day usually irritated her, but she suddenly recalled him quoting these words in the radiation cellar as he sent his goodbye message to his family. The acute sense of grief and loss returned. She stood watching him as he moved back from the window and stretched his shoulders. She wondered how a man who had so much faith in science could really believe that he was in daily communion with his brother.

As he turned, his face was peaceful, but when he saw her, his expression changed.

'Have you had breakfast yet?'

'I'm not hungry.' Sally walked over to the floor to ceiling window and stared out. 'It looks so real, doesn't it? Perhaps we truly are in Sydney. Perhaps the angels don't create things at all; they just send us to wherever we want to go.' She turned away from the beautiful view.

'It's just an illusion, like everything else here.' Alistair spoke impatiently.

Sally protested; 'The food we eat isn't an illusion. Otherwise we'd be dead! And how can you be so sure? Perhaps they have portals or something to other places – and that's how they travel to Earth. Maybe they just beam us up!'

'I've tried to explain to you. There's a rational explanation for everything we've seen so far. The technology is almost beyond belief, but it does make sense. Instantaneous transport, portals into other worlds – that's just nonsense.'

Alistair's matter of fact tone infuriated Sally. Every time they argued, he would back away, as though it was beyond him to make her understand.

Alistair glanced at her and changed the topic. 'We should eat before we leave.'

'Where are we going this time?' Sally tried to speak calmly.

'Round to the eastern hemisphere; I want to look at the area where the ice thins out.'

'Why there? What do you expect to find?'

'I don't know, but I'm starting to get an idea of how this planet works.'

'And then?' Sally hated herself for speaking so sharply, but she could feel the irritation rising again.

Alistair sighed. He had answered this question so many times. 'If we can figure out exactly where the angels and gods get their power from, we might be able to do something, to find some way to warn earth. That's one of the reasons we decided to stay. Remember?'

'And do you think you're making progress?'

'I don't know.' Alistair's voice rose slightly. 'It would help if you took more interest. You have such a phenomenal memory; you could help me with the calculations.'

'What if that's just an illusion, like everything else in this place.' Sally hadn't meant to repeat Alistair's words back to him but she was starting to lose control.

'I believe that what the probe recorded is real. We have to trust something. And I can't stay stuck inside all the time; I need to get out where I can see the real sky.'

Sally tightened her jaw to restrain herself from another retort.

'At least you always enjoy the flight. Come on, cheer up.' Alistair turned away and gestured towards the small dining table. 'You should try to eat something.' Sally followed him and sat down. She felt helpless and lethargic again, and the smell of Alistair's cooked breakfast nauseated her. She lifted the cover off her own plate. As if someone had guessed how she felt, the dish contained a selection of fresh fruit and toast. She banged the lid backed down and stared at Alistair. He did not look up.

'I can't stand this.'

Alistair placed his knife and fork carefully on to his plate. 'We don't have a choice. We've tried everything. There's no way out. You know that.'

'There must be a way.'

'Do you have any new ideas?'

'There must be something we can do.'

Alistair started eating again. 'If you think of something we can do, I'm willing to try it. Otherwise…' He suddenly banged his fork down. 'It's hard for me too, you know. I hate feeling so helpless, but I said I would look after you and that's what I'm trying to do.'

'I never asked you to stay,' Sally muttered. 'I told you not to.'

Alistair stood up abruptly. 'What did you say?'

Sally turned away. 'Nothing. It doesn't matter.'

Alistair grabbed her arm. 'Yes it does. We agreed. And if we stay calm, we will find a way through this.'

Sally wrenched her arm away. 'How? How do we know anything? How do we know they're telling us the truth about anything?' When Alistair didn't reply she continued. 'And don't tell me it's because they're angels and they have access to some higher bloody wisdom.'

Alistair remained silent, looking downwards. Sally felt her control slipping away. 'You still believe that, don't you? In your heart you believe we're safe, as long as we do as we're told.'

Alistair looked up. 'I believe what I've always believed. I do believe it's safer for us here than anywhere else.' He frowned and his freckled face flushed slightly. 'Aren't you forgetting what Zeus tried to do to you? We wouldn't stand a chance against him.'

'Ceres would help us.'

'Be reasonable Sally. We've been through all this before.' Alistair breathed in deeply, sat down again and returned to his food. In between mouthfuls he said, 'We can't get out of here. And even if we could, how could we get to Northland from here? Swim?' He ignored Sally's reddening face and continued calmly. 'Remember what the angels showed us. Can we really trust Ceres?' Alistair paused as he remembered Ceres warning him not to reveal Hercules resemblance to Jeremy. He had never told Sally.

'You've changed,' Sally interrupted bitterly.

Alistair banged his fork down on his plate. 'I haven't changed. It's you. You throw yourself into things and then everyone else has to pick up the pieces. You're the one who dashed into the tunnel.' He grasped the table as though trying to control himself but his voice rose angrily. 'You're the one who insisted on staying. You didn't believe that we would love each other again if we lost our memories, if we forgot what happened to us here. I never thought that. But you were so certain. So certain! I stayed for you, because I love you. Sometimes I think you don't know who you are or what you believe in. Sometimes I wish I'd never met you.'

Sally's faced paled, but Alistair continued relentlessly. 'I gave up my family, my whole life for this.' He gestured around the room. 'And for what?' His face flushed with anger. 'Why did you come with us Sally? I've never been able to work it out. You didn't have to come. You never seemed to want to. You're not interested in any of the things that we want to do. Why did you come at all?'

Sally stared at him incredulously. 'I don't know. I just felt I had to.' She recalled the moment when she heard that Pierre Meyer had died and her anger when Thomas told her he didn't think she was suited to the mission. She started to sob. If only she had listened to him. Why had she felt compelled to prove him wrong?

Alistair watched as she covered her face with her hands. He stood up again and put his arm around her. 'I'm sorry. I didn't mean that. I can't imagine life without you.' He hugged her tightly and then gave her a small shake. 'You really are being very brave. I know it's harder for you. There's nothing for you to do here.'

He continued to hold her until her sobs ceased. She raised her face and he kissed her. 'We just have to keep our nerve. The Millennium must leave soon and then we can at least use the wall. You can find out who your father is. Remember how much you want to do that. We can find out all sorts of things.'

Sally wiped her eyes and nodded. 'I'm sorry too.' But in her heart she felt a coldness growing. Alistair didn't understand. She couldn't go on like this.

Alistair pulled her to her feet. 'Get your jacket and let's get moving. At least it will keep us busy.'

'No. I'm still tired. I think I'll stay here this time.' Sally hated to see that Alistair looked faintly relieved.

'Are you sure? Do you want me to stay a while?' When Sally shook her head he said softly, 'I won't be away long.' He kissed her briefly on the cheek 'Don't think so much. It does no good. Do something nice for yourself.'

Sally nodded. 'Don't worry, I'll be fine.'

Alistair gathered his gear and called out. 'I'm ready.' The door opened and an angel entered. Beyond him all was white. Alistair turned, looking uncertain and Sally tried to smile. Alistair hesitated and then walked to the doorway. As the angel enfolded Alistair in his wings Sally felt a sudden panic. She ran to the door and pulled. As usual it opened onto a white wall.

For a few moments Sally lost all consciousness. When her mind cleared she was again looking down over the harbor. She felt as though she were dreaming.

Alistair's words rang through her head. 'It's just an illusion,' she whispered. She stood rigidly for a moment, staring down at the small ferries as they disappeared into the shadow of the Sydney Harbour Bridge. 'It's all an illusion,' she repeated loudly. The scene seemed to waver for an instant. She pressed her hand against the window and was not surprised when it passed through the surface as if it were water. Her fingertips felt suddenly cold and she withdrew her hand. The glass rippled as her fingers brushed across the window and she thought she glimpsed a dim landscape, like a reflection, beyond it. The glass started to frost over and the view of Sydney Harbour faded.

She turned and looked behind her at the room she and Alistair had occupied for these long weeks. She felt numb but her mind was clear. She linked her thumbs above her head, rose to her toes, leaned forward and plunged through the tall window.

3

'Sally!' Alistair flung open the bathroom door and pulled back the shower screen. He felt his legs give way and he sat down hard on the tile floor. 'Stay calm, stay calm.' He breathed in hard through his nose and puffed the air out through his mouth. After several breaths the tension in his chest eased and he stood up. He emptied his mind of all thought and moved through the suite of rooms making a systematic search of every corner. Sally's breakfast was untouched. Everything was as he had left it that morning. There was no message, no sign of a struggle. As the search revealed nothing, his actions became more frantic. When he found himself on his knees looking under the bed, he stopped and repeated the deep breaths. This time the panic did not ease and he opened his mouth to shout for help. Then he stopped abruptly. If the angels found out Sally had gone, what would they do? Contrary to what Sally believed, Alistair was deeply suspicious of the angels' motives.

    He sat down on the couch and clutched his head. He had to think. If Sally had found a way to get out surely she would have left him a sign. He stared around the room and felt a sudden sense of relief. She must have called an angel and gone outside. No! Even if she were still angry with him, she would have left a message. The sharp taste of bile filled his mouth. Zeus or one of the other gods had abducted her. His head pounded. Surely none of the gods would risk entering Iceland?

    He heard a sharp knocking sound and looked up joyfully. But it was not Sally. One of the lesser angels appeared near the entrance door and behind him stood Thomas, in human guise again and dressed in his black body suit. Alistair looked frantically towards the bedroom, and saw with relief that he had slammed the door behind him.

The angel looked at him blankly. 'You appear distressed. Do you need anything?'

For a moment Alistair could not find his voice, then he croaked, 'No! Sally and I had an argument.' He looked towards the bedroom. 'She's in there, sleeping it off.'

The angel did not move. 'Thomas is here to give you news about the Millennium.'

Thoughts raced through Alistair's mind. Finally he asked, 'Could you leave Thomas alone with us, please.'

Thomas spoke a few words. The angel gave a small nod and retreated through the wall.

Thomas sat opposite Alistair and stared at him. 'You don't look well.'

Alistair tried to conceal his feelings. 'What did you expect? Why are you here?'

'I have finally managed to convince John that the Millennium should leave.' Thomas rubbed his head in a way that Alistair had never seen before. The angels did not touch their faces or bodies as humans did.

'You don't look so good yourself.' Alistair leaned forward and saw that the fine lines on Thomas's face had deepened and his skin appeared dry and flaky.

'I have spent too much time away from the choir. I took certain actions ...' Thomas paused. 'I had hoped to stay here but it is agreed that I should return with the Millennium crew to Earth.'

Alistair could feel the tension building. 'Well, I guess it's goodbye then.'

'I will make my farewells to Sally.' Thomas stood up and moved towards the bedroom.

Alistair caught him by the arm and then let go abruptly. He had forgotten the strange sensations which touching an angel caused. 'I wouldn't wake her now. You're not her favorite person you know.'

Thomas ignored him and opened the bedroom door. After a moment he asked, 'Where is she?'

Alistair looked down at the floor. He still suspected Thomas could read his thoughts. Suddenly everything turned white. Thomas had restored the area to its original form and it was obvious that Sally was not there.

'Where is she?'

'I don't know. When I came back she was gone. I don't know what happened.'

There was a long silence and Thomas rubbed his head again. Finally he said; 'The choir must not discover that Sally is missing.'

Alistair stared at him suspiciously. 'What?'

'You were right not to tell them. It is complicated. I will explain later. Now we must leave.'

'What! Gabriel won't let me leave!'

'We will not tell him. We must hurry. We must find Sally.'

'We should contact the Millennium.' Alistair reached forward and grabbed at Thomas's watcher, but Thomas evaded him.

'No! It would take too long.'

For the first time Alistair saw real emotion on Thomas' face. He backed away as Thomas leaned forward slightly and gave a small gasp. A pale blue light shot above his head and spread out as his wings unfurled. The body suit strained against his lengthening legs and torso and Thomas pulled at it impatiently until it split. He waved his hand around the room and all the details of the hotel suite returned. Alistair shook his head but Thomas reached forward and grasped Alistair by the neck.

'I will explain later. We must leave now.'

Alistair knew there was no point resisting. He submitted numbly, closed his eyes. Once again he felt an unpleasant squeezing sensation as they passed through the walls of ice and the pressure of their rapid acceleration. When he opened his eyes they were high above the ocean, the small ice covered islands far below, strewn like diamond chips across the dark blue ocean. Iceland loomed to the south. They hovered for a few moments and Alistair heard Thomas exclaim loudly in his strange tongue. Without warning Thomas enfolded Alistair in his wings and dived towards the surface.

Alistair lost consciousness for a few moments. When he came to, he was lying half covered by a drift of snow and Thomas was sweeping more snow over him. He struggled to free himself but Thomas pushed him down. 'Be still. They will see us.' He swept the snow up into a small wall and threw himself down beside Alistair.

Alistair looked around. Although it was mid afternoon and the sky was clear, the light was growing dim. He heard an immense rustling noise. He gasped and Thomas put his hand across his mouth. Alistair struggled and then lay quiet as the vast crowd of angels rose and sped north, covering the sun.

After endless minutes the sky brightened and Thomas straightened up. 'We will have to take another way.' He did not explain but turned Alistair face down and seized the back of his jacket. He sprang lightly off the pile of snow and flew west at high speed, staying close to the water. When Alistair shouted, 'Where are we going?' Thomas shook him like a cat and did not reply.

Alistair had become accustomed to the angels' mode of flying on his explorations of Iceland. They would ascend steeply to a great height and then descend just as sharply and with amazing precision to their target. This was completely different. Thomas weaved between the icebergs and skimmed over small islands only a few meters above the surface. The sickening speed made Alistair nauseous. He closed his eyes and bowed his head against the rush of air. He managed to clasp his hands against his chest but his legs dangled helplessly, buffeted to and fro by the sharp turns and twists of Thomas's flight. He gritted his teeth and tried not to think.

When he next looked they were over solid land. Thomas did not slow down and Alistair shut his eyes again as they skimmed over the tree tops. He yelled in panic as Thomas plummeted downwards. They had entered a complex of deep, winding canyons and Thomas wove between the pillars of rock like a player in some giant virtual reality game.

Alistair had no idea of time or distance until they swooped up out of the canyon and he glimpsed the huge cloud of angels, some distance to the left. He realized that Thomas had flown over the North Pole and was approaching the gods' city from the north. Below him he saw the valley where the Millennium crew had landed weeks before. His heart raced but there was no sign of the shuttles or the camp. Thomas slowed down abruptly and Alistair's feet brushed across a soft surface. He landed heavily and fell sideways onto the sandy incline. Thomas hovered over him for a moment and then seemed to disappear. Alistair sat stunned. He staggered to his feet; fell down again, his head spinning. Finally he pushed himself up and looked around. Thomas was standing just inside the opening to the cave where he and Sally had been trapped. The rocks blocking the entrance had been cleared away.

Alistair looked back down the valley and saw the cairn of rocks which the crew had constructed as a memorial to their missing friends. Alistair recognized it immediately from the images that Thomas had shown them. He stumbled down the sandy slope. Thomas called out but he ignored him. Beyond the cairn he saw the communications pyramid. He knelt down overcome by emotion and pressed the top. The input hatch slid open and he stared at it longingly. If only he could leave a message here! But his watcher was still inactive and he had hidden his data pad in the gods' city.

'We must conceal ourselves.'

Alistair looked at Thomas in astonishment. The angel had retracted his wings and was dressed in the style of the village people. He appeared shorter and thicker. His features were fuller and his complexion and hair were darkened.

Alistair closed the pyramid and stood up reluctantly. 'Where are the crew?

'As I told you, they have returned to the Millennium. They are preparing to depart. We must hide in the village here.'

'Damn it Thomas! Why can't I go back to the crew?'

Thomas ignored him. He strode quickly up to the path which followed the line of foothills and headed towards the stream. He crossed over the rough bridge and followed the path towards the forest.

Alistair ran to catch up with him. 'Wait! Where are we going?' He stopped and looked around. He had an excellent memory for landscapes but he felt disoriented. 'The village is the other way.'

'No, not now. Zeus erased it and has rebuilt it nearer the hills'

'What? Why?'

Thomas did not reply. He disappeared as the path wound between the trees. Alistair swore with frustration and hurried after him.

4

Sally hit the water with such force that she gasped. Icy water filled her mouth as she plunged downwards. The shock propelled her upright and she kicked vigorously, her lungs heaving until she thought they must burst. Then her head rose above the water and she sucked in the cold morning air. She flailed her arms to stay afloat, and looked around. A small ice floe was drifting towards her. Suppressing the rising panic, she swam towards it. She groped along the smooth surface until she felt a crevice and heaved herself onto the shelf. She sat panting for a few moments, shaking with cold and fright. The bright water stretched to the horizon dotted with icy chips. For a moment she was completely disoriented. She turned around. Some twenty meters to the north the immense walls of the angels' domain loomed, blank and featureless.

Numbness crept up her legs. She clambered to her feet, jumped up and down and slapped her arms across her chest. As feeling returned to her body she was filled with a strange euphoria. She had done it. She had escaped.

She almost slipped over as the icy platform bumped against another ice floe and her feeling of joy was immediately replaced by a sense of incredulous horror. She was free but what could she do now? As if in answer to her question, she saw a group of angels emerge from the building and pass over the huge plaza. In unison they took to the air. Before she could stop herself she screamed for help but they had already turned northwards and did not hear her.

For several moments her mind was blank but she continued to move around and gradually the coldness faded and she felt a growing resolve. She would return and make up some story about how she had got out. Then she and Alistair would be free to leave again whenever they were ready. The sense of victory returned. She had overcome the angels' trap. Their illusions were not as powerful as they believed. She laughed out loud and gestured obscenely towards the angels' domain.

She made an easy leap to the next ice floe and three more jumps brought her within a few meters of the shore. She was glad that she was not wearing her dark body suit. The pale tracksuit rendered her almost invisible against the ice. She looked around again, to decide which way she should go. The ice was drifting very slowly to the east and would soon pass by a long peninsular jutting out from the plaza. She stepped back and prepared to make a running jump and then screamed as something circled her neck and wrenched her upwards. She gagged for air and struggled to free herself. The tall walls of Iceland receded rapidly as she was hauled back and upwards. Her legs and arms flailed helplessly for several moments. Just as suddenly whatever was holding her plunged down and she was deposited onto the ice.

She leapt up and turned around. For a moment she did not recognize the two figures, dressed in white skin tight garments, their hair concealed beneath hoods. Diana stood, her arms folded, glaring at her. Ceres showed a more sympathetic expression.

'So, now we have her. Now we can continue.' Diana turned away.

'What the hell?' Sally stuttered in astonishment. 'How did you find me?

Diana snorted. 'We were not looking for you. Ceres saw your stupid antics and thought we should rescue you.'

'We will explain later. Diana is right. We need to get away from here as quickly as possible.' Ceres took Sally's arm and Sally felt warmth spreading through her.

Sally turned to look back at Iceland, several hundred meters away. 'We can't leave Alistair there. We have to find him. Or at least let him know where we're going.' She felt panic rising in her.

'Are you mad? The Diptera must never know we came here.' Diana was checking a long silver rod attached to her waistband. Several other objects hung from a sash across her chest.

'But we must ...' Sally gasped as Diana struck her a stinging blow across her cheek.

'Be quiet. When I want your opinion, I will ask for it. If you do not cease your babble, I will dump you back in the ocean.' Diana ran lightly across the ice to the edge. She waved her hand and a wide vessel like a deep white saucer appeared. She stepped into it and looked back at the others. 'Hurry up.'

'No! I can't leave Alistair.' Sally clutched her face and looked helplessly back at Iceland.

'Do not be a fool Sally. I cannot understand how you escaped, but the Diptera will not let you free again.' Ceres took Sally's arm and once again she experienced a sense of warm safety. She stumbled across the ice, looking back at her prison, imagining Alistair returning to find her gone.

Ceres pushed her into boat. There was a small jolt and then the boat moved smoothly through the water. Diana shouted suddenly and pointed upwards. In the northern sky a small gold cloud drifted. Diana waved her hand and the sky disappeared, concealed by a thick white fabric.

'What was that?' Sally asked. 'I've seen it before.'

'Zeus's spies,' Diana replied shortly. 'How he dares send them so close to the Diptera!'

They sat in tense silence for a few moments, then Diana spoke rapidly to Ceres, glancing angrily at Sally. Finally Ceres said in a calm voice. 'Sally may be useful to us. If the worst happens, we can take her back to earth and she can intervene for us.'

Diana's black expression deepened. 'If it comes to that …'

'It will not help to keep her ignorant. She needs to understand the danger.'

Diana did not reply. She closed her eyes and leaned back.

Ceres spoke slowly as though Sally might have difficulty understanding. 'Zeus is planning a war against the Diptera – those you call angels. He believes that he can win. He is of course completely mad. Athena, Hercules and some others will try to prevent it. But we are not strong enough to fight Zeus.'

Sally could not reply. For the last weeks she had thought of nothing but how the angels might deal with her and Alistair. She had pushed the gods to the back of her mind. She shuddered as she remembered Zeus's face, looking down at her in his huge marble palace.

'Sally! You must understand this. Diana and I are going to seek an alliance with the immortals in the south. If they agree, we may prevent Zeus from embarking on this insane war, which can only lead to our total destruction. You must promise to do as we ask. Nothing must stop us from reaching the southern land.'

'Could Zeus really defeat the angels?' As she spoke the words, Sally's head reeled and she almost laughed out loud. She couldn't believe what she was hearing.

'Do not call them "angels",' Diana said impatiently. 'I know what that word means to you.'

Ceres interrupted 'We do not believe so. But Zeus maintains that he has discovered a weakness in the Diptera of which we were unaware. He has confided in Poseidon but he will not reveal it to us.'

'Who? What?' Sally felt again a hysterical desire to laugh.

'Zeus's other brother, of course.' Diana spoke contemptuously. 'Don't you know any history at all?'

Sally felt her control slipping. If she could only find the right words, she could send these characters back where they belonged, in the pages of a fantasy novel. Ceres gave her a warning look but she could not stop herself. 'We were taught history, not mythology. Perhaps you don't know, but no one on earth, practically no one, believes any longer that any of you ever existed.'

Before she could continue, Diana leapt across at her and the boat rocked violently. Sally felt something sharp digging into her side and Ceres cried out in alarm.

'Does this feel mythical?' spat Diana. 'Make up your mind, mortal. Is this real?' Sally gasped as she felt her skin puncture. Ceres swiped Diana across the side of her head, knocking her to the bottom of the boat. To Sally's surprise Diana did not retaliate. She pulled herself up and sat down again. Her expression was calmer, as though the moment of violence had given her some sort of release. She looked sardonically at Sally as she sheathed the short dagger. Sally rubbed her ribs and looked down. The cloth was torn but there was no blood. She caught her breath and said calmly, 'You've made your point.'

Diana stared at her and then laughed loudly. She leaned across and slapped Sally on the knee. 'Ceres is right. There may be more to you than meets the eye. At least you can keep us amused.'

'Are you sufficiently warm?' Sally nodded at Ceres sympathetic question. Ceres turned away, hissed softly and made a gesture. She passed Sally a small white roll and Sally bit into it eagerly. The taste reminded her of the night she and Alistair had spent confined in the god's city, and tears sprung to her eyes. She closed her eyes and leaned back. She felt exhausted. Her head sank on her chest. She looked down at the white bread in her hand. The image faded and she slept.

When she woke Ceres and Diana were speaking quietly in their own language.

Ceres noticed her stirring. 'It is almost noon. We are travelling too slowly, but we are not yet far enough from The White Land to risk another mode of transport.'

Sally felt refreshed by her sleep, and strangely calm. 'You told me how you travelled to earth. Can't you just conjure something up; imagine some faster way to get to Southland?'

Diana laughed harshly. It depends on who's got the best imagination. I've never beaten my father in a battle of wits.'

'We have crossed the line of ice. This is not our domain,' Ceres explained. 'We have less power here and if we use it, Zeus may discover us.'

'Would he harm you? Why would he do that?'

Diana laughed again. 'Perhaps not, but Hera would.'

'If he finds out that we are plotting against him.' Ceres spoke rapidly to Diana in her own language and Sally decided not to ask any more questions. The situation was too strange. She thought of Alistair returning, searching desperately for her. She closed her eyes to conceal her feelings. The warmth and slow rocking movement of the boat made her drowsy and she drifted off again.

A sharp jolt jerked her awake. The cover was drawn back and Diana and Ceres were gone. She looked around in panic. A few meters away, the two white figures stood on the stony beach and stared towards the north. Sally scrambled out of the boat and joined them. The light was dim. Far to the north a huge cloud covered the sun and Sally saw with a sense of dread that the angels were massing. The cloud spread out until it covered most of the northern sky and bands of light rippled over the surface.

Ceres muttered something in her own language and then remembering Sally was present, said, 'Perhaps they have discovered you are gone.'

Diana chortled. 'They must think that Zeus has seized you. That will keep him occupied.' As she spoke the bands of light began to pulsate more rapidly. 'Which reminds me; how did you get out? The Diptera are never careless.'

Sally hesitated. She had assumed that the Diana and Ceres had seen her dive. It could be to her advantage if they had not. 'I don't ...'

Ceres cut in. 'Look!' The white cloud seemed to split apart and a tongue of red fire shot through the gap.

'Mother of life!' Diana swore. 'Zeus must be mad. What does he think he's doing?'

'He never thinks. That is our problem.' Ceres gazed steadily at the cloud. Her face remained calm.

Sally was transfixed by the spectacle. A small black cloud had emerged from the east and bolts of red light pierced the mass of angels. They retreated north at enormous speed and vanished only to re-emerge moments later from the western horizon. The black cloud receded to the north and disappeared. Then a huge bolt of light shot over the horizon and rocketed skyward. Sally followed its path and a few seconds later saw a bright flash.

Diana turned towards the boat and waved her hand. It sank beneath the water and quickly disappeared. 'It will be faster to travel by land now.' She started to move away, but Sally stared up at the sky. Strange lights glinted for a few seconds.

'Come!' Diana was insistent and Ceres pulled at Sally's arm. They had reached one of the larger islands and the ice had given way to barren rock. The two immortals raced away across the rough surface. Sally tried to keep up but she kept looking back, fascinated by the drama in the north. The black cloud raced around the perimeter of the cloud of angels, sending out brilliant flashes of red light. Long ribbons of light, bands of angels, their distinctive colors pulsating, pursued and withdrew. Part of the white cloud swept south towards the equator and Sally turned and fled. For long minutes she pounded over the uneven surface but she could not catch up with Diana and Ceres and finally she stumbled and fell to the ground. She staggered to her feet and saw with relief that the sky was clear again.

'Sally!' Ceres and Diana had stopped and were gesturing for her to hurry up. Sally pointed to her feet. She could not go much further without shoes. Diana swore loudly but Ceres made a strange whistling noise and gestured. She threw the pair of leather sandals to Sally.

As soon as Sally had put them on Ceres shook her arm. 'We must hurry!' She sped off and Sally ran after her. Every time she neared them, Ceres and Diana increased their speed. The ground was rough, littered with small stones. Sally stumbled frequently but managed to stay upright, amazed that she could keep going. She was breathing evenly and her legs felt strong. After a while she thought of nothing but the rhythm of her legs and arms and the fresh cool air in her face.

'Sally!' They had finally reached the southern end of the island. Ceres and Diana were silhouetted against the late afternoon sky, their shadows long and dark. A bright light was descending towards them. Sally crouched down as it grew into a huge fiery object. As it screamed overhead she realized that it was the Millennium, glowing bright red as it tore through the atmosphere. Sally watched in horror as the doomed spacecraft arced across the sky and plunged into the ocean, some distance to the south. Bright plumes of water gushed skyward.

'There go your friends.' Diana spoke without emotion. Her expression dared Sally to give way to grief.

For long moments Sally shook with speechless rage. Then a strange calm overcame her. She closed her eyes and thought hard. The distinctive silhouette of the Millennium was still imprinted on her retina, and she realized that the distinctive bulges of Radon and Xenon were missing. Her heart jumped. The crew must have detached the shuttles before the Millennium's orbit had decayed.

Ceres touched her arm as she looked back up in the direction of the Millennium's descent. There was no sign of any more debris. She composed her face and looked defiantly at Diana. 'The Millennium may be destroyed but the crew will return to Earth in the shuttles. And then they will be back. Whoever did this will be sorry.'

'Yes, and we will make Zeus pay for all this trouble.' Diana slapped Sally on the back and set off at a run.

5

The wail of the alarm resounded again through the control room. John punched the green button, the deafening blare ceased and there was a moment's silence. Then the computer warning system continued. Vicki listened in stunned disbelief as it detailed the damage to the ship. She started to pull her visor down but Sima stopped her.

'The breach has been sealed. Don't use the suit's oxygen until you need it.'

John's fingers flew over the screens. 'I've launched the comms capsule and the emergency beacon.' He turned to look at the crew. As usual, his face was calm, showing none of the urgency of their situation

'Sima – you prep the ECRV. Mohun! Check the supplies. We can take another 200k plus.' His voice was unemotional but sharpened as he turned towards Vicki. 'Are you listening, Vicki? Help Mohun. Figure out what else we should take.'

Vicki stared at John's impassive face and her breathing steadied. She nodded and then looked away. Beyond him the landscape of the planet was still sliding across the viewport, although the rolling had slowed down.

'Sharon and I will check the AGD. I'm going outside to take a look,' John continued. 'It's a long shot but we may be able to make repairs.' He pushed a toggle forward. 'If not, we have three hours until orbit decay.' He released his harness and pushed away towards the hatch. 'Three hours maximum. Make the most of it.'

Vicki felt numb as she followed Mohun. She knew that the 200k referred to the combined weight of Sally, Alistair and Thomas, and the extra supplies might mean the difference between life and death. The events of the last few weeks flashed before her eyes and the image of Thomas appeared as clearly as if he was standing in front of her. 'Sorry', his last message had read, but he wasn't sorry for anything. By some odd association, Poseidon's strange face merged with Thomas's and she felt a sharp sense of danger.

'Vicki!'

With enormous effort she shut out these morbid ideas. Mohun had pulled open the door to the main store. He pushed a mule towards her and handed her a data pad. 'Call them out and I'll pass you the stuff.'

Vicki scanned each item as she loaded it onto the mule; weapons, medical supplies, enzymes, mobile desalinators, space blankets, tools, hard food and their supply of harvested spirulina. She checked her data pad. 'Ninety k; we're almost through the list.'

'OK, we'll finish then go back for more.' Mohun sounded calm but his voice shook slightly. Vicki put her hand on his arm but he shrugged her off. 'We need to focus. If we forget something ...'

Vicki nodded. They spent some time calculating the last few items. Finally Mohun said, 'That's it. We should let everyone take a couple of personal things. Something light. Say 1k each.'

Vicki helped Mohun steer the mule towards the main airlock where Sima was checking the ECRV controls. She left Mohun to secure the mule and pushed back down the walkway. The Millennium was stable again and she kept feeling that they didn't really have to leave, but she knew it was an illusion. The ship already had an air of abandon. Packets of food had floated out of an unsecured locker in the galley and miscellaneous items thudded softly against the metal walls. Every few seconds, the metallic voice of the main computer sounded, detailing the malfunctions and vainly reminding the crew that they had not performed routine jobs. Vicki felt as though she were floating through a graveyard.

She opened Sally's locker and searched inside. If things went wrong, if they found that Sally and Alistair really were dead, she would make an offering. She pulled out the thin volume of sonnets that Sima had read from at the memorial service. Sally's father had written inside the cover; "Love, Dad" and the date, some twenty years earlier. Vicki wiped her eyes and opened Alistair's locker. She sorted through the contents and selected two vid disks. She slipped the disks and book into a small satchel and carefully removed the shrine from her own locker. She made a swift obeisance and touched each item, remembering clearly how she had acquired them. She looked for a long moment at the framed print of a young couple and a small boy. Her mother and father had never again looked so happy. A few months later and several years before her own birth, her brother had drowned. She thought of her parents' faces as they had made their final farewells and her stomach clenched.

'What are you doing?'

Vicki looked up at Sharon. 'I only need this photo, so I have taken something for Sally and Alistair too.'

Sharon's expression did not change. 'We're leaving now. We can't repair the AGD even if we had more time.'

Vicki kept her eyes fixed on Sharon's back as they made their way to the airlock. John and Mohun were already there and they stood awkwardly in the narrow space. It seemed unfit for such a solemn occasion.

'We've made the final checks, and we've uploaded all the data to the satellites. We'll take the ECRV down as close as possible to Northland.' John spoke calmly. 'We can't expect Rick Jones for several weeks. If he's delayed, well then, we might be safer in Southland but we'll go through our supplies quicker without access to fresh water and soil.' He looked around. 'Any questions?'

Vicki fumbled with her visor. She wished she could speak to Sima before they left but he was already in the ECRV's cabin. A strange feeling of dislocation was growing in her and she recognized the initial symptoms of shock. She checked her satchel for her Rescue Remedy. The others had laughed at her supply of yellow capsules. She closed her eyes for a moment and savored the faint aroma of grape juice on her tongue. The effect was immediate. She snapped her visor down, squeezed through the narrow opening and pulled herself along to the couch that had been assigned to her, back in Geneva. Mohun and Sharon flanked her. The door thudded shut as she pulled the restraining bar up between her knees and snapped the horizontal rung into place.

'Parameters set for descent.'

'Check that Sima,' John replied. 'Ok, we will hear three loud sounds as we descend, each one accompanied by a reduction in speed.' John was stating the obvious but Vicki was glad to hear it. She closed her eyes and used his steady voice to slow her breathing.

'On my mark; three, two, here we go.' There was a sharp series of forward movements, a sensation of pressure as the ECRV exited the spacecraft and then no sense of motion at all as they started the long glide to re-entry. John called out a series of figures and Sima replied 'check!' tersely to each one. Vicki counted the seconds, the minutes. Only moments after she expected it, the vehicle shook as the propulsion unit was jettisoned. Her heart raced as the acceleration increased and a dull rushing noise increased to a deafening roar. The vehicle shuddered, settled into a bone shaking, jarring vibration. Vicki had experienced this several times in the flight simulator on Earth but then there was always an audience, faces she could look at. Sweat ran into her eyes. She closed them and started to count again but was interrupted by John's calm voice, checking the data screen. Sima replied and the duet continued until the ECRV lurched violently.

'Drogue released.' John sounded pleased. 'Prepare to engage steering.'

Vicki heard a few murmurs as the vehicle swung erratically, dragged back by the parachute. She felt the pressure of their descent and an immense feeling of relief filled her, as intense as joy.

Sima's voice replied, in a much lighter tone. 'In place and ready to execute.'

There was a short silence before John continued his readings. Sima answered briskly and Vicki imagined the planet passing below them. She had a sudden burst of hope. Perhaps this would all end well. They would find Sally and Alistair, or at the very least what had happened to them. The pressure varied with each swing of the ECRV, as though they were descending in a lift but the speed was inconstant. Vicki wondered for a moment why AGD drives were not installed on the crew rescue vehicles. She remembered being told but could not recall the details.

'We are on course; engaging the parafoil.'

'Parafoil engaged.' The vehicle lurched again and began to swing erratically.

'Jettisoning drogue.'

Vicki exclaimed in alarm as the vehicle shot forward but a moment later it steadied and the movements became smoother.

'On course. Wind at ten. Heading north.'

'All ok. We will ...' The ECRV jerked and shot upwards. 'What the hell? Sima!'

Sima exclaimed as they lurched again and swung violently. 'Parafoil's functional. Steering does not respond. We've changed direction; heading south. It must be a storm.'

A sharp 'No!' from John. 'No abnormal weather readings. It can't be wind.'

'Descending rapidly and still heading due south.'

There was a long silence. They were still swinging, but more gently now, in a strange rotating movement. Vicki felt a stinging in her mouth and realized she had bitten her tongue.

'Altitude twenty four hundred. Leveling off. No steering!'

'I'm going out.' John's face emerged from behind Mohun's boots. Vicki glimpsed his grim face as he groped towards the door. She leaned forward and saw Sima sliding out from his position below.

'I'll secure you.' Sima clipped a tether to one of the stanchions and attached it to John's webbed belt. They were both pushed back by the rush of wind as they slid the door open. John turned his back to the opening, grasped the brace with one hand and leaned out. Vicki glanced at Mohun. His face was drained of color. Perhaps he was thinking about the day when he and John had lost the shuttle.

'I can't see what's happening.' John's voice was hoarse with effort. 'Something has seized the parachute.'

Sima stepped back. 'We'll have to free it manually.'

'Could you be more specific?' Sharon spoke calmly.

'There's something up there. Whatever it is, it's moving, perhaps alive. We have to scare it off. Sima! Take manual control. Sharon! Hand gun!'

Sharon leaned forward and unclipped a weapon. 'What the hell?'

'Stop!' Mohun fumbled with his harness.

'Stay where you are!' Sima pushed Mohun back. 'If we lose the chute, we'll drop like a stone.'

'No!' Mohun's voice was agitated. 'John! You know what happened last time! We can't use force. We'll be killed.'

'Shut up!' Sima shouldered Mohun back and snapped the lock on the restraining bar. He took the gun from Sharon and checked its settings. 'Maximum stun.' He handed it to John.

'For god's sake, John.' Mohun struggled to release the lock again. His hands were shaking.

John did not reply. He disappeared through the opening. Sharon joined Sima and clutched at the doorway.

Mohun was muttering incoherently. When Vicki put her glove on his arm, he turned to her. 'It's mad. We can't just pretend ...'

Vicki heard the loud pinging noise which the MUDs made when a body suit had been breached. A deafening bang resounded though the cabin and a purple light shot through the opening. Sharon and Sima were flung back as the ECRV lurched and plummeted.

The flare raced around the cabin, fading suddenly into violet glow. Sima struggled back to the hatch. He braced himself and leaned out. 'The chute's gone. I can't see John.' He ducked back inside as fragments of the parafoil whipped across the opening. 'Taking manual control now.' He slid out of sight. The ECRV lurched violently, steadied for a few seconds, lurched again.

'Help me! Mohun!' Sharon was pulling on John's tether. Mohun released his harness and scrambled over to her.

Sharon swore violently as they both heaved. 'He's caught on something.'

Vicki heard a series of soft thuds and yelled out. 'Oh god! He's banging against the side.'

'One thousand meters.' Sima was shouting. 'Get John inside! Quick!'

Sharon leaned out, her helmet buffeted by the wind. 'He's caught on the lower rail.'

Mohun pulled her back. 'I'll climb down and free him.'

Sima yelled. 'No time, you'll be crushed. We are coming in too fast, crash landing.'

As Mohun clambered onto his couch Vicki could hear herself moaning. 'No, no, no.'

Sharon grabbed the door to pull it shut but fell back against Mohun. John's helmet appeared in the opening and then he fell through, knocking Sharon to the deck. Behind him Vicki saw a bearded face and bright blue eyes staring directly at her. The face widened into a brilliant smile. Long pale hair whipped in the wind, there was a loud roar of laughter and the face disappeared.

Vicki clutched Mohun's arm. 'Did you see that – that man?'

Sima yelled. 'What's happening?'

Mohun did not reply. He wrenched open his harness and leaned down to Sharon. A sudden jolt flung him back against his seat and a bright light filled the cabin. Bands of color pulsated across the opening and radiated through the cabin. The ECRV swung violently again and the clear blue sky reappeared. Vicki gasped as the sky seemed to turn green; the blur of grass or trees raced past. There was a sharp bump and several gentler thuds. Then the vehicle was still.

'Sima, help me.' John's crumpled body pinned Sharon to the floor. His space suit was slashed and singed down to his waist.

Sima slid out from the control couch. 'Careful! Mohun.' They lifted John onto Mohun's couch and Vicki removed his helmet. John's face was pale and slack.

'He's badly burned.' Sima reached up for the medical kit. 'Get him outside. We have to stabilize him.'

John groaned loudly as they maneuvered him through the hatch. Vicki clambered after them and watched as Sima and Sharon crouched over the still figure.

'Where are we?' Mohun asked in a shocked voice. 'I thought we were heading south.'

Vicki suddenly realized that she was standing, not on the bare rock of the southern continent, but on lush green grass. It shimmered around her feet as though water flowed across it; rippling yellow, blue, violet and orange. She slowly pulled off her helmet and looked around. The sky was clear. The position of the sun meant that they were well south of the equator. She felt giddy and disoriented.

'Look!' Mohun shouted.

Less than fifty meters away, a brilliant rainbow arched across the grassy plain. Vicki shaded her eyes and stared at it. The vivid colors descended in an enormous arc like a waterfall and faded off into a vast distance. She had never seen anything like it. It was too big. It was the wrong shape. Mohun stared back at her blankly, his eyes round with amazement. She looked back at Sima and Sharon, working intently on John's still form.

'It's no good. He's bleeding internally.' Sima started to swear. He pulled off his helmet and threw it to the ground. 'Mohun! Get my kit.' His voice rose as he stood up. Sharon remained kneeling, staring down at her commander.

Mohun grabbed Sima's arm and pointed. Two figures had emerged from the glare of the rainbow and were walking slowly towards them.

For one moment Vicki thought the men were clothed in the rainbow. Then she saw that they wore long capes which reflected the colors of the arc. Her heart thumped in her chest as they approached. 'That's him. I saw him.' She pointed at the figure on the left. 'He's the one. He pushed John inside.'

The two men stopped. The man with long blonde hair pointed at the ECRV. He bellowed with laughter, slapping his thighs. The taller man's hair was concealed by a strange horned helmet. He ignored his companion and raised a long curved horn to his mouth. A piercing sound rang through the air, increasing in volume until the whole plain resonated. The sound died away as he lowered the horn.

Vicki looked around. Mohun, Sharon and Sima were gazing at the rainbow. She felt her legs start to shake. The ground was vibrating and a dull rumbling noise increased until it became a thunderous beat. The rainbow seemed to pulsate with the same rhythm and where it touched the ground a dark band spread across the grass. Above the loud thudding, a clanging and clashing rose. Just as Vicki thought she could stand it no longer, the noise ceased.

She heard Sima gasp. As her eyes adjusted to the rainbow's glare she saw the dark band was a line of armed men. She saw faces, pale and hard, long plaits of yellow hair, tall helmets with long curved horns, leather kilts, corselets of chain mail, thick legs and huge arms. And weapons; hundreds of weapons. Sharp tipped spears, daggers stuffed into wide belts, axes flung over massive shoulders, long swords, huge round shields with strange markings in red and black.

The figure slammed their weapons against their shields three times and shouted something.

Sima gasped. 'Heimdall! They called him Heimdall. It can't be.'

Both of the caped men now raised their right fists and shouted in reply. Sima sucked in his breath. 'Thor's hammer,' he whispered. He swore in Russian.

The tall man addressed as Heimdall stepped forward and spoke sharply. In response a dozen of the warriors raced towards the crew. There was no time to retreat, to find their guns. Sharon hunched over John and Sima pushed Vicki behind him. But the pale haired warriors ignored them. They encircled the ECRV and the crew and stood roughly to attention. Heimdall walked unhurriedly towards them while the blonde man looked on, an amused expression on his handsome face.

As Heimdall approached, Vicki saw that his long cape was woven from metallic thread, embossed with strange, intricate patterns. His helmet gleamed with gold tracery and the long curved horns were tipped with gold. She felt a strange reluctance to look at him and turned away quickly when she met his eyes. His pale face was perfectly symmetrical like the Anomees' but his features were large and strong and his eyes a brilliant blue. She felt his magnetism even as he looked away at the rest of the crew.

No one spoke for a long moment. A loud cawing noise made Vicki look up again. Two of the large ravens, which they had seen in Northland, were circling Heimdall's head. One landed on his shoulder. Heimdall spoke to it and the bird flew off as though responding to a command. The other bird flew into the ECRV. It squawked loudly and flew back to Heimdall. Then it too disappeared behind the rainbow.

Heimdall uttered something in a language which sounded vaguely familiar to Vicki, and to her amazement Sima responded. There was a short exchange before Heimdall said loudly, in heavily accented but very clear English; 'I am Heimdall, the god of light and the son of nine mothers. I am the guardian of Bifrost, the rainbow-bridge. He turned and pointed to the rainbow. 'Beyond lays my domain and Himinborg, my great hall. I can see one hundred miles around me, day and night and I can hear the grass grow.'

Sharon swore. 'What the shit is this? Sima?' She leapt up.

Sima muttered something and put out his hand to restrain her.

Heimdall's face flushed unpleasantly. His voice became harsh. 'We stand in Midgard, the realm of mortals. Only through Bifrost may you enter the realm of the gods. In Asgard sit the Aesir, mightiest of the Norse. You are commanded to enter, and there you will find Thor, guardian of Asgard.'

Sharon insisted. 'Sima! What is he talking about?'

Sima ignored her, as Heimdall continued. 'And you have been here before, though three of you are not here now. I saw how you came from the moving star above. I heard and saw all that you said and did here in our realms.' He pointed to small hillock a few meters from the ECRV. 'Your gods have no power here. But we respect your beliefs. We have allowed their sign-shape to remain here.'

Sima exclaimed and ran over to the pyramid.

Heimdall shouted and four of the warriors encircled Sharon and John. Sharon screamed out to Sima and pushed one of them back. He threw her aside, drew his long sword and pointed it towards John's chest.

'No!' Vicki shrieked.

In one flowing movement Sharon leaned forward, grasped the warrior's wrist, dropped down onto one knee and threw him over her shoulder. The man landed with a great thud on his back as Sharon straightened up, gripping his sword.

There was a huge guttural roar from the warriors and several of them banged their axes against their shields, their faces split in wide grins.

Sima ran past Vicki and to her amazement he pulled Sharon back. 'Stop!' he shouted. 'You don't know what you are doing.' Sharon was so taken aback she did not resist when he took the sword from her.

The warrior had regained his feet. His face was flushed with anger and embarrassment. He took the sword from Sima, bent over John, placed the tip between his feet and the hilt beneath his hands.

The crew stood frozen as four of the warriors braced John's body with their spears and secured him with wide leather belts. They lifted the prone figure and walked slowly towards the rainbow. The line of warriors approached them and formed a guard of honor, banging on their shields and calling out in unison. The group disappeared into the glare of the rainbow and the line of warriors resumed their positions.

Sima said slowly. 'If I understand anything, I am certain that John will be safe.'

Sharon could hardly speak. 'John is dead.'

The blonde man strode between them and shook his long corn colored hair. 'He will be reborn!' He waited a moment and when no one spoke, he said, 'Perhaps you do not know me. My name is Loki.'

'Loki the Trickster!' breathed Sima.

Loki's smile flashed. He moved closer to Sharon and when she backed away, took hold of her chin. He brushed the damp hair from her forehead and leaned towards her.

'Leave her alone!' Mohun rushed forward. Sharon slapped Loki's hand away and pushed him back. He rose into the air as though seated on an invisible chair. The crew watched in disbelief as he floated in a slow circle and shouted out in mock fright; 'A Valkyrien! Help me! A Valkyrien!'

The warriors laughed, shouted, and drummed their shields with their weapons. Vicki saw Sharon and Mohun flush with anger but Sima was gazing intently at Loki.

Heimdall shouted sharply and Loki drifted down to him. They talked quietly for a moment. Heimdall turned back to the crew. 'I sense that you have questions which you wish to be answered?'

'Where have you taken our commander?' Sharon shouted hoarsely.

Sima signaled Sharon to be quiet. He spoke slowly and calmly but Vicki felt a growing alarm. She glanced at Loki and saw him regarding her with amusement. His face was as handsome and well formed as Heimdall's but his smile repelled her.

'When we were here last and ...' Sima gestured towards the pyramid, 'When we worshipped at our sign-shape, this place was barren. There was nothing here. No rainbow-bridge, no grass, no people. How must we understand this?'

'We were asked to hide, to conceal our realm.'
'Why? Who?'
'Because you were coming.'
'Because *we* were coming?'
Heimdall nodded.
'Who asked you to do this?'

'If you do not know the answer to this question, I am not the one to tell you. When the time is pregnant, all will be revealed to you.'

Sharon interrupted. 'I've had enough of this. What do you want with us? Why did you fire on our ship?'

'We did not. You have powerful enemies.'

'What?' Sharon shouted.

Heimdall ignored her. 'Loki will now take you to meet your fate. Stand on your ship and hold tight.'

Sharon glared defiantly at Heimdall. Sima muttered, 'I know it sounds mad but I think we will be all right. Anyway we have no choice. We're outnumbered.'

Sharon clenched her fists. She looked at Vicki and Mohun and nodded grimly. She stepped up on to the lower rung and grabbed one of the braces.

Mohun helped Vicki up and she squirmed around so she could see what was happening. She caught Sharon's eye. 'I told you. They're not human. There are other beings here.' She clutched the brace as they bumped across the grass and rose from the ground. Loki was pushing the ECRV with one hand as though it were a small toy. When he saw Vicki staring at him, he gave a malicious smile and pushed again. Heimdall looked up at them as the ECRV shot towards the rainbow. He raised his arm in a salute and the line of warriors parted. Vicki glimpsed their faces washed by the colors of the rainbow.

'Behold Bifrost! Rainbow Bridge of the gods!' Loki called out.

Vicki panicked as the rainbow engulfed them and she lost sight of the others. Her hands, slick with sweat lost their grasp on the brace. But the pulses of color were like powerful waves, holding her firmly against the metal hull. A low sound throbbed, changing in pitch as they moved through orange, yellow and green. Her skin prickled painfully and she squeezed her eyes shut. The humming rose in intensity until she cried out in pain. She lost all sense of time and place, suspended in the thick, vibrating cloud.

Suddenly there was silence. Vicki opened her eyes. The sky ahead was clear. They were floating along a wide grassy valley. To left and right the steep hillsides were covered in trees. Vicki stared incredulously – ash, birch, fir; trees from Earth.

She grabbed at the brace when the ECRV abruptly changed direction. The daylight dimmed as they entered a narrow canyon. The vertical cliffs were so high that only a narrow band of sky could be seen. Before them the canyon sloped up, narrowing at its apex into what looked like a cave or tunnel.

They landed with a thud. Vicki let go and fell painfully. She tried to stand but her legs were shaking. Sima pulled her against his chest and held her close for a moment. 'You have to be brave.' He kissed her cheek and then thrust her away. 'You must trust me. We will survive.'

Loki stood at the rock face, next to a large timber frame. Long and short swords, axes and bows hung in rows. Above them, round shields, helmets and chain mail shirts gleamed dully in the dim light. 'Look closely and choose wisely.' Loki spoke seriously but his expression was gleeful.

'What now, Sima? Do you want to tell us what's going on?' Sharon's voice was hoarse with rage. 'Where did they take John?'

Loki interrupted. 'You warriors from far away are about to meet your fate - the Berserks. Choose your weapons.'

'Berserks?' Sharon shouted. 'What the hell is this?'

Sima let out a deep sigh as though he had been holding his breath. 'Please give us some time. I need to prepare my friends.'

Loki laughed. 'There is no time. Choose now.'

'Listen very carefully.' Sima spoke more loudly as Sharon tried to interrupt. 'If I am right, we have to do this. It's as Vicki said. It's mad but it must be true.' He paused. 'Listen! Do you hear that?'

Vicki felt as though she would collapse. As she strained to hear, screams rang out, very faint at first but rapidly becoming louder. The voices were accompanied by strange clanging noises.

'The Berserks are Norse warriors. They whip themselves into a frenzy, become insensitive to pain. They dress themselves in bear skins and howl like animals.' Sima spoke in a strange clipped voice.

Loki interrupted 'Most importantly - they live to fight and take delight in killing.'

'For heaven's sake,' Mohun burst in. 'You can't do this. We came here in peace.'

Loki laughed again. 'Your fate has been decided by the Aesir. Choose your weapons.' He sprang from the ground and settled on a narrow ledge some five meters above them.

Vicki felt her legs give way and she sat down with a thud. The screaming and crashing sounds were now much louder.

Sharon spoke briskly. 'I understand.' She seized an axe off the timber frame and pulled down one of the chain mail shirts. 'Sima! Take care of Vicki.' She grabbed another axe and threw it to Mohun. He caught it awkwardly and stared down at it in disbelief. She yelled, 'Mohun! Pull yourself together.'

As she spoke, the roaring and screaming became ear splitting. Four men burst out of the narrow opening at the top of the hill; gigantic figures dressed in animal skins and furs. They flung themselves against the rock face, heaved up stones and smashed them against the ground. Vicki shrieked in terror and the group paused. There was a dreadful silence and then they bellowed more loudly, some hitting themselves with their own weapons, tearing their hair and beating their fists on the ground; others biting their shields, their faces contorted with rage.

Sima shouted. 'This is Norseland. We have to die. They believe they can bring us back.' He pulled Vicki to her feet and pressed the hilt of a dagger into her hand. 'Keep hold of your weapon,' he shouted. 'When you fall, whatever happens, don't drop your weapon.'

Vicki stared at him aghast. She looked helplessly at Sharon. She was like a stranger; her face was grim, her eyes shone strangely. She nodded curtly at Vicki. 'Do as Sima says!' Behind her, Mohun's face was ashen with terror.

The Berserks were suddenly silent. Then they let out a mighty noise and rushed down the hill. For a moment the crew stood, horror struck. Sima shouted, 'Don't lose your weapon!' and ran forward. He called out in Russian and swung his axe above his head, brought it down in a wide arc and cleaved the shoulder of the foremost Berserk. The huge man bellowed and knocked Sima off his feet. As he brought his club down on Sima's head, Sima thrust his dagger upwards and the Berserk fell dead across him. Bright blood gushed across the grass.

Sharon leapt over the bodies and with a loud yell hacked at another of the Berserks. Mohun stood rigid with fear but when Sharon fell, he touched Vicki's arm and ran forward. Vicki stumbled back until she was pressed against the ECRV. She looked up. Loki was gazing down at the scene with amused interest. Time seemed to slow as she saw Mohun fall to his knees next to Sharon and the two remaining

Berserks stride towards her. The dagger dropped from her numb hands and she reached down desperately to pick it up. She felt an agonizing pain in her head and the horrible sensation of her dagger sinking into the stomach of the foul smelling beast. His scream rang in her ears. His coarse hair grated her cheek and his bloodshot eyes stared into hers. Then darkness overwhelmed her.

6

The air in the small room was stifling, and full of strange, alien smells. Five Anomee were lined up near the door. They listened attentively to Thomas, although as usual, their faces were expressionless in the flickering light of the oil lamps. Alistair could not be sure that he knew them. All the Anomee looked so similar to him; the symmetrical faces, handsome features and well formed bodies.

For a long time, Thomas had harangued the Anomee. Alistair had no idea what he was saying but he guessed that Thomas had started by interrogating them. Now he seemed to be giving detailed instructions and trying to make sure that he was being understood. He repeated the same phrases over and over. The Anomee replied shortly. A sound like 'ohee' seemed to mean 'yes.' Thomas ignored Alistair when asked for a translation and finally Alistair gave up and sat down on one of the narrow beds. He leaned back against the wall and closed his eyes. Sometimes he still felt that he might wake from this nightmare.

'Alistair!' Thomas was standing over him. 'Pay attention! This is very important. They will take you through the caves.' He gestured at the women. 'They will find Ceres and ask her to hide you.'

'What about you?' Alistair shook his head. 'What about Sally?'

'I will find Sally. It is safer if I go alone.' Thomas spoke sharply. 'You must not tell Ceres or anyone else about Sally. No one must know. Do not tell anyone about me.' His voice rose. 'Do you understand?'

Alistair was amazed at Thomas's agitation. The angel's face was creased into deep lines and he looked sick.

'They will kill you and they will kill Sally if I do not find her first. When I find Sally, I will come back for you. I am your only hope of returning to Earth. Do you understand?' Thomas repeated.

'No! I don't understand anything. We should contact John.'

'There is no time. I cannot explain. I must leave now and so must you. You must go with the Anomee.'

'I'm not going anywhere till you explain what's going on.'

'Any delay will endanger Sally. I must find her.'

Alistair's heart pounded. He felt acutely that he was about to make a wrong step but he had no idea what to do.

'By now the Millennium will be out of range.' Thomas opened the door. 'Come, I will show you.'

Alistair shook his head. 'What about the angels?' He grabbed Thomas's arm and then jumped back. The usual feeling of repulsion was stronger than ever, as though Thomas was giving off some form of electrical charge. 'Thomas! Why do the gourds call you "Diptera"?'

Thomas ignored the question. 'The Millennium is gone. Come, look.' They went out into the night. The lane was empty of people and most of the houses were dark. The moons had not yet risen and the stars burned brilliantly in the clear sky. Thomas pointed up to the northeast where the Millennium should be visible as a small slowly moving light. Alistair scanned the sky, his heart pounding again. The Millennium was gone.

Thomas ignored Alistair's stricken expression. 'It is as well that they are gone. You do not need the Millennium to return to Earth. I have other ways.'

'I can wait for Rick,' Alistair said stubbornly.

'You cannot survive here alone; if he comes at all you will be dead by then. You must find Ceres.'

When Alistair did not reply, Thomas said impatiently, 'I must leave. Tell Ceres that you escaped when you were out on one of your trips. Invent a story that Ceres will believe. Do not tell her about Sally. Do you understand?'

Alistair felt that there was something glaringly wrong with Thomas's argument but he did not know what. He shuddered as he remembered the image of Ceres' enraged face on the angels' wall. He felt a rising panic. 'I can look after myself. I would be safer here. I saw what Ceres did to earth.'

'It is not as you think. If you had moved to another place in the room, you may have seen another view.' Thomas was scanning the sky. 'I must leave. I will return with Sally.'

Alistair looked up at the sky again. 'Why would John leave without you? You told me that you were meant to return with them.'

Thomas paused. 'They think I am dead. I arranged it that way.' He did not wait for Alistair to reply. 'I must leave now. You must find Ceres.'

Thomas walked rapidly towards the arch, looked back for a moment and disappeared into the dark. Alistair stared after him for a few minutes. The street remained empty. He looked up at the sky. The stars were in their familiar positions. He could have been in a small European village, but for the unfamiliar odors, and he was suddenly overwhelmed with a terrible homesickness. Then the door opened and the two Anomee men stood silhouetted in the rectangle of soft light. They stood aside as Alistair entered the room.

The three women were packing clothes and food into bags. When they saw Alistair, the tallest of them put her hand against her chest and said 'Marisura.' She pointed to the other women and repeated the gesture - 'Elisura, Anisena.'

Alistair looked at each in turn and saw minute differences in their faces. He felt certain that none of these women was the one who had taken Sally and him through the caves. He copied the gesture, and said slowly 'Alistair.'

The three women repeated the name tentatively, softening the hard 't' sound. Marisura took a pile of clothing from the bed and gestured to the adjoining room. Alistair took the clothes and shut the door behind him. He changed quickly into the calf length brown trousers and pulled a lighter brown tunic over his head. The clothes draped softly against his skin. He relieved himself in the night bucket, splashed some water on his face and stood for a moment, looking around. He shrugged. What else could he do?

The lane was still empty and no one looked out to watch them leave. The women turned left up the laneway, away from the arch and paused where the lane ended in a small clearing. Three narrow paths led into the forest. There was a brief discussion and the women took the leftmost path and quickly disappeared into the gloom. Alistair ran to catch up. The women used no light and their pale clothing was only dimly visible in the starlight. He stumbled a few times but the women did not notice and kept up a steady pace. Finally they exited the trees and stopped abruptly. Selenis had risen in the north and illuminated the valley. The women conferred again for a moment and then set off at a fast pace, skirting the trees as they headed towards the hills.

Alistair cursed softly as he stubbed his feet against rocks and tree roots. The women looked back at him from time to time to make sure he was following before quickening their pace again. They were obviously worried about being seen.

As he stumbled on, a sense of unreality grew in Alistair. His time in Iceland seemed like something that had happened a long time ago, his home and family a distant dream. Then he thought of Sally and his stomach lurched. He wished violently that he had asked Thomas where Sally might be. The angel seemed so certain that he could find her. Perhaps he knew who had taken her.

Alistair was suddenly so frightened for her that he gasped and stopped. Terrible images of Zeus's domain, of Sally sprawled unconscious on the white marble floor, almost overpowered him. He leaned forward retching and finally sank to his hands and knees, shaking violently. He made a massive effort to regain control and breathed deeply. When he looked up, he saw that two of the women were some distance ahead while one of them walked back towards him. Marisura stopped a few feet away and gazed at him without expression. She waited until he started forward, then turned and went on.

The range of hills was now clearly visible in the moonlight and they walked more quickly. After several minutes they came to a small stream and Alistair recognized the rough log bridge that Sally and he had discovered the day before they first met the Anomee. They crossed over and turned left, following a well-worn path parallel to the hills. Finally they arrived at the entrance to the caves. Alistair looked inside. The women walked past him and into the darkness.

Alistair entered the cave. The moonlight cast a small circle of light. Beyond it was pitch black. He retreated and called out. How did they expect him to walk in the dark?

Marisura turned back and followed Alistair out of the cave. He pointed first to the moon, and then into the cave. He shut his eyes and pretended to fall. Marisura regarded him impassively but when he held his hands out and shrugged, she reached into her bag and pulled out a garment similar to her long tunic. She held the end of one sleeve and handed him the other. She turned away, pulling on the tunic and he understood. He sighed with frustration but followed her.

As he walked blindly through the tunnel he was reminded painfully of his journey with Sally and his stomach churned. Several minutes later he heard the faint sound of water, Marisura dropped the sleeve and they entered a faintly lit cavern. The women drank from the small stream of water, but backed away as Alistair approached. He cupped his hands to drink. The water had a slight metallic taste. He splashed his face and drank again. He felt exhausted, but he took hold of the tunic cuff when Marisura handed it to him.

Alistair remembered the two tunnels behind the small spout of water, but this time the women chose the one which veered right. Alistair pulled on the shirt and Marisura turned around. He pointed to the other tunnel. They stood for a few moments but Marisura turned back to the right hand tunnel. Alistair followed reluctantly. He had no way to make them understand. Perhaps this tunnel led to a different part of the gods' city.

The tunnel wound on, ascending gently. They passed through several caverns, some small and dimly lit, some larger and more brightly illuminated with a small spring and a basin to drink from. Alistair wondered again about the source of light. After a while, he ceased to think of anything. His legs felt like lead and he stumbled frequently. When the women stopped in a yet another cavern to take a drink, he sat down heavily. The three women looked at him and talked quietly. Marisura reached into her pack and pulled out a small bag. She untied the fastening and offered it to Alistair. He shook his head and leaned back against the wall. His eyelids drooped. He tried to stay alert but his head sank heavily onto his chest.

He felt a sudden sensation of happiness. He was sitting in his favorite café in Nantes; a delicious scent of coffee filled the warm air and sunlight glinted on the glass tabletops and chrome railings. Therese Larroque sat opposite him, her beautiful eyes gleaming over her demitasse. He had persuaded her to slip away from her husband's office and meet him for lunch. If the Professor discovered their affair it could mean the end of his studies at the best exogeology institute in Europe. He didn't care. His research project was almost complete and soon he would have to leave anyway. Meanwhile here was Therese; exotic, exciting, irresistible.

Alistair reached across the table to take her hand but she withdrew it quickly. She smiled provocatively, and shook her head. 'Tu deviens tout a fait folle!' Her voice sounded strange. Alistair looked at her questioningly and glanced behind him to see who she was speaking to. The café was crowded and no one was paying any attention to them. The scene blurred and he heard another woman speak in a low, soft monotone. 'Non, Marie.' He turned back but Therese was gone. Alistair's eyes flew open. He was not in France. Opposite him the three Anomee women sat in a small circle. Marisura whispered, 'Il faut que nous ...'

'What!' The shock made Alistair leap up. 'What!' he shouted again. 'You're speaking French!' The women looked at each other and then rose to their feet. Marisura tried to hand him the end of the shirt, but he grasped her arm. 'Vous parlez francais!' he repeated harshly. Elisura gasped and ran towards the far end of the cavern but Anisena caught up with her and led her back.

A strange scene followed; the women talked rapidly in their expressionless voices. They turned back and forth, shuffling in the sand, looking sideways at Alistair, and making minute gestures, their faces expressing little of their agitation.

Finally he shouted 'Parlez francais! Speak French, damn you.' He swore several times. Sally and Sima spoke French fluently. How ironic that they had never tried speaking in any other language to the Anomee. But why would they? Who would have thought that a group of aliens on another planet would speak a European language? He laughed bitterly and then swore again.

The women suddenly quietened, sat down and looked at him silently. Alistair's heart raced. For a moment he could not find the words. 'Of what are you speaking? Why do you speak French?'

There was another long silence. Then Marisura said, 'It is necessary that we tell him all.'

Alistair had spent almost a year in France and had visited most of the major cities. Marisura's French was blurred and strangely accented, with none of the usual nasal tones.

Anisena spoke briefly in Anomee and there was another silence. Finally Marisura said, 'You are English. Where did you learn to speak French?'

'I lived in France during one year when I had twenty five years of age.' When Marisura did not reply, he continued, 'Et vous? And you?'

Anisena spoke again but Marisura interrupted her. 'I was born Marie-Madeleine de la Trave. I was born in Paris. I was brought here when I was thirty years old.' She paused and continued in the same neutral tone. 'Elise and Anne also were born in Paris. The greater part of the people in our village lived in Paris when they were first born.'

Alistair ground his teeth. If only they had known. With great effort he restrained himself and looked closely at the two women. It seemed impossible to him that they were really from France. Their behavior, their voices were so completely alien. 'I do not believe you.' He struggled to find the right words. 'You are completely different to all the French people that I have met.'

Anisena avoided his gaze. 'We have been here a very long time.'

Alistair sat back. A suspicion was growing inside him that made him feel sick.

'Did you go to France with Thomas?'

Alistair stared at Marisura. He could not understand the question or why she would ask it. 'No. I have known Thomas only two years. I am now thirty five years of age.'

The women looked at each other and spoke rapidly in Anomee. Alistair tried to form questions into French but he was distracted by the women's behavior. They seemed to be changing in front of him. Subtle movements, the turn of the head, suddenly seemed overwhelmingly familiar to him.

'How long have you lived here?' Alistair tried to soften his voice. 'How long have you known Thomas?'

Marisura took some time to answer. 'I was brought here at the time of the great change. My thread ...' she paused. 'My life has been mended three times. I am not certain how much time I have spent here.' She paused again. 'But it is too long.'

Alistair's stomach heaved. 'And Elise, and Anne?'

'The same time.'

Alistair's head spun. He had an awful sensation of impending danger.

'How did you go to France?' Marisura's voice did not change but Alistair sensed the appeal in it. 'Thomas told us no one could return.'

Alistair immediately realized that Thomas had not revealed his own identity or that of the Millennium crew to these people. He repeated his question. 'For how long have you known Thomas?'

'For almost three years; since he came out of the islands. He told us he would help us, that there were more people like him, but we must tell no one about him.' She paused again. 'He told us that when the new star was born, our time would be near. We saw the star, traveling across the sky. Then you came, in your strange clothes, with your strange machines.'

Alistair interrupted. 'Please speak more slowly. I do not understand.'

Marisura repeated what she had said and then continued. 'We thought you had come to help us but you said nothing. We thought you were some new gods, playing some new game.'

'Did you not understand our language? You did not recognize that we spoke English?'

'Your language is so strange. I learned some English when I was at court but I could not understand any of you.'

Alistair thought hard. He could not figure out how this fitted with what had happened to him and Sally in the gods' city. But for certain, these women did not know Thomas was an angel or that the Millennium crew were from Earth. He shook his head, searching for some clue that would help him understand. He must be very careful not to reveal too much.

'Where are we going? It is safer in the village, is it not?' At least he could communicate with them now.

'Thomas told us to take you to Ceres. She will hide and protect you. You look so different. If the gods come to our village they would see at once you are not one of us. You must not tell anyone you speak our language. Not Ceres, nor anyone.' She paused again. 'You will help us, when you are able?'

Alistair nodded. 'I understand.' He picked up the sleeve of the tunic. 'Let us continue now.'

As he stumbled through the dark his mind raced, but he could not reach any conclusion. He kept returning to the same idea. He could trust no one. Thomas was obviously playing a double game, both with the angels and the gods. Why was he so anxious to find Sally?

They passed through several more small caverns and the number of tunnels leading out of them increased. Alistair guessed that these formed a network of caves that the Anomee might use to hide from the gods. He checked his watcher; it was more than three hours since they had left the village.

The tunnel suddenly rose steeply and Alistair stumbled and dropped the cuff of the tunic. He felt his way along the wall until it turned sharply to the right. One of the women stood outlined against a dim circle of light. When he reached her, she said 'Wait.' They stood for a few moments until another of the women appeared. She spoke first in Anomee and then in French. 'Anisena went ahead to find Ceres, but no one has seen her today. We must wait here until she returns. Anisena will bring some food.'

Alistair felt very uneasy but he followed the two women into the cavern. He waited until they sat down, then headed back towards the light. A few meters on the tunnel ended abruptly and he stood blinking up at Selenis's bright disk. Marisura came up beside him as he stared down at the gods' city and the white-capped island in the centre of the lake. A steep rough path led down the side of the cliff towards the maze of small houses some twenty meters below. Beyond he saw the wide alley leading down to the plaza. He felt again as though he were dreaming.

'Venez! Come!' Marisura did not touch him but he sensed her alarm. 'You will be seen.'

Alistair stepped back out of the moonlight, but continued to stare out over the gods' domain. 'Do not worry yourself. I will stay here with you. But I need some air.'

Marisura did not reply but remained watching him.

7

Pain tore across her belly, burned up her throat, escaped in a roaring gasp and was gone. Her head jerked up. Shaking with cold, she struggled against the darkness. Her chest heaved and she dimly heard her panting breath. Something soft brushed across her back. Warm sensations on her arms and legs became hands, gently stroking.

'Open your eyes. Oh brave one, open your eyes.' A low, calm voice was joined by others. Her eyelids trembled. She shook violently. The chant grew louder. She cried out in fright but her voice did not carry. A hand grasped her shoulder. She flinched.

'Hail Vicky!' Her eyes flew open. Vague shapes loomed. Strange movements flashed in the corners of her eyes. She stared into a woman's face; pale, unsmiling, huge blue eyes. She gasped and retched. The arm around her shoulders tightened and lifted her to sit.

'You have entered the realm of the gods and the site of the brave.' The woman spoke in a calm, cool voice. 'Tell your story.'

Vicki stared at her incredulously. Her hands touched a cool surface and she pressed against it, trying to push herself up. She could not move. Her arms and legs felt like lead. The woman's silvery hair fell across her shoulder as she leaned towards Vicki. 'Tell your story!'

'I am Xaio Law. I was cold, but now I am warm. I left my family and everything I know to come to this place.' Vicki realized she was speaking Mandarin. The words poured out of her as she looked around wildly. She could not understand anything she saw. Long white shapes lay to her left and right. Ahead, wide stone stairs rose steeply but the scene blurred as figures emerged and faded again.

She recalled her last moments and sobbed with terror. 'I am in the house of the dead,' she wailed.

'No! You are in the realm of the gods.' Vicki looked to her right. Another woman, with the same pale fall of hair and light blue eyes took her hand. She lifted a cup to Vicky's mouth and waited. Vicki gulped down the liquid. It flowed warmly down her throat. She drank again. The taste of grapes and honey filled her mouth and she felt a sudden joy.

'Tell us your story,' the woman repeated.

Vicki spoke again; her childhood, her parents, the long years of studies, friends, holidays, her favorite music, affairs she could scarcely remember, and finally the journey to Earth 2. Her voice went on and on but it gradually slowed and became calmer.

'Hail Mohun!'

To her left, a white shape jerked upright. With enormous effort she focused on Mohun's face. He was staring around, his mouth agape. He looked past her as though he did not recognize her. Two women supported him and placed a shawl around his shoulders. Their arms gleamed palely, almost as white as their long robes.

Sandaled feet approached. Vicki watched as two more women walked slowly past. The words still gushed from her mouth but the women did not look at her. They stopped at the white draped figure to her right. One woman knelt. The other dipped her hand into a large golden bowl and sprinkled the contents over the still form. Golden dust hovered in the air for a few seconds, and then the white form was engulfed in a rainbow of colors, pulsating in a slow rhythm. Vicki clutched her chest. Her heart was beating in time. She suddenly recalled how she had travelled from the landing site and heard herself describe the terrifying moments as they were pushed through the rainbow to face the Berserks.

The white form was shaking now. The covering fell back from Sima's naked body. His pale skin shimmered unblemished in the dim light. Vicki screamed. She tried to move, to reach him, but was held back.

The rainbow of colors faded one by one until only a scarlet haze remained. Sima jerked convulsively and gave a hoarse shout and the red mist flowed in through his open mouth. The two women helped Sima sit upright and whispered to him. There was another ringing cry. 'Hail Sima!'

Vicki looked up. On the stone stairs three tall men with long yellow plaits and a woman with a stream of golden red hair sat quietly, gazing down at her. Metal circlets around their hair and arms glinted in the golden sunlight.

Vicki gazed around. Now she could make sense of what she saw. The crew had been brought to a small amphitheatre and lay in a line across the smooth dark paving. Wide stone stairs circled the arena and rose steeply into the surrounding hills. The sky above was a dusky blue and the setting sun sent brilliant shafts through the small fluffy clouds. Vicki blinked against the light and lowered her eyes. Two white robed women emerged from an archway cut into the stairs. Like the others they were tall and fair, their long hair falling past their strong shoulders. The women paused and glanced up at the seated figures. The redheaded woman gestured, and the two women retreated into the archway's gloom.

'Hail Sharon!' The four seated figures raised their right arms in a salute. Intense beams of light shot out from their hands. Vicki squinted against the brilliance; it was the reflection of sunlight on rings which each of the four wore. She turned towards Sima, who was now sitting up and speaking very fast in Russian. He stared back at her without expression and her heart beat faster as she remembered that she loved him.

Beyond Sima, Sharon was drinking from a metal bowl. Further away John's figure remained unmoving; two women sat at his feet. Vicki shook with relief when she saw the commander lift his hand and pass it over his face.

To her left Mohun was speaking rapidly in his own language, his face blank. His expression changed when he saw Vicki. His voice slowed and faded, he swallowed several times and his face twisted with emotion. 'Vicki?'

Vicki slid across the stones and put her arms around him. He put his head on her shoulder and they both wept. 'It's alright,' Vicki murmured. 'I don't know how, but we're all here. We're alive.'

She felt gentle hands on her back and her mind misted over again. A slow, swinging movement woke her. Bright lights flickered. She saw flaming torches against a dark wall, casting deep shadows of moving figures. She gasped and groped around. She was being carried on some sort of stretcher.

'Be calm. It will not be long.' A pale face emerged from the shadows and Vicki's breathing steadied as she recognized the woman. The calm blue eyes gazed steadily into Vicki's. The wide shoulders hunched as she shifted her grasp on the long handles. Vicki lifted her head and glimpsed the file of women and stretchers winding up the path behind her.

She drifted in and out of sleep and could not tell how much time passed before she felt herself lifted onto a soft bed. She felt no alarm or fear, only a profound and peaceful joy. She sank back into the pillows and gazed up. Thick beams supported a high pitched roof. Smoke drifted up through the small vent, occasionally dispersing to reveal a dark sky sprinkled with brilliant stars. Shadows flickered on the ceilings and walls. A fire was burning brightly in a large central hearth. In its warm light Vicki could see that she lay in a circular room, surrounded by high couches. A cup was held to her mouth. She saw Sharon clasping her cup and gulping eagerly. Vicki tasted the same sweet wine and at once fell into a deep sleep.

8

The cock crowed loudly. It repeated its intense and piercing cry several times and the sound seemed to hang in the air long after it ended.

'What the hell was that?' Sharon had been dreaming that she was on her uncle's farm in Iowa. She sat up and shook her head. Her watcher showed four am. She tapped it and shook her head in frustration when the screen did not change.

The room was softly illuminated by the embers of the fire and sunlight slanting through the narrow doorway. Eight couches circled the walls. Three were empty. To her left and right Vicki and Mohun were stirring. Across the room John and Sima were sitting on the edge of their couches. She saw John staring at her and looked down at her loose brown robe. She had no memory of how she came to wear it.

'You have heard Gullinkambi. Every morning he awakes the heroes in Valhalla.' A blonde woman stood in the doorway. She gestured to her left and right. 'Here are rooms where you may refresh and clean yourselves. I will call for food and drink.' She turned and disappeared from view.

The crew gazed at each other in silence for several moments. Each showed a different reaction. Vicki and Mohun appeared calm and unconcerned. John's face was rigid with shock or disbelief. Sima frowned as though puzzled. He glanced at the empty couches and looked inquiringly at Sharon. She shrugged and shook her head.

Sima slid off the couch and went to the doorway. 'There's nothing nearby.' He looked at each of the crew in turn. 'Well, then. We all seem to be ok; which is amazing after what we went through.'

John took a deep breath. 'I don't remember a thing after climbing outside. Where the hell are we?'

Sharon gave a short laugh. 'According to the people here, what that woman said, we're heroes; we're to go to Valhalla.'

John gave an explosive snort and there was long silence.

Sima spoke slowly. 'This is what happened.' He gave a brief outline of the events as he recalled them, looking at the others for confirmation. Sharon nodded several times but John's expression became more impatient. Finally he interrupted. 'This is unbelievable.'

Sima started to reply but Vicki cut in. 'They killed you all. I was the last.' She gasped with the memory. 'I saw it, before…' She swallowed several times and then finished in a husky voice. 'And I saw you all before …. They did something to us.'

As John shook his head Sima continued, 'We've discussed before what has been happening since we arrived. John, you have to consider the possibility.' He looked around the room. 'You don't know what we went through. Does anyone remember it differently? Sharon? Mohun?'

'I saw Sharon die. She could not have survived.' Mohun shuddered as he remembered. He looked appealingly at Sharon and she nodded.

Sima shook his head. 'It is incredible but it all fits. As soon as I saw the one who calls himself Loki and the man called Heimdall, I realized. These people are right out of the Norse legends. They will tell us we are in Asgard. In Norse mythology that is the land of the immortals.'

John stood up. 'You can't be serious!'

'It doesn't matter what we think. These people speak Old Norse. The rainbow – you all remember that? All the sagas tell us the same thing. It is a bridge between the realm of the living and those killed in battles. Loki, Heimdall; it's completely consistent. Whether they simulated our deaths or whether we really died and they have brought us back. They must have some advanced medical knowledge, technology. As far as they are concerned we are in Asgard, the land of the Norse gods.'

Vicki rushed in. 'I do remember. Last night. The pain when they … whatever they did … They called us brave. They said we had entered the land of the gods.' She took a deep breath. 'I saw it all. Those women, they cast something over us and we breathed it in. Then we told them everything.'

'What do you mean?' Sharon frowned.

'Don't you remember? The woman said, "Tell me your story" and I kept talking. I told her things that I hadn't thought of for years. I remember I was speaking Chinese.' Vicki turned to Sima. 'And you were speaking Russian, very fast. And you too Mohun, in Konkani. And you John, you were whispering something.'

John cut in, his voice harsh. 'That's it. This is the same conspiracy. And now we know. They've done this to interrogate us. No one died. It's part of the same elaborate hoax.'

Sharon spoke in a flat voice. 'You died, John. I heard your last breath. I saw you die.'

Sima stood up. 'There's something you all need to see.' He went to the doorway and beckoned.

To the left and right of the entrance, narrow openings led to small rooms. Vicki peered inside; shelves held bowls, cups and other dishes. Several round stools were set against a small scrubbed wood table. The other room she guessed to be a washroom and toilet.

She blinked as she passed through the doorway. The sun was bright in the clear sky. Beyond the paved entrance, lush green grass sprinkled with small wildflowers spread out to the horizon. She stepped forward cautiously and looked around. Their hut was one of many buildings which dotted the valley; small circular houses with wide eaves and what appeared to be thatched roofs. There was no sign of the inhabitants. The valley was silent save for the faint whisper of breeze ruffling the long grass.

'I woke up before the rest of you. The women followed me but they did not try to stop me.' Sima gestured up a path to a small hill. 'Over there is what they call the Hall of the Gods. I couldn't tell how far away it is but it's huge.' He turned. 'Look at this.'

To the left of the entrance, in the shadow of the eaves, hung a variety of weapons and some dark shapes. Mohun moved closer, gasped, backed away. The silver space suits and black body suits were stained with dried blood, slashed and ripped.

'Look!' Sima reached up and pulled down one of the space suits. The insignia showed that it belonged to John. Sharon took it and examined it closely. Her face paled as she handed it to John.

Vicki made a choking noise and clapped her hand over her mouth. Particles of singed flesh and hair still clung to the suit and it gave off a shocking smell of burnt meat.

'I don't think that we need DNA tests to show us what happened.' Sima looked at Vicki as though for the first time and put his arm around her. 'We were all killed or at least fatally wounded. These people have the technology to … some sort of cell regeneration process.'

John fingered his suit and stared at the bloodstains. He clutched his chest and let out a muffled shout. His eyes gaped as he ran his hands over his torso. He tore at the ties on his robe and stared down. The skin was clear and healthy. He put his hands to his face and rubbed his short hair. His eyes were wide and staring. Vicki had never seen him so affected.

Sima continued. 'It's not so difficult to believe. We've known for several years the theory of how to stop cells from degenerating when they replicate. We just don't have the technology to do that or to regenerate dead cells.'

Only Sharon and Vicki listened. Mohun lifted the other suits down and checked each one. The black body suits were in the same condition. He shuddered as he recalled staring down at Sharon's body. The Berserk's axe had slashed deep into her neck and shoulder. Her skin now was unblemished. He clapped his hand over his mouth as he started to retch.

'Don't think about it. It's over.' Sharon took his arm.

John stumbled away, stopped abruptly and stood motionless. Just as suddenly he turned and walked rapidly back. He had fastened his robe and his face was calm.

'We need to make a plan.' Sima positioned himself as though taking command. 'I can brief you on how these people might act. We need to be prepared this time ...'

John interrupted. 'Yes. Thank you, Sima. It's quite obvious that we can't defend ourselves. Still, they must have let us live for some reason. We need to find out why that is and use it to our advantage. The first thing is to send a message to Rick.' He lifted his watcher and started to speak.

Sima laughed harshly. 'Inactive. I think you'll find none of the watchers work – except for the local time.'

The others stared down at their watchers and there was a moment's silence.

'Right,' said John grimly. We have to find a way back to the pyramid to send a message. We need to let Rick know what's happening. We just have to survive; weeks or months. We just have to get through it until Rick gets here. And we have to …'

'And who is Rick?' The question was followed by a loud peal of laughter. Loki emerged from behind the hut. His face was shadowed but Vicki felt again a strong revulsion and stepped behind Sima.

No one spoke. John stared without expression at the tall blonde man.

Loki stepped forward. 'Well? I asked you a question.'

'Who are you? Why did you bring us here?' John tried to keep his gaze steady but his eyes dropped.

'You are the leader of your people, but I could finish you with a wave of my hand. Do not challenge me John.' Loki laughed at John's surprise when he heard Loki speak his name. He extended his arm to the rest of the crew. 'Let it be known to you all. I am the god of fire. Defy me and you will burn.'

John stood frozen for a moment, but as Sima started to speak John cut in. 'I acknowledge you. Tell us what you want.'

'I want nothing,' Loki replied in an amused voice. 'Perhaps in another time, elsewhere' He shook his blonde hair and looked regretful. 'But no, that is not allowed to me.' Just as quickly his mournful expression was replaced by a malicious smile. 'You will all be taken to Gladsheim where you will be questioned as to why you left your homes to intrude in our realm, and …'

'We intended no disrespect.' John stopped as Loki's face turned red with anger at the interruption. He bit his lip, staring hard at John for several moments. Mohun felt his heart turn cold at the expression on Loki's face.

Loki suddenly smiled again and waved his hand as though dismissing John from his mind. 'Listen carefully. You will be taken to the great hall of Gladsheim where the Aesir, the immortals, meet to decide the fate of the realms. There you will be questioned. You will answer all questions honestly, and you will freely tell us all we desire to know; where you have traveled, what you have learned of the ice land, and all the realms beyond. If any one of you conceals the truth or attempts to deceive us you all will be cast out from Asgard. You will meet the Berserks in battle again and this time the Valkyrien will not be there to bring you back from the realm of the slain. You are mortals and you will remain slain.' Loki looked around. The crew stared at him silently.' Return to your couches. In a short time, others will come and you will be prepared for your meeting with the immortals.'

He made an elaborate gesture and rose into the air, his arms and legs extended as though seated on a large chair. He hovered a few feet above them and smiled at each in turn. Vicki flinched as her eyes met his.

'Take care, mortals. Choose your words wisely.' He continued to smile as he accelerated towards the hill and his laughter rang out again as he drifted out of sight.

9

Alistair rubbed his neck. The effort of speaking and listening to French was giving him a headache, but he felt a frantic need to learn as much as he could before these women left him. Anisena had just returned, bringing more supplies, but no news of Ceres. She had spent all day searching and would go out again at dawn. The Anomee were not permitted to be out after dark, unless on the immortals' business.

He reflected on what he had been told. According to these women, most of the people on Earth 2 had been brought here several thousand years ago from Neolithic settlements in Iraq and southern Turkey. It was their language, modified greatly by their interactions with the immortals, which formed the basis of the Anomee speech. Some of the people in this city however had been abducted from ancient Greece.

Beyond that, these women knew very little about their world. They had never traveled beyond the surrounds of their village and the gods' city. They knew nothing of the people whom Thomas told them lived secretly in the northern islands; the people which they believed Thomas and Alistair belonged to. And they shuddered when Alistair mentioned the angels; the Anomee feared the Diptera even more than the immortals.

Marisura explained that Anomee who were injured or who showed signs of aging or disease were mended. After this mending, the Anomee could not reproduce and almost no one remembered when the last Anomee children had been born. Her expression did not change when she said this but Alistair received a distinct impression of distress. He could understand why. The thought of living for hundreds, even thousands of years in this situation disgusted him. How could he trust Ceres or anyone else who allowed such things to happen?

'If you cannot find Ceres, then what will we do?'

'If so, we must wait for Thomas.' Marisura handed Alistair a flask from the bag that Anisena had brought back with her.

Alistair thought for a moment and decided to risk a question. 'Can you tell me; why did one of your people, another woman, take me and my woman friend to the god's city?'

'Thomas told us to take you to the caves.'

'Why?'

'I do not know.' Marisura looked at him impassively. She continued to unpack the satchel and offered him some food.

Alistair took a bite from an oval fruit which tasted remarkably like a pear. 'Is it possible that these people, from Turkey, from Iraq, truly can live for thousands of years? How many times can the gods make these repairs?' Alistair tried to sound conversational.

Marisura spoke slowly. 'We do not know. I have heard that sometimes people are taken away for a long time. When the gods return them, they look much younger but they cannot remember much of their earlier life. This has never happened to our people.'

'Do you remember what happened when you were mended?'

Marisura paused. 'Each time, I was taken to the island.' She waved her hand towards the exit. 'Below the mountain there are long tunnels and caves, great caves. Many people went. We were told to sleep. We slept. When we woke we were given food and drink. Time passed. I cannot remember how long. When I returned home I felt very well.'

Alistair chewed for a few moments and took another drink. 'So you are happy? You are not angry because the gods took you from your home in France and brought you here?'

Elisura interrupted. 'You must understand. If we had not come here we would have died. Perhaps you have learned some history in France. We served at the court of Marie Antoinette, in Paris. The Parisians rose up against the king and we had to flee. Many of our friends were killed on the road to Versailles.'

Alistair nodded. 'Yes I do recall. I learned something at school. Not much.'

Elisura continued. 'When I awoke here, I thought we had come to heaven. But we have been here too long. It is not natural to live like this; to have no children to care for, nothing to hope for, to never die.' Her voice quickened slightly and Alistair could not understand what she said next. When he asked her, Marisura cut in. 'There is nothing we can do to change the situation; unless Thomas can help us. He said he would.'

'What did he say?'

'He did not tell you?' When Alistair shook his head, Marisura said, 'He told us the Diptera do not approve of how we live and that he would ask them to free us from the gods.'

Alistair nodded as though he agreed, and his uneasiness increased. It made no sense. Thomas had never showed any interest in the Anomee and their welfare.

'I will try to sleep now,' he said. 'Thank you for the food.' He spread out one of the thin blankets and lay down.

He was very tired. He had hardly slept since leaving Iceland. And when he did he had strange dreams about France and his affair with Therese. His mother's face, as he had seen it on the angels' wall continuously flashed before his eyes. Each time she looked more anxious.

But he could not sleep. His mind buzzed with what he had learned. Somewhere there must be a clue to what Thomas intended and he needed to be ready to take action. He cast aside the idea that still plagued him – that this was all a delusion – and tried to review what he knew. Despite the angels' assertion that they could not lie, Thomas had deceived everyone.

But some facts seemed clear. The immortals and possibly the angels had visited Earth many times and had abducted large numbers of humans. They had advanced technology, could modify the appearance of the material world and their own appearance, and regenerate human life indefinitely. The angels tolerated the immortals' existence but did not approve of them. Alistair's stomach clenched. Why was Thomas so concerned about Sally?

He sat up abruptly. This was getting him nowhere. He had to wait. He had kept his patience in Iceland, even as Sally became increasingly agitated. He breathed deeply and tried to calm himself, using every technique he knew to clear his head. Nothing helped and his frustration grew until he thought he would strike out.

'I have need of some air.' He walked past the three women and groaned as Marisura got up to follow him. 'I need to be alone for some moments.' Marisura sank back to the ground and then sprang up again as Alistair passed the passage way to the small cavern which they had used for waste, and headed for the exit tunnel. She ran forward and pushed past him as though to bar his way. When he stopped just before the opening she relaxed. She said, 'It is dark. No moon yet.'

'What do you call the moons?'

Marisura spoke a few words in Anomee, and said in French. 'Simply, small and grand.'

'We named them Artemis and Selenis, as the ancient Greeks did.'

'You should not call them so here.'

Alistair shrugged; another piece of information that might be useful. He leaned against the wall and stared at the pale outline of Marisura's face. Why did her people look so similar? They must have been very different originally. Was she telling the truth? As though she knew what he was thinking, she turned away and peered out of the tunnel. He heard her gasp. 'Quickly. Hide. Someone is coming.'

Alistair ran back to the cave and into one of the passageways. He fumbled along the dark tunnel for a few meters and then listened intently. Someone was entering the passage. He held his breath and pressed against the wall, then relaxed as he heard one of the Anomee whispering. 'It is all right. Come.'

The cavern was illuminated by a brilliant device, which fastened the garment on a tall figure in the centre of the cavern. Pale arms emerged from the dark cloak and pushed back the hood, revealing long blonde hair. Alistair sighed with relief, but the figure turned and Venus's radiant face smiled at him. He recoiled but was immediately drawn towards her. He felt at once the overwhelming power of her beauty and an urgent sense of danger.

'Where is Ceres?' he asked hoarsely. He turned to Marisura. 'Why did you let her come here?'

Marisura shook her head as though she did not understand. She stood passively, her eyes downcast. As

Venus walked towards him Alistair backed away. 'Where is Ceres?'

Venus stood so close to him that he could feel her breath on his face. He felt dizzy and closed his eyes. Venus ran her hand down his cheek and he started to shake. With enormous effort, he turned his head away. 'Stop that! I need to see Ceres.'

'Ceres is gone. She has gone with Diana. Hercules has sent them to seek an alliance. Zeus is become mad.' Venus spoke English, her beautiful melodic voice lilting as though she were reporting some pleasant news. 'Hercules will tell you. He will be here soon.' She placed her hand on Alistair's shoulder and he felt a violent shudder pass through his whole body. He wrenched away and staggered over to the other side of the room.

'This is not what we agreed.' He turned to Marisura. 'Take me back to the village.' He started to repeat what he had said in French, but she cut in quickly. 'No. Please.'

Venus spoke sharply and the three women began to gather up their belongings. She turned to Alistair and her voice softened. 'You will stay here with us. Hercules will tell you what to do.'

Alistair thought frantically. If he followed the women, Venus would use her powers to make him stay, and that idea made his skin crawl. He looked at the women as they sidled around the room, but they turned away from him.

A loud clanging noise suddenly reverberated through the chamber and Venus smiled. 'Hercules is here.' She gestured to the women and they backed against the wall, their heads bowed.

Several sharp noises followed and Hercules emerged from the tunnel. He stood for a moment, looking around. He was dressed in the same manner as in Zeus's palace; a short kilt of some sort of animal skin and laced sandals. His bronzed skin shone and his pale gold hair and his round shield glistened in the light of Venus's clasp, as though an ancient Greek statue had come to life. Alistair clenched his teeth as he met the brilliant blue eyes. He had tried to forget how much Hercules resembled his brother. The familiar face darkened into a scowl when he saw the Anomee. He spoke harshly to Venus and then strode forward and seized Anisena by the throat. He shouted at her in a thunderous voice and shook her like a rag doll.

Alistair was frozen with surprise for a few seconds. He ran at Hercules. 'Leave her alone! She did as she was asked.'

Hercules flung his arm out and knocked Alistair to the ground. He dropped Anisena and roared at Alistair. 'How did you escape from the Diptera?'

Alistair gasped for a few seconds, winded by the blow. He looked at Marisura but she turned away. Elisura cowered behind her. Anisena lay motionless, covering her head with her hands.

'I don't know. How would I know? I don't understand anything. Something, someone took me away, to their village.' He heard a grating noise. Hercules was unsheathing a short sword. The huge figure reached down and dragged Anisena upright. He held the sword to her throat and shouted. When she did not answer, he shouted again. She tried to speak but she could not make a sound. Her face was still without expression but her eyes were staring. Finally she whispered 'Thomas.'

Hercules did not let her continue. He shook her violently and this time Alistair heard the name Thomas repeated several times. Venus stood by, showing no reaction. Alistair pulled at the hem of her cloak and whispered, 'What does he want?' Her face warmed as she looked down at him and

Alistair felt again his involuntary response. 'He wants to know where Thomas is. Thomas, the traitor. He was seen here two days ago.'

There was a long silence. Hercules kept the sword pressed against Anisena's neck. Alistair felt paralyzed. To say anything could be a terrible mistake, but if he kept silent, Hercules might kill one of the women.

'I saw the man you call Thomas.' His voice cracked and he coughed. Marisura turned to look at him. 'I saw Thomas. When I was dropped near the caves, I saw him. He went inside.' He made himself look up at Hercules. 'That is the truth.' Hercules lowered his sword as Alistair continued. 'No one else was there. I did not follow him. I went to the village to look for my friends but they had gone.' He pointed to Marisura, 'So these women brought me here.'

Hercules' amazing blue eyes fixed on him for a long moment and then he waved dismissively at the women and spoke sharply. Marisura help Anisena to her feet. They both glanced at Alistair before following Elisura out of the cave. Alistair felt a pang to see them go, but there was nothing they could do to help him. Hercules prodded him roughly towards the exit. When he reached the opening, Alistair resisted. 'I can't see the way. Do you want me to fall?'

Hercules muttered something and Venus went ahead, lighting the narrow path. Alistair followed, balancing himself against the cliff face. He wished violently that he and Sally had spotted this path when they were trapped in the city but he guessed that it was barely visible from below.

The path did not lead down to the maze of small houses. It leveled off for some fifty meters or so, ascended steeply and ended on the flat roof of one of the larger buildings which butted the eastern headland. The bright crescent of

Selenis was ascending above the cliff and Alistair instinctively moved to the shadows of the rock face.

Hercules hissed something and then repeated in English. 'Stay here!'

Alistair sat down and leaned against the rock. Every time he looked at Hercules he felt a terrible pain in his heart. He had tried to maintain his daily ritual but this morning he had felt no connection with Jeremy. He could hardly imagine how his family would feel when John sent the news of his disappearance. Would they believe he was dead?

Venus had extinguished her luminous clasp and was barely visible against the dark rock. Alistair could hear her whispering and Hercules' sharper replies. Her pale hand emerged from her cloak and reached up to the tall god. Hercules moved away abruptly and Alistair wondered if she had the same effect on the gods as she had on him. Their faces, made pale by the moonlight, turned towards Alistair, He averted his eyes and felt a sharp pain as Hercules kicked him.

'So, mortal. Are you ready to tell us why you are here?'

'I don't know anything; only what I told you.'

Venus spoke rapidly to Hercules in the immortals' language and took Alistair's arm. 'You can trust us. Tell us what you know.'

Alistair tried to pull away but his head was spinning from Venus's scent. 'Let me go. I feel sick.' He turned away and started to retch. Venus started back as though he had hit her. He wiped his mouth. 'The angels, the Diptera took us; you saw that. They imprisoned us. They told us nothing; only that we could not return to our ship. Then, somehow, something took me to the village. I have no idea why.'

Hercules snorted in disbelief but Venus spoke more kindly. 'It is important that we know everything. We are all in great danger. Zeus has decided to make a final stand against the Diptera. For some reason, he thinks he can overcome them. But this is madness. They are not flesh like us. They are indestructible. They want to be rid of us but something restrains them. But if we attack them they will have good reason to destroy us.' She continued slowly, as if to ensure that Alistair understood. 'Therefore we must stop Zeus. Diana and Ceres have gone south to ask the immortals there to help us. But every time we turn around, there is Thomas, working against us. We don't know why he conspires with the Diptera. He can gain nothing from them. They care nothing for the Anomee.' Venus's voice rose. 'Or for us. They care only about their own mysterious purposes.'

Alistair at once realized that the gods, like the Anomee, did not realize Thomas was an angel, or that he had travelled to Earth 2 with the Millennium crew. He wondered for a moment why that was so, but was interrupted by another sharp nudge from Hercules.

'Take heed, mortal. Tell us how we can reach your friends. They may have something to help us.'

Alistair hesitated. There was no point concealing what would soon be obvious. 'They have left Earth 2. They must think I am dead.' He pointed up. 'See! Our ship would cross the sky, right there, every few hours if they were still in orbit. But it's gone.'

As Hercules stared up at the sky, Alistair continued in a rush. 'But they will come back and if you harm me, you will …'

Hercules interrupted him. 'Well then. You stay here. If you move from this place before I return, I will find you and kill you.' He nodded at Venus and then appeared to walk off the side of the flat roof. Venus glanced at Alistair and sat down sedately, arranging the drapery of her cloak around her. She pulled the hood across her face and was silent.

Alistair shivered. He crouched down and clasped his arms around his knees against the cool night air. The two moons now hung over the city, casting long shadows and adding mystery to the strange landscape. The symmetrical cone of the mountain shone brilliantly but no other lights showed on the island or in the city. Alistair closed his eyes and wondered where Sally was. He was so exhausted he could hardly think. He leaned to one side and tried to pillow his head on his folded hands. The rock grated against his cheek but he fell into an uneasy sleep.

He awoke to a terrible roaring noise and a brilliant flashing light. For several moments he had no idea where he was, and he could see nothing through the glare. Then he glimpsed Venus, standing pressed against the wall, her eyes wide with fright, her hand over her mouth.

The dawn sky was pale and clear, but above the lake a dark cloud had formed. It roiled furiously, revealing a deep purple interior from which bolts of dark red light were fired. They struck the western headland with ear splitting cracks and huge slabs of rock slid down into the water, sending up fountains of spray. The city below was deserted; its inhabitants had fled or were hiding.

Venus screamed and pressed back against the rock.

'What is it? What's happening?' Alistair could hardly hear his voice above the noise. He ran to the edge of the roof. The wall of the house dropped a sheer twenty feet. He looked around frantically but there was no way off the roof except to go back along the narrow path.

More crashing noises followed and then a loud low whine like enormous gears scraping against each other. Beyond the western cliff a brilliant object shot into the sky and sent a volley of what looked like golden spears into the dark cloud, which retreated at amazing speed and disappeared behind the snow capped mountain. Pulses of light - red, gold and purple – flashed out behind Olympus like some huge fireworks display.

'Zeus has evoked his aegis against us,' Venus said bitterly. Her face was wet with tears. 'Now it is war. It cannot be avoided.' She pulled away from Alistair. 'This is what you have done to us. I would pray to Gaia to send her furies, but she is not here.'

Alistair shouted at her, asking her what she meant, but she pressed back against the wall as though she did not hear him and as the noise increased she became almost insensible with terror. She pleaded and cursed, calling out names that he recognized; Diana, Apollo, Athena.

Alistair himself became numb as the battle raged on. The golden vehicle raced back and forth across the sky, narrowly avoiding the bolts of lightning which issued from Zeus's storm cloud. They detonated with ear splitting cracks and Alistair clapped his hands over his ears. Zeus could be seen dimly within, clad in vivid purple robes, his face lurid with anger. As the dark cloud and the golden aircraft wheeled and dived above the lagoon the sky became thick with smoke and strange bursts of colored fire. The air reeked of sulfur and other vile smells, which Alistair could not recognize.

As the sun rose towards the noon, the cloud seemed to diminish. Venus sprang forward, shook her fist and shouted 'Apollo!' in a triumphant voice. A golden torrent rained down on Zeus's dark shield and finally the cloud retreated to the island and disappeared. The golden craft made one last triumphant dash across Olympus, streaked above their heads and out of sight. As the sky gradually cleared to reveal the wreckage of the town Venus spoke in an excited voice. 'Zeus must know now that he cannot prevail. Even his youngest son can best him.'

Alistair could not speak. The plaza was littered with broken columns and piles of stones and the surrounding buildings were ruined. Great gaping holes showed smashed interiors, the wooden floors and furniture burning furiously. He felt sick, suffocated, his throat burning and his eyes streaming.

Venus looked at him without sympathy. 'Now we must wait for Hercules.'

Alistair clutched his head. 'Can you at least get me some water?'

'I dare not. Not with Zeus so nearby. I would reveal myself. We must wait for Hercules.' Venus sank down and leaned back against the wall. She gave Alistair an almost hostile look. 'I will not risk anything for you. Diana warned me.'

'What?'

'If you had not come, Zeus would not think to challenge the angels. We have lived in peace with the Diptera, even though we hate them. We could have gone on so, and forgotten your people. You are to blame.'

Alistair stared at her aghast. 'What the hell do you mean?'

'I cannot explain.' Venus's voice was flat. She pulled her hood over her head and folded her arms across her chest.

Alistair stumbled forward and stared over the city. The plaza and the lanes remained deserted. No one emerged to fight the fires; the inhabitants had fled or they would not show themselves. Thick smoke clouded the lake and obscured the white-topped mountain. He looked down at the maze of cottages below him and recalled how he and

Sally had come to this place. The events since that time raced through his mind like a speeded up movie. He felt a tension mounting in him until he thought he would burst. He could not continue like this.

He walked across the roof and carefully stepped on to the narrow pathway. At its lowest point the path was only a few meters above the eastern end of the maze of Anomee houses. Alistair glanced back. Venus had not moved. He took a deep breath. Keeping his back pressed against the wall and his eyes on Venus he edged down the steep path. As he emerged from the shadows he moved more quickly. He felt terribly exposed, like a fly on a bare wall. But nothing stirred in the town below and the lake was still veiled by smoke.

When the path started upwards towards the caves he stopped and looked down. The cliff face was rough but not vertical. He did not hesitate but dropped to his knees and swung over the edge. He felt around for a foothold, and slithered painfully down to the ground.

He opened the door of the nearest house. There was no one within. He drank a full ewer of water and then crept along the small laneways trying to stay parallel to the cliff. After a few minutes he groaned with frustration. It was impossible to remember exactly where he and Sally had left the pack. The interior of each house was almost identical. He looked up towards the rooftop. There was no sign that Venus had missed him. He started a systematic search of all the houses in the area where he and Sally had been held.

The tension became unbearable but finally his hand touched the pack, still stowed under the bed where he had left it. He pulled it out and sank down on the floor. The pack was untouched, and the lock responded to his thumbprint. His hands trembled as he pulled out the contents.

He had not thought beyond this point. Should he return to Hercules and Venus, or should he try to find Thomas and Sally?

He shook his head. He had no real choice. It would be insane to travel alone and unarmed on this planet. He looked longingly at his scanner and tool kit. They were too large for concealment. He activated the data pads and sighed with relief when he saw that they were still functioning. He transferred Sally's data to his pad and checked the communications icon. No signal. He cursed softly, thrust the data pad into his trousers and secured it beneath the waistband. He returned everything else to the pack and pushed it back under the bed.

When he emerged from the lane he saw Venus descending the path towards him. Her face was anxious.

'What are you doing? You cannot escape Hercules.'

'I had to relieve myself.' Alistair replied roughly. 'I am not an animal to piss in public. I have feelings.'

Venus crouched down and extended her hand as he clambered back up. She pulled him up the remaining few feet as though he was a small child. He stumbled against her and she clasped him for a few moments until he found the will to push her away. Her slender figure was misleading. She was as strong as the other immortals. Fortunately she did not seem inclined to use force to get her way.

Alistair ran quickly ahead of her, back up to the roof. There was still no sign of life but he was glad to be off the exposed cliff face.

Venus stood in front of him in an alluring pose. When Alistair looked away she frowned. 'We must remain concealed and wait for Hercules. Can I trust you to stay here?'

The data pad pressed against his waist, Alistair felt a new confidence. 'What do you think? You blame me for your problems. If you give me something to drink and eat, I promise to stay here until Hercules comes back.'

Venus hesitated, then she gave a soft hiss and made a quick gesture. She put the flask and bowl at his feet and moved away, pulling her hood over her head again. 'Be quiet now.'

Alistair drank the same invigorating liquid he remembered from the nights he had spent in the city. His head cleared and he felt his strength return. The bowl contained a warm thick soup. He took a sip and stood up. 'What if Hercules does not come back?'

'He will return.' Venus was almost invisible in the cliff's dark shadow. 'Drink your broth.'

Alistair drained the bowl and almost immediately a warm sensation spread through his body. It rose through his chest and throat and his eyelids drooped. He shook his head but the outline of the city blurred and he felt his legs go weak. 'Damn it! What did you ...?' The bowl clattered on the rock as he slumped to the ground.

10

For three days and nights they had travelled with very little rest. The islands were growing larger and closer together and were now patched with cushions of dark moss and tiny purple, yellow and blue flowers. In the distance Sally could see more vegetation on the islands to the south. She wondered again at the ability of the immortals and angels to change the appearance of things. When the crew had flown north in the shuttle, the islands between Southland and the ice belt had been devoid of life.

Her questions to Ceres and Diana were always met with the same answer. 'We will tell you when you need to know' or 'there is no time for that now.' Perhaps they didn't know; like people on earth who used cars and watchers but had no idea how they worked. She had watched carefully each time Diana or Ceres conjured up food or drink and had practised the gestures when she was alone, but with no success.

As usual Ceres and Diana were well ahead of her. They waited occasionally for her to catch up but then sped on. Sally was amazed at her own endurance. After several weeks of idleness in Iceland she should have been suffering from sore muscles and aching feet. Instead she felt invigorated. The few hours of sleep snatched during the short boat trips between the islands seemed sufficient. She awoke each time with a clear head and a burning desire to move on.

Her eyes searched for the two figures in the distance. Yesterday all three of them had changed to close fitting tunics and trousers in a light grey brown color, camouflage against the rocky surfaces of the islands. Sometimes only the glint of Diana's weapons showed her location, but Sally did not mind. She was glad of the time alone, judging her progress by the movement of the sun or the march of the two moons across the night sky. With every step she took she felt nearer to her purpose – to find out what was happening on this bizarre planet, to rescue Alistair and return to Earth. Sometimes her confidence wavered and she wondered again if she was suffering from delusions. But the feeling soon passed; she had no choice.

A silver flash caught her eye. She ran faster and within moments she had caught up to Diana and Ceres, standing near the water's edge. As usual Diana had created a circular vessel, which from above would resemble a large rock. She seemed to be listening intently and suddenly hissed, 'Down! Get down.' She and Ceres threw themselves face down into the boat and pulled their hoods over their bright hair. Sally did the same and waited, aware only of her pounding heart. They remained that way for several minutes and then the boat moved slightly as Diana straightened up and looked around.

'Hermes!' Diana spoke several words emphatically.

Ceres translated. 'Hermes would never willingly pass over The White Land. Perhaps we are too late.'

For several minutes she and Diana spoke in their own language, and finally Diana said, 'What choice do we have?' She pushed the boat away from the shore. When Ceres went to pull the cover back over them, Diana stopped her. 'I would rather face my doom than have Hermes slay me like Argus in the dark. That bitch Hera has set him on to us.'

Ceres shook her head. 'Letting him take Sally will not help us now. When Zeus has finished with her, Hera will still want revenge.'

Sally's heart thumped but she kept silent.

Ceres noticed her reaction. 'Do not be alarmed. We would gain nothing by giving you up. It would reveal our plans.'

Sally's temper rose at this casual dismissal. 'If we could somehow return to Earth, we could get help. We could end all this.' She glanced at Diana who regarded her with a calculating expression.

Ceres shook her head. 'That is our last resort.'

Diana sneered. 'And to be exiled to your world, as it is now, would be a living hell for us. Better to go back to from where we came. I would rather …'

Ceres cut in sharply. Diana argued but finally slumped down making the boat rock wildly and as if in response to her mood, the vessel accelerated through the water. She looked at Sally through narrowed eyes. 'Get some rest mortal. You will need it.'

The boat settled into a long swaying motion. It was hard to judge the speed at which they travelled until they passed by another island. Instead of landing, the boat veered to the right and quickly passed along the island's western shore. Small shrubs and bushes flashed past. The sun was nearing the horizon as they reached yet another island and once again the boat passed it by. Sally stared up at the clear evening sky and watched the steady rise of Selenis. The constellations to the south were more familiar and she searched for the Southern Cross, but it was not yet visible. Suddenly she saw a streak of silver to the east, moving more slowly than a falling star. Diana cursed again as the light disappeared over the horizon. 'By Gyges' ring, does that thief never rest?'

Sally ventured a question. 'Would he really harm you? Isn't he your brother?'

Diana laughed shortly. 'Ha! So you do know some history. No, I don't own him as a brother. My father spawned so many, on anything that moved; I am sister to half the world, if I cared to believe him. Hermes is Hera's slut and no friend to me.' She looked shrewdly at Sally. 'And what of you? Do you have brothers who would come to your rescue?'

Sally thought briefly of the handsome woman whom she could still not accept as her mother. 'I don't know who my real parents are,' she said, 'or if I have brothers or sisters.'

'An unwanted child. That explains many things.'

Ceres interrupted and spoke at length in the immortals' language. Sally listened closely. She was starting to hear patterns but the meanings of individual words escaped her. When Ceres paused, she asked quickly, 'With regards to history, I am rather confused. You and several other gods use names which we believe the Romans called you by. But Zeus and Hera and others, they call themselves by names which we think of as Greek.'

Diana looked at her in amusement. 'We call ourselves as we please. Zeus likes to think of himself as an almighty deity.' She laughed. 'When we have time I will complete your education; but not now.' She stood up on the seat, and the boat tipped alarmingly. 'We should disembark soon and travel overland again.'

Sally wondered how far south they had travelled but did not want to display her ignorance. Her knowledge of the night sky was too casual for her to estimate where they were. She dozed off again and was awakened by a light shower of rain. The boat was slowing down and she saw they were approaching a dark land mass. Diana waited impatiently and then jumped down into the shallow water.

The white beach sloped up gently up to a dark forest which extended like a wall in both directions. Ceres followed more cautiously and signaled for Sally to wait. She looked around, making a loud sniffing sound. 'There is a strange smell here. Perhaps we should continue by water.'

Diana shook her head. 'It will take us much longer. We will have to go too far to the west to find a passage.' She ran lightly up the beach and disappeared. A few moments later, her head and shoulders appeared above one of the dark trees. She clung swaying to the branch for a few moments and then they heard her jump to the ground. She was hissing with frustration as she stamped back onto the beach. 'The forest goes far to the east and west. If you do not wish to enter the forest at night we should wait here until dawn.' She pulled her hood over her head and flung herself down on the sand.

Ceres sank gracefully into a cross-legged position and stared to the north. Sally climbed out of the boat, wondering what the blond woman was thinking about. She looked at Ceres' serene face. She found it hard to dislike her. But Diana was another matter. She knelt down and fingered the sand. How strange life was on this planet. She tried to picture herself back on Earth, this great adventure behind her, but her imagination failed her. All her thoughts were focused on the immediate future. Beyond was blank.

She felt a sudden agitation and looked around. A dim light was growing in the east. Soon they would be on their way again. The forest looked less threatening in the pre-dawn light; slender trees spread out across a carpet of short grass and small bushes. The treetops rose gently to some small hills several hundred meters away. Sally could not smell any unusual odors, just a faint scent like eucalyptus in the fresh salty air.

Ceres got up, approached the trees, stared into them; she leaned down to Diana and spoke quietly to her. Sally pulled off her sandals and walked a little way along the beach. She enjoyed the sensation of sand and cool water on her feet and splashed happily for a few moments. A slight breeze ruffled her hair, making her shiver and as she sat down to wipe her feet the water suddenly receded down the beach. A little way away two small silver fish flopped helplessly on the wet sand. She pulled on her sandals and stared as the water sank further down the gentle slope. She remembered Alistair talking about the effect of the moons on the tides but she had not taken any notice. Several more small fish wriggled at the water's edge. Suddenly the water level dropped dramatically, exposing a steep rocky slope. The light breeze quickened and Sally felt the hair stand up on her head.

'Oh fark!' She leapt up and raced up the beach. She shouted more loudly. Ceres turned towards her and Diana jumped to her feet. For a moment the two women did not move, and then Diana seized Sally by her tunic and shot upwards. She felt a branch whack painfully against her leg as they cleared the treetops and soared towards the hill. She stared back across the water. The ocean floor was now exposed for several hundred meters and a wall of water raced towards the island. She heard Ceres shout out and Diana cursing. Her stomach lurched as they plunged downwards and then swept up the side of the hill. Diana let her go and she slid down the ground.

Diana landed gracefully beside her and without a word, dragged her to her feet. 'Run, mortal! Save yourself.' Diana pushed through the dense bushes and Sally staggered after her. She glimpsed a flash of light brown as Ceres raced ahead up the heavily wooded hill. A loud rushing noise made her look back. The wave was just below them but it was now receding, dragging everything with it. Strange shapes struggled in the water and she thought she glimpsed a human face before it was submerged under the tangle of branches and greenery sweeping back across the flooded island like a gigantic raft.

Ceres stared down at the receding flood. 'We must find shelter. If Poseidon has come so far south, he will not want to return empty handed.'

'Why would Poseidon help Zeus? I thought they were enemies.'

Diana laughed harshly. 'Oh, they would fight over a woman or a good wine, but not about anything serious.'

Ceres urged them forwards. Sally slipped and slid as they traversed the muddy slopes of the hill, finally climbing down into a small ravine.

'We will wait here until night fall.' Ceres leaned against the rough rock face, her expression serene as usual.

Sally squatted down, staring up at the narrow patch of blue sky above the ravine. If Poseidon sent another wave, she would be drowned. But Diana and Ceres looked quite nonchalant and she had to assume they knew what they were doing; or else their immortality made them fearless of something as trivial as a flood. And her death, she supposed, would simply remove a nuisance. She felt herself becoming calm. She had no choice. These beings' motives were still a mystery to her but she had to follow them. She straightened up and wedged herself into a crevice, stretching her legs across the narrow gap.

She wondered about her own feelings. The rock digging into her back and legs did not bother her. As a child she had disliked getting dirty and hated camping. Wherever her work took her, she had insisted on good food and accommodation, and she always thought of her herself as physically rather lazy. She had gone three days without washing, almost no food and hardly any rest, but she felt full of energy. She was also losing the need for constant distraction. Just days ago she could not have borne so many hours with nothing to do. Now she sat still, her eyes focused on the mossy patterns of the rock above her feet. The hours passed, the sky darkened and then the first stars appeared.

When Artemis's gold crescent rose above the ravine, Ceres and Diana climbed out and set off. Sally stayed close behind, watching her feet in the rough dark terrain. They stopped briefly at two small streams. Each time, Ceres stared into the water, muttering some words and running her hand rapidly across the shining surface. Diana looked at her questioningly but Ceres shook her head and they continued on without speaking.

On the south side of the island the forest thinned out, punctuated by small glades of soft grass and flowers that gave off a sharp but refreshing scent. They skirted these open spaces, running quickly from tree to tree. Selenis was now also high in the sky and the two moons gave off as much light as a winter sun.

As they entered yet another small clearing Diana held up her hand. Ceres stopped at once and when Sally started to speak, put her finger across her lips. They heard a crashing in the trees ahead, and Diana, without turning waved them away with her hand. Ceres grabbed Sally's arm and pulled her back into the forest. They hid behind a large tree.

The crashing noise grew louder and Diana backed away, pulling her long silver sword from its sheath. An enormous creature suddenly emerged from the trees. It stopped dead and stood swaying from side to side, blinking in the moonlight. Sally could not believe her eyes. This was the first animal she had seen on Earth 2, but it was no beast. It wore clothes – leather boots, a sort of shirt and ankle length trousers in a smooth dark material. It was at least two meters tall, hairless, with a huge pig like head. A long spear rose above its shoulder, secured by a leather band around its chest. It snorted as it looked around the clearing.

Diana had positioned herself so that the moonlight was in the creature's eyes and before it had a chance to move, she leapt forward and thrust her sword into its stomach. The creature shrieked and flung up its arm to grab its weapon. Diana pulled her sword out and leapt back, sheathing the blade as she did so. The beast staggered towards her, waving its spear. She ran forward again, ducked down and seized its right wrist. It roared and bent its great head down towards her neck. She lifted one foot up and drove it into the huge stomach, twisted the wrist sharply and pulled the monster off balance. It fell heavily forward and hit the ground with a loud crash. She threw herself astride its back and pulling out her sword again, drove it between the huge shoulders. The creature heaved and writhed but it could not shake Diana off or dislodge the sword. She leaned down hard, her face strained with the effort, until the creature ceased to move. Then she stood up and bracing herself with her foot on its back, she pulled out the sword. A spurt of green liquid shot up, narrowly missing her face. She ripped a large leaf from a nearby tree and wiped her sword, looking at the body. Then she leant down and searched its pockets. The sound of Sally vomiting made her turn.

Sally leaned up against the tree, trying to recover her breath. When she straightened up and saw the body, covered in its green blood, she retched again. 'Did you have to kill it?' she gasped finally. It was her first experience of violent death.

Diana looked at her with contempt. 'What did you have in mind?'

'How did you know it was going to hurt us?'

'Look at it,' said Diana, waving her sword towards the prone animal. 'Why do you think it was here? I've never seen anything like it before. It's something that Hera or one of her cronies dreamed up. If you want to survive here, you'll have to toughen up. Haven't you ever killed anything?'

Sally shook her head and Diana gave a rather unpleasant smile. 'A vegetable eater!' she said scornfully. 'Well, you'll learn. Next time it might be you. Unless you'd rather give up right now and run back to your angels?' she added.

Sally stared back at her resentfully. 'Why couldn't you just conjure it away?'

'I told you before. It depends on who's got the best imagination.' Diana laughed shortly. 'I'd rather trust my sword.'

She left the clearing the same way the creature had entered. Ceres followed her and Sally sidled around the body. The beast had flattened the bushes into a good track for several hundred meters and they followed the trail until they came to the foot of a cliff, about ten meters high. It was covered with patches of small bushes and thick rope like vines. Diana looked around. There were cave openings in the cliff face to both sides of them. 'There may be more of those things around here. I think we'd better go straight up.'

She grasped one of the vines, tested her weight and climbed rapidly up the side of the cliff. Sally looked up and saw some large trees at the top of the cliff. She pulled herself up and scrambled to find a foothold. Diana called down for her to hurry. Sally gritted her teeth and hauled herself up. Ceres followed.

They kept up a fast pace for the rest of the night, helped by the bright moonlight. When the sun rose they approached the edge of a plateau and could see that the island extended far to the south, covered in dense forest. Diana looked challengingly at Sally. 'Ready for more, or do you need to sleep?'

Sally shook her head. She refused to rise to the bait. 'But I do need something to eat.'

Ceres crouched down and gestured towards the soil; a green shoot appeared and grew quickly to almost half a meter, two pinkish buds emerged and swelled to the size of small apples. Without a word Ceres plucked them from the vine and handed them to Sally. As Sally bit into one of the fruit the vine withered and dropped to the ground.

Diana and Ceres disappeared over the edge of the escarpment. Looking down, Sally saw that the steep slope was covered with small bushes. She hastily finished the fruit and lowered herself over the rim.

The forest was dark and empty; the only noise was the sound of their feet crushing the undergrowth and the occasional thwack of Diana's sword as she impatiently thrust through the dense foliage. The pace was slower and Sally had no trouble keeping up with Ceres and Diana. She gazed at the ground ahead of her to avoid tripping over the roots that spread like large veins between the trees. She walked quickly and lightly, swerving between the tree trunks, dodging beneath low hanging branches. Ahead, Ceres walked in a measured pace while Diana danced from side to side, pushing at the branches and occasionally lopping one off to clear the path.

The hours passed and the sun was well below the treetops when they emerged from the forest into a wide clearing, about fifty meters in diameter. Large slabs of corrugated rock jutted against each other, like enormous stairs around a wide flat area in the middle, which sloped gently down to the forest on the other side. There were a few low bushes but it was possible to see from one side of the clearing to the other. Diana walked towards the center and looked around. 'We can rest here.'

Ceres sat down on one of the rocky slabs and Sally joined her. They watched as Diana roamed around the clearing. She heaved boulders in to a large circle, muttered a few words, gestured, and then kicked each one until it became a glowing red. 'For Zeus's little friends,' she said, glancing at Sally. She loosened her belt, removed the sword and several smaller implements and placed them carefully on the stone. Then she reached beneath her tunic and drew out a pale cloth. She drew the sword, wiped it carefully with the cloth and sheathed it. She repeated the process with a dagger and several smaller weapons.

She noticed Sally watching her and grinned. 'You are thinking that I could just wave my hand, but it is not the same. Every action has consequences.' She shook out the cloth and folded it neatly. Sally sucked in her breath and without thinking stretched out her hand.

Diana grinned again. 'You recognize this, do you?'

She handed the cloth to Sally. The border of the linen square was decorated with marks similar to those Sally had seen on the plates and cups in the gods' city. They had seemed familiar then and she recalled them now as the symbols which Pierre Meyer had found at Helike, which he believed to be a written language. Pierre had watchered them to her, and after his death she had seen them again, reproduced in the many tributes to the famous French linguist. She turned the pale green cloth over. It was very finely woven and the narrow, angled characters appeared embossed. She felt a terrible weight on her heart as she thought of Pierre, but also a strange sense of relief. Here was concrete evidence of the immortals' presence on Earth.

She was not delusional. Everything that had happened to her was real.

'So, mortal?'

Sally evaded the question. 'I am not expert in this script. What does it say?'

Diana laughed harshly. 'Why, it says "Artemis, daughter of Zeus, Olympian born and bred, sister to the bow-god Apollo." Bah bah bah.' She took back the cloth and tossed it in the air, catching it on the point of her dagger. 'Which is why I use it to wipe the filth from my weapons.'

Ceres made an abrupt movement, walked over to the hot stones and returned a few moments later with some toasted bread. Diana shook her head but Sally took a piece and bit into it. The bread, like the fruit, was delicious. She turned the toast in her hands and looked at it. She should have listened to Alistair. They needed to know how this planet worked. How could Ceres produce food from thin air, or by plucking it from the soil?

There was a long silence. Ceres' face was radiant in the light of the glowing stones and even Diana looked peaceful. Sally risked a question. 'Can you tell me about the people in the south? Will they help?'

'Oh yes,' laughed Diana. 'Thor will help. He has many reasons to teach Zeus a lesson.'

Sally digested this information. They were heading south to meet the Nordic gods. She tried to recall what she knew of the Scandinavian myths.

Diana stood up. 'I need to hunt.' She leapt over the outer ring of stones and ran towards the forest. Only a few moments later, she returned holding a small animal by its long ears. It screeched as Diana slit its throat and Sally looked away. As though she sensed Sally's disgust, Diana threw the animal down in front of her and proceeded to disembowel and skin it. She tossed it onto one of the heated rocks. The smell of blood and burning fat nauseated Sally. She stood up. 'I'm just going to stretch my legs' she said. 'Otherwise, I'll get stiff.'

Ceres followed her to the outer circle of stones. They stood in silence for a few minutes. Then Ceres said quietly, 'Try to understand Diana. She may sound cynical but she tries to lead a noble life. She has a deep sense of honor, and unlike many Olympians she does not use her powers frivolously.'

Sally looked towards Diana. The hunter was sitting with her elbows on her knees, gnawing meat off a large bone. Sally suddenly saw her in a different light. She tried to imagine what it must be like to be Diana, or Ceres, in an endless battle of wits and will power with Zeus and Hera. The world shifted and for a moment she saw a thin-faced woman in a frantic struggle for survival.

She tried to smile at Ceres, and walked back to the centre of the circle. 'Is there any meat left?' she asked, in what she hoped was casual voice.

'Not a vegetarian, then?' Diana used her dagger to spear a piece of meat off the stones. Sally took it and sat down. Now the meat was cooked, the smell was no longer offensive. It reminded her of chicken and tasted very good. She tried not to think how Diana might have conjured it up, just for the pleasure of killing it.

11

Alistair twitched and shivered, as in a nightmare. His body jolted from side to side. It was pitch dark except for some tiny sparks of lights which danced tantalizingly around him. He tried to move but his arms and legs felt like lead. He fell in and out of consciousness, and as his eyes adjusted to the darkness, moving figures slowly became visible. He heard heavy breathing and the occasional grunt. He groped around and realized that he was slung in some sort of stretcher.

More time passed and his mind gradually cleared. His head pounded and his mouth tasted sour. He suddenly recalled standing on the rooftop, looking out over the ruined city, drinking the broth. Venus must have drugged him. He ground his teeth in rage.

Something bumped his leg and he squinted sideways. The sparks of lights were minute reflections off the metal trappings and weapons of the men who ran alongside. Beyond – nothing.

Sensation was returning to his body and he could tell that he was not injured or bound. He felt no pain, except for a fading headache. He considered his options. If he called out, what would happen? Better to stay quiet. He remembered the battle over Olympus, and Venus's accusing face, just before he drank the broth. For some reason the immortals believed the Millennium crew were responsible for Zeus's crazy plan to attack the angels. Thank heavens John and the others had escaped.

His eyes pricked with tears in a moment of weakness as he thought of Sally and then he steeled himself. There was no point speculating about what he did not know. He could only pray that Thomas would find her and keep her safe. His thoughts started to cycle back and forth – angels and gods - and he felt a growing sense of panic. He groped across his tunic. The data pad had slipped sideways but was still secured by his waistband. He felt a huge relief and almost immediately fell asleep again.

He was awakened by a sharp voice and the swinging motion slowed down. Suddenly it was light and his stretcher was set down with a painful thud. Alistair risked a look and saw that they had exited a tunnel onto a grassy hillside. The brief glance revealed Hercules and several men dressed in what looked like the uniforms of ancient Roman soldiers, similar to the guards in the gods' city. Their long shadows showed that it was early morning. Alistair closed his eyes again. No escape here. And if they wanted him dead they would surely not have bothered to carry him this far.

Voices grew louder as the speakers approached him. He waited, feigning sleep as they stood over him, and then his stretcher was lifted up again. The pace was slower but the stretcher jolted and tilted alarmingly as though being carried over rough ground. Hercules shouted commands several times and the stretcher changed direction abruptly. Alistair started to feel nauseated from the endless motion and a terrible thirst from the heat of the sun beating down on his uncovered face. Just when he thought he could bear it no longer, the stretcher was set down again. Alistair waited a moment and then half opened his eyes. Huge legs were striding towards him, and he felt his shoulder squeezed in a harsh grip.

'Wake up mortal ' Hercules shook him violently. Alistair wrenched himself out of his grasp and jumped up off the stretcher. He looked around wildly. They had descended a steep rocky slope and were only a hundred meters or so from the coast. There was no sign of habitation here or on the small green islands sprinkled across the blue water. Four tall Anomee stood nearby, dressed in leather shirts and short kilts, and armed with swords and daggers. Another Anomee draped in a long white toga stood apart.

Alistair composed himself. 'Where are we?'

Hercules did not reply. He barked some orders at the guards and they set off down a narrow path. He gestured to Alistair to follow. They entered a grove of trees and proceeded along a trail that zigzagged down a steep incline. Alistair was stiff from his hours on the stretcher and he stumbled. The Anomee in the toga grasped his arm to prevent him falling and when Alistair thanked him, he smiled. Alistair was so surprised that he stopped. The man was typical of the Anomee, tall and handsome with a light olive complexion, dark eyes and curly hair worn long. But his face was mobile and expressive. He smiled again and gestured ahead. Alistair went on, but glanced back at the man several times. Each time he smiled slightly as though to reassure Alistair that he was not unfriendly.

As the trail leveled off Alistair heard the sound of water and soon saw a wide stream flowing along the bottom of the gully. He ignored Hercules' shout and scrambled down the slope towards the gushing water. The Anomee reached him just as he was about to dip his hands into the stream.

'No! It is sacred.' He grasped Alistair's tunic and pulled him back. 'Here. Drink from this.' He pulled out a flask from his satchel and gave it to Alistair.

Alistair eyed the flask suspiciously. 'You speak English.'

'Of course. I speak many languages.' As though he understood Alistair's suspicions, he took the flask, drank from it, and handed it to Alistair.

While Alistair drank, the Anomee called out something to Hercules who had been regarding them from the path. The great figure turned away and walked on.

Alistair returned the flask. 'Who are you? Are you one of the immortals?'

The man looked back as climbed up to the path. 'No. I am a servant of … well you will soon see. My name is Althamas, formerly of Helike.'

'Helike?' Alistair stared at the young man, trying to recall why the name sounded familiar.

'Yes. Thus I owe loyalty to Hercules, and to others.' Althamas frowned. 'We must hurry.'

Alistair followed him back up to the path, feeling somehow better, either from the drink, which always had an energizing effect, or from meeting another person he could communicate with.

'Where are we going?'

Althamas looked back briefly. 'We must hurry. We will be there soon. Do not be alarmed.'

The path suddenly widened and opened into a small clearing. At the far end a wide bridge crossed the stream and beyond it Alistair could see an arch, which seemed to penetrate the other side of the ravine. Hercules and the others passed rapidly over the bridge and a glow appeared beyond the archway. Althamas took Alistair's arm. 'We are almost there, and then you can rest.' His voice was warm and sympathetic, with only a slight accent. Alistair felt certain he had heard the name Althamas before but he could not recall where. As they entered the archway Althamas reached up and drew down a lamp. He turned the base, and it emitted a dim light. Ahead, Alistair could see other lights bobbing in the darkness. They walked for a few minutes, the lamp illuminating the smooth floor a few yards ahead.

'Take care. Here are steps.' Althamas lowered the lamp and Alistair saw steep, wide stairs cut into the rock. He ascended them awkwardly, feeling like a small child. They obviously had been made for much taller people. Gradually the light brightened and he stood blinking in the midday sun.

'Get down,' whispered Althamas and prostrated himself. Alistair saw that they were in the middle of a large glade, facing the ocean and surrounded on the other three sides by tall trees. At the centre stood a grey stone building shaped like an ancient Greek temple, the roof supported by narrow columns. The guards were already lying face down, their arms flung forward, palms upwards. Hercules was down on one knee, his head bent.

'Quickly,' Althamas hissed and Alistair imitated his position.

There was a long silence. Alistair's heart pounded in his ears. Then he heard Hercules speak, in a much softer voice than he normally used.

'Do not move,' Althamas whispered. 'Wait.'

Hercules said a few more words and then a woman spoke, very slowly, as though considering each word. The voice was low and musical but very strong and it made Alistair tremble.

'Get up now, but keep your head lowered.' Althamas spoke so quietly Alistair could hardly hear him.

Alistair stood up and waited. He was conscious of someone approaching him and saw a long sandaled foot and the embroidered hem of a white robe. He felt a hand on his head and he shook violently.

'Alistair.' For some reason, the voice reminded Alistair of his mother's, when she had something serious to tell him. He kept his eyes downcast.

'Alistair, look up.'

Alistair clenched his jaw and lifted his head slowly. He saw pale skin and a circular metal disc, finely engraved with the image of an owl. He raised his eyes and looked straight into the woman's face. Large grey eyes stared down at him from a perfectly formed, wonderfully beautiful and yet totally frightening face. It was like the face of a child, unmarked by experience and yet knowing everything. The woman gazed at him for several long moments. He felt dazed and he fell almost forward as she turned to Hercules. She spoke in the immortals' language, then said, 'This one is a good spirit. No one should harm him. You were right to bring him.'

Alistair heard Althamas let out a deep breath. The woman turned back. 'Well done, Althamas. Well done.'

To Alistair's amazement, the tall man put his face in his hands and sobbed violently, 'Athena, Athena!' and flung himself down at the woman's feet. She stooped down and raised him up, but he did not uncover his face. She spoke again to Hercules, more sharply this time and walked away. Hercules followed her and they disappeared behind the grey columns of the pergola shaped building. The guards stood up and took up positions along the edge of the cliff, looking out over the bright water.

While Althamas wiped his eyes, Alistair sat down a few feet away and waited. He wondered if the man was embarrassed but when Althamas looked up, his face was joyful. Alistair gave way to confusion. A series of images flashed before him; the expressionless features of the Anomee in the village, Michael's livid anger and Zeus's defiance, Hercules' contemptuous stare, the blank gazes of the angels, the sad circle of faces at the memorial service and Sally's tears. He suddenly felt weak and put his head down on his arms.

'Alistair. Do not despair. Athena will help us.'

Alistair raised his head. Althamas was looking at him with the same sympathetic expression. Alistair felt a violent need to talk to him, to feel some trust, but he suppressed it. Nothing here was as it seemed. Whatever this man's motives, they were unlikely to coincide with his.

'It is no one person's fault. Remember that. So many mistakes have been made and we must resolve them, or at least prevent worse happening. That is all we can try to do.'

'And how can we do that?' Alistair would not admit that he had no idea what Althamas was talking about.

'Athena will tell us what to do.'

Alistair looked away to conceal his feelings. 'Yeah, right' he muttered. The effect of Athena's presence was wearing off and he now thought of it as ruse, like Venus's, to control the Anomee and any other humans who came into their power.

'Where is your faith?'

Alistair felt shocked by the question. He suddenly remembered his sister Claudia, arguing with her husband at the farewell gathering.

'My faith is with my people, and they are not here,' he replied shortly.

'Then you must put your faith in us. Ask me anything. Unless it is sacred, I will tell you.'

'How do I know you're telling the truth?'

'Why should I lie? Perhaps you think so, because you cannot trust us. You have spent too much time with Thomas.'

'I hardly know Thomas.' That at least was true, he thought.

'No one knows Thomas, or where he is gone to.'

Alistair could think of no reply to this. He stared at his feet. The Anomee sandals were hardly marked by the journey. His freckled skin looked strange to him, surrounded as he was by these beautiful, olive skinned people. He wondered what Althamas really thought of him. 'Why did Athena say "well done" to you?'

'She asked me to decide whether you should be allowed to come here. If I had decided against you, Hercules would have disposed of you.' Althamas saw Alistair grimace and continued quickly. 'No! He would have taken you back to the village or some other place where you could do no harm.'

'Do no harm? What could I do to any of you?'

'I do not believe you mean harm, but the Diptera took you from Zeus and he wants you back, even more than before. Zeus is insatiable.'

Alistair shuddered. Should he tell Althamas about Sally? What was the best way to protect her? If only he knew what was in Thomas's mind. He shook his head. There was no point thinking about it. He would go mad. He stared at Althamas' graceful face. He appeared to be around thirty, like most of the Anomee. 'Who are you? Were you born here?'

Althamas shook his head. 'I was born in the land you call Greece, more than two thousand years ago. Poseidon destroyed Helike in a fit of jealousy against Hercules. I was the only survivor; my family and friends – all gone in an instant. Great numbers were brought here and reborn as slaves to serve Poseidon.' Althamas spoke in matter of fact tone, but his face was sad when he mentioned his birthplace. 'Hercules carried me from Helike to Athens and placed me in Athena's care. When the Diptera commanded all the gods to leave the mortal domain, Athena took me with her.'

Alistair suddenly recalled Pierre Meyer. 'I know about Helike. The ruins were found late last century.'

'So long a time,' Althamas murmured. 'My beautiful city!'

Alistair stared at him. Althamas's face was so expressive, but it was unlined and showed no marks of his great age. He could not imagine living so long. He remembered what the Anomee women had told him. 'You are not like the other Anomee.'

Althamas frowned. 'We are Athena's people and we do not call ourselves by that name. The Anomee were primitive people when they were brought here and they have been given little opportunity to develop further. You have not seen all the mortals on this planet. We are as different as you are.'

Alistair thought for a moment. This was a chance to solve some riddles or at least get another version of what was going on. 'Why did the angels, the Diptera make the gods leave our planet?'

'Zeus and Poseidon, and other immortals caused great destruction and suffering. We all agree on that. They do not always follow the code, and they have broken the contract between the immortals and the Diptera many times. I cannot tell you why this contract was made, or what purpose it serves. Perhaps the immortals know but I think not. I believe that the Diptera's motives are as mysterious to them as they are to us.' Althamas looked directly at Alistair but his face was now in shadow and Alistair could not see his eyes. 'You may know more than any of us. You have spent more time with the Diptera, than any other creature.' He added as an afterthought, 'apart from Thomas.'

Alistair looked away and Althamas continued, 'you are not ready to tell us what you know. Perhaps you are our doom.'

Alistair thought carefully. 'Gabriel told me that the angels are instruments of the good; that they act only to restore harmony, to move life in the right direction. But I honestly don't know what they mean by that.'

Althamas sighed. 'Perhaps it is beyond our comprehension; ineffable. Perhaps only a Dipteros can understand.'

Alistair continued quickly. 'I do know that they make all their decisions as a group, that they exchange information through something they call a choir. They chant endlessly until there is total agreement. You must have noticed – they turn their heads aside whenever they make a decision. I think they are consulting the choir.' He felt his mouth go dry but he rushed on. 'Also, they have a wall, some sort of huge screen - everything that happens on Earth is recorded on it. Nothing on this planet, only Earth. And just images, no sound.'

Althamas looked shocked. 'That explains many things.' He jumped up. 'I will tell Hercules.' He started towards the stone building but stopped as Hercules emerged and beckoned to him. They conferred for a moment. Althamas returned to Alistair. 'Come. It has been decided. We go to war.'

As he spoke Alistair saw Hercules kneel down and Althamas followed suit. Alistair, still feeling ridiculous at the gesture, did the same. He did not look up when Athena spoke.

'Hercules will return to Olympus to gather our allies.'

Hercules stopped in front of Alistair. 'Get up, mortal.'

Alistair stood up and stared into Hercules' brilliant eyes. 'My name is Alistair and I am your kin.'

Hercules made a loud snorting sound. 'Then let me see you prove it. If you are false I will command the eagles to rip out your liver.'

Alistair refused to flinch. What would be, would be. He stood with his arms akimbo and glared up at the handsome face.

'Alistair will stay here with us.'

Hercules frowned but bowed his head towards Athena. The guards followed the tall figure back over the bridge and disappeared into the tunnel.

Athena was regarding him gravely from the stone steps. She had pulled on a short chain corselet and concealed her cloud of dark hair under a tall fronted leather cap. A large grey owl sat on her right wrist. She spoke to the bird, raised her arm, and it sailed into the air and east, over the trees.

'Althamas. You will be responsible for Alistair's conduct and safety.' She walked swiftly but gracefully down the steps and entered the wooded area beyond the temple.

Althamas ushered Alistair ahead and they hurried after her. As they wound through the trees they heard shouting in the distance, which gradually became a rhythmic chant, backed by what sounded like loud drums. Alistair glimpsed daylight through the dense wood and a few moments later they emerged on to small grassy knoll overlooking a great plain. Flanked by the ocean to the south, it was enclosed to the east and north by a line of hills. Athena walked deliberately towards the crest of the knoll and halted at its edge. Althamas stood a few feet behind her.

For a moment Alistair did not understand what he saw. Something shimmered along the horizon and then long lines wove across the distant plain. They joined and thickened. He looked in the direction of the noise and saw a huge contingent of soldiers approaching from the north. They banged their fists on their shields as they ran, calling out the goddess's name. The long lines converged rapidly into a solid mass, so that within minutes the plain was covered by thousands of men, in full battle gear.

Althamas beckoned to Alistair and he walked reluctantly to join them. The noise was deafening and the sight of the soldiers just below them was overwhelming. He felt again a sense of dislocation, as though what he saw was some huge computer simulation. But the smell of sweat, dust and leather drifted up to him and he saw each man's face as real, flushed from the journey. Like Althamas, their faces were expressive and now they were gazing up in adoration at the goddess.

'I will tell you what Athena says,' Althamas whispered as Athena raised her arm in a salute. The host of soldiers was immediately quiet.

Athena's voice rang out and Alistair knew at once that this was not the language of the Anomee or the gourds.

'Men of Athens, men of Sparta, men of Troy,' Althamas translated quietly but clearly. 'For two thousand years we have maintained order. We have dreaded this moment but we are ready for it. My father, the obstinate old wretch, whom I love dearly and worship with all my heart, has gone mad. He has armed himself, and with his reckless brothers prepares to drive the storm cloud, the flood and the fire over the domain of the Diptera. We must halt this wild and thoughtless plan. We must prevent his destruction, and our own. We must not rest until Zeus returns in peace to his own domain.'

Athena looked from north to south in a long sweeping gaze. The soldiers waited in silence. She raised her hand again. 'Are you with me?' The soldiers beat on their shields with the hilts of their long swords until Athena silenced them. 'Now turn you each to your fellow and say the words of forgiveness. Forget Troy. Forget Achilles and Hector. They are not here.' There was a great stirring on the plain and each man clasped the hands of those to his left and right. Then they were silent again and looked up expectantly at Athena.

'Zeus and his brothers are ancients. Hermes and Ares are young, but they are treacherous. We have Apollo, lord of the air and the warrior Diana who is already gone to seek a treaty with the immortals of the south. Ceres herself supports our cause.' The men cheered and rattled their spears and shields but Athena put up her hand. 'And we have something more. We have the one true man.' She turned towards Alistair and Althamas pushed him forward. They stood next to Athena and Alistair looked down at the massed men. Athena took Alistair's hand and held it high. 'This is your future. If you defeat Zeus, he and his like will sing your praises for evermore. Now swear! Let no harm come to the one true man.'

Alistair's hair stood up on his neck as the crowd roared. Athena released his hand and leaning down, beckoned to one of the soldiers below. He climbed quickly up the slope and knelt before her. Athena spoke quietly to him and he stood up and placed himself next to Althamas.

Athena's voice rang out. 'When the dawn mist lifts, the ships will be here and you will make ready. I go now to shake the fringes of my aegis at the trickster Hermes and the wicked Ares and they will wish that Zeus had never known their mothers.' Althamas translated quickly but Alistair could not help staring at the other soldier. Like the other Anomee he was handsome and well formed but there was something different about him.

'I will enter the bronze-floored palace of my father and beg him to listen. If he ignores my counsel, I will return here to lead you to victory.'

The men roared again and Athena acknowledged them, but Alistair saw her face as she turned away. Her bright grey eyes were filled with tears and her mouth was trembling. She strode past them and disappeared into the forest.

The great mass of soldiers started to disperse and unpack their gear. One group of men headed south and passed in single file over the edge of the cliff. Alistair guessed that there were jetties below from which the ships would depart.

'We will camp here tonight.' When Alistair did not respond, Althamas took his arm and gave him a questioning look.

'I'm all right. I'm just a bit knocked over by all this. Why did Athena call me the one true man'?

Althamas sighed. 'There is so much to discuss. Let us set up camp and eat first.'

Several more men had climbed up to join them and were starting to set up a bivouac. They glanced sideways at Alistair but did not speak. All across the plateau rows of small tents had sprung up and the soldiers milled around organizing their equipment. In the distance a large area had been left clear and as Alistair watched, lines of men entered it and began a series of drills. Alistair grimaced. Would anyone believe that he had seen this? He shook his head. Would he ever get the chance to tell them? The possibility of returning home seemed less likely with every day.

'Ready for some chow? You must be done in.'

Alistair whirled around. The soldier who had spoken to Athena was regarding him with amusement. 'Probably time for me to introduce myself,' the man continued in a pleasant drawl.

Althamas spoke sharply in another language and the man laughed. 'He'll be fine. Looks like an ok guy to me.' He held out his hand. 'Sam Mousalimos, at your service.'

Alistair swallowed painfully. 'I'm glad you think this is funny.' He looked at Althamas. 'If you don't tell me what the bloody hell is going on here, I'm leaving.'

Althamas frowned. 'As I told you, I will answer all your questions. Sit down and we will start.' He waved his hand. One of the soldiers brought three wooden chairs and placed them in a semicircle under the boughs of one of the larger trees. Alistair took the centre chair and another soldier immediately brought a tray with three flasks.

Althamas sat down. 'Tell me what you know and I will try to explain.'

Sam Mousalimos cut in. 'Why don't I tell him my story. Perhaps that will help.' He drank heavily and as he wiped his face, Alistair suddenly understood why Sam seemed different. All the Anomee were clean shaven but Sam wore a beard.

'And then,' Sam continued, 'he can tell us how he got here and how he escaped from the Diptera.' He looked challengingly at Alistair.

'I've already told Hercules. I don't know.' Alistair found it hard to look Sam in the face.

Sam's drawl sharpened. 'I don't believe you. But never mind. Let me tell you how I came here.' He drank again and then stared ahead for a few moments. 'I'll try to be brief. I was born in 1919 in Philadelphia. Have you heard of it?'

'Yes,' Alistair confirmed. 'I've been there several times; a beautiful city.'

Sam stared. 'You must tell me sometime, what it's like now ...' He broke off. 'First things, first. My parents were born in Greece and we always thought of ourselves as Hellenes. I was one of the Americans who volunteered to join forces with the Greek resistance. We were dropped into northern Greece, May '44; to harass and impede the enemy – that was our mission. Anyway, one night I got separated from my group. It was my fault. I got careless and my number came up. The bastard didn't finish me off, just left me there to bleed to death. I remember lying on the grass, looking up at the moon through the trees, thinking that this wasn't such a bad way to die. I felt sorry for my parents, you know, but I didn't feel any pain; just sort of cold. So, all of a sudden, this woman appears from behind a tree; a tall pale woman in a long white gown. I thought I was dead already. She didn't say anything, just knelt down and stroked my face. Then I woke up here.'

He drank again and laughed. 'Sounds crazy, don't it? There were a whole bunch of us; soldiers mainly, but some women and children too; people who'd been hiding from the Nazis. Anyway, here we all were, in perfect health. We thought we were in heaven; until I saw Athena.' He looked at Alistair. 'Your turn.'

'I already knew the gods abducted humans, and that they keep them alive against their will.'

Althamas started to speak but Sam cut in. 'Hell, they aint gods. Not real gods; nor angels neither. They just call themselves that because we did, back in the old times, that is.'

'Why do you call the angels, "Diptera"?'

'It is the Greek word for creatures with wings,' Althamas explained.

Sam grinned. 'And they're everywhere, just like flies.'

Althamas continued. 'Athena does not force mortals to remain alive if they wish to die. Not all the immortals on this planet are the same. Just like mortals, some are good, some are not so good. But they are different from us. They call us mortals because we are easy to destroy.'

'It's nigh impossible to end an immortal. Believe me, I've tried.' Sam paused as one of the soldiers approached and set up a small table. While they had been talking a large tent had been erected and another soldier emerged from it, carrying a tray of dishes.

'I'm starving. Been running half the night to get here. Let's eat.' Sam tore apart a roll and stuffed it into his mouth.

Alistair took some grapes and chewed slowly. Soon he had to decide what else he would reveal. He stared at Sam. 'You don't look so old to me.'

Sam laughed.' Of course not. Some people are happy with three score years and ten. Not me. I'll go on as long as I want to.'

'How do they do that? How is it possible?'

'Oh come on. You must have some schooling or you wouldn't be here. They just know a lot more than we do, or at least more than we knew when I was young. What's it like back on Earth now?'

'Never mind that. So you're telling me, that it's just luck that the angels – the Diptera and the gods, as they call themselves, just happen to be on this planet and we never knew about them until now?'

Althamas interrupted. 'The Diptera and the immortals come from elsewhere. The Diptera came here for some purpose; even the immortals do not know why. For some reason your planet is important to the Diptera. They allowed the immortals to live there, to show themselves to us mortals. Then they changed their minds. After Poseidon destroyed Helike he brought hundreds of citizens here against their will. So, the immortals are forbidden to go back to Earth, although as Sam told you, Athena and some others have defied them on occasion. When the Diptera told us that your starship was coming to us, we were commanded to conceal ourselves, to keep our existence secret from you. If Zeus had not broken his word … '

Alistair thought for a moment. 'So, the problem now is that if Zeus attacks the angels, then the angels may destroy all the immortals. That doesn't make sense either. They are really weird, but I wouldn't call them vindictive. And also, they have this dedication to something which they at least call "the good". Wouldn't that stop them?'

Sam said slowly. 'You'd better tell him. He needs to know how serious this is. Perhaps then, he'll tell us what he knows.'

Althamas sighed heavily. 'The immortals believe that the Diptera only allow them to live as part of their plan. But no one knows what these plans are.'

'They talked to us about harmony and the progress of the good.' Alistair wondered if the angels might have told them more, after the Millennium left. He would never know. 'But they would not tell us more until our space craft had left.' He sighed heavily remembering the day he and Sally had made their decision to stay.

'You are worried about your woman?' Althamas's tone was sympathetic.

'I am. I don't trust Thomas.'

'What do you mean?' Althamas stood up abruptly. 'Why should Thomas have anything to do with this?'

Alistair groaned. He had given himself away with a slip of the tongue.

Sam leaned forward and grasped his arm. 'Speak up. What are you hiding?'

Alistair's stomach churned and he could not speak.

'Tell him, Althamas. Tell him everything.' Sam spoke sharply.

Althamas looked distressed. 'You must understand. It is not only the immortals who will be destroyed. The Diptera will destroy all the mortals on this planet.' He paused. 'And on yours, also.'

'What? No! That's not true. Why would they do that?' Alistair leapt up and seized Althamas by the throat. 'Who told you that?'

Sam dragged him off and shook him. 'Pull yourself together, man.'

Althamas rubbed his throat. 'The mortal called Thomas told the gods. This Thomas was taken by the angels some time ago. They let him go, if he promised to help keep the peace. He has acted as our intermediary. But we believe he has betrayed us. He has disappeared and no one can find him.'

Alistair's head whirled. Why was Thomas deceiving everyone? Was it possible that the angels would destroy all life as he knew it, for the sake of some mysterious plan? If only he had stayed in Iceland. He might have discovered what was going on. He shook his head. He remembered Athena looking down at him and how her voice recalled his mother's. 'It's not in you, Alistair, to be dishonest,' she would say. 'And remember, the truth will always out.'

He looked up. Althamas regarded him sympathetically but Sam's expression was hostile.

Alistair took a deep breath. 'Thomas is an angel; a Dipteros.' Althamas's face paled while Sam looked incredulous. 'I'm sorry I concealed this. I don't know who to trust and I don't understand what is going on.' He slowly described his first meeting with Thomas and all the events since. 'So you see, Zeus may have captured Sally. Thomas told me he would find her and bring her back.'

Sam stared closely at Alistair. 'No way! Zeus couldn't get into The White Land, let alone get anyone out. Are you telling us the truth?'

'Have you considered that Thomas himself took Sally?' Althamas asked. 'Are you absolutely sure Thomas is a Dipteros?'

'As sure as I can be of anything in this mad place.' Alistair's stomach jerked. 'Why would Thomas take Sally?'

Sam laughed bitterly. 'To make you leave, of course. It's obvious you're mad for her.'

Alistair recalled Thomas's face when he learned that Sally had gone. He had thought then, that Thomas looked strange, almost ill. 'I don't think he took her. You know the angels, the Diptera seem to have no emotions, no feelings, but Thomas – well I think he's frantic to find her. She's very important to him, but I don't know why.'

There was a long silence and then Althamas said, 'But why would he not tell the other Diptera? Why search for her alone? Why remove you from Iceland? It makes no sense.'

Alistair shook his head. 'I had no time to ask him. It doesn't make sense to me either.'

'If Zeus has your woman … 'Althamas sucked in his breath. 'Then he will make her talk. She will tell him everything.'

Alistair winced but Althamas continued. 'Perhaps that is why Zeus thinks he can go against the Diptera. He may have knowledge about the White Land which he has not shared. But Athena will find it out. If Zeus has taken your woman, he will not be able to resist boasting to Athena.' He frowned. 'I wish Athena knew this but now we must wait for her.'

They ate and talked as the sun descended the sky and night fell. Althamas described what he knew of the immortals and their role in human affairs. Some of it sounded familiar to Alistair, some of it contradicted the little he had read about the ancient world. He now understood why the fate of humanity was bound up with that of the immortals. The immortals had intermarried, fathered and borne thousands of children in the millennia they had spent on earth. To the angels, there would be little difference between them.

'A child fathered by an immortal would live much longer, be stronger than other mortals.' Althamas looked intently at Alistair. 'Have you never wondered why some mortals are so extraordinary? But after a time, the effect weakens.'

In turn, Alistair gave a brief history of events on Earth since Sam's death in 1944. 'There are so many problems on Earth – pollution, hunger. We had great hopes for this planet.'

When Alistair described the latest developments in computing, genetic engineering and cloning, Sam observed, 'You see – it's pretty much what they do here. They're just way ahead of you.'

Something niggled at the back of Alistair's mind; some clue to understanding the source of the angels' and gods' enormous powers. The struggle to remember made him long for sleep. He looked at the two men. They were gazing out over the ocean, each lost in their own thoughts. Althamas's expression was calm and resigned but Sam's face wore a deep frown. There was nothing alien about either of them. Alistair felt a great sense of release. He had to put his trust in someone.

He yawned. 'I've never thought to ask this. What do the gods, what do you call this planet?'

Sam's face lit up. 'Can't understand a word of the immortals' lingo. Even Althamas can't speak it. But us mere mortals, well of course, we call it Elysium.'

12

'Mother of Life! What have we here?'

Sally had never heard Diana speak with such emotion. For weeks they had scurried from island to island, endlessly deviating from their journey south, blocked at every turn, backtracking and hiding, fleeing from flood and fire, while overhead strange apparitions haunted the night skies and each morning brought bizarre and disgusting changes to the natural landscape. Ceres and Diana had cursed and vilified Zeus and his allies – Ares, Poseidon, Vulcan and others. But in the last few days they had hardly spoken and Sally knew they were enraged and humiliated by their lack of progress. She kept silent; relieved that they did not take their anger out on her.

They had just emerged from two days in a forest where every plant was covered in a reeking slime and the trees were infested with stinging insects. Now they stood on the edge of a small cliff, overlooking a narrow valley. The land below them roiled with sickening movement. Sally's stomach heaved.

'We must go back,' Ceres said in a flat voice.

'We cannot.' Diana drew her sword and brandished it. 'I will deal with this.'

Ceres pushed the sword down. 'You will reveal us and play into his hands. Zeus must be desperate.'

Diana sheathed her sword. 'This is Vulcan's work. Look!' She pointed downwards.

Sally shuddered as she caught the eye of one of creatures, just a few meters below her. It was scantily clothed in some rough cloth and much of its skin showed bright red and raw as though it had been flayed. It was roughly the same size and shape as a human but the face and limbs were hideously deformed as though parts of different bodies had been tacked together. But amongst its awful features Sally recognized parts of the typical Anomee: a patch of smooth olive skin, a clear almond shaped eye, a beautifully proportioned hand. The creature stared at her with a blank look, as though it lacked all feeling. She flinched and looked away.

'They are monsters.' Diana spat. 'There must be a thousand or more. Only Vulcan could do this.'

Ceres let out a deep sigh. 'So Vulcan has joined Poseidon to pursue us. That leaves Zeus more vulnerable. We assist Athena in that, at least.'

Diana stamped her foot. 'We must reach Odin's domain. We must pass.'

They had reached a crisis. A retreat would mean a delay of days or even weeks. Sally watched the two women carefully. Diana's face was flushed with anger. She fidgeted with the hilt of her sword and hopped from one foot to the other as though limbering up for a fight. Ceres stared down into the valley; the tightness of her expression showed that she was very anxious. Diana spoke, slowly at first and then in rising tones until Ceres pulled her away from the edge of the overhang, back towards the forest.

Sally stayed where she was. The creatures nearest to the cliff stood still, gazing around aimlessly. They had seen the three women but made no move to attack. Further back they shifted restlessly, jostling and pushing each other. There was no organization, no sense of an army prepared for battle. She turned to Ceres and Diana. 'I have an idea.'

Diana sneered but Ceres looked at Sally inquiringly.

'Look! Look at them. Do you see a leader, a commander?' When neither Ceres nor Diana replied, Sally rushed on.

'I suppose you're right. Zeus is trying to get you to show yourselves. But you don't have to.' She paused. Diana was staring at her. She pointed towards the middle of the valley where a small fight appeared to have broken out. She felt sick but she continued. 'I'll show you.' She untied the wide sash which secured her tunic and knotted the ends. She looked around and found some stones.

Diana hissed. 'I understand you, mortal. There is no honor in this. I will not be party to it.'

Sally folded one of the smaller stones into the looped sash and swung it tentatively. 'You won't have to. I'll do your dirty work for you.' She spun the circle of cloth, gradually raising it to circle above her head. A quick flick of her wrist released the stone and it whistled through the air. A scream and a sudden flurry of movement showed that it had hit a target. Sally flicked off two more stones and searched around for more. As she had hoped, the creatures took no notice of her. They assumed that their neighbors had struck the blows and they hit back. The creatures nearby turned to see what was happening and Sally fired off more rocks. One of the brutes fell to the ground and was trampled as its mates rushed to join the fight, brandishing short swords and clubs.

Diana stood back, her arms folded and her expression contemptuous, but Ceres started to gather stones. Sally swung her slingshot like an automaton and tried not to think about what she was doing, tried to ignore the screams, wails and grunts of the creatures below. The only time her father had been truly angry with her was when he had discovered her slinging stones up at the crows which sat cawing outside her bedroom window. 'Shameful' David had called it; hurting creatures which knew no better and could not defend themselves. Sally wondered what he would think of her now. She clenched her jaw. She had no choice. The plain was now a mass of heaving bodies. She had been more successful than she could ever have imagined.

Diana suddenly gave a loud cry and leapt over the precipice. She bounded over the piles of bodies and cut a swath through the creatures still standing. Ceres put her hand on Sally's shoulder. 'Diana will finish it. Put down your weapon.'

They stood silently while Diana whirled through the mass, slashing, hacking and screaming like a banshee. It was no contest. The monsters fell in heaps until Diana stood alone on a field of corpses.

Ceres spoke calmly as usual. 'You are not to blame. Zeus allowed this. He is determined to prevail.'

'But what does he want?' Sally's throat was dry. She could hardly speak. 'How could he want anything this much?'

'He wants to break the power of Diptera. He wants to return to Earth and take up his old life there.'

Diana reappeared. Her tunic was unsoiled but she wiped her bloodied sword and hands on the short grass. Sally felt as though she would vomit. She sat down and put her head between her knees.

'We should pass through now; before my wretched father sees what we have done.' Diana poured water over her head and pushed back her shining black hair.

Ceres pulled Sally to her feet. 'First we will acknowledge our debt.' She punched the air and then struck her left collar bone with her clenched fist. She looked sideways at Diana, who reluctantly repeated the gesture. 'And today will be recorded for Athena to hear.' Ceres unwound her own sash and tied it around Sally's waist.

For more than an hour they wove through the dead and battered bodies of Vulcan's monsters. Sally followed Ceres closely so she could avoid looking down. But she stumbled a few times and once almost fell onto a mutilated corpse. Nightmarish images of severed limbs and crushed faces were burned into her mind. Diana took the lead, occasionally stooping to examine one of the bodies and constantly looking skyward and down the stretch of the valley. She urged them on.

Finally they reached the southern rim of the valley, where the land sloped gently up to yet another forest. Sally paused. Her head was reeling.

'Hurry! We should not remain unconcealed.' Diana ran up the hill and into the trees. She reappeared a few moments later and called down to them. 'There is a strange smell here. Even so, we must enter.'

As if to defy her, a wind arose and the trees rustled loudly. Sally's hair whipped around her face as a distant whispering noise grew rapidly into a thunderous roar. Ceres pushed Sally forward. As they neared the edge of the forest, Sally turned. The eastern end of the valley seemed to shimmer and then a wall of water rushed towards them. It carried all before it, trees, rocks and bodies.

'Damned Ares! Will this never cease?' Diana screamed long and loud in her own language and drew her sword. Ceres shouted but the roar of the water covered her voice. Diana leapt down the slope and launched herself into the flood. She sprang up a moment later on the deck of a wide flat vessel, lurching and jerking against the swift torrent. Immediately a dark column rose out of the water and whirled over the deck like a twister. Diana swung her sword and hacked at the column. It wavered and reformed and Diana swung her sword again, parried and thrust as the twister wove around the deck. Suddenly it widened and thinned, like a cloud of smoke, and the figure of a huge man haloed by a dark red light appeared within it. He shot across the water towards them. Sally watched in terrified fascination.

Ceres shouted again and pushed Sally towards the trees. She stumbled and slipped on the grass and felt a searing pain. The cloud of dark vapor spread over her and her arm was caught in a vice like grip. Ceres grasped her other arm and pulled her away. The pain blurred Sally's vision but she glimpsed Diana racing up the hill, slashing at the cloud. A scream of rage almost deafened Sally and then her world exploded in agony. She fell backwards staring in disbelief at the bronze blade protruding from her stomach. Splintered images flashed before her; Ceres' white face, contorted with fury, Diana whirling her sword above her head, shiny green leaves only inches above her, and finally her own hands smeared with bright red, reaching up, disappearing into the gloom.

'Sally!'

She opened her eyes. Diana stood over her. In her left hand she gripped the bronze hilt of a bloody sword. Her own weapon pointed down towards Sally's chest. 'It is better that I finish you now. Ares' blade has poisoned your blood. You will die screaming.'

Sally stared at the bloodied blade and saw again the strange symbols from Helike, engraved across the hilt. She felt very cold. She turned her head slowly. The water had receded. There was no sign of the vessel or the dark cloud. Ceres face came into focus. She nodded slightly as if to agree with Diana.

'Can't you help me?' Sally could hardly speak.

Ceres shook her head. 'Nothing can be done against such a blow.' Her wide blue eyes were filled with tears.

Sally looked up again. Diana was slowly lifting her sword as if to increase the force of the deathblow. Her face was impassive but her eyes showed a grudging sort of respect.

'You have come to an honorable end. Your name will become legend.' Diana paused. 'If you cannot speak, give me a sign.'

'Wait.' Sally tried to clear her throat. 'Wait. Wait until I feel something.'

Diana shook her head but she averted her sword a fraction. Sally fumbled across her tunic until she touched the sticky wet of the wound. She pressed her hands over her stomach. 'Wait. I need to ask you something.' She felt suddenly warmer. Ceres had knelt down beside her.

'Tell me the truth. Why are you here?' Sally cleared her throat again. 'Where did you come from?'

'What good can it do you now?' Diana spoke harshly but she stepped back as Ceres lifted Sally's head and supported it with her arm.

'We have told you. The Diptera brought us – so long ago we have almost no memory of where we came from.'

'Do not speak of it,' Diana cut in.

'I'm a dead woman. I can't know?' Even as she said it, Sally could not believe she was going to die. Ceres' arm infused her with warmth. 'Why did you come? What do you want with us?'

Diana flung the bronze sword down and slashed at the grass with her own sword. Ceres ignored her and stroked Sally's hair. 'The Diptera have never disclosed their plans to us. They brought us and many other creatures to your world.'

'Other creatures?'

'You must have heard of them – giants and small beings, dragons, peri and others.'

Sally started to feel faint. It was hard to concentrate while she was expecting pain to strike. 'Only in fairy tales.'

Diana made a contemptuous sound.

Ceres signaled Diana to be quiet. 'It was very strange. When we first came to your planet, we found you mortals alone in your knowledge. No other species matched your intelligence. That is not the way things should be. The Diptera commanded us to stay with you, to help you progress. But Zeus and his brothers, and some others, angered the Diptera so they brought us here. Since then it is forbidden for any of us to visit your planet and we do not know what the Diptera intend for us. But if Zeus provokes them, they may destroy us all.'

Sally coughed. Her throat felt tight and she found it hard to keep her eyes open. Still she felt a burning desire to understand. 'The angels – the Diptera - showed me. You almost destroyed the Earth. Could you really wreck a planet, kill us all, just to get back at Zeus?'

Ceres gave a sharp laugh. 'It is time for the truth. How could you know that?'

'There is a device in Iceland - what you call White Land - a wall, like a huge screen. It shows the history of Earth.' Sally gasped. A strange burning feeling was spreading across her stomach. 'Everything that has happened there.'

Diana sucked in her breath. 'So, it is true. Almighty furies!' She muttered angrily. 'What else are you concealing; you who should be dead by now?'

Ceres stood up. 'The Diptera showed you what they wanted you to see. I did not cause the meteorite to hit your planet. I used my power and that of my followers to divert it to where it might do the least harm.' Her voice hardened. 'If you thought so ill of me, I wonder that you would willingly remain with us.'

Sally gritted her teeth. The tingling sensation was now almost agonizing. It was like the pins and needles she had experienced as a child when she had sat still for too long, but a thousand times worse. 'I don't believe everything the angels have told me.' She panted with the pain. 'If I did, I would have stayed with them.'

Ceres looked down at Sally, a puzzled expression on her face, but Diana cut in. 'It is of no matter now. You will be dead within minutes.' She continued rapidly in her own language while Ceres listened, shaking her head.

The buzzing in her stomach suddenly eased and Sally stared up at the clear blue sky. Apart from the circle of pain where the sword had penetrated, she felt nothing; no fear or anger, no emotion at all. She moved her hand and winced as her tunic caught on the wound. She waited patiently, thinking that she ought to do or say something; to make her farewells. She tried to fix Alistair's image in her mind but she was distracted by the continuing argument between Ceres and Diana. Every few moments they glanced at her and finally Diana asked abruptly, 'Who are you?'

The shock of the question made Sally sit up. Diana backed away and drew her sword. She shouted harshly, then repeated. 'Who are you?'

Sally looked down. The bloodstain covered the front of her tunic, but it was turning dark. She was no longer bleeding. She looked up and met Diana's hostile gaze. 'I don't understand,' she whispered.

Ceres came forward and helped her to her feet. She pulled Sally's tunic up roughly and examined the wound. Then she turned away and took Diana aside. They stood, staring at Sally. Ceres spoke quietly and Diana answered in a harsh voice. Sally looked around. The floor of the valley had been swept clean by the flood and nothing remained of the monsters or their weapons. The forest behind was bright and green and the air was fresh. There was no sign of anything malevolent.

Diana cursed loudly. 'Why are you still alive?'

Sally tried to think about what had happened but she could not focus. 'I don't know. What do you think?'

'I think you are a lying bitch!' Diana sprang forward but Ceres restrained her. Diana shook with rage.

There was a long silence. Sally felt gradually stronger but she became uncomfortable under Ceres' steady gaze. 'I don't know what happened,' she repeated. 'I thought I was going to die.'

Diana snorted in disbelief. 'You are a liar, a traitor. This is how we have been led along like little sheep, to and fro, while our father laughs at us.' She turned to Ceres. 'Use your aegis. Make her talk.'

Ceres shook her head. 'I don't believe she knows.'

Sally shivered. 'What don't I know? What do you mean?'

Ceres took her hand and looked into her eyes. Then she sighed. 'You were struck by Ares. The power of his hand is second only to Zeus's. There is only one explanation for why you still live. You are not mortal.'

Diana cursed again but Ceres ignored her. 'You are not mortal,' she repeated to Sally. 'No mortal could survive such a blow.' She paused and looked closely at Sally's face. 'You may be of some sort unknown to us.' She shook her head. 'No. I think you are a child of Olympus.'

Sally's knees gave way. She sat down heavily and gasped for breath. For the last few weeks she had accepted her situation as real, however bizarre and unbelievable. She was on a strange planet, surrounded by aliens, who had played a covert and often malicious role in Earth's history. She had escaped the angels and formed an alliance with two beings whose motives and actions made some strange sort of sense. Now the whole edifice had come tumbling down and once again she was in a world of deception and illusion, a plaything in some hateful game. She clutched her face. If only she had stayed with Alistair.

A sharp blow to her head knocked her sideways.

'How did you get out of the White Land?' Diana's face was furious. 'Find a weapon, bitch. Perhaps you are my sister, but I will kill you anyway.'

'Desist!' Ceres dragged Diana back. 'I tell you, she does not know.' She looked sternly at Sally. 'Stay here. We must decide what to do. If the Diptera find out that an Olympian has once again visited earth, has fathered another child with a mortal...' She continued in her own language, pushing Diana ahead of her. They turned their backs to Sally as though suspecting she would understand what they said.

Sally sat for a few moments, panting with fear and shock. She lifted up her tunic and stared down at her stomach. Pink streaks radiated out from the livid gash of the stab wound. She touched the damaged flesh and winced. It was tender but not painful.

Her head pounded. She could not think. She looked around for her satchel. It was lying under a tree, near where she had been attacked. She took out her water flask, leaned against one of the trees and drank. Ceres and Diana were gazing back across the valley but there was nothing to be seen. As she replaced the flask, a movement caught her eye. A figure was standing in the darkness of the trees. Before she could move the man threw himself at her and clapped his hand over her mouth. She struggled frantically as he dragged her into the forest. Beyond the trees she glimpsed Diana and Ceres still looking away. She grabbed at a bush and dug her heels into the ground.

'Be quiet!' the man hissed. 'They must not see me.' Sally stared in amazement.

Thomas covered her face with his hand and she lost consciousness.

13

'Let no spear leave your hand that does not find its mark! Let your arrows fly true and your swords sate their thirst!' Athena turned towards Alistair and nodded. As he had done a dozen times in the last weeks, he raised his right arm above his head and pounded his left fist against his chest. The men roared in approval and banged the shafts of their spears against their shields. Despite himself, Alistair felt a rush of exhilaration.

The Spartan warships lay thick across the water. Each time they set out, fewer vessels returned but they still numbered in the hundreds. Many of the Spartans had been destroyed but that did not seem to diminish the passion of the survivors. For the first time in over two thousand years, they were doing what fate intended for them – fighting an impossible war. Alistair had watched in astonishment as the Spartans, in between the battles, had lazed around the decks, oiling their bodies and endlessly combing their hair. But he had seen them at the battlefront. Zeus's superior numbers had no chance against the fearless Spartans.

'Remember Thermopylae! Remember Xerxes!' Athena's voice roared out and her face was livid with passion. 'Look to your Law. Each of you is worth a hundred, no, a thousand of Zeus's men. Pity those poor fools but do not let that pity stay your hand. If Zeus overpowers us, you will all become slaves. Conquer or die!'

In response, a thousand sails rose and the air resonated with the beating of oars against the water. Alistair watched as the shining black triremes moved out of the bay, following the same strict formation as ever. The hundreds of blue eyes on the ships' bows stared back at him. He shivered in the cool dawn air.

'Go say your words to your brother. Then find Althamas.' Athena's mouth tightened into a grim line. Her spies had advised her that a huge armada was moving east. What Zeus intended was not clear but Athena was determined that the fleet should not pass through her domain. 'We will watch the battle.'

Alistair tried not to show his revulsion. It was always the same. Athena insisted on his presence and the endless slaughter sickened him. Many of the men were brought home and regenerated but increasing numbers could not be saved. And for every Spartan lost, a hundred of Zeus's men died in agony, only to be regenerated and flung back into the battle a few days later. Still, Alistair could not disagree with Athena's strategy. The Spartans welcomed death in battle - if they were revived to fight again, so much the better. Their spirits rose with every conflict. But Zeus's Anomee were not military by nature. Athena knew that they were losing heart and their resistance was weakening. Zeus would soon have no army fit to mount an attack on the Diptera.

Meanwhile Apollo and Hercules harried their father, in the hope that he would give up his reckless plan.

'Is there any news of Diana and Ceres?' Alistair still found it hard to look at Athena directly. Her gaze confused and disoriented him. She so often seemed like a normal, although extremely beautiful young woman. But when she commanded her people, her superhuman powers were obvious. She could see vast distances. Her voice carried for miles. And she could go for long periods without rest or food.

Now she gave him a sympathetic glance. 'No. Nor do we know where Poseidon and Vulcan have gone. Find Althamas and join me within the hour.'

Alistair saluted Athena, turned away from the view of the great armada and ran towards the eastern hills. He did not bother to ask for news of Sally. Athena was sure that neither Zeus nor any of his followers had her. He could only hope that Thomas had found her and was keeping her safe. The thought of her dead or suffering tortured him. In the first days he had looked obsessively at the images from her data pad. He had listened to her favorite music and read her notes over and over again. Now he tried not to think of her at all or to wonder what Thomas's motives were. No Diptera had been sighted in Northland since their confrontation with Zeus several weeks ago. Either they were preoccupied with what was happening on Earth or they were waiting for the outcome of the struggle between the immortals. Alistair shuddered and resolutely tried to think of something else. The idea that the angels would destroy this world and his own was unthinkable.

He paused to catch his breath, bent down and plucked a stem of rosemary from the bushes that covered the hillside. He crushed the flowers and breathed in the odor. It reminded him sharply of roast dinners and family gatherings. Were there any native fauna here or was everything imported or imitated? His eyes watered as he thought of Vicki and Mohun. Were they safe? Had Thomas deceived him about that as well?

He cast the sprig away and walked more quickly up the path. The rolling hills east of the great plain were named Salonica. Further north were other settlements – Arcadia, Ithaca, Sparta and Dardania, named after the areas of ancient Greece from which the inhabitants had been brought. There was no commerce between the Greeks and the Anomee; the Greeks regarded them as backward and weak. Nor were they curious about the regions south of the ice belt. Alistair was surprised by their lack of interest in the rest of the planet, until he realized that the constant battles between the gods kept them occupied.

Salonica was mainly populated by the hundreds of Greeks whom Athena had rescued during the Second World War, and their descendants. For almost two thousand years Athena had honored the Diptera's command to leave Earth alone. But, according to Althamas, news of the Nazi occupation of Athens and the starvation of its people had maddened Athena and she had intervened. The Diptera had not punished her disobedience. They were either ignorant of her activities or had decided they were unimportant.

Sam Mousalimos and his compatriots had been encouraged to establish families. Those who tired of life here were permitted to age and die, but most accepted the option to be regenerated, so that several generations often lived side by side, the old appearing as young as their descendants.

The regeneration process greatly improved physical health and strength and eliminated diseases and deformities. But it had several other side effects, including the elimination of facial hair, a fact lamented by the Greeks who had valued their beards highly. A more serious consequence was that it ultimately caused sterility and the birth rate was declining. Many men and women had been killed or needed repair during the endless clashes between the immortals. But there were still hundreds of children here and Alistair was greatly consoled by their company. They laughed at his attempts to speak Greek and teased him about his sandy, receding hair and freckled skin.

'Alistair!' Melissa stood at the doorway of her house; a toddler perched on her hip. Alistair smiled and waved but did not stop to talk. Sam's great granddaughter had lost her husband in a skirmish with Zeus's Anomee more than a year ago and she had made it plain that Alistair would be a good replacement. Alistair was happy to enjoy the Salonican women's hospitality but he could not commit himself to a more serious relationship. It would be unfair to Melissa. He had tried to explain to her that he was still in love with Sally. She smiled and shook her head. 'You take life too seriously,' she had said.

He heard her laughing now as he passed along the paved lane towards his home. The Salonicans were a light hearted people. Alistair felt sometimes that he was living in ancient Greece where the people took for granted that most of the gods were capricious and often downright malicious. In such an existence, every moment had to be lived for its own sake. They worshipped Athena and Ceres as true and just, and admired Hercules, Diana and Apollo, even if they did not quite trust them. When they compared their existence with that of the Anomee, they were even more grateful that they had not fallen into Zeus's hands.

Alistair pushed open the door to his house. No need for locks here, where nothing was scarce and anything the people wanted could be replicated. They grew their own food, wove cloth and made most of their necessities by hand. And domestic animals flourished here. But if need be, they could conjure up anything they needed.

He passed through the living area and into the small walled garden, sat down on an ornately carved bench and composed himself. For the last few weeks he had strange feelings after this daily ritual. He had always been able to imagine Jeremy at home or with friends and his imaginings cheered him. But recently his vision of Jeremy echoed that of the poem. His brother was in a confined space, surrounded by darkness, anxious and tense. Alistair wished violently that he knew what was happening on Earth. What were the troubles that the angels had alluded to; what events had taken them to Earth and led to the present conflict?

He breathed deeply and composed himself again. He spoke the familiar lines in an even voice, but they did not comfort. He was certain that Jeremy was in trouble. For a few moments he sat dispirited. Then stood up abruptly, found his thick poncho like garment that could also serve as a blanket, and filled a satchel with food and flasks of water. Like the Salonicans, he preferred to eat naturally grown food even if he could not taste the difference. And it frustrated him that he could not yet understand how the immortals created material objects. Althamas believed that the immortals themselves did not understand the process. They had no curiosity about such things.

Alistair avoided Melissa's house and took another path to the agora. At this hour Althamas was probably there, enjoying a debate with some of his contemporaries. Althamas had been studying logic and rhetoric when Helike had been destroyed. When Hercules took him to Athens he had joined Plato's academy and aspired to become a master. He had been amazed and delighted when the modern Greeks had told him that Socrates, Plato and Aristotle were still widely read and admired.

Alistair paused as a young man ushered a small flock of sheep across the path. The man greeted him and made a reverence. Athena's people still treated him with a respect that he often thought he did not deserve. But he was an important symbol of what they were fighting for; freedom from Zeus and Hera's capricious disregard for mortal life, even the survival of human life on this planet.

He smiled back at the young man and realized with surprise that there were many moments when he was almost happy. The air was clean, the weather pleasant and the food tasted wonderful. He had interesting company and there was so much to learn. He had no instruments but he was a keen observer with a good memory. Every night he entered the day's findings into his data pad.

The view from the top of the hill still amazed him. He wondered again how the immortals could mould the landscape to so closely resemble Earth's. He had questioned Althamas closely but he professed ignorance. None of the people here seemed interested in how or where the immortals had acquired their technologies.

The valley below was a junction for several regions and from a distance resembled an ancient Greek town. The central agora was paved with white marble and surrounded by banks of seats. Four broad colonnaded avenues led out of the agora, punctuated by narrower streets, which led to the large rectangular buildings where many of the ancient Greeks preferred to live. Unlike the modern Salonicans, they welcomed the immortals' ability to replicate anything they desired. Athena did not approve of slavery and no mortal was compelled to work for another. So the ancient Greeks lived in luxury thanks to the bounty of the immortals. No wonder they called this land "Elysium", Alistair thought.

The agora was busy and Alistair could see a flock of white togas seated on the lower benches. He looked up at the sun, ran down the hill and entered the city. He ignored the Hetaerae, calling out from their balconies. Thanks to Athena, women in this society enjoyed similar status to men but the Hetaerae maintained their traditions. Alistair was fascinated but also repelled by the idea that they would willingly continue such a trade for more than two thousand years. Althamas had tried to explain. 'These are not prostitutes. They are accomplished women. Even Hercules respects them.'

A wonderful scent of roses drifted out of a nearby garden. The large houses were built in the Ionic style, with central courtyards. Alistair had spent many evenings with Althamas, in his splendid courtyard garden. Such beauty was very tempting but Alistair resisted it and returned each night to his small house in Salonica. Perhaps he was deluding himself, but it seemed more real.

As he entered the Agora he saw Althamas surrounded by his admirers. He was very open-minded and had welcomed the new knowledge brought by the modern Greeks, but he found some of Alistair's ideas unsettling. In particular Althamas objected to Alistair's ideas about scientific method. 'You ignore purpose,' he would say reproachfully. 'You are too preoccupied with material causes. Consider the Diptera. Who knows how they live? What is important is the purpose for which they were created.'

'Or which they created for themselves,' Alistair had contradicted him. 'Since we don't know exactly what they intend or why, we should try to figure out how they work, what they can and can't do.' Alistair had long abandoned any hope that the Diptera might resemble the angels he had learned about as a child in Sunday school. 'And stop them!'

Alistair waved. Althamas responded and rose to make his farewells. Alistair admired the graceful figure as it descended the seats and weaved through the crowded agora towards him. It was hard to think of Althamas as being old. He looked the same age as Alistair and still had boundless enthusiasm for life. He also had a very sweet nature and was not offended by Alistair's refusal to become his lover. Instead they had become firm friends.

When Alistair told him of the forthcoming battle, Althamas's smile disappeared. 'How much longer can this continue?'

'Athena is very patient. One of the advantages of immortality, I assume.'

'But Zeus is not patient.'

Alistair stood by as Althamas returned to warn his friends. Within moments the news spread through the agora and the crowd had dispersed.

'I would like to visit the pyramid again. My friends need to know what is going on.' Alistair took Althamas's arm. 'Will you come with me, after the battle?'

Althamas nodded. Alistair had explained how the data pad and pyramid worked; how the Phoenix crew would be able to read his messages when they arrived in their star ship. Althamas had conveyed this news to Athena and had been assured that a watch would be kept for any signs that the spacecraft had arrived. On each occasion Althamas had accompanied him and kept guard. But the valley was deserted. The Anomee had been taken from their village or had fled.

Whatever had affected the watchers had also disabled the data pad's ability to receive or transmit, so Alistair had to use the relay cable to transfer data directly to the pyramid. Nor could he retrieve any data which the Millennium crew might have recorded for him. Sometimes Alistair wondered whether anyone would read his messages. How had Thomas persuaded John to leave? He shook his head. Thomas might not be able to lie, but he could deceive. Had the Millennium really left Earth 2? Was Rick Jones already on his way? He hoped they would take his warnings seriously. He wished violently that the pyramids had been designed for two way communication, but they could only store and transmit data to the satellites. He would have to be patient.

'Alistair! Are you unwell?'

'No; just thinking. Let's go.'

As they reached the crest of the hill they paused to look out over the sea. The black swarm of Spartan warships was marking time at the entrance to the bay. To the west, a long line, like a thin brown snake was moving rapidly towards them. As they watched, the line split in two.

'Hades!' Althamas swore. 'Where has Zeus been hiding all those ships? We are vastly outnumbered. Hurry!' They ran along the path, and leapt up the rough steps towards the white rostrum at the top of the hill.

Athena was alone. She did not comment as Althamas and Alistair entered the elevated platform, but pulled down the clear screen which magnified the view and sound.

The Spartan triremes were now on the move. They lowered their sails and sped towards the double line of Zeus's fleet. The three banks of oars hit the water in perfect unison, sending streaks of white across the calm water.

Althamas swore again. 'What are they doing? They will be outflanked.' As though the enemy commander had heard him, the brown lines separated further as though to enclose the faster black ships.

Alistair heard Althamas hissing with dismay as the lines converged. He grasped his friend's arm. 'Wait and see. They have been learning new tactics.'

The Spartan warships raced through the gap between the two brown lines, which moved to close behind them. Suddenly they took on new speed. In perfect formation, the Spartan ships flew left and right and rammed the unsuspecting Anomee before they could turn their vessels to face them. The blue eyes rose triumphantly as the sharp prows pierced their enemies' hulls, lifting them out of the water. Within minutes the forward line of the enemy was routed. Some of the brown ships turned frantically to flee but the black ships pursued them and impaled them from behind. The Spartans threw down their oars and leapt onto the decks of the stricken ships. Alistair turned away. The

Spartans took no prisoners. With the banning of slavery, there was no point. He could not watch the slaughter.

Athena gave a furious cry. Alistair looked towards where she was pointing. A dark cloud was moving over the surface of the water. Streaks of lightening flashed across it and shot down to the water. It swept down over the ships and there was a deafening noise of cracking timber and screaming men. The cloud swirled for a few moments and then retreated at enormous speed. Across a great tract of water the fleets lay ruined. To extinguish the legendary Spartans, Zeus had sacrificed his own people.

They watched helplessly as the black triremes foundered and pitched violently. The water hissed as the flaming wrecks sank.

Athena screamed with rage. 'He has broken the law. He is no longer my father.' She swept her cloak around her shoulders and Alistair glimpsed the edge of Athena's dreadful aegis, which terrified all who faced it.

Althamas groaned. 'So many men. We will not recover them in time. They are lost to us.'

'It is ended.' Athena's voice was calmer but her face was livid. 'I will find my brothers and sisters. I will go directly to the Diptera and beg that they rid us of this tyrant.'

'No! Surely there must be...' Althamas was silenced by an angry look.

'There is no other way.' Athena beckoned imperiously. 'You, mortal, will come with me. Althamas, warn my people. Be their shield.'

Alistair felt the heat rise to his head and for a moment he could not speak. As Athena reached for him, he said quickly, 'Althamas should warn my people too. Let him go first to send a message.'

Athena nodded.

Alistair grasped Althamas's hand. 'You know how to do it. You will find the pad in my pack. Tell them everything. Please.' Overcome with emotion, they embraced. Athena pulled Alistair away and covered him with her cloak.

14

'What are you looking for?'

Thomas did not answer. After their frantic and dizzying flight through the forest, he had dropped Sally onto this narrow ledge overlooking the ocean. She sat shaking and nauseated for a few moments. As her eyes adjusted to the light she saw his tall figure. He was staring southwards, his wings half extended. Beyond him, she could see the dark outline of a large land mass. There was no sign of Diana or Ceres, no movement on the shining water.

Sally looked down and drew back quickly. Below her feet, the cliffs fell more than twenty meters to the water. She swiveled around. The dense trees fringed the cliff in both directions. 'Thomas!' She shivered. It would soon be dark.

Silence.

'Thomas! Where are we going?' Sally edged forward carefully and pulled at his tunic.

He turned awkwardly towards her and she gasped. She had not seen him clearly in the forest. His face was gaunt and furrowed. 'I cannot move my head,' he said in a low voice. His wings were trembling as though agitated.

'What?' Sally started back in fright and almost overbalanced. She clutched at a branch to steady herself. 'What's wrong with you? I thought you couldn't get sick.'

Thomas moved his shoulders slowly as though they pained him. 'I cannot retract my wings.'

'Can you still fly? We have to find Alistair.' Sally could not look at Thomas's face.

'I need to rest.' Thomas turned away. His wings were still moving and now she could see that his whole body trembled.

Sally shivered and the caked blood on her tunic grated against the stab wound. 'Can you at least give me something to eat and drink, something warmer to wear?'

'I cannot commune with the choir. I have lost contact. I can do nothing.'

Sally shook with fear. Her heart pounded so violently she could not speak. She pulled at Thomas's arm and flinched at the touch. She felt the strange sensation she had always experienced when she came into contact with an angel, and the trembling ran up her arm like an electric shock.

'What do you mean? Why did you bring me south?'

Thomas shifted slightly but he remained facing the sea. 'I did not understand what was happening to me. I thought I could get back to the choir in time.' He paused and Sally made an impatient sound. He said abruptly. 'But it is too late. You must stay here with me. There is something you must know. You must never tell anyone, not even Alistair.'

'So don't tell me. I won't keep secrets from Alistair.'

'Will you tell him that you are not mortal?'

Sally shuddered again. Despite her bloodstained tunic she still could hardly believe what had happened. She raised her chin and stared defiantly at Thomas's back. 'Yes, I will. It's not like I'm the only one. From what Ceres told me, Zeus and the others had hundreds of children on Earth. My mother was just one of their victims.' She thought of the image of her birth mother on the wall in Iceland; the angry expression on the young woman's face as she spoke to the father, her sharp movements as she handed the baby to the nurse.

Thomas was silent for a moment. 'If you tell Alistair, the choir may take the knowledge from him, and you will be in great danger.' He turned stiffly to look at her and she flinched at the sight of his haggard face.

'I don't understand.' For a brief moment Sally saw herself as from above, a tired, desperate woman arguing with an angel, like a scene from a fantasy movie. She shook her head. 'I don't understand,' she repeated. 'Why should I be blamed for what some gourd did to my mother?' She thought of Zeus and her stomach churned.

'Who do you think is your father?' Thomas's voice was slightly stronger.

For a moment Sally couldn't speak. She stared into Thomas's eyes and a series of images flashed before her.

She heard her voice as though someone else spoke 'It was me who should have been shot in Geneva.' She almost choked. 'Did you kill Pierre as well?'

'No. Pierre Meyer's heart failed.' Thomas moved his head slightly and grimaced as if with pain. 'You were the greatest danger. With your talents ... We knew that you might discover our secrets. We took actions to prevent the Millennium from leaving Earth. But the protocols and conditions did not produce further solutions.' He paused again as though speaking tired him. 'The choir is ...' He broke off.

Sally took a deep breath. 'So then, you tried to make sure that the mission would fail; we would go home thinking that something on the planet caused hallucinations. Did you really think that would stop us? John will come back.'

'The Millennium crashed.'

'I know. I saw it. But the shuttles were gone. The crew can get back to Earth on those. And then they will come back.'

'You are mistaken. The shuttles were destroyed. The crew landed safely but they cannot return to Earth.'

'I don't believe you.' Sally's heart thumped.

'You know that if I speak, I can use only the data I have collected. The crew are in the southern land somewhere.' He pointed to the south, towards the dark outline of the island.

'Well, Rick will come. He will be here soon.'

'Richard Jones ...' Thomas did not continue.

Sally felt sick. 'What have you done to him? Have you killed him too?'

'No instructions to dispose of him were issued.'

'If you wanted me dead, why didn't you kill me later?' She wondered at her recklessness. Even in this weakened state, Thomas could probably finish her with a mere beat of his wings.

'Sima showed me a photograph of your parents. You may remember that he was sick during the voyage. I deleted his memory of the event.'

'Why? Did you recognize my father? Who is he?'

Thomas continued as though she had not spoken. 'My attempt to trap you in the hills failed. I could not inform the choir; therefore I could receive no further instructions regarding how to dispose of you.' Thomas gazed at her. 'Your mother was the instrument of my corruption.' He ignored her shocked face and continued in the same unemotional tone. 'Michael will end us both if this information enters the choir.'

Sally clutched a branch. She thought she might faint, but she had to get him to repeat what he had said. 'Are you telling me, you are my father?'

'I fell.' Thomas closed his eyes for a moment. 'I was corrupted. I warned Gabriel not to leave me on your planet, but my input did not affect the consensus. I have lived many times on your planet and during one of those times I met your mother. I knew I had fathered a child but your mother gave you away. I could not inform the choir. It is forbidden to … Without the choir, I could not trace you.'

Sally cut in. 'It can't be true. I've seen my DNA – it's the usual – European, Asian.'

'Your tests are inadequate. They would not show my contribution. I speak the facts. I was the first being who penetrated your mother and …'

'Shut up! I don't want to know.' Sally clutched her head.

'You must tell no one. Michael will end us both,' he repeated. 'And Michael may judge this as the final proof that the great trial has failed. If so, Michael will order a cleansing. A new trial will be undertaken, but the gourds, the mortals here and on Earth, will be erased.'

For several moments Sally could hardly breathe. Her heart thumped so violently that she thought she might die. Then Thomas's face loomed in front of her and she sucked in a great gulp of air. Thomas leaned back and watched silently as she tried to steady her breathing.

Finally her head cleared, although her heart was still pounding. 'Let me get this straight. Are you telling me that if the other angels, the choir, finds out that you had sex with a human, then they will blame us for your weakness? The fact that you can't obey your own laws, will cause Michael to judge us as failures, to justify destroying us?' Her voice rose to a shriek.

Thomas's expression did not change. 'It is the logical conclusion. It is who you are, what you have caused to happen. You have not progressed in the approved manner. Your influences are unpredictable, difficult to control.

We have tried to correct you but we have failed.' He closed his eyes again. 'So many variables, so many unintended consequences ...'

Sally stared at the unemotional face. 'I've never heard anything so bloody ridiculous in my whole life. You're all farking mad!'

'You may be correct. I believe we are faulty. Michael has ...' He paused. 'But the consensus will continue to operate until the termination condition occurs, and I have no information on that.' His eyes opened wide and Sally had to look away. 'If you assist me, I will make no more attempts to dispose of you. But I must rest and compose myself. I may be able to continue without the choir. I do not wish to end.'

'No. We don't have time.' Sally pulled at his tunic, and then pulled harder as he teetered at the edge of the cliff. 'We have to get Alistair out of Iceland. We have to get help.' Part of her mind was still screaming – it can't be true. Symptoms of shock were starting to overwhelm her and she wrestled frantically to stay calm.

'Alistair is no longer with the choir. When you escaped, I took him to Northland.'

Sally felt as though he had hit her. 'You bastard!'

'He told me he did not know where you were. I thought he lied. If the choir interrogated him ...'

'Zeus will get him.'

'That may occur. Or he may avoid notice.'

Another mammoth effort to collect her thoughts: 'You have to take me to Southland. We'll find Ceres and Diana. They told me that Hercules and some others are fighting Zeus, to stop him going up against the angels. They're trying to get to the southern gods, to get them to help. We can find John and the others too.' Sally felt her mind clear.

To be able to talk to the crew seemed like the most joyful thing she had ever hoped for. John and Sharon would know what to do.

'I cannot travel as I am now. I need to rest.'

'How long?' Sally carefully moved forward and peered up at Thomas. He was shivering violently. His profile was very pale and the blonde curly hair was flat and lifeless. His wings twitched as though he was trying to extend them. She felt an enormous revulsion. She could not bear to think about how she might have been conceived.

She looked south towards the island. The sun was dipping below the horizon and Selenis had already risen. They could travel by moonlight. Her eyes watered at the prospect of seeing the crew again. She couldn't wait. The dark forest loomed behind them. 'We should leave now. It could be dangerous here.'

'No! I must rest.' Thomas reached out and grasped her wrist.

She tried to pull away and winced as he tightened his grip. His hand shook and painful tremors run up Sally's arm. She felt again that his flesh was not in quite the same reality, as though they were out of synch. 'Let me go. I can bring back help.'

Thomas did not release her. 'No. You must stay here with me. I must give you more information.'

Sally felt an awful panic. She wrenched away from him with all her strength and Thomas reeled backwards, thumping against a tree. The wood reverberated with a strange ringing noise and Thomas shook violently. Sally grabbed his hand and tried to force open his fingers but they were clenched hard, like an iron ring around her wrist. He muttered something and tottered towards the edge of the cliff. Sally screamed and pulled frantically back. She was dragged forward and just as she thought they would both topple over, Thomas stopped abruptly.

'Let me go!' Sally shrieked. She punched Thomas's arm and yelled with pain. He had stiffened so that his flesh was as hard as rock. He did not react. He stood motionless, his left hand stretched out in front of him, his right hand still circling Sally's wrist. She pushed him again. He was no longer trembling but stood still as a stone.

The setting sun slipped below the horizon, sending a flash of green light over the ocean and the great orb of Selenis shone brilliantly in the dark blue sky, turning the water and the forest to silver. Sally felt an awful stillness as though time had stopped. She put her hand out to pull at Thomas's tunic. The fold of cloth was cold and hard under her fingers. She leaned forwards to look up at his face. The lines and furrows were gone, the skin smoothed out as though he were a young man. The eyes were blank, the face calm, the lips set in a serene half smile. She had seen him a hundred times before, in cemeteries and churches, in stone or paint. She reached up. The skin was smooth and cold, the surface slightly elastic, like clay that had not quite hardened.

She bent down and wrenched a piece of rock out of the crumbling edge of the cliff. Her breath caught in her throat as she smashed the rock down on Thomas's right arm. The first blow dented the smooth surface. Two more blows shattered the wrist and the severed hand dropped heavily. Something clanked against the stony feet and she picked up Thomas's watcher. Her heart thumped as she turned it over, but like her own watcher, it was inactive. She hesitated, slipped it onto her right arm, then knelt down and chipped at the stiff fingers which still enclosed her left wrist. A few moments later her hand was bloodied but free. She swept the shards into the ocean and then touched the half extended wings. There was nothing to suggest that a living being had once occupied this shell.

She sat on the edge of the cliff and gazed out over the silver sea. For a long time she thought of nothing. Then she looked up at the still figure and Thomas's words rang in her head. 'Live forever,' she breathed and trembled with shock. Her mind shied away from the idea, replaced by images of her childhood flashing before her eyes, faster and faster as though she were watching a movie. Her parents had never hidden the fact of her adoption. There was no point. None of her family had Sally's pale olive skin, her exotic beauty and mental brilliance. She had always felt out of place, bored by the local school and her classmates, driven to search for the answer to some indefinable question. She couldn't wait to leave her comfortable home, to find her real identity. Now, perhaps, she had found it. As she thought of her parents' cozy, old-fashioned living room, loneliness gripped her like a physical pain and she felt tears running down her face. She wiped them away and stood up. 'I am what I am,' she muttered.

The familiar constellation of the Southern Cross had escaped Selenis' brilliance and dominated the southern sky. She stared up at it for a few moments and then slipped over the side of the cliff. Footholds seemed to meet her feet as she descended and within a few minutes she had reached the narrow strip of sand. She tried to imitate the gesture which Diana had used to conjure up a boat. A faint whisper of wind was the only result. She looked out over the calm water to the southern land mass, a dark shadow, no more than a few miles away. She slipped off her trousers and unfastened her sandals. The water was cool but not unpleasant. She walked out until the water reached her waist before looking back. The stone angel stood shining in the moonlight, like a guardian of the island. She turned away and started to swim south.

15

Sharon stepped sideways as neat and nimble as a dancer. She ducked under the whistling blade and drove the hilt of her sword into the man's back. He fell forward with a grunt of surprise. The audience roared with approval as Sharon set her foot on the Viking's neck and thrust the point of her sword against his throat. She let him squirm for a few moments before stepping back. The man jumped up, leapt for his sword and charged. Sharon skipped away, grinning.

'Your friend takes great care not to be slain.' The statuesque blonde leaned closer to Mohun and fingered his dark curls.

'It is not our custom to seek death,' Mohun replied coolly. He waited a moment before standing up. Ylva had been eyeing him for several days and he did not want to encourage her. Nor did he want to insult her with a flat refusal. He called out to Sharon and she blew him a kiss, her face alight with pleasure. Her Viking opponent stood like a stone as Sharon teased him, dancing around him and making beckoning gestures. Each time he thrust at her, she dodged away. Finally he shook his head in frustration and lowered his sword. He strode back to the benches, seized a goblet and poured the contents over his head. Sharon did a little victory dance and ran up the wooden seats towards Vicki and Mohun.

'But to be reborn! To be forever young! You cannot deny the pleasure each new day brings,' Ylva insisted.

Mohun secretly agreed. He would never forget the deep sense of joy and peace which the regeneration had given him. But he could not pay the price. He was no warrior. He could not bear the idea of taking another's life or willingly giving up his own, even if only for a few hours.

When Mohun did not reply Ylva grunted, rose to her feet, and adjusted her leather jerkin. She pushed through the people below her and stepped out onto the arena. She looked back at Mohun and shrugged as he continued to ignore her.

'Good show Sharon!' Vicki grimaced. She and Mohun had managed to avoid the daily competitions. The Aesir had been so impressed by their knowledge of animals and plants they had given them special status as sages. Still, they were both expected to make regular appearances at the Hall of Warriors to witness the combat and attend the feasts. For the first few days, the sights, sounds and smells had made Vicki feel ill. She had tried to close her mind to them and gradually the spectacle ceased to affect her.

But this life suited Sharon; battle without grief or guilt. Her face was glowing. She flung her arms around Mohun's neck and kissed him passionately. Mohun felt the same drowning sensation he had experienced from the moment Sharon had entered his hut and declared her intentions. He could not imagine what attracted Sharon to him but he had no desire to resist. For the first few days after their landing Mohun had seen little of Sharon, Sima or John; endlessly discussing tactics and making plans for Rick's arrival. Vicki and Sima slept together from the first night and Mohun started to feel his solitude. But on the day John presented their plans, Sharon moved her gear into Mohun's hut.

As the weeks passed they settled into the routine of life in Asgard; early morning rides through the misty birch forests on the small but sturdy Icelandic horses, marches along the windswept beaches, long afternoons in the Hall of Warriors, the twilight processions to carry the slain to the hall of rebirth and the wild feasting that followed. Every few days they would be summonsed to Gladsheim to be questioned closely by Thor and the other Aesir. Mohun shivered as he thought of their first meeting with the gods.

On the morning after their rebirth the Valkyrien had dressed the crew in pale linen robes and had given each a distinctive amulet to wear. The runes on the amulet, the Valkyrien explained, symbolized some quality which the Norse gods assumed the mortals to possess. They had mounted the small horses and ridden to the top of the small hill north of the hut. From there they had a spectacular view of Gladsheim. The hall of the Aesir was so immense that it was impossible to judge how far it extended. It filled most of the wide valley and the sheer grey walls receded into the distance until they merged with the dark blur of the mountains beyond. Mohun's heart thudded in his chest as they passed through the great arched entrance and the huge wooden gates slammed shut behind them with a dreadful finality. They were led through a hall so vast and featureless that it seemed to belong to a different reality, and when they entered the meeting room Mohun felt as though he had indeed entered another world.

Five figures sat in a group on carved thrones at one end of a brightly lit room. Hundreds of candles, and huge lamps which appeared to be suspended in midair showed a great open space. The vast chamber was unadorned except for strange carvings around the pillars which supported the high vaulted ceiling.

Mohun recognized Loki and three others who had witnessed the crew's regeneration. But here their demeanor was quite different. The woman with the radiant fall of red hair was smiling at Loki. She laughed and gave Loki a small slap across his shoulder. Two massive men with long pale plaits talked loudly to a stunningly beautiful man with corn colored hair, and threw back their heads to drink from large goblets. The crew stood in stunned silence in the doorway until the Valkyrien pushed them forwards. At once the five became quiet and stood up. As they did so there was loud long note as though from a horn and two other men entered. One appeared much older; he walked slowly, leaning on a thick spear which he used as a staff. His long hair was white and his yellow beard was streaked with grey. The younger man's hair and beard were dark red. They wore similar clothes to the other Aesir, the metallic embroidery and gems glittering in the candlelight as they mounted the stairs and seated themselves. The elderly man made an elaborate gesture and the younger man stood up and called out in a loud voice. 'Come nearer to us and say your names.'

John stepped forward and stood stiff and erect. He gave his name, rank and serial number as though preparing for interrogation by an enemy. 'And before I continue,' he added. 'I want to know to whom I am speaking and why my crew and I were assaulted and kidnapped.'

Sima gasped in dismay but the man seemed to treat John's question seriously. 'There are great changes taking place in our world. What part you will play is not yet clear, but we may have need of your advice.' The tall red haired man leaned forward, his long plaits swinging across his shoulders. He stared intently into John's face. Then, as if satisfied by what he saw he raised his head. 'I am Thor, son of Odin.' He gave a half bow to the older man. 'Here are the other Aesir, those who remain on this planet.' He gestured to the seated figures. 'Freya, for fruitfulness, Balder for peace and beauty, Tyr for justice, Vidar, god of war, the silent one who keeps the book of reckoning and Loki, who holds the power of fire.'

He paused. 'Have you no memory of us?' He looked directly at John. 'Your people lived far to the south of our domain on your planet. But many of you travelled to our lands and accompanied us on our voyages. Have you forgotten the stories?'

To Mohun's surprise, John answered in a respectful voice. 'We have not forgotten, but it is so long ago that the stories have grown dim. Why did you leave us?'

Loki cut in. 'We are asking the questions ...'

Thor silenced him. 'We lived in harmony with your people, but the dark immortals, the Olympians, caused terrible damage. The Ice Giants were greatly angered and commanded all immortals to leave. Now we live out our allotted time, awaiting Ragnarok.'

'The Ice Giants; who are they?' John leaned forward, his face intent.

'Later.' Thor turned to Sharon. 'Give your name and your purpose.'

Sharon and Sima gave clear but terse summaries of their roles in the Millennium mission. Mohun felt an enormous relief that Vicki had recalled their awakening and the telling of their stories. This interrogation might be some sort of test of their honesty.

Thor asked Vicki apparently random questions about different areas of Earth, the oceans, vegetation, animals and human settlements. Her answers did not seem to please him and Mohun saw that all of the gods except Loki and Odin were frowning. Loki retained his usual amused expression and Odin was staring downwards, his eyes half closed.

'And what of the great lizards?'

Vicki hesitated. 'There are many types of lizards.'

'I speak of those that fly. Do they still harass the peoples of the North?'

Vicki looked around as though seeking an answer from the crew.

'Well?'

'There have been no lizards which fly, in living memory, although there are many stories about them.' Vicki stammered slightly and her face flushed.

Thor's frown deepened. He continued to question Vicki. As her answers revealed the explosion in the human population, the resulting pollution and the number of species which had been made extinct, his expression grew angrier. Vicki's voice weakened and she hesitated. Sima moved to her side and put his arm round her waist.

'Enough!' Freya stood up and made a placating gesture. Her ring flashed in the lamplight. 'This young woman is not responsible for the earth's ills.' She smiled at Vicki. 'Indeed her knowledge tells us that she has spent her life trying to remedy them.' Thor nodded and ran his hand over his face as though tired.

When it was Mohun's turn, Freya had smiled at him and said quietly, 'You have already told us all we need to know. We see plainly the avatar within you.' She raised her right arm. 'Hail, son of Krishna.'

Mohun had stuttered with shock. 'What do you mean?'

'Not all the immortals returned with the Ice Giants. A few live among you still. Some of their children have become like you – frail and mortal.' Freya smiled again. 'But always surprising.'

Mohun shivered again as he recalled the expression in Freya's eyes.

Sharon leaned back. 'What's the matter?'

'Nothing; sometimes I can't believe I'm really here; what is real and what is not.'

Sharon stroked the back of his neck. 'Don't worry. We've been over this so many times. We have to work with what we know.' She silenced him with another kiss.

Vicki looked up as the Vikings roared again. Although she could not see them, she knew that John and Sima were playing their parts, on the far side of the hall. She could not bear to watch. John had been killed twice, Sima three times. Each time she had accompanied his body on the torchlight procession she had felt she would never see Sima again. But the following morning she would awake to find him, full of joy, loving her as though it were their first time together.

She stared around at the jubilant throng. These people were happy. For millennia they had lived like this, in an endless cycle of death and rebirth, but their love for life had not weakened. They were quarrelsome and easily offended but they could settle their grievances each day in the Hall of Warriors and wake the next morning with a clean slate. Vicki flinched as one of the Vikings, Berse, landed on his back with a thump which would have killed a weaker man. His opponent Ulf raised his sword to finish him while those nearby stepped back to watch. This was a famous dispute which months of fighting had not settled. Berse had taken Sigrun, Ulf's daughter, without his agreement and although Sigrun was happy to stay with Berse, Ulf took her back and would not return her until Berse paid a ridiculously heavy bride price.

Shouts rang out as Berse rolled quickly aside and knocked Ulf off his feet. Vicki wondered how the Vikings could bear their existence if it were not for these passionate feuds and the daily promise of revenge and rebirth. There was no boredom, no tedium in these people's lives. They were child-like in their enthusiasm, for food, adventure, romance, and the beauty of the natural world. The Aesir had created the stark beauty of northern Scandinavia in the southern continent. Thick forests, deep fjords soaring up to snow tipped mountains, long white beaches pounded by the windswept sea. Vicki still could hardly believe it. She often thought back to their first days in Southland, surrounded by barren rock and the calm ocean. She understood in principle how the gods had managed to conceal their country but the source of their power remained a mystery.

The only shadow on the Vikings' lives was the absence of children. The regeneration process affected their fertility. Vicki would have loved to investigate why this was so but only the Aesir and the Valkyrien had knowledge of the substance and process which allowed the cells to regenerate so perfectly and at such an amazing rate. This knowledge was forbidden, even to Vikings fathered by the Aesir. None of the Vikings seemed worried by their situation. When Vicki had questioned Tyra, one of her new friends, the woman had laughed and pointed to a handsome young man. 'There is Ivar, my son, born before my fourth rebirth.'

'Don't you miss your home?' Vicki had asked wonderingly.

Tyra shook her head. 'I can hardly remember my family. We were poor. Often there was not enough to eat. Thieves slew me when I fought to defend my cattle.' She laughed. 'Why would I want to leave? What could be better than this? Besides, after Ragnarok, we will all start again. Then there will be babies.'

Ragnarok! Sima had told Vicki what he remembered from his studies of the Norse sagas. 'It's puzzling. From what I have read, it's meant to be the end of everything, not something to look forward to.'

Vicki sighed. So many things they did not understand. Their combined knowledge of Norse mythology sometimes supported, sometimes contradicted what the Aesir told them. For example, Balder, whom Sima believed to have been slain by the devious Loki, was alive and well. The blindingly beautiful young immortal sat close to Freya and said very little. When questioned about his supposed death, he had laughed quietly. 'We are not so easy to end. I would guess that when we left your planet many mortals made up stories to account for our disappearance.'

Vicki looked around again. The wooden benches were crowded but there were no Aesir present at this event. Usually, one or two arrived during the afternoon, and seated themselves on the huge ornately carved chairs facing the entrance. No special attention was paid when they arrived or departed, unless Odin himself came. Then the crowd would become silent and the warriors would pause, until the old god seated himself and nodded for them to continue. Of all the immortals only their leader showed signs of age. He walked slowly, leaning on his spear, but Vicki felt that Odin's appearance was misleading. He radiated an awesome aura of strength and power. She had never heard him speak. He communicated with gestures, similar to those all the people here used when they wished to create something.

Vicki had watched Loki when he signaled for his invisible chair. She had tried to imitate his gestures. She felt some movement in the air but nothing else happened. Sima believed that the hand signals evoked some sort of vast program, that the Aesir had technology which could convert energy to matter. He had questioned Balder and his brother, the one handed Aesir named Tyr. But although the Aesir had explained many things to the crew, they were not forthcoming about their technologies.

Sima emerged from the crowd and waved his sword at Vicki. She frowned when she saw him. He looked down at his blood stained tunic and made a gesture to indicate that he would bathe before joining her. As he moved towards the entrance the crowd hushed; the clamor of weapons and bellowing ceased. All heads turned to the wide, arched doorway. A younger warrior called out 'Odin! Odin!' and slammed his sword against his shield but one of his fellows silenced him with a blow. Sima scrambled up to sit next to Vicki though she flinched at the stink of blood on his arms.

Odin led the way, banging the shaft of his spear on the rammed earth floor. Freya and Thor followed. Vicki saw that Freya's face was downcast as though worried about something. The brilliant Balder entered last flanked by his brother Tyr and the massive Vidar. The Viking warriors fell back in silence to let their Aesir pass.

Vicki held her breath. She had never seen the Aesir arrive in such a state. They wore the full ceremonial robes which she had not seen since their very first meeting. Jeweled headbands glistened in their hair and their rings gave off a fiery light. They passed through the Hall of Warriors without a word. As Odin stepped up to his throne, Loki entered hastily and ran to catch up. Freya turned and gave him an angry look. For several moments the seven Aesir sat silently regarding the warriors; then they turned as one to face the Millennium crew. Odin made a sweeping gesture and Thor stood up. 'Where is your leader?'

John had pushed through the crowd and stood just below them. He raised his arm. 'I am here.'

Thor nodded and turned back to his people. 'The ravens have brought dire news. The age of wind is upon us.'

At once a great shout went up. 'Ragnarok! Ragnarok!'

Thor raised his hand. 'No, no. Not yet. We have lived through the age of the axe and through the sword age. The wolves have not yet found us. But the Olympians have left their domain and entered Iceland. They seek to challenge the Ice Giants. For a thousand years and more we have honored the contract. Now they have broken the contract. We must defeat the Olympians or the Ice Giants may destroy us all. Prepare for war!' As the Vikings responded with a great roar, Thor beckoned to John and the crew. Vicki's heart thumped as they passed between the Viking warriors. She glimpsed familiar faces but now they were transformed by the call to battle and they looked back at her as though she were a stranger.

Thor waved his arm to silence the Vikings and stared down at the crew as they lined up before him. 'This is your concern as much as ours. You must give us counsel and aid. Tell me when you expect your mortal friend to reach us.'

'I expect him daily,' replied John. Vicki wondered at John's nerve. His plan depended on Thor's conviction that Rick would bring superior military power. How could Rick's weapons match the Aesir's power; even if Rick came at all?

In the first few days they had argued for hours but John was unshakeable in his faith; Rick had said he would follow. In the end Sima had put a stop to the discussion. 'What else can we do? We must put on a show of strength. We can't admit of any weakness to these people. We have to assume that Rick will come.'

Vicki had been amazed that Thor believed John so readily until she heard of his admiration for all dark skinned people or "blue men" as he called them. 'Wise counselors all, and the truest of the true.'

'If I could send another message,' John added in the same calm voice, 'I know Rick would make the utmost effort to reach here as quickly as possible; if you would let me cross the Rainbow Bridge.'

'Yes. We must cross the Bifrost this day. Someone awaits us there.' Thor stared down at the crew. 'Someone who may interest you.' He silenced John's question. 'Clean yourselves and clothe yourselves as before.' He raised his arm again and addressed the Vikings. 'Men and women shall sleep apart tonight. There will be no song or music of any kind. Eat only the food and drink only the drink your forefathers lauded. Ready your weapons. Speak only to the brave. Prepare yourselves. Tomorrow we may go to war.'

Thor stepped heavily down the stairs, and held out to his hand to Odin. The two mighty figures stood, arms upraised while the warriors chanted their names. Vicki saw Thor finger his amulet, the gold and silver hammer he wore on a heavy chain. Her eyes watered and she felt weak as she remembered holding the same figure in a silversmith's shop in a little town in Denmark. She could taste the coffee and the apple pastry she had eaten before she and her friend had gone to search for souvenirs.

'Fear not.' Freya put her hand on Vicki's shoulder. 'Death is never the end.'

Sima took Vicki's hand as they followed the Aesir from the hall. John marched wordlessly ahead and did not speak until they reached the hut where they had spent their first night in Valhalla.

'As I expected.' John pulled down the black body suits which still hung there. The cuts and slashes were gone and the stains cleaned away. 'Whoever we are going to meet, they don't want us mistaken for Vikings.' He entered the wash room. 'We'd better hurry.' Sima and Mohun followed him.

Vicki slumped down on a bench and stared at her body suit. The last few weeks now seemed like a dream. Suddenly she was back on the Millennium. She thought of Alistair and Sally. For a long time she had tried not to think about them at all. She had been living in a sort of limbo, and now it was over she regretted it; except for Sima, she could never regret that.

'It's hard to believe, isn't it?' Sharon sat down next to Vicki and patted her arm. 'What we've been through and all.'

'What does it mean? What's going to happen?'

Sharon shook her head. Her face had lost its rosy hue and was almost as pale as her hair. 'I don't know but I guess it's time to face the music.' She pulled Vicki close to her and they sat quietly.

Vicki opened the faucet and stood under the stream of cold water for as long as she could bear. She rubbed her hair dry with the rough towel. 'I wonder what I look like,' she thought. The Vikings did not use mirrors. The admiration in their mates' eyes was sufficient. She dried herself hastily and pulled on the black body suit.

Two Valkyrien approached leading the small Icelandic ponies. The crew mounted and led the way across the valley. At the top of the hill, Odin, Thor and Vidar waited, three great figures mounted on massive black horses. Their faces were grim, and without a word they thrummed their mounts with their heels and rode pell-mell down the steep slope towards Gladsheim. The small ponies followed carefully, picking their way down the stony hill. As they approached the tall grey walls the three Aesir veered off to the right and entered the dark ravine which Sima and John knew led to the rainbow bridge. They had been this way only once before. Shortly after their arrival, they had been permitted to return to the pyramid, to send a message to Rick. Although their watchers remained inactive, the pyramid appeared to be functioning perfectly. The Aesir could not or would not explain why this was so. John had asked several times to send further messages as he gained new information, but had been told to wait.

Mohun tightened his calves against the pony's flanks and clung to its mane as they thundered through the stony passage. He might be a son of Krishna but he lacked that god's skill with horses. He lowered his head and took a swift look behind him. Sharon sat lightly, almost upright, her face set and determined. The bizarre but joyful weeks were gone, he thought. For the hundredth time, he wondered what might come next. The events of the last two years ran through his head like a movie, from the day when his father had persuaded him to join the Millennium project. Who would believe their stories, if they ever got the chance to go home? He wondered how his father felt now.

The Valkyrien who flanked him suddenly reined back their mounts. Ahead the pulsating colors of the Bifrost filled the narrow ravine. Mohun closed his eyes as his horse plunged forward. He felt a sudden dislocation as the hooves left the ground. Then the rainbow overwhelmed him. Vicki gave a gasping cry and Sima responded. Mohun clenched his jaw and closed his eyes as the tingling sensation covered his body. The humming noise became almost unbearable. He pressed his fingers over his ears and almost fell from his horse. Vicki cried out again and Mohun desperately tried to recall how long the journey across the bridge lasted. A sudden calm took him. He laid his head against the horse's neck and let the sensations stream over him. Time passed but he was not aware of it until he was aroused by the jolt of their landing. The humming ceased abruptly and he felt the fresh breeze on his face.

The rainbow's reflection washed across the grassy plain. Odin, Thor and Vidar had dismounted and were talking to the Aesir named Heimdall. To the left and right the crew sat, still mounted and disoriented.

Vicki looked around. Her heart gave a painful lurch as she saw that they had returned to the place where their ECRV had been forced down, where John had died the first time. Suddenly she screamed. 'Look!'

Beyond the Aesir, three women stood by a hillock, next to the communications pyramid. Heimdall gestured to them and they walked slowly forwards. A slim pale haired woman in a closely fitting dull brown garment led the way; behind her, a more athletic figure similarly dressed, a woman with a shining bell of straight black hair. A third woman, who had been examining the pyramid, pushed back her short dark hair and followed.

'Sally!' Vicki yelled again. She jumped down from her horse and ran towards the women. Sima pursued her and grabbed her before she reached the Aesir. She struggled in his arms.

'Wait!' Sima held her tightly.

'It's Sally! Don't you see her?'

Sally suddenly noticed them. She stared at them for a few seconds, covered her face and sank to the ground. The other dark haired woman nudged her with her foot and when Sally did not respond, dragged her to her feet.

Thor looked intently at John. 'Is this the woman whom the traitor took?'

John nodded. During the long questionings, he had told Thor about Thomas and his belief that he had kidnapped Sally and Alistair.

Vicki wriggled free, darted past Heimdall and flung her arms around Sally. 'You're alive!'

Diana stood back, her expression sardonic. 'Take care, mortal! She is not who you think she is.'

Sally wept violently against Vicki's shoulder. Vicki stroked her head and kissed her. 'It's alright.' She took Sally's hand. 'Come on. Everyone is here.'

She started to lead Sally towards the crew but Heimdall stood in the way. 'Stop! This one may not pass.'

'What?' Vicki could not meet his eyes. She stared past him at the crew. Their faces showed stunned surprise. No one moved.

John called out. 'Sally! Where is Alistair?'

Sally started to reply but Ceres interrupted. 'He is safe. He is with my people.'

There was a long silence. Odin made several elaborate hand movements and Thor spoke again. 'These are the Olympians; the dark immortals. Why they are here we will soon discover.' He gestured to Vicki. 'Return to your people.'

Sally whispered. 'Yes, you go on. I'll tell you everything later.' She wiped her eyes and gave Vicki a small push.

Vicki stumbled back to Sima. Diana laughed harshly and Sally looked away.

Thor waved his arm at the crew to remain where they were. He suddenly roared out. 'Speak plainly and hide nothing.'

Diana and Ceres showed no signs of fear and gazed steadily at Thor. After several moments Ceres spoke in a loud clear voice. 'We are Ceres and Diana, children of Olympus, spawned by Zeus but owing no allegiance to him. We are here to warn you of great peril. Athena sent us to request your aid.'

Another long silence. Then for the first time Odin spoke. 'So, it is true.' His voice was very deep and rumbled resonantly. He leaned his head against his spear for several moments. 'I will cast the runes.'

No one moved and Mohun felt as though time had stopped. At length Odin struck the earth with his spear. He beckoned to Heimdall; they spoke quietly together for a moment and then Heimdall ran swiftly towards Bifrost and disappeared into its colors. Thor and Vidar mounted again. They looked at Odin as though waiting for further orders but he stood still and silent as a rock. They wheeled around and galloped back into the rainbow.

John and Sharon conferred in whispers while Sima held Vicki. Mohun stared at Sally. Her expression puzzled him. He thought she would be overjoyed to see them. Instead she looked confused and almost ashamed. 'Olympians! Diana, Ceres!' Mohun suddenly blurted. He looked intently at John. 'And Hercules. Remember Hercules?'

John shook his head. 'I still believe there is something else behind all this.'

'What else could it mean? It all fits.'

'And there is a logic to the whole thing – the myths and legends. They had to come from somewhere.' Sharon paused.

John shook his head again. 'I accept what you say. What I don't understand is how Thomas fits into all of this and why he took Alistair and Sally.'

'Why won't they let Sally come over to us?' Vicki stood up. 'She may know.'

'They may not trust her – because she arrived with the others. And of course we don't know where she has been; what she has been doing.' John looked over at Sally. She sat hunched up, her head on her knees.

Odin suddenly roused himself. He struck the earth again with his spear and beckoned to Diana and Ceres. 'Approach and tell me everything I need to know.' When Sally remained seated, Odin added, 'you also. If you speak the truth you may return to your friends.' He made an elaborate gesture, the air shimmered and his throne appeared. He seated himself and waved his hand at the three women.

Ceres made a low bow to Odin and knelt at his feet. She gave Diana a warning glance and the dark woman frowned but obeyed. Sally sank to the ground somewhat behind them. Odin leaned down and spoke in a quiet intense voice.

John hissed with frustration. He could hear only the occasional word. 'Why are they speaking English?' he wondered aloud.

'Perhaps they have no other language in common,' Sima replied. 'Or it may be for Sally's benefit.'

Odin was now questioning Sally and his voice rose suddenly. 'Speak clearly now. How did this Thomas die? How could he die? The Ice Giants are immortal.'

The crew strained to hear Sally's reply, but she spoke too quietly.

'Did you hear what he said; about Thomas?' Mohun was interrupted by a loud humming noise. Beyond Odin the earth was moving. The grass rippled as though a huge snake was passing beneath the surface. The ground rose slowly in a smooth wave to a height of more than twenty meters but the grass covering remained intact.

For a moment Mohun felt as though the huge mound was sweeping towards them; that it would crash down on them like some terrible tidal wave. But the movement ceased and the new hill stood solid as though it had always been there.

With a rush of wind, Thor and Vidar rode past, followed by Freya and Tyr. Their horses high stepped up the steep hill and came to a halt at its peak. Odin mounted his horse and followed them. Diana started forward up the slope but Ceres called out and Diana strode back down, her face sullen. Odin turned in his saddle and signaled for them to remain where they were. But he beckoned the crew to come forward.

Sima helped Vicki mount and the line of horses trotted towards the hill. Vicki paused when she reached Sally. Sally's face was still white but she gave Vicki a faint smile. 'Don't worry. I'm ok.'

Diana snorted rudely while Ceres touched Vicki's hand and gave her a sympathetic look. A calming warmth spread up Vicki's arm and she felt reluctant to move but her horse was jostled forward.

The little horses did not hesitate as they reached the sheer hillside. They picked their way through the lush grass, in a zigzag path which took them quickly to the summit.

The valley beyond was unchanged and Mohun wondered why the hill had been created. The peak was so narrow that the horses stood in a single line, facing away from the Rainbow Bridge. John had positioned himself between Thor and Vidar. Mohun's horse stirred restlessly and Freya leaned across to quiet him. Her face was grave but she smiled kindly at Mohun.

Odin dismounted, leant on his spear and closed his eyes. The air became very still and Mohun realized that he had become accustomed to the constant noise in Valhalla. The Aesir had imported not only the landscapes of Scandinavia but also many of the birds and animals. Most of the Vikings kept songbirds near their houses so their music rang out from early morning to late evening. Now there was nothing to be heard and Mohun was aware of a growing sense of something awesome about to happen.

Odin unfastened a small cloth bag from his waistband. Unlike his robes and sash, the bag was plainly made; no precious gems or embroidery adorned it. He pulled at the two draw strings and looked inside. He grasped his spear again and started to speak; softly at first and then louder. The words meant nothing to Mohun but he heard someone give a soft gasp. Sima was watching Odin with intent concentration; his lips moved as though he were repeating some of Odin's words.

Odin's voice rang out. He repeated a short phrase three times, thrust his hand into the small bag and flung it forward. Small dark objects flew through the air. As they fell down they increased in size so that the silver and gold markings on each became visible. Just above the grassy floor they hovered and spread out, as though each one possessed its own independent purpose. Odin called out again and the dark rectangular tablets rearranged themselves. He called out a third time, but the pieces remained motionless, floating just above the grass.

'Odin's runes,' Sima whispered.

The attention of all the Aesir was fixed on the dark tablets below. Mohun looked back down the hill. Sally, Diana and Ceres gazed up at him. Beyond them, he saw a glint of blue; they were not far from the coast.

Odin spoke one word and the runes rose rapidly. Mohun could not tell how it happened but they seemed to fly straight back into the bag which Odin held open for them. He suddenly recalled Arthur C. Clarke's maxim; that any sufficiently advanced technology is indistinguishable from magic.

Odin refastened the small bag to his waistband, mounted his horse and wheeled it around on the narrow grassy platform. He called down to Diana and Ceres. 'The runes have spoken. We grant your request.' He laid his hand on John's bridle. 'We will not wait for your friend and his starship. Send your message. Prepare him.' He nodded in Sally's direction. 'Take that woman back with you. I believe she has told as much of the truth as she can.'

'But we will go with you?' John insisted.

'Yes. All of you will travel with us. And you will bring your sign-shape so that your friend can find us.'

Odin took Thor's hand and raised it high. The other Aesir lifted their arms in a salute.

Odin's voice resonated in the still air. 'The runes have spoken. Tomorrow we go to war.'

16

The crew woke to the sound of Heimdall's horn. After a long evening of talk, they had fallen asleep on blankets spread on the soft green grass of the Midgard meadow, and had slept soundly to dawn. The morning air was fresh and the sky was clear, with no sign that a battle was imminent.

The horn sang again – a long note rising and descending. Without speaking the six stood up and stretched, looking this way and that, their glances meeting and veering away again. Sally's revelations; her escape from the angels, her journey south and her final encounter with Thomas, had astounded them. There seemed little more to say. Their ordinary lives, extraordinary as they might seem to others, were now behind them. Each one, in their own way felt that they were about to enter the realm of myth and legend.

Thor had spoken to them briefly and confirmed Ceres' story. The Ice Giants had the power to end all life on this planet and Earth. If Zeus was not halted in his reckless course, the Ice Giants might well take action. 'This is not the Ragnarok we awaited,' Thor had concluded. 'None of us foresaw such madness, not even by the Olympians.' He looked fleetingly across to where Ceres and Diana had constructed a small pavilion for their night's shelter. 'At least some of them have kept their wits.' He gave a deep sigh. 'The strength of our armies may be too little to stop Zeus, but we must try.' He turned to Sally. 'You have concealed nothing regarding the Ice Giant's death?'

Sally had nodded though she found it hard to face Thor. When Diana and Ceres had plucked her from the ocean close to the southern continent they had interrogated her for hours. She had told them everything except for Thomas's assertion that he was her father. They were interested only in how Thomas had died. The news that the Diptera were not indestructible amazed them.

Thor was more concerned with why Thomas had pursued her and not any of the other crew. He gazed into her eyes as he repeated his questions. It had taken all her will not to give way in the face of his magnetism. The thought of how he might react to her real parentage gave her strength. She felt certain that if the Aesir or the Olympians found out she was half angel they would kill her. So she doggedly repeated what Ceres had concluded; Thomas had seen Ares attack Sally and realized that she was not fully mortal. So he had taken her as living evidence that at least one of the gods had broken the contract and fathered a child on Earth. She wished it were true.

As Thor remained silent, she finished in a rush. 'I was nothing more to him than that. He would have killed all of us if he'd been told to do it.'

'How did you escape from the Iceland?'

Sally was able to answer truthfully. 'I don't know. I don't understand how anything happens there.'

John had also regarded her suspiciously, especially when she described her time with the angels. She remembered then that John was a devout Christian. 'They're not what you think,' she tried to explain. 'Alistair thought they might be partly artificial. They behave like machines, as though they are part of some huge system. They have no personal opinions, no feelings.' She shivered as she thought what this might mean to her. 'The Olympians call them "Diptera".'

'Diptera!' exclaimed Vicki. 'Why would they call them that?'

'The scientific name for the order which includes flies, gnats and so on,' Mohun commented thoughtfully. 'The Greek word for two-winged. That is strange. It makes you wonder where the Greek language came from.'

'And the Diptera speak some strange version of Aramaic,' Sally added. 'Alistair and I, we both asked them where they came from, but they were very vague; not from Earth or here. They wouldn't tell us anything else until they were sure you had all left Earth 2. I don't know why.'

She suddenly remembered the watcher she had taken from Thomas's body. She slipped it off and gave it to John. He looked at it casually but his face paled as he turned it over. He squinted at the tiny inscription on the back of the casing. 'What the hell?' He turned away and muttered a sequence of numbers.

'Look at this.' John's face was rigid with anger as he handed the watcher to Sharon. 'It's a command level watcher. How the hell did he get that?'

'I don't understand.' Sharon thumbed the screen. 'It's inactive, just like ours.' She shook her head.

Sima smiled grimly. 'Now we know how Thomas could access the codes and take the shuttle.'

Sally cut in. 'I think the angels were the ones who sponsored this whole thing. Thomas didn't say so, but it makes sense. That way they could control what was happening. They must have organized for Thomas to get that watcher. They tried to sabotage the mission. Thomas as much as admitted that they were responsible for David Liu being killed. Why they didn't just kill us all, I don't know. They seem to have some bizarre set of rules for making decisions ...' Her voice trailed off as the crew stared at her.

'What about Rick?' John suddenly shouted. 'Have they hurt him?'

'I don't think so. I asked Thomas. He said Rick didn't matter. I don't know why.' Sally swallowed. 'From what Thomas said, the angels seem to have lost control of events.'

John muttered angrily. 'What else haven't you told us?'

Slowly Sally told of her journey south, Ares' attack and Ceres' conviction that she must have been fathered by an Olympian. The crew looked disbelieving and for long moments no one spoke.

Finally Mohun had sighed. 'It's not impossible. Look at what we've seen in the last few weeks. We probably all have some DNA from these creatures. Remember what Freya told me about Krishna. And don't forget Hercules – the image of Alistair's brother.'

Their talk had turned staccato with agitation as they considered the implications of what Thor had told them. Each of them thought of their families and friends on Earth. It was impossible to grasp the idea that everything they knew could be destroyed by entities they had never seen; that the fate of their planet might depend on beings that still seemed to belong in the pages of a storybook.

John tried to rally them but their angry voices finally attracted the attention of the Aesir. Heimdall brought them mulled wine and advised them to rest. The drink had its usual effect. They became calm and resigned. As they drifted off to sleep Sharon had summed up their feelings in a drowsy voice. 'What will be, will be.'

The horn sounded a third time. The Aesir had climbed with Diana and Ceres to the peak of the new hill. A group of Valkyrien emerged from the rainbow bridge. They looked briefly up at Odin and then galloped away towards the coast. A few minutes later a line of warriors came into sight, followed by another and more. Soon the valley was filled with men. They walked briskly, not marching in time, but upright and orderly. They wore full battle gear and bristled with weapons. The crew saw many familiar faces; Tyra's son Ivar and his friends, Sven and Jens. Thorkel, who had killed Sima in the first week, saluted him grimly. The red haired brothers Per and Orm walked alongside their father Sigurd. For what seemed like hours, the ranks of warriors, fifty deep, passed by, shouting to Odin as they went. The crew watched as they faded into the distance.

Next the women emerged, calling out to Odin and Freya. Almost as numerous as the men and as heavily armed, they strode forward. Their shining hair was pulled back under metal helmets and they wore short chain mail jackets and leather kilts. Ylva shouted out to Mohun. Ida, who had helped Vicki ride the tough little horses waved her spear at her. Jonna, Tyra, Asa, Sif, Mirah; all the women who had eaten and sung with them, had told their tales and listened to the crew's stories, marched past.

Finally the Berserks came, brandishing their axes. They were dressed as before, naked except for rough animal skins, but they were silent and their repressed anger showed only in the occasional violent shudder or the jerk of a head or limb. More than a hundred of the huge men stopped in front of the hill and were addressed at length by Odin. They banged their axes against their shields but he quieted them with a gesture and slowly descended the hill side. Thor and the other Aesir followed him, with Diana and Ceres at the rear. Only Heimdall remained behind.

Odin mounted his horse and with a sweeping gesture gathered the Berserks behind him. The strange company headed off in the same direction as the Vikings.

Thor offered mounts to Ceres and Diana but they declined them and set off at a run. John strapped the communications pyramid to his back. He beckoned the crew nearer and said quietly. 'Remember, we owe these people nothing. Keep your eyes open and stick together. Nothing is certain. If I give an order, I expect you to remember that I still command this mission.' He looked around until the other five nodded. 'OK. Let's go.'

The crew mounted and followed the Aesir out of the valley. John gestured to Sharon to lead the way. He took up the rear, watching Sally closely.

The grassy plain sloped gently down, giving a clear view of the hordes ahead and the wide bay. The sun shone brightly in the clear sky. There was no breeze but white breakers scudded across the blue water. The shoreline was strangely edged with a thick black smudge. When they neared the coast, the crew could see that the dark lines were dozens of long narrow ships. Fifty oars flanked each side and the curved prows bore the heads of dragons. As they reached the beach the warriors strode into the water to board them. Wide dark sails were raised, filled with wind and the long ships moved out into the bay.

The Aesir halted where the long grass met the sand. The crew sat silently on their restive mounts, watching the fleet move into formation. When most of the warriors had embarked the Berserks boarded one of the longest of the ships and Odin took his place at the prow. Two huge ravens circled above his head several times before flying northwards.

Thor signaled to John that the crew should board the last of the ships. As they waded out they heard angry voices. Diana stood, arms akimbo, staring defiantly up at Thor. She pointed towards the Millennium crew and shouted. Finally she strode off, made an elaborate gesture and a small, gracefully shaped boat materialized at the water's edge.

She called out but Ceres continued talking to Thor. The tall Aesir slapped his sword against his leg, his face red with anger.

'Quick!' John leaned down and heaved Sally into the ship. He dropped her unceremoniously onto the wooden deck and ran lightly up to the prow where Tyr and Vidar were standing.

The ship rocked violently as the Vikings took to the oars. Sima and Sharon edged their way forward to join John while Sally, Vicki and Mohun sat uncomfortably, trying to balance themselves on the rough boards. The ship was not designed for passengers and there was nothing to hold on to.

Sally peered over at Diana's boat and met the Olympian's baleful glare. Ceres and Freya were climbing aboard and Diana gave the boat a vigorous push into the water before joining them. The small vessel took off at surprising speed.

'She doesn't like you, does she?' Vicki commented.

'I don't think she likes anyone. She's a hunter.' Sally did not look at Vicki.

The ship suddenly lurched forwards. Thor was now aboard, talking to the Viking at the helm – the long rudder board at the rear of the ship. A rope whipped past Sally's cheek and the crew flattened themselves against the deck as the elaborate network of ropes flailed with the raising of the dark sail.

Odin led the way through the headland, followed closely by Thor and the small white boat which Diana had invoked. Sally looked past Freya's streaming red hair to the crowd of long ships which followed. She guessed there must be more than a hundred, each jostling for a position near the Aesir ships.

It took more than an hour for all the ships to reach open water. Finally the dark sail billowed and the Vikings rested their oars. A huge man with red hair and a bushy beard reached out and took Sally by the ankle. 'Hey, lovely! Where did you come from?' His English was thickly accented but clear. 'I haven't seen you around. Come here and I will show you what a real man is.' Sally pulled away and the man laughed, winking at his friends.

The wind remained favorable and for several hours the ships cut a rapid zigzag path between the larger islands. Gradually the islands became smaller and further apart, and the ships could follow a more direct course. When they were not rowing the Vikings ate and drank and played with small tokens shaped like knucklebones.

More than once a fight broke out. During one argument two men were tipped overboard. The others laughed heartily, making gestures towards the nearest island as though encouraging their friends to make a swim for it. The men shook their fists, then resigned to their plight, pulled off their heavy gear and flung it at the ship.

Thor ignored the scuffles. He remained at the helm, his red hair streaming behind him, his eyes fixed on Odin's ship. Twice the ravens had returned and flown north again. Each time Odin's ship turned westwards.

'Tell me what happened ...' Sally ignored the lascivious comments of the oarsman who was still trying to attract her attention. 'When did you first suspect Thomas?'

Vicki was watching Sima standing at the prow with John, Sharon and the two Aesir. He had let his hair grow in the weeks in Southland and he could easily be mistaken for a Viking. She turned to Sally and continued her account. Mohun interjected a few times but otherwise remained lying on his back, one ankle crossed over his knee, staring up at the small puffy clouds.

When Vicki described how Poseidon had tried to kill Sima and take her, Sally shuddered. The scene in Zeus's palace was still vivid in her mind.

Mohun sat up abruptly. 'Do you trust those two?' he asked, pointing towards Diana's boat.

'I don't know.' Sally shrugged. 'But they seem to hate Zeus and are terrified of what he might do. I guess that's all that counts right now. And Alistair told me that Ceres rescued me from Zeus and Poseidon.' She grimaced.

'Those are fine tales you tell.' The red haired Viking laughed. 'Perhaps you are poets, in your own land?' Several of the other Vikings looked up and one of them called out, 'Yes, give us a poem, or even better a song. We have no wine, and the women row their own ships. We need a song.'

'I will sing you a song about the women of my country,' Mohun volunteered and launched into a plaintive but strong melody. The others looked at him in surprise, not knowing that he had such a good voice. Even John smiled and called out at the end, 'Well done, Mohun.'

To the crew's surprise the Vikings were quiet while Mohun sang. As his voice faded they wiped their eyes and shook their heads, as if overcome by emotion. The red haired man reached out and touched Mohun's amulet. 'You must be a prince in your country. I am Sigtrygg and I will defend that voice to the death.' Tears ran down his face. 'These are my brothers in blood – Ulfarr, Tyrfingr and Erik. My vows are their vows.' The men nodded their heads solemnly. Mohun winced as each of the big men squeezed his hand.

Sally broke the tension. 'You now, sing us a song that will blunt our enemies' swords.'

Sigtrygg squinted at her. 'Ah! So you know our songs, do you?' He sang a few words in Norse.

'Some,' Sally admitted. 'Nor will their weapons wound us,' she translated for the benefit of the others.

Sigtrygg needed no more encouragement. He launched into a long ballad, with the other Vikings echoing every fourth or fifth line. When Thor signaled that they should take up their oars again, they continued to sing, emphasizing the words with each down stroke.

As they sped past another small island Mohun observed, 'These ships go much faster than they ought to. Something else is at work here.'

'Certainly,' Vicki agreed. 'But if the situation is so urgent, why are we travelling by water? Why not conjure up something faster?'

Sally sighed. 'I asked Ceres that while we were travelling south. It seems to have something to do with a sort of battle of wits. If you break the rules you draw attention to yourself and bring your enemies down on you. Also they have some rule about keeping to your own domain. I told you what happened to us on the way down. There has been some kind of contract with the angels, whatever, that the gods should not cross the ice belt. They should stick to their own territory. But Zeus, Poseidon and the others are ignoring that.'

Vicki interrupted. 'Right now, all I can think about is how I'm going to pee.'

Sigtrygg laughed. 'Go the stern, where we make water. There you will find a thwart, which the women use, and some ropes to hold on to.'

Vicki grimaced. 'Not the first time do I wish these suits were not one-piece!' She tottered back down between the two rows of oarsmen, kicking away the hands which snatched at her. The men laughed merrily and made offers to accompany her. She disappeared behind the helmsman.

Mohun sat up. 'Perhaps I should have gone with her.'

Ulfarr spoke up. 'Have no fear, friend. No Viking takes an unwilling woman.' He smiled broadly. 'Luckily for us, most women are willing so we have no need to bother the others.'

As if to make him a liar, Vicki gave a piercing shriek and reappeared, pulling up her body suit. Thor swung round while Vicki gabbled and waved her arms.

The ship rocked wildly as the Vikings rose to their feet and stared towards the stern. Behind them the sea was black with the dozens of Viking long ships. For a few moments no one could see what Vicki was pointing at. Then the crew gave a collective gasp. Far to the south, between two islands, the water was bulging skywards.

'It's Poseidon!' Sally yelled. 'He'll drown us all.' She called out. 'Ceres! Ceres!'

Diana's boat had already turned and was speeding south. Ceres and Freya clutched the sides. Diana's scream came thinly across the water as she shook her fist at the giant wave.

Thor roared out some commands and another ship came alongside, bumping and smashing against the line of round shields. Sigtrygg picked up Sally like a doll and tossed her towards the other ship. She was caught and dropped onto the deck. Moments later Vicki and Mohun thumped down next to her and lay winded. Sally jumped up to see what was happening. John was struggling with Vidar as he and Tyr pushed the astronauts down the gangway. Thor called out to John. 'You mortals can do nothing. Do not hinder us. Your time will come later.'

Sima and Sharon were flung across. Sigtrygg seized John and with a massive leap they cleared the gap between the two ships.

Thor's helmsman pulled mightily on the steering board and the oars came down with a crash as the ship started to turn. Odin's ship was already heading south, the sail flapping and the Berserks rowing furiously. Odin stood at the prow, his white hair blowing wildly, his spear glittering strangely in the sunlight.

'Flee! Flee for your lives!' Thor's voice boomed as his ship raced into a narrow gap between the lines of the Viking fleet.

Sigtrygg called out to his friends, sat down heavily and seized an oar. 'I said I would defend you and I will. But it makes my heart sore to see my brothers going against that monster, without me. Will we ever see Valhalla again?' He pushed the end of his beard into his mouth, bit down hard and struck the water with his oar.

The Millennium crew stood looking back as their ship sped north. The two Aesir ships snaked southwards through the thick crowd of their fellows. Thor gesticulated wildly, urging his people to row faster. In the distance Diana's small white boat gleamed on the empty sea.

'I've seen this before,' Sally said dully. 'Last time we just ran. We escaped to high land. I don't know what Ceres can do.'

Beyond the fleet the water loomed up like a mountain. Diana's tiny boat met the wave, rose sickeningly like a carriage on some giant rollercoaster and disappeared over the foamy crest. Sally felt suddenly bereft. The Vikings groaned loudly.

'Freya!' Vicki whispered. 'Freya!'

Odin and Thor passed the last of their fleet and emerged into open water. Their long ships looked like toys against the vast wave, the Vikings small mechanical men wielding matchstick oars.

A brilliant beam of light shot out from one of the Aesir ships and penetrated the wave. The water parted and great fountains of foam shot skyward. The Vikings let out a huge cheer and shipped their oars, certain now that the Aesir would triumph. More jets of light hit the wave and it started to collapse. Huge billows of water raced towards the southernmost long ships and they started to pitch violently.

For several minutes Odin's and Thor's ships disappeared behind the spumes of green water. They emerged from the watery veil, speeding across the tumultuous waves. Behind them a huge dark figure emerged, riding the breakers like some hideous surfer. The Vikings groaned again and watched breathlessly as Poseidon neared the Aesir. There was a giant cheer from hundreds of throats as Diana's boat reappeared over the crest and then an awful shrieking.

'Cover your eyes! Cover your eyes!' Sigtrygg threw out his great arm and knocked Mohun and Vicki to the deck, pushing Sally and the rest of the crew forward.

The screaming that followed was terrible to hear and the crew covered their ears as well. It seemed to go on forever but finally faded to whimpers and sobs.

Mohun was the first to raise his head. He shouted something, rushed to the side and vomited violently into the water. Sigtrygg's face was black and his eyes were gone. The huge man murmured something and collapsed face down on his oar.

All around them, the men who had not heard the warning in time were clutching their faces and moaning with pain. Others lifted their heads and shouted with anger when they saw what had happened.

'Where are the Valkyrien?' Vicki stood up and looked around wildly. The huge wave had gone. The ocean to the south was rough as though a storm was brewing but the sky was clear. There was no sign of Poseidon, the two Aesir ships or Diana's boat.

A very young man, his face scorched red on one side answered. 'The Valkyrien will come but they are very few for so many.' He picked up his sword and before they could stop him, ran it through the throat of a man who was rolling around in agony.

John leapt up. 'What are you doing?'

The young man plunged his sword into the chest of an unconscious man whose face was a black space. 'I am sparing them,' he replied faintly. 'It is not only the hurt to their flesh that causes their pain. They saw Ceres' shield. They may wake tomorrow in Valhalla, but they may wish they had not.'

Another Viking whose forehead was burned strode down the gangway. 'Tonne is right,' he said. 'The shields of the dark gods are legend. Few can survive a glimpse of an aegis; even at this distance.' He pushed past John and dispatched two more men who were calling for help. The crew watched in numb silence.

A ship bumped alongside and without a word the Vikings wrapped the dead and wounded men in their cloaks and lifted them across to the other vessel. Other men leapt aboard to take their dead comrades' places at the oars and then the ship of the dead turned south to seek the Valkyrien. The Vikings lowered their oars and rowed slowly on, their faces downcast.

Mohun wept and clutched his amulet. 'He said he would defend me. I never thought …Why would Ceres and Diana do that?'

'It may have been the only way to stop Poseidon.' Sally wondered what had happened to Diana's boat. 'You told me, Mohun, what happened to you and John. Zeus's shield is a terrible weapon but Ceres' is worse. Diana told me that the image on her cloak can burn the mind as well as the body.'

Mohun covered his face and John looked away. No one spoke. The Vikings stared at Sally as she continued. 'On our trip south, several times when we thought we might not make it, Diana asked Ceres to use her aegis but she wouldn't. She must have used it now because she was desperate, thought it was the only way.'

The Vikings rowed in gloomy silence to the nearest island. They flung down their anchors and waded ashore. The sun was low in the sky. John scrambled up the mast and hung off the cross beam, counting the ships until it became too dark to see.

They spent a melancholy hour on the narrow beach, but gradually fires sprang up and voices became louder. The Vikings shouted cheerfully when a ship rowed by women arrived. 'Now our luck will turn!'

Soon the bay was thick with ships and the beach crowded as the Vikings came ashore carrying provisions, passing around food and ale, looking for their comrades. Finally a woman's voice rang out and a long song started. Sharon put her arms around Mohun who was still shocked at Sigtrygg's fate, and Sima pulled Vicki back to rest against his chest. Sally wondered where Alistair was and looked at John. The commander's dark face shone in the firelight but his eyes were closed and his brow wrinkled as though he were thinking hard about something.

The song rose and fell and faded away. Mohun stood up and said unsteadily, 'I want to sing something for Sigtrygg.' He sang nine ascending notes and repeated the refrain. He sang in Konkani and only Sally knew that the song was really about a son's longing to see his father. As the beautiful melody soared Mohun raised his arms as though beseeching help from above. Finally his voice broke and he sat down abruptly.

The long silence was broken by splashing. 'I would know that voice anywhere.' Ulfarr strode out of the water and into the firelight. 'Ale for the weary, if you please. We have jumped across a hundred ships to reach dry land and what do we find? Here are you laggards lolling around as though you are in the feasting hall.'

Two more figures waded out of the water. 'Where is the ale? Have you louts drunk it all?

There were joyful shouts. 'Ulfarr, you old fool. Erik! Fari! What news? Where is Odin? Where is Thor?'

Ulfarr waved his sword above his head. 'Now hear this. The Aesir defeated the great green god of the north and brought his ocean down upon his head.' He added in a quieter voice, 'with the help of the lady Freya of course and those dark gods.'

The Vikings roared and smashed their swords against their shields. Ulfarr signaled for quiet and continued, 'even now the Aesir and the dark gods are holding counsel on their ship and tomorrow will lead us against Poseidon's brothers. We have lost many ships but we will overcome. Yes!'

The Vikings yelled until Ulfarr called out again. 'Be quiet now and do not bring our enemies down upon us.' He turned and pointed out to sea. In the distance they could see a small shaft of light. Some of them murmured, 'Odin! Odin!' and then were silent.

Ulfarr and Erik approached the Millennium crew. Mohun spoke first. 'We have bad news.'

Erik put his hand on Mohun's shoulder. 'We know. We saw the sad ships go by. But not all those men and women will be lost. Perhaps you will meet Sigtrygg again.'

As if by mutual agreement the Vikings disposed of their rubbish and set to polishing their weapons and arranging their gear. Then they stretched out around the fires and slept. The crew stayed awake longer, discussing what had happened and speculating about what the next day would bring. Sally was thankful that they were too concerned with the immediate future to question her further. But she often felt John's thoughtful gaze upon her.

The next morning's journey was uneventful. The crew were taken back to Thor's ship and once again Odin led the way. The ravens hovered overhead and the fleet headed directly north. Diana's boat kept its distance but the crew could see that the three aboard were unharmed.

The sky was clear again with cheerful little puffs of cloud, and the ships were sped along by a brisk wind and by the strenuous efforts of the oarsmen who did not ship their oars at any time. Gradually the islands disappeared and they entered the empty ocean south of the ice belt.

The mood this day was different. The Vikings sang as they rowed but the tunes were harsh and the Norse words sharp. Sally translated some of the verses but they mainly recounted the deeds of their ancestors. The men were obviously bracing themselves for the battle ahead.

When the sun reached the zenith, the Vikings raised their oars for a few moments and passed around the ale. The strong brew gave them strength and they did not need to eat. Sally shivered as the wind rose sharply and the light fell. Vicki and Mohun helped the Vikings secure the ropes to the net braces as the sails strained against the wind. The air suddenly became colder and the Vikings' faces whitened. They shipped their oars again and sat very still.

'Get down, get down,' Vidar, who rarely spoke, called out. 'The Ice Giants are passing.' He threw his cloak over his head and pressed against the deck.

'Look,' Sally whispered. The angels filled a quarter of the sky. As they descended, a rustling noise filled the air and bands of colored lights flashed across the crowd.

Sally cowed down as the throng hovered over the ship. A humming noise grew louder and faded. Then the angels rose rapidly and sped northwards. The crew watched as they disappeared over the empty horizon, but the Vikings turned their faces away and muttered to each other.

'My god!' John spoke for the first time in hours. 'That was impressive.'

The expression on John's face reminded Sally of Alistair's reaction to their first encounter with the angels. She spoke fervently. 'Forget everything you've ever believed about angels. They look beautiful but they don't care about us. They have no feelings, no emotions. They're fixated on some purpose that no one here understands. They would have us all killed in an instant if they thought it was the right thing to do.'

'Not so different from a lot of people on earth, then,' Mohun observed.

Ulfarr punched Mohun's shoulder. 'Don't be foolish. Remember who your friends are. These Ice Giants belong to another world. We are nothing to them.'

Towards the middle of the afternoon rocky islands appeared just above the water line, and the ships were forced to tack between them. The waves washed across the dark rocks, making them difficult to see and the helmsman cursed as he heaved on the long oar. As the islands grew larger and more frequent, the ravens circled above, landing frequently on Odin's shoulder and then soaring up again, and the atmosphere became tense. Small ice floes floated past and finally the mountains of Iceland loomed on the horizon. As they stared at the forbidding sight the sun clipped the western range and the temperature dropped sharply. The crew wrapped themselves in thick cloaks and shivered on the cold boards.

The fleet dispersed as they entered the narrow passages between the icy islands but Thor's ship and Diana's boat followed Odin closely. The wind had dropped and the oarsmen sweated and panted with the effort to keep up. Fine webs of ice formed on their hair and beards. Tyr and Vidar kept watch at the bow and called out as small icebergs loomed up. Thor's helmsman pulled mightily on the steering board, swinging the long vessel left and right; even so, the ship was constantly jolted by collisions and the Vikings yelled out as their oars jarred painfully against the submerged ice. Soon they were winding through narrow courses, the sheer white walls rising ominously on either side. The Vikings muttered. 'This would make a fine place for an ambush.'

'Listen!' One of the Vikings suddenly stood up, and the rest raised their oars. Above the creaking of the ice they could hear the sounds of battle; clanging, smashing, wild yells and screams.

Odin's ship shot forward and disappeared behind a huge iceberg. Thor called out and his oarsmen redoubled their efforts, sweeping around the icy wall and into a narrow stretch of open water. The ship pitched violently as the crew and most of the Vikings rose to their feet. No one present would ever forget the sight before them. They had finally reached the battleground

17

Directly before them was a great icy plain, flanked to left and right by snow covered hills. At the peak of the eastern slopes a huge pavilion had been erected, the purple, rose and gold walls contrasting garishly with the pure white of the surroundings. Beyond the plain, in every direction, the mountains of Iceland rose, curving and soaring up to the clear blue sky.

The Vikings and crew stared in wonder. Two armies were embroiled in an intense battle, from the steep ice wall in the north, down to the water's edge. The line of the battle could be seen clearly near the western foothills, where a ridge in the mountain range reduced the plain to a narrow strip of smooth ice. Higher up the western slopes hundreds of arrows rained down, a black cloud against the snowy backdrop. Below the archers, dark clad soldiers fought hand to hand with a bizarre foe; huge semi-naked men who looked barely human, who screamed terrifyingly as they were cut down. But they could not retreat; they were pushed onwards by their pale comrades who flowed down the eastern hills and across the plain like water pouring over a dam.

Odin raised his spear and gestured to advance, and the Vikings cheered and rowed furiously towards the shore. The crashing noise of thousands of oars hitting the water reached the armies on the plain and they turned to look southwards. A wailing rose from the pale army as they saw that the long ships were heading towards them. The dark clad soldiers let out a roar of triumph and pushed forward, hacking at the enemy with renewed energy.

'Athena!' Diana's voice carried across the water and her boat veered west. On the crest of the hill to the west of the battlefield, what looked like a crag was revealed as a white building, as large as the pavilion on the opposing slopes. Its columns were almost invisible against the snowy peaks, but now the sunlight struck the elaborate fluting on the ridge of the roof and the whole building gleamed.

Thor signaled, the helmsman strained, and his ship turned to follow Diana's. The Vikings bent to their oars while the crew gazed in amazement at the battle.

'Spartans!' Sima yelled above the noise. 'They are Spartans!' A group of dark clad men was running towards them, their bronze greaves and round shields glinting. The crew could clearly see the fearful images on their shields but their faces were invisible behind their metal helmets, the horse hair crests streaming behind them. The pale giants chased them, brandishing huge swords.

At the water's edge the Spartans stopped abruptly, spun round and launched a volley of spears against their pursuers. The giants crashed to the ground, screaming and clutching at the protruding shafts. The Spartans gave out a cry of triumph, leapt over their bodies and ran back to the main battle front. The Vikings roared approvingly and brandished their weapons at the pale warriors.

Mohun exclaimed, 'Damn it, what the hell are those things?'

Sally leaned forwards. 'They are Zeus's army. They have been reconstructed, thrown together so they can fight again. Zeus doesn't give a shit about his people.' She pointed back to the eastern foothills. 'Look! Over there.'

Streams of pale figures moved up and down the slopes to two enormous fires. 'That's where Vulcan does his work,' Sally continued. 'We came up against an army like this, just before Ares attacked me.'

Mohun and Vicki looked at her in amazement. 'Good god! How did you get past them?' Vicki asked. Before Sally could reply, Tyr loomed over them.

'Get you out now and send a message to your friend.' When John started to protest, Tyr stopped him. 'You will be of no use if your friend comes and finds you all dead.'

The ship slammed against the stony beach and the crew jumped ashore. Ceres and Diana were already running up the hill towards the temple, treading lightly over the snow, but Freya waited.

As the crew hesitated, Freya held up her hand. 'When you meet Athena, show her the same respect you show to Odin.' She pointed up the slopes to the shining white temple. 'If we win this day, she will rule over half the world.' She turned away and started forward to where Odin's and Thor's vessels had beached. When John went to follow her, she waved him back. 'Send your message to your friend. We need help. We are greatly outnumbered.'

John waved the crew forward and they started up through the deep snow of the western hill. Vicki screamed and clapped her hands over her ears as a blood freezing shriek rang out and they turned to look back down at the battlefield

All of the long ships had now entered the eastern end of the bay. They had formed into a single line and were approaching at great speed. A large force of Zeus's men rushed to the water's edge to stop the Vikings from landing. As the ships approached the shore line they suddenly veered away, parallel to the beach; half of the Vikings shipped their oars, rose to their feet and sent volleys of arrows into the enemy. The front lines of Zeus's men collapsed, and the remainder screamed with rage as the Vikings continued along the coastline and out of range.

'What's happening?' Vicki cried. They can't land there! They'll be slaughtered.'

Sima shook his head. 'They're creating a diversion. Look! They've forced Zeus to divert some of his force away from the Spartans. But they don't know how these Vikings fight. Look how many have been brought down! And the Vikings are gone before they can strike back.'

'I think we've arrived just in time.' John pointed down to the narrow stretch of plain where the dark army maintained a dogged battlefront. 'The Spartans are pretty hard pressed.' Like Sima, his face was alive with interest and amazement. 'I can't believe I'm seeing this.'

As they watched, the long ships gathered on the western shore. In what seemed like only a few minutes the ships were secured in rows, and planks were set across each ship, so that the Vikings could quickly disembark and offload their provisions and equipment.

Sima shouted in admiration. 'That's something to see!'

John nodded. 'The Vikings act casual but they are well drilled units.'

Freya had joined the Aesir on the foreshore and they stood in a huddle with several of the Spartans. Thor stepped forward and quickly slashed some lines in the snow with his long sword. They showed clearly in the deepening twilight; several rows and a square.

The Spartans pointed at the lines and appeared to question Thor. Suddenly the whole group stepped back into a rough circle and clashed their weapons together with a mighty bang; then the Spartans ran back to the battlefront.

Tyr shouted and waved his sword. The Viking men turned en masse and followed him, running at a brisk trot towards the northern end of the plain, past the Spartan force and behind another large group of men clad in similar gear but with different shaped helmets.

'It's like watching a movie,' Vicki exclaimed. 'Those men are Athenians. They won't take orders from the Spartans.'

The Vikings continued behind the Athenian force until they reached the northern flank of Spartans and then formed quickly into two lines behind them.

When the men had passed, Freya quickly stepped a little way back up the snowy slope, held her sword high and called out. The Viking women responded with a roar and gathered below her, looking up expectantly.

'Come on! It's getting dark.' John turned from the amazing scene and started up the hillside.

They heard a strange piercing call; 'Cooee!' and Sally yelled. A figure draped in a bright blue cloak was descending from the temple; the crew broke into a floundering run as they realized it was Alistair. John reached him first and hugged him hard. He wiped his hand over his eyes as Alistair greeted the crew. When he saw Sally, Alistair stared for a moment and then put out his hand. Sally hesitated, then leaned against his shoulder and whispered something.

'It doesn't matter. None of that matters anymore.' Alistair's face was haggard in the dim light but as he looked around his usual cheerful expression returned. 'I'm sorry about the Millennium. Ceres just told me. But it's bloody wonderful to see you all again. Sometimes I thought I never would. I thought you had left me here.' He hugged Sally. 'I hear you brought the Vikings. We're going to need them. What you see down there is our last line of defence; the last of the Greek army. We have no more fighters.'

They were suddenly aware that the noise of battle had dimmed and as they listened it died out.

'Thank god,' Alistair said fervently. 'They won't fight in the dark.'

To the east the pale army was still, although the massive fires burned on. In the distance, Zeus's pavilion was dimly lit but nothing could be seen of Zeus or his allies. One by one, small fires sprang up as the armies prepared their bivouacs. The crew could see the Vikings massed into two groups behind the Greek army; the men at the northern end of the valley and the women nearer the shore. A line of Greek soldiers bore the dead and wounded up the steep path to the temple.

'I can't imagine the Vikings sitting back and letting the others fight first,' Mohun commented.

'They won't,' promised John. 'See down there; the Vikings are building something. This must be a part of the battle plan.' He smiled thinly and glanced at Sharon. 'I'd like to be down there with them.'

'No!' Alistair cut in. 'Athena told me to bring you to her.' He took Sally's hand and they pushed up through the heavy snow.

'I warn you,' Alistair panted as they neared the temple. 'You're going to find all this hard to believe. Just follow my lead.'

John laughed. 'I don't think anything could surprise us. Wait till you hear where we've been.'

Alistair kicked the snow off his high leather boots and mounted the wide white stairs to the portico. As they passed between the columns, the air became much warmer. The interior of the white temple consisted of a spacious hall, lined on all sides by columns and lit by braziers. Long couches were grouped around some small tables but otherwise the room was quite bare. Three tall figures clad in long dark cloaks were standing in the eastern portico, gazing out over the battlefield. To the crew's surprise Odin, Thor and Vidar stood nearby.

Alistair crossed the room, knelt down and bowed his head. 'Lady Athena! Here are my friends.'

The crew knelt behind Alistair, and there was a moment's silence.

'Good! Come here and give me your names.'

This prosaic reply startled the crew. They stood up and stared at the tall dark haired woman in the strangely shaped helmet. Her face was white, dominated by her huge grey eyes. One by one they felt compelled to look down.

Diana stepped forward and took John's arm. 'This is their commander. You should speak first to him.'

Athena frowned slightly. 'Quickly, then.'

John could not face Athena. Instead he glanced sideways at Diana who was gazing at him with an admiring, speculative expression. For the first time in months he felt a strong surge of desire and his face reddened. Diana smiled and her grip on his arm tightened. He clenched his teeth in an effort to regain his self control and presented the crew.

We had no knowledge of this planet until two years ago,' he added. 'Our purpose here is peaceful. We came to explore. That is all. Our mission was sabotaged; first by Thomas, one'of our crew. We know now that he was not human but an Ice Giant.'

'A Dipteros,' Diana interjected.

'First by Thomas.' John continued. 'Then our spacecraft was destroyed. We escaped and were taken by Loki, one of the Aesir. We have spent the last weeks in Valhalla with the Norsemen and the Aesir. We are waiting for a friend, who will be here soon.' When Athena did not comment, John added, 'From Earth. He is coming from Earth.'

He lifted his face to look at Athena. She nodded. 'Come and confer with us. We would welcome your advice.' Diana led John forward, Thor nodded, and the group disappeared behind the columns. Sima and Sharon followed.

Ceres took Sally's hand. 'Remember who you are,' she said very quietly. 'You must tell Alistair.' Sally nodded as Ceres smiled faintly at the crew. 'I will leave you now. I must attend to the dead and wounded.'

As Ceres turned away, a white robed figure emerged from the shadows and Alistair introduced him to the crew. Althamas greeted them joyfully. 'At last! Poor Alistair has been melancholy all this time without you.' He looked closely at Sally. 'So you are the one who holds his heart and causes so much trouble.'

Mohun and Vicki looked at Sally in surprise and Sally flushed. She had not told them of her relationship with Alistair. She had not told them so many things.

'Now,' said Alistair, 'tell me everything.' He gestured to the circle of couches around the brazier.

'Wait until they are refreshed.' Althamas made a hissing sound and gestured. He passed around one of the dishes which appeared. 'Try this. You must be weary of barbarian food.'

They ate in silence for a few moments until Mohun said, 'Something is puzzling me.' He gulped down warmed wine as he spoke. 'How did you get here? I thought there was no passage through the ice belt?'

Althamas shook his head and sighed. 'You know that Athena went to the Diptera and laid everything open to them; Zeus's raids on our people, his transgressions against our laws, even his plan to attack the Diptera themselves?'

'We heard something of the sort from Thor,' Mohun replied. 'But not much.'

Althamas summarized the events of the last few months and then Alistair took up the story. 'I was with Athena. It was humiliating. The Diptera ignored her and questioned me for hours about Thomas. They weren't interested in Zeus or any of our problems. Athena tried to get Gabriel to agree that Zeus is the source of the problem, that he should be eliminated. But they weren't interested. They just wanted to know about Thomas. Of course I had no idea where he'd gone to ...'

Sally felt that Alistair's disillusionment with the angels must distress him. She gave his hand a sympathetic squeeze.

'Anyway,' Alistair continued. 'There was nothing we could do. We started back north but Zeus had already set sail and our boats were chasing him. There was a hell of a battle just north of here. Most of the ships were wrecked. We landed and fought our way across the mountains, just falling back all the time.' He shuddered. 'It was ghastly, but Athena drove us on. She saw Odin's ravens and was sure that he was on the way.' He moved closer to a brazier and rubbed his hands. 'God! It's good to see you again. They've been very kind to me but ...' He broke off, shaking his head.

'I don't understand,' Mohun said slowly. 'The angels have got this device, they can see everything. Why couldn't they find Thomas?'

'The word only records and displays what has happened on Earth,' Sally replied.

'So, the trouble on Earth; do you know what that's about?' asked Vicki.

'Something big. The angels wouldn't tell us anything more until the Millennium left Earth 2.' Alistair shrugged. 'I don't know why. Their logic is beyond me. I guess Sally has told you. The angels came to Earth, from somewhere else – we never found out where. Apparently they had to come because things on Earth were not going the way they should. It has something to do with what they call the "good", the way things ought to progress. But their plans didn't work out. They told us that they brought other species that should have helped us but somehow we destroyed them. They believe we caused the gods to go wrong; something in our natures, whatever. I know it sounds mad.' He looked at Sally. 'Is that how you see it?'

Sally nodded. 'Yes. And also, everything Ceres and Diana told me, and then Thomas...' She shut her eyes for a moment. The memory of Thomas's death still made her shudder. 'But Thomas also said something which I think might be important. I've just remembered. Just before he died, I told him I thought they were all mad; to blame us for what went wrong, when they've made so many mistakes. And he sort of agreed. He said I might be right. He was going to say something about Michael and then he just froze.

Sally hesitated. The memory of Thomas's revelation could still shock her; that her mother's "seduction" of Thomas would be seen by the angels as further proof of humanity's flawed nature. 'The way he spoke,' she continued, 'it's like the angels are programmed to operate in a particular way, to make sure that the "good", whatever that means, is kept going. But in our case it just hasn't worked. And something seems to have affected them. Perhaps they've been here too long.'

Alistair looked at her intently. 'Why did Thomas take you south? He told me he would come back and get me as soon as he found you.'

Vicki exclaimed. 'What? I don't understand any of this? Why would he do that? Why not take you straight back to the angels?'

As Alistair shook his head, Sima stepped into the circle of light. 'John's going to send the latest data up to the satellite, for Rick.'

'We'll be lucky to last that long,' Alistair said bitterly. 'The Greeks are much better fighters than the Anomee but Zeus can regenerate the dead much quicker. You can see the results – body parts thrown together; it's horrendous. Athena and Ceres won't do that, so it's just a matter of time before Zeus wears us down.'

'Don't be too sure,' Sima replied. 'Thor and Athena have a plan. There will be some surprises.' He looked around the group. 'Can any of you think of anything which might help Rick?'

'I just hope he believes what we tell him,' Mohun observed. 'Otherwise he's going to arrive here totally unprepared, and if Zeus or one of the others sees him, they'll bring the Phoenix down as they did the Millennium.'

'I'm more concerned about the angels,' Alistair cut in. 'How will they react to Rick's arrival? He needs to know what he's up against.'

Sima nodded. 'Of course. But I am sure he'll believe whatever John tells him. They've been friends a long time.'

Alistair was looking at Sally intently. 'What is it? Are you ok?'

Sally felt a sudden cold. She had just remembered something. If she was right it could give them a weapon against the angels. But if Thomas had told her the truth, if she really was half angel, any action taken against the angels might affect her too. She could die or at the very least her real identity might be revealed. For some reason she thought of David and Hilda and her birth mother in New Zealand. She had no choice.

'I have an idea. It might be worth telling Rick.' She swallowed hard. 'We know the angels make all their decisions through consensus, what they call the choir.' Alistair started to speak but she continued. 'But I think it may be also connected to the colors that they show when they group together. You remember when they flew overhead? Different groups of angels exhibit different colors. And when they were chanting, I could hear that different groups used different tones. Now I think about it, the tones and the colors are used consistently.'

'I never realized that.' Alistair looked puzzled.

'I didn't take much notice at the time. But I do have a good memory for those sorts of things. Thomas said that separation from the choir was what was killing him. And just before he died, or froze or whatever, he gave out this sort of ringing sound, like a bell.'

'What are you saying, Sally?'

'Think about it. Perhaps we could disrupt the choir, using different tones and colored lights.' Sally flushed. 'I haven't thought it through properly ...'

Sima interrupted. 'Yes! I think you may have something there. There are lots of theories about the association between sounds and colors. If Rick can interfere with their communication, it would give us some time ...' He strode back to the portico where Sharon and John were bent over the pyramid.

'Why don't you tell Athena your idea?' suggested Mohun. 'There's no reason why the gods couldn't try the same thing.' He wondered if they were all thinking the same thing: that Rick might never have left Earth.

Alistair shook his head. 'I don't know. Perhaps you're right.' He put down his cup and stood up. 'I'll ask John what he thinks.'

Mohun and Vicki took some more wine but Sally was too agitated to sit still. She glanced at the group standing around the pyramid, and the shadowy figures in the portico, and felt a sudden need to be alone. She wandered over to the western porch, brushing her hand over the elaborately decorated couches as she passed, noting again the angular inscriptions around the edges of the small tables. She leaned against a column and stared down the snowy slope towards the ocean. Selenis cast a wide band of light across the water and the stars shone brilliantly in the clear sky. The beauty of the landscape drew her on and she stepped down onto the wide stairway. The icy air shocked her and she stumbled back. At once the air became warm and fragrant again. She felt sharply that she was on an alien world. She shivered. Until she discovered the truth, all worlds would be alien to her. Where did the angels come from? If she could go there, would she feel some sense of identity with their home?

She could not believe it. She hated everything they stood for; conformity, mindless consensus, rules and regulations, all for the sake of some abstract principle which even they could not explain clearly. What about life? Did human beings count for nothing? She thought about her parents' uneventful existence, full of small blameless pleasures, and difficulties faced with quiet persistence. She thought about the happy days after Alistair told her he loved her. What about Shakespeare and Mozart? What about Joni Mitchell, Edwin de Souza? What did the angels have that could match any of them? She felt a rage growing inside her. The angels would not destroy all this for some higher bloody purpose; not if she could prevent it.

She turned and crossed the room quickly. 'Did you understand what I meant?' she asked abruptly.

John replied quietly, 'I understand exactly what you mean, and unlike us, Rick has the resources to look into it. If he can find the right resonant frequency and the corresponding colors ...' He gave a slight warning nod towards Athena. 'But I think we'll keep this to ourselves for the moment.'

Sima detached the relay cable and smiled grimly at Sally. 'This could well be our best shot.'

Sally felt relieved and numb at the same time. She had done what she could. The future stretched out, unknown. Someone touched her shoulder and she took the goblet gratefully. Alistair put his arm around her waist but when she looked up at him, she saw that he was staring across at the two cloaked figures next to Athena. She glimpsed a radiant face framed by short golden brown curls – a face too beautiful for a young man. The youth looked at her curiously and turned to his companion. She gasped as the other figure faced them.

'No, it's not my brother,' Alistair said to her, his voice harsh. 'He calls himself Hercules. What do you think of that?'

Mohun came up behind them. 'I told you what he did for me and John. He saved us. I'm sure we would have been killed.'

Sally leaned against Alistair as Mohun related the crew's experiences. Before Mohun had finished describing how Thomas had stolen the shuttle, Vicki was already dozing on one of the couches. Sima stroked her hair, his eyes half closed.

Finally Alistair said; 'Your turn Sally.' He squeezed her arm. 'What's this I hear about you fighting an army and being wounded by a gourd?'

Sally's heart jumped and she could not speak. To her enormous relief Althamas stretched and yawned, commenting, 'enough for now. We should get some rest.'

She breathed deeply. She was not ready to tell Alistair about Ares' attack, and what the crew believed about her parentage. She was not ready to lie to him; not yet.

18

Something awakened Sally while it was still night. She sat up, not sure for a few seconds of where she was or why she had woken. Alistair lay stretched on the couch to her left. Sima had fallen asleep sitting up, his hand still resting on Vicki's head. As her eyes became accustomed to the dim light she was startled to see Diana, naked under her cloak, lying in John's tight embrace.

She heard a piercing whisper. Althamas and Athena were standing on the western porch. Beyond them Selenis was a huge disc in the western sky, and as she watched, the smaller globe of Artemis touched the rim of the larger moon and started to cover it. Athena exclaimed loudly, and immediately John and Sima awoke. Diana jumped off the couch, pulled her cloak around her and disappeared into the shadows.

Athena walked rapidly through the room, her mouth set in a grim line.

Vicki was rubbing her eyes. 'What's the matter?'

'It is a fearful omen,' groaned Althamas.

'Nonsense!' John said curtly. 'It is only ...'

He was interrupted by a series of shouts from the eastern portico. Althamas and the crew rushed towards the cries and found the Olympians and the Aesir staring down at the battlefield. Zeus's Anomee had risen in the dark of the moon's eclipse and were running across the plain towards them. The Greeks and Vikings shouted and screamed as they scrambled to find their gear and meet the assault. The Spartans raced left and right and within moments had reformed into the same two solid flanks at the north and south ends of the ice. The Athenians pushed forward to fill the gap between them while the Vikings took up their earlier positions behind the Spartans.

Thor cursed in Norse while Diana cried out, 'To fight at night! It is an obscenity. He has broken every rule. He has rejected us entirely.' She shook her fist at the bright pavilion on the distant hill.

Odin said loudly, 'We respected your laws and this could bring us undone.'

Athena's face was flushed. She bit her lip. 'My father has forgotten what it means to be Olympian.'

Suddenly the sky brightened as Artemis uncovered Selenis, and at that moment the left and right flanks of the Spartan army seemed to panic. As Zeus's army approached, the Spartans broke formation, turned and ran back towards the Viking lines, swerving at the last moment towards the centre where the Athenians were holding firm. Zeus's men hesitated for a brief moment and then surged forwards in pursuit of the fleeing Spartans.

'What are they doing?' Alistair yelled.

The Spartans stopped abruptly and within seconds the two flanks lined up, forming into a perfect square with the Athenian force.

'Just watch!' To Sally's surprise, a grin spread across John's face and he put out his hand and hugged Diana against his side. When he saw Sally watching him his expression did not change. Diana smirked triumphantly at Sally.

In an instant Zeus's men ran into the Vikings on either flank. The watchers could see clearly in the bright moonlight that the Vikings had constructed a solid wall of shields and timber which protected their front lines. The pale army now crashed against this barrier. But it did not waver. The few Anomee who managed to penetrate the wall were quickly disposed of by the axe wielding defenders. The second line of Vikings had mounted their ramparts and rained arrows and javelins down on their bewildered foe.

'This is a classic Viking defence,' shouted Sima, 'Just like the battle of Hastings, when the English king Harold fought the Norman invaders!'

It was clear that this strategy had completely confused Zeus's army. They could not break through the Viking wall and were hemmed in on two sides by the Athenians and Spartans. A major part of Zeus's force was now trapped.

Meanwhile Odin was crying out in a loud voice and gesturing furiously. His long ship emerged from the shadows of the far eastern coast and sped towards the now lightly defended eastern beach. As the boat reached the shore the Berserks leapt out and raced towards the enemy. Each of them carried a torch in one hand and a battle axe in the other. The crew could hear their bellowing roars and the screams of Zeus's men as the Berserks hacked and burned their way forward, hardly seeming to pay attention to the pale soldiers who flung themselves in front of them as though they were seeking death. The Berserk targets were now obvious. They headed directly for the dark mounds where the huge fires were still burning.

Althamas explained in an awestruck voice. 'They are mad! They challenge the servants of Vulcan! Those are the furnaces in which they remake the army.'

The crew watched the distant drama in silence. The Berserks onslaught was clearly silhouetted against Vulcan's huge fires, leaping, thrusting, weapons flailing. The Anomee were scattering in panic; objects and bodies flew through the air as the Berserks pursued their relentless mission. When the crew looked back down to the spectacle below them, even John flinched. The Vikings and Spartans encircled more than half of the Anomee army, while the Athenians chased the remainder back across the plain. But there they were confronted by the terrifying Berserks. The horrible screaming rang across the plain.

Zeus's pavilion was shaking, as though struck by a strong wind, and the front wall suddenly parted. A dark figure appeared, stood for a moment, shaking its head and looking around and then charged down the hill towards the fires.

'Zeus,' Sally whispered. Her skin crawled with fear and her eyes widened as she noted the lurching gait of the huge man.

Diana shouted in her own language. When John shook her arm, she repeated in English. 'It is Vulcan. Misshapen wretch! He has come forth.' She turned and called out to Athena who was staring as if transfixed by the battle scene below.

The dark figure lurched and lunged down the slope, raised an enormous hammer shaped weapon above his head and flailed at the Berserks. Two of them fell instantly and when they did not rise again, Odin let out a roar. The resonant sound rumbled round the ice walls, seeming to increase in volume so that the men below them looked up and Vulcan paused in his attack. But only for a moment. The Berserks were upon him. He brandished his hammer and a great axe above his head, brought the weapons down in a wide arc and the Berserks flew through the air.

Odin called out again, and gestured furiously to Thor. Vidar gasped and stepped forward but Thor pushed him back. He wrenched his amulet from around his neck and flung the hammer forward. It shot across the plain like an arrow, hit Vulcan and threw him into the hillside. Great plumes of snow shot skywards and for a few moments the dark figure disappeared.

Thor did not wait to see if his enemy had survived. He drew his long sword and using it as a vaulting pole, took a great bounding leap and hurtled above the heads of the astonished soldiers and into the northern foothills. As if he had been freed from gravity he sprang along the almost vertical walls of ice, past the Spartans and the Vikings, past the Anomee, and onto the eastern slopes.

Vulcan was waiting for him. He swung his mighty hammer and Sally heard John groan as Thor appeared to fall under the crushing blow. There were cries of relief as Thor emerged a moment later racing up the hill towards the pavilion, his long red plaits shining silver in the moonlight. When Vulcan tried to seize him, Thor turned, used his sword to propel himself upwards and sprang over Vulcan's head, delivering a crushing blow with his axe.

Vulcan dropped to the ground and Thor stepped back.

'Finish him!' shrieked Diana. 'Dog faced fiend!'

John took Diana's arm. 'It is not the Aesir way. Vulcan must die on his feet.'

The battle below them had almost ceased as the armies turned to watch the conflict between the Aesir and the Olympian. Sally stared across at the pavilion. Were Zeus and Hera there?

Vulcan staggered to his feet, feinted at Thor and then turned and ran. He stumbled up the northern slope until he reached an outcrop of rock which provided some defence. As Thor climbed up towards him he swung his hammer and when Thor dodged the blow, Vulcan flailed furiously with both the axe and the hammer. Thor appeared to retreat and stood for a few seconds looking up at his opponent. Then he ran forwards, clasped the hilt of his sword in both hands and used it again to vault over Vulcan's head.

The Viking armies roared in triumph as Thor swung his sword at Vulcan; but the Olympian was not finished. His axe met Thor's sword with a loud clang and once again Vulcan scrambled away across the rocky slopes.

For endless minutes Thor pursued him, trying to force Vulcan to face him and fight. Vulcan responded by seizing huge chunks of rock and ice and flinging them down on his foe. Up and down the icy slopes they fought, clambering, slipping and sliding, Vulcan's great bulk and strength matched by Thor's long legged agility. As they approached the western hill, the Anomee wailed in alarm and pushed back at the Greeks who surrounded them.

As though to draw Vulcan away from his camp, Thor suddenly turned and raced back over ridge. Vulcan cried out triumph and pursued him. They disappeared from view and for long moments the watchers saw only the bright sparks of their weapons clashing and heard their loud grunts and gasps. Suddenly the tip of Thor's long sword appeared above the ridge and there was a terrible shrieking noise. For several seconds there was complete silence and then Thor reappeared, bent over as if in great pain. In his left hand he had hold of Vulcan's leg. He dragged him over the crest of the ridge, picked up the still figure and hoisted him above his head. He stood for a few moments, his chest heaving with Vulcan's weight. Then he flung Vulcan down into his own fire. Loops of flame shot out of the blaze with ear splitting cracks and sparks cascaded down the white slopes.

Sally could not contain herself. 'Where is Zeus? Why is he letting this happen?'

Her words were drowned out by the cheers of the Vikings as Thor bounded back across the northern hills. The Spartans and Athenians responded by turning on their enemy. The terrified Anomee were surrounded. There was no escape. The rest of the Anomee army did not come to their help. They turned and fled, pursued by the Vikings.

Diana shouted something in her own language, then repeated in English, 'we must stop this. There is no honor in it.'

Athena stood silently but Odin nodded in agreement. 'You are right.' He leaned down and grasped Thor's arm as the tall man gained the top of the cliff. Thor brandished his amulet and embraced Odin.

'Zeus must be defeated,' Athena maintained.

For the first time, Apollo spoke. He threw back his hood and his short curls shone like silver in the bright moonlight. 'Yes! But let the mortals decide how it should be done. Speak to them.'

Athena sighed deeply and stepped down the wide stairs of packed snow. She halted at the edge of the cliff and called out in a ringing voice. The fighting below her faltered for a moment and then as Odin joined her, the noise of battle died away. Greeks, Vikings and Anomee all turned to look up at the two figures.

Athena called out again and several of the Spartans shouted back hoarsely, staring up at her in disbelief.

'She is telling them to lay down their weapons,' Althamas explained.

Diana waved the crew forward imperiously. 'Show them,' she commanded.

John smiled and stroked Diana's cheek. She flushed and her face softened as he took her hand. The crew followed slowly, shivering in the cold air.

Athena's voice rang out again and the Spartans flung down their swords. The Vikings stared up at Odin, and at his signal they laid down their arms. The pale army shuffled in confusion but when Athena called out in Anomee they too became still. Their disfigured faces stared upwards. Vicki shuddered as she looked at the patchwork of flesh and scars that made up their bodies and limbs, and thought of her first sight of the beautiful Anomee.

Athena now raised her arms and spoke rapidly. She pointed to the crew and gestured violently.

'You will become whole again as these people are whole,' Althamas translated. 'I will give you back your mortality. You may live or die, as you wish.'

'I swear this to you.' Althamas continued rapidly. 'Look at the men and women you are fighting. They have children. They can love or fight or die, as they choose.' Athena's voice rose to a roar. 'You have been betrayed. Leave Zeus and become whole again.'

Freya and Tyr had climbed back up the hill and now the five Aesir raised their arms and linked them as though to give support to Athena's words.

John punched the air, shouted and hugged Diana. The Vikings cheered in approval as she pulled his head down and kissed him passionately. Sharon threw back her hood, flung her arms around Mohun and kissed him. Sima looked on incredulously but Vicki suddenly laughed and she too waved her arms. 'Do it!' she shouted, forgetting that no one below would understand her. 'Do it! Be free like us!'

Athena spoke again and the Anomee let out loud groans and wails. Some of them sat down and covered their heads. Others stumbled around as though disoriented. Athena's voice carried over the noise of their distress and gradually the Anomee became quiet. Athena held up her arms and for a few moments there was complete silence.

Suddenly the hair rose on the back of Sally's neck and she looked out across the plain. Above Zeus's pavilion a dark cloud was forming, an evil shape against the snow covered hills. As it rose, it blotted out the stars.

Sally grabbed Alistair's arm. 'Look!' she cried, her voice hoarse with fear.

Dark red sparks spread across the cloud and a bright light shot out of it. It streaked across the plain and crashed into the western foothills. Bodies flew skywards and fell with sickening thuds onto their fellow soldiers. As Zeus's cloud approached, another bolt of flame shot overhead, narrowly missing Athena's temple, and two more bolts crashed into the snow below them.

Sally saw Mohun shouting and gesturing at John but she could not hear him above the great confusion of noise; screaming from the armies trapped on the plain, shouts and curses in several languages, the whistling shriek of Zeus's missiles and great crashes as they hit their targets. Smoke rose from the plain, covering the awful prospect and suddenly the whole scene seemed to turn red. Athena had flung off her cloak and was holding it up between her outstretched hands. Her head was lowered and her arms strained as though she was holding a mighty weight. Hercules and Apollo stood behind her, their hands on her shoulders. To her right, Odin stood, supported by Thor, pointing his staff towards the cloud.

'The aegis! The aegis!' someone shouted. 'Get down!'

The lightning bolts ceased abruptly. A ghastly red light filled the valley and the pale army fell like wheat before a harvester. From east to west the air shimmered like a heat wave. Between the dark cloud and the figures on the western hill, arcs of light emerged, spiraling back and forth, fading and reforming; and the air vibrated with tension as if two giant magnets were struggling to repulse each other.

The silence was complete. The armies were dead or prone with fright as the struggle between light and dark went on above their heads.

Someone whispered. 'What is it?'

As if the voice had triggered something, a brilliant light shot out of Zeus's pavilion, whizzed across the valley and hit the snow in front of the crew. A tall silver skinned figure materialized and seized Sharon's hood, lifting her off the ground. Mohun screamed, flung his arms around Sharon's waist and was dragged upwards with her. The trio hung there for a moment. Then the silver clad man kicked out violently and Mohun dropped onto the snow. John bellowed something, leapt over Mohun and grabbed the silver legs. He swept a sword from beneath his cloak and hacked at the strange man. There was a loud booming noise, a blossom of green smoke and all three fell to the ground.

'Hermes!' shrieked Diana. She raced over to the struggling figures and kicked Sharon's attacker in the head. He seized her ankle and they rolled away across the snow. Diana landed on top, knelt on the man's chest and chopped at his neck.

Sally stood stunned as Alistair and Sima dashed towards their crewmates. She could hear Diana shouting with rage and then her voice was drowned out by a loud ringing noise. Zeus's cloud was retreating and within moments had disappeared behind the veil of smoke which hung over the plain. Odin had lowered his staff and stood with his head bowed. Ceres leaned over Athena, who had dropped her cloak and sunk to the ground.

Apollo and Hercules pushed past Sally. She caught at Hercules cloak, tried to speak but she could only point. Flashes of light raced along the eastern peaks and the foremost angels appeared over the ridge behind Zeus's pavilion. The throng grew quickly until it filled the eastern sky. They flew slowly inland and then halted, hovering just above the icy wall.

'Athena!' Hercules stopped and stared at the sight.

Sally stumbled forward. She could hear violent sobbing from the group surrounding John and Sharon. Diana had flung herself on John's body and was trying to breathe life back into him. Sharon and Mohun lay winded and gasping nearby. The silver figure was half buried in the snow, Diana's dagger protruding from its throat.

Apollo pushed through the group and put his hand on Diana's shoulder. He spoke gently to her but she ignored him, her chest heaving as she ran her hands frantically over John's face.

'Can't you help him?' Sharon staggered to her feet and stumbled across the snow towards John.

Apollo shook his head. 'He has been struck by Hermes. We cannot revive him.' He lifted Diana up. 'Come away sister. There is nothing you can do.' Diana screamed and tried to pull free but he carried her away.

Hercules uttered some angry words and then looking back towards the sky, cried out in alarm, 'Athena!'

The angels were moving towards them. The lights, all the colors of the rainbow, flashed rapidly across their ranks and a series of long notes could be heard. They increased in tempo as the angels descended.

'Athena!' Hercules called again. 'We are doomed.'

Odin gestured to Thor and Vidar and the two Aesir ran forward, disappearing over the steep incline. Odin lifted his staff and a great beam of light shot from it, streaked across the valley, and hit the western hill, narrowly missing the purple pavilion. The angels halted and hovered just above the icy wall. Sally felt as though there were a long silence even though the air was filled with the terrified screaming of the Anomee.

The lower ranks of angels appeared agitated but Sally could see clearly the red and cream of Michael's robes and Gabriel's blue gown above him. She waited in dread. Michael suddenly moved forward from the throng and his staff flashed. The great pavilion burst into flames. The staff flashed twice more and the eastern hill exploded showering the valley with huge chunks of ice and rocks. Ear splitting crashes rang out and then the scene disappeared behind a mist of vaporized ice.

Time seemed to slow down as Michael rejoined the throng and the angels turned west towards Athena's temple. Sally heard shouts and felt hands on her arm but she could not look. She gazed down at John's still face. Sharon was now cradling his head and preparing to close his eyes. In the dark orbs Sally saw a strange reflection.

'My god! Look!'

The crew stared up. A hundred small aircraft darted across the smoky sky. Above them a huge craft hovered. Colored spotlights swept across the plain and the southern ocean, and suddenly deep rumbling noises boomed out. Sally looked back towards the angels. They were receding into the distance, the bands of lights flashing and pulsating in a way that she had never seen before.

Alistair called out. 'It must be Rick! What on earth …?'

As if in answer, a deafening voice roared out. 'Stand down! Stand down! Or we'll blast you off this fugging planet!'

19

The Valkyrien prepared John last. The Vikings slain in battle and beyond revival were already arrayed in small boats soaked with ceremonial oils, their prows turned to the south. Friends and families surrounded the vessels; some silent with disbelief that their loved ones could not be regenerated; others sobbed and cried out at the prospect of parting forever from lovers and children with whom they had lived for hundreds of years. Artemis and Selenis were hidden behind heavy cloud. Bright torches cast flickering reflections on the black water and the air was oppressive. The Aesir watched in silence; Odin as usual appeared deep in thought.

'Now is the time for us to say goodbye as our heroes take the long journey beyond Valhalla.' Thor's words were greeted by a great wailing. The boats were set alight and pushed out until they were seized by the current and carried away. Several Vikings screamed out and flung themselves after the boats, splashing and flailing in the still water, but their friends pulled them back.

Amid these dismal scenes the Valkyrien gestured for the crew to remove their amulets. One by one they were placed around John's body.

'You will thus accompany your leader into the great unknown,' Ulfarr said sadly. He drew one of his daggers and placed it at John's feet.

'Damn it John.' Rick Jones' voice cracked. 'You could have waited.' The tall man thrust something into the boat, turned away and strode up the small rise which overlooked the bay.

Sally handed over her small book of Shakespeare's sonnets, which Vicki had kept for her. 'I never knew him,' she muttered as Ulfarr continued to collect tokens. 'I never tried to know him.' She felt cold as ice despite her heavy clothing.

Sharon touched her arm. 'John didn't want it any other way. I've known him for more than ten years but I was never close to him. He never allowed anyone to get near him, apart from his family, and a very few friends.' She glanced up at Rick who was pacing up and down in an agitated manner. Loren hovered behind him while three of the Phoenix's marines stood at a respectful distance.

'That's why John never married. He believed our type of work was incompatible with that sort of emotional commitment. But he died for me and I would have done the same for him.' Sharon rubbed her eyes. 'Now look at him. Perhaps that's who he really was.'

The Valkyrien had clothed John as an Aesir, in a thickly embroidered robe, with a coronet sparkling against his short dark hair. His hands clasped the hilt of a shining sword. His face was calm and serious.

Sally glanced across at Alistair. She longed for some sign of affection. Their reunion had been passionate, but since he had learned of her apparent parentage he had avoided her. And the appearance of his brother Jeremy amongst Rick's crew had overwhelmed Alistair; now the two brothers stood shoulder to shoulder, as though unwilling to be separated again.

Jeremy was gazing at Athena's group. Hercules had not yet spoken to Jeremy although he was obviously fascinated by the young man's resemblance to him. The disposal of the Anomee bodies and the ceremonies for the Spartan and Athenian funerals had kept the Olympians occupied throughout the day. Now the funeral byres had been cleared away and the Olympians had come to pay their respect to the Norse heroes. Athena and Ceres wore their usual calm expressions, but Diana looked enraged as she stared at John's funeral byre. She gave Sally a baleful look and turned abruptly to speak to Apollo. Athena signaled for her to be quiet and Diana complied with a frown. Althamas stood with his head bowed, his face twisted in grief. Sam and many of his friends had not survived the battle.

Sally looked up at the dark sky. Few stars were visible through the dense cloud and it was impossible to tell whether the angels might be nearby. They had not been seen since Rick's arrival. For two days, while the Vikings and Olympians prepared for the funeral rites, Rick had sent his crew out to search the planet. There was no sign of life. The impending battle had sent the Anomee and Athena's people into hiding, probably into the network of caves and tunnels near the gods' city. And Alistair had explained to Rick that if the angels wished to conceal themselves, they would be impossible to find.

Rick had been furious. He wanted revenge for his friend's death. 'What sort of creatures are they? According to you they are all powerful, they have some great mission they are carrying out but they just watch while people slaughter each other; attack without provocation.'

The Phoenix crew were suffering from massive psychic shock. In three days they had had to adjust to ideas which the Millennium crew were only now starting to accept, after months on the planet. Loren in particular had been very distressed by Alistair's account of his time with the angels.

The wailing grew louder as the lights of the last Viking funeral boats disappeared into the darkness. Thor's voice boomed above the cries. He spoke for some moments in Norse and the Vikings slowly became silent.

Now it was John's turn. In special recognition of his heroism, Thor strode out into the icy water and placed his hand on the boat.

'Wait!' Loren shouted. 'We can't let him go like this. John was a believer.' She pulled her crucifix over her head and ran down to the water. She waded out to the boat, her teeth chattering with cold, lifted John's head, and placed the gold chain around his neck. She could not look at Thor. She clutched the side of the boat wishing she could think of something to say but it was too cold. She started to shake violently.

Thor shouted something and another man splashed out through the water. He smiled sympathetically at Loren and said, 'Let me.'

Loren thrust her cold fingers against her mouth and stared at him. The man was as fair skinned as most of the Vikings but he had black hair and bright blue eyes. He was silent for a moment. Then he placed his hand on John's forehead and called out loudly.

'That which we can see lasts but a moment, but the unseen will endure forever.' He raised his other hand toward the sky. 'This man walked the path of honor and laid down his life that another might live. Oh heavenly father, receive now thy humble servant, John Armstrong, who lived and died in the sure and certain conviction ...'

The rest of his words were drowned out by a fresh bout of wailing from the shore, but Loren watched his mouth and took comfort from the familiar words. He looked at her questioningly and she nodded. As Thor lowered his torch to the boat she felt warmth against her arm. Rick had joined her and with Thor they pushed the boat until it started to drift away. Rick picked her up just as her legs gave way and carried her back to the shore.

Sally looked around. Sima held Vicki close as she wept silently. Mohun and Sharon stood, their arms entwined, staring out to sea as John's boat drifted south and burst into flame. Jeremy draped one arm over Alistair's shoulder and hugged him. Sally stepped back. The Olympians stood around Diana as though to restrain her. Rick and Loren were talking intently to the marines. Thor had rejoined Odin and the other Aesir. Freya's red hair gleamed in the torchlight but her face was in shadow.

Sally shivered and without thinking, walked rapidly away, past the groups of Vikings, through an outcrop of jagged rock and out of sight. She emerged onto the rim of a hollow as perfectly shaped as a fine china bowl. On the opposite side, the wind or water had carved the deep snow into strangely regular shapes, like the carved columns of Athena's ice temple. She thought of the elaborate structures which she and Alistair had seen when they were first taken to Iceland. Nothing remained of them now. Had the angels really left the planet? Did they know that Rick's huge fleet was merely a projection? Rick's sound and light show had had not affected her and they had no way of finding out how much it had disturbed the angels. Perhaps Michael's bizarre behavior had caused their retreat. Perhaps even now they were planning how to eradicate life here and on Earth.

She shook her head. It did no good to think about it. Rick had explained his technology to the Olympians and the Aesir, and was ready to repeat his performance if the angels reappeared. Everyone was agreed. There was nothing else they could do.

Her feet felt numb and she stamped up and down. She looked back at the rocky entrance. No one had noticed her absence or come to find her. Perhaps they would never really trust her or feel any real friendship for her again. She was stuck, half way between the human world and the world of the Olympians, to which everyone assumed she belonged. She sighed. That was the most likely explanation for Alistair's change of heart.

She pulled her fur lined hood further over her head and made her way around the rim of the snowy bowl, slipping and sliding, looking for distraction from her thoughts. She came to a halt where the snowy columns blocked the way. Beyond them, the snow extended for several meters and then rose steeply to another outcropping of dark rock. She felt the need to keep moving and climbed awkwardly a little way down the slope, stopping in shock as her eyes drew level with the base of the first pillar. It was formed into the shape of a pair of feet. The resemblance to a sculpture was so strange that she put out her hand to touch them. She gasped as the shapes moved and a cold hand grasped her neck and pulled her upwards. She yelled as she recalled Thomas's vice like grip and yelled again as Gabriel emerged from the pillar. He shook off the snow, showing that he was dressed as usual, his wings tightly folded behind him.

'Be quiet.' Gabriel put a finger to his mouth. 'I must speak only to you and to Alistair.'

Sally heard a panting sound and saw Alistair scrambling up the slope towards her. He did not speak but stood staring at Gabriel.

'I have very little time. The choir has been disrupted and cannot reach consensus. We must leave this place.'

Alistair gasped. 'What?'

'We must leave but we will return.' Gabriel held up his hand. 'Listen carefully. It has been agreed that you should be given certain information which may help remediate the situation.'

'It's a bit late for that,' Alistair panted.

Gabriel ignored this. 'Where are the remains of Thomas?' he asked Sally.

'Don't tell him anything,' Alistair cut in, but Sally replied, 'I'm not sure; somewhere on the southern end of a large island, a few miles from the southern continent. Ask Diana or Ceres. They may know more.'

Gabriel shook his head. 'There is no time. We must leave here very soon. We will return when the choir has been reformed and full functionality has been restored.' He turned his head sideways for a long moment. 'But if you wish to avoid destruction and attempt your own repair, you should pay attention to what you have been told.' He looked aside again. 'That is all.'

'What?' shouted Alistair. 'What the hell does that mean?'

'We told you before. Your domain has not progressed satisfactorily. We came here and found you alone. We provided instructions. We brought other species to assist in your progress but you destroyed or corrupted them.'

'I have no idea what you are talking about.' Alistair's face was red with frustration despite the cold.

Sally interrupted, trying to speak calmly. 'Could you be more specific? What must we do? Please repeat the instructions.'

'At important times in your history you have all been told, in many ways, in all languages. It is written as a commandment in the books. Go forth and multiply.'

'What?' Alistair shouted again.

'You have multiplied but you have not gone forth. Thus your multiplication threatens your existence. If you cease to exist and this domain is emptied of intelligence, it will affect all contiguous domains.'

'So, you're saying that what we've done wrong is to remain on earth and not go anywhere else?' Sally spoke slowly, feeling that at any moment the pieces of this puzzle would fall into place.

'That is correct. Your progress was impeded by the lack of other intelligent species. We attempted to provide these but the experiment failed. If you continue to multiply, the earth will not sustain you, you will be extinguished and this domain will lack intelligence. This must not happen. If you cannot progress, we must replace you with others.'

Sally could hear Alistair still panting, as though in panic. 'How long do we have, to show that we have made progress?'

Gabriel turned his head again. 'We estimate that we cannot return here before a hundred of your years.'

Sally asked huskily, 'Are you telling us that we are alone in the universe; that there is no other intelligent life?'

'That is correct. All information indicates that domains, what you call universes, originate from a single planet from which intelligence spreads in an orderly manner.'

'What? Nobody else? Nowhere in the universe?' Alistair's voice rose. 'How could you know that? I don't believe it.'

'The evidence is clear.'

Alistair persisted. 'So, where do you come from?'

Gabriel turned away while Sally and Alistair stared at him. The silence seemed endless.

'I have told you before that you would not understand. We are not from this domain although we must concern ourselves with its progress.'

Alistair started back as though he had been hit. 'You come from another universe? There are theories that…' He took a deep breath. 'How did you get here? That's impossible.'

'Only a thought separates the domains. Only Michael can think that thought, and then we follow.' Gabriel looked briefly aside again. 'But Michael has been damaged and we must leave before he deteriorates further.'

Sally shuddered as she remembered the slaughter. 'Is that why he killed Zeus?'

Gabriel looked aside again. When he faced them his eyes were turned skywards. 'I have provided the information which the choir considers necessary. I will leave now.'

'No! Wait!' Sally and Alistair spoke at once. Alistair continued. 'Give us a moment to think. There may be something else we need to know.'

'You need only to follow the instructions. You cannot make progress by ceasing to multiply. You must go forth.'

'But what if we make the same mistakes? You need to tell us more; where we have gone wrong.'

'You must go forth. Is that not clear?' Gabriel shook his wings as though preparing to unfurl them.

Sally heard Alistair gasping with frustration. She longed to ask about Thomas's death. Was it just a coincidence that he resembled the thousands of stone angels that could be seen on earth? But she did not dare.

As though she had spoken aloud Gabriel said, 'Thomas is verification that our choir has become faulty, our instructions corrupted. I will not provide you with further information in case that too is defective.' The angel's wings started to lift above his shoulders and the familiar grating sound grew louder. 'I will see you in one hundred years, if you have not destroyed yourselves.'

'One hundred years? Sally may live that long but I'll be gone.' Alistair spoke bitterly.

'The technology is here that will prolong your life. You must persuade the gourds to let you use it.' Gabriel's wings were now fully unturled and a pale blue light spread out in a fan shape over his head.

'What about your contract with the immortals, the gourds? What about them?' Alistair shouted above the rustling noise.

'Null and void. The experiment failed.'

'The word wall; is that still here?'

'Gone, all gone.' Gabriel closed his eyes and shot upwards, sending a cloud of snow into the sky.

20

Alistair turned without speaking and edged past the collapsed columns.

Sally pulled at his arm. 'Wait! Can't we talk for a moment? I've hardly seen you since …'

'We should get back to the others and tell them.' Alistair kicked at the pile of snow as if to confirm that nothing else was hidden within.

'If you don't feel anything for me anymore, just tell me.'

Alistair stared at the snow. 'I don't know. It's a lot to take in.'

'How do you think I feel?' Sally swallowed. 'But it's not like I'm the only one. Just look at Hercules.'

Alistair's face tightened. 'Jeremy is the spitting image of my grandfather; and I've seen pictures of other relatives …'

Sally regretted speaking. 'I didn't mean that. But all of us probably have Olympians and Aesir too amongst our ancestors.'

'I need time to get used to it.' Alistair scrambled part way down the slope. 'Are you coming?'

'I want you to tell the others what Gabriel said.'

Alistair finally looked at her. 'Why?'

'They'll believe you. None of you seem to trust me anymore.' Sally slid past him and climbed back up to the rim.

Gabriel's flight heavenwards had caused a panic and it took several minutes for quiet to be restored so that Alistair could be heard. At his first words, the Vikings let out a great cheer but the Aesir and Olympians stood like stone as though stunned by the news. Alistair waited until the cheering had died down and then summarised what Gabriel had told them. When he reached the part where Gabriel said that their contract was ended, the Vikings cheered again.

Finally Athena called out to Alistair, 'you have done well. Now we can plan for our survival.'

Odin struck the ground with his staff and Thor gasped for breath. 'Agreed. We must work together to combat this threat. Tomorrow we will gather for a moot.'

* * *

The Phoenix crew had set up their habitat domes at the top of the rise, in the shelter of the northern foothills. The simple round shapes and drab colors contrasted strongly with the colorful pavilions and tents now erected by the Aesir and Olympians. The flat area where the funeral byres had been prepared was swept clean and two of the Vikings had dragged a stone pedestal to the centre. The white stage remained empty, while the immortals conferred inside their tents. The Viking and Greek armies had been sent home. Only the long ships of Thor and Odin were anchored in the icy bay.

The crew waited nervously, endlessly discussing the possible outcomes of today's conference, and checking the empty blue sky for any sign that Zeus or his allies had survived. Nothing disturbed the moot space, other than the occasional gust of wind drawing new patterns on the fresh snow.

Rick had welcomed the news. 'It makes sense,' he said. 'The drive to explore is natural for humans; probably for all species. With the immortals to help us, we can be on our way in no time.' He grinned at Loren. 'That'll show those bureaucrats on earth.'

When none of the Millennium crew replied, he continued. 'Look, I know you've been through hell. But it's over now.' He waved his arm towards the horizon. 'Can you believe it? A whole new world to explore and this is just the beginning.'

Mohun stared at him. 'Let's wait till we hear from the others,' he said. 'We are not the only ones affected by this.'

Sally spent most of this time outside, hunkered down in one of the deckchairs. She was painfully aware that every time she entered the communal dome, all eyes turned to her, as though the crew believed she had some secret knowledge that she was keeping to herself.

The deep note of a horn sounded and there was a sudden stir in the Aesir camp. Thor and Odin emerged and almost immediately the Olympians also appeared on the opposite side of the snowy field. One of the marines called out to Rick and the crew filed out of the dome. For several moments the three groups looked at each other. Then Thor walked slowly towards the round table. Vicki shivered. She felt as though she had viewed this scene before, as though some ancient memory was stirring in her head.

Thor picked up the speaking stone from the centre of the table and held it above his head. He spoke loudly in English. 'On behalf of my father, the all powerful Odin and of the remaining Aesir, I, Thor, claim all lands south of this icy waste, and the command of all peoples, immortal and mortal, living therein. We swear to support the alliance, to prepare for the return of the Ice Giants.' His voice rang out. 'Your allies are our allies. Your enemies are our enemies. We will pursue them and bring them to their doom.' He bowed slightly to the north and east, replaced the stone on the pedestal and returned to the Aesir who stood on the western side of the moot space. Freya touched his arm and he grasped her hand.

Athena stepped slowly forward. She touched the stone and stared at it for a few moments. Then she too picked it up, cradling it in both hands. 'I am Athena, ruler of Olympia, daughter of the previously great and mighty Zeus. I claim authority over all the lands north of the White Land and all the people who reside there. I will bring the followers and allies of Zeus to justice. I will support the alliance whatever my fate.' She bowed and retreated.

'Good grief!' Rick muttered. 'Do they always carry on like this?' He jumped to his feet.

Alistair grabbed his arm. 'Be careful. They are easily offended.'

'Ah! What the heck.' Before any of the crew could answer Rick loped forward and picked up the stone. He looked around defiantly. 'I am Richard Jones, commander of the Phoenix and representative of the people of Earth. We lay claim to the lands surrounding the equator, since the angels, or whoever they are, seem to have abandoned them.' He looked around as though he expected to be challenged but no one spoke. Ceres and Hercules stood behind Athena, their faces impassive. Odin as usual seemed lost in thought, staring at the ground. Thor and the other Aesir retained their grave expressions.

'That's it, then.' Rick grinned, replaced the stone and returned to stand with the crew.

There was another long silence. Finally Thor stepped forward and picked up the stone again. 'It is agreed. None will trespass on the others' domains, except to give aid.' He looked around until he met Sally's eyes. 'We will conceal nothing that concerns our mutual fates.' Sally was unable to meet Thor's gaze, relieved that when she looked up he had turned towards the Olympians. 'Are we agreed?'

Athena nodded and called out. 'We agree.'

Rick stepped forward again. 'In that case, there are a lot of questions I want answered.'

Thor looked at him for a long moment. 'We also want answers to our questions.' He glanced at Sally again. 'But we have more urgent matters to set right. We must clear this world of those who would work against us. We will meet here again in thirty days and decide what is to be done.'

The Olympians nodded and bowed slightly. Ceres gestured to the tent and called out to Rick Jones. 'We will leave this here for your shelter and for our use when we return.' She did not wait for a reply but walked rapidly towards the water and disappeared behind a drift of snow. Athena nodded again towards the domes and followed her. Hercules stared for a few moments at Alistair and Jeremy. He seemed on the point of speaking, but he shrugged and turned away.

Althamas gave the crew a sad wave. 'We will meet again. Do not forget me.'

Alistair's eyes watered as he thought of Melissa and her children. He embraced Althamas. 'Don't forget me; don't forget who we are,' he whispered.

'Never,' Althamas replied solemnly. 'Have no fear. We will prevail.'

Rick took his hand and shook it firmly. 'I won't forget what you did for us.'

Thor and Freya walked over to the crew, followed by a Viking who looked like a bear in his thick furs. Freya kissed Vicki on the forehead and stroked her hair. 'You see?' She waved her hand upwards. 'The sun still shines. Keep well, little one, until we meet again.'

'I will leave Ulfarr with you, with one of our ravens,' Thor was telling Sharon. 'If you should need anything; if danger approaches, Ulfarr will know what to do.'

The tall Viking beamed. 'And I will keep you well supplied with ale and wine.' He grasped Mohun's hand. 'I am glad to stay with you a while longer.'

Rick watched these proceedings with some skepticism and remained behind when the Millennium crew accompanied the Aesir to the shore. He joined them as the two long ships disappeared behind a cliff of ice.

'No offence, Ulfarr, but I would like to talk to the crew in private.'

Ulfarr shrugged. 'I am not offended. I will help you as I can. While you speak I will look around. I do not like to sleep in a place which I have not cast my eye over.' He adjusted his hood and strode off.

Mohun frowned. 'There was no need to be rude. We need all the friends we can get. It's not as though you have enough room to take us all home.' He was referring to the fact that Rick had packed the Phoenix and the shuttles with his own private army.

'Is that what you want? To go home?' Rick sounded incredulous. 'After everything that's happened, you just want to leave?'

Mohun looked startled.

Alistair interrupted. 'Why don't we sit down and talk about it. Everything has happened so fast. We've had no chance to talk.'

Rick nodded curtly. He signaled to the three marines to wait outside and thrust his long form through the dome's hatch.

Mohun gathered some mugs and took them to the urn. He was annoyed to see that his hands were trembling. 'Tea, anyone?'

Vicki came to help him and passed out the hot drinks. The six Millennium crew sat together, flanked by Jeremy and Loren. Three of the Phoenix's scientists sat slightly apart. Their clean uniforms and alert expressions were in stark contrast to the disheveled clothes and tired faces of the Millennium crew.

Rick took the seat nearest the door and stared down into his cup.

'Imagine this.' He looked around the circle of faces. 'Just imagine it. We return to Earth. We somehow convince them that our stories are true. Overnight we reveal that we have knowledge which can end disease, bring immortality and allow us to create almost anything we want to. What do you think will happen? Have you any idea what it's like back there? The US is in chaos and it's only a matter of time before the trouble spreads to Europe and Asia, if it hasn't already. We have to think this through but we don't have much time; thirty days and then those immortals will be back, with their own ideas.'

'Are you saying that we should make the decision, as to what to tell humanity? What about democracy? We should allow the UN to decide how to handle this.' Sima spoke firmly.

Vicki cut in. 'And think of the hope it could bring to people, to know that we can solve problems like pollution. We have no right to keep this to ourselves.'

Rick did not seem to hear her. 'If some of you still want to go back, I'll refit one of the shuttles.' He shook his head. 'I just want you all to realize what the situation is like back on Earth. And it's probably worse now.'

'I agree with Rick,' Sharon said.

'Don't you want to see your family again?' asked Mohun.

'Of course I want to go home. I couldn't bear it if I thought ...' Sharon swallowed and continued, 'but we have to think about what might happen. We have to make plans. We can't just go back and blurt it all out.'

'And another thing; why should we trust these immortals.' Alistair gulped his tea. 'I think Athena and Ceres are pretty straight, but the others ... well ... they don't think the way we do. What's to stop them going back to Earth and taking over again?'

Sally nodded. 'Also we don't know whether Zeus and the others are really dead.'

Vicki cut in. 'And if you had seen those creatures; what Zeus did to the Anomee. They've been making genetic changes, treating people like lab rats. Earth could be in great danger.'

Rick stirred restlessly. 'I do understand how you feel.' He had seen the remains of Zeus's army on the blasted site of the battlefield. 'I agree we need to warn Earth. But believe me, it would be hard to get them to agree on anything right now. They're too busy trying to sort out the problems in the States.'

Jeremy interrupted. 'A lot of this is hypothetical anyway. How could we mount expeditions to populate other planets? Where would we go? How would we live? It would take huge resources.'

'We've got those, right here,' Rick retorted. 'We already planned for a scientific settlement on Mars. We just need to expand it.' He turned to Alistair. 'From what you've told me, a lot of the geology of Earth 2 has been manipulated. And the gods ...' He raised his eyebrows as though he still could not believe he had spoken the word. 'And the gods have been travelling back and forth to earth. They must know how it's done.'

Alistair shrugged. 'I don't think they know how their technology works, but they know how to use it. There's a lot about this planet that's odd. No northern lights for example. Also they must have some control over the climate; the way they produced that cloud cover when we first got here. That wasn't natural. Plus, there's been hardly any change in temperature since we arrived, and there should have been - the way the planet's tilted. That's what Gabriel said – we need to get the immortals to let us use their technology.'

Jeremy cut in again. 'That may be so, but after all these months, none of you are any the wiser about how they do it. Do you think these gods are going to teach us? Can we trust them?'

'That's another reason for staying. We can learn just by watching.' Rick turned to Loren. 'Show them.'

Loren hissed quietly, and made a quick gesture. The air shimmered and she caught the cup before it dropped to the ground. There were gasps of surprise.

'How the hell did you do that? I lived with the Olympians for weeks and I couldn't work it out,' Alistair looked at Loren in amazement.

'One of my older brothers is deaf, so we all learned Auslan – the Australian sign language. I guess I'm just better at imitating the gestures.' She made the strange hissing noise again and another quick gesture. A small table appeared. 'You try.'

Alistair imitated the sound and the gesture; the air before him stirred for a moment. 'See? Nothing happens.'

'Move your hands closer to your chest and slightly down. Do it quicker.'

Alistair repeated the gesture and yelled in triumph as another table appeared.

There were excited shouts and laughter as the others attempted the gestures. Finally Rick interrupted. 'Ok that's enough. I suggest we keep this quiet. No reason for the gods to know. One thing they seem to lack and we have plenty of, is curiosity. They may not realize what fast learners we are.'

Alistair frowned 'That's odd. That's what Gabriel said – that our curiosity was what ruined things; what brought them here, to interfere.' He looked at Jeremy. 'I want to see my family and I hate to think of things getting worse on Earth if there is anything we could do to help.' He shook his head. 'But there's also a million things I want to find out – the moons – they're very strange, and how much of this planet is original, how much they've changed it and how they do it; just for starters. I mean, just think about what we found when we first landed. It was as though the southern continent had been wiped clean.'

No one spoke. The Millennium crew had found it difficult to explain to Rick and the Phoenix scientists exactly what had happened.

'Also,' Alistair continued, 'I would like to make sure that the Anomee get a fair go. I respect Athena and I was treated very well. But it gets my goat to think of any human being depending on the good will of another species. I would like to give them the choice to go back to Earth.'

'Or with us,' Rick suggested. 'Those Vikings would make great settlers.'

There was a long silence. Sima shook his head and stared at his feet. Rick turned to his three scientists. 'You don't have any preconceived ideas about this planet or its people. What do you think?'

The dark haired woman whom Sally recalled was named Sarah cleared her throat. 'You have to understand that it's still very difficult for us to believe what is happening.' She glanced at the two men next to her. 'If we believe what the angels ...' Like Rick, she grimaced, as though she found it difficult to speak the word. 'These beings who resemble angels appear to be logical, even if they have developed faults.' She shook her head. 'It's hard to understand. The whole business with the watchers; why did they have to do that? With their technology they could have just …'

Alistair cut in. 'I realise it doesn't make sense to us. But from what they told us, they have a way of making decisions and then they are all bound by that. They seem to have complicated rules and procedures for what they can and cannot do and how they do it; impossible for us to figure out. But I think that until now their main idea was to make sure we didn't find out about them. Again, I'm not sure why.'

Rick's lead scientist, an older man spoke. 'Be that as it may, if we believe what they told Sally and Alistair, and it's probably best that we do; surely our first priority must be to plan for the next hundred years, how to work with the others. If we're sidetracked from that major goal, then nothing else we do will matter anyway.'

Loren interrupted. 'You're assuming, Russell, that we have to do what they tell us. Rick showed that we can disrupt them. We should work on that.'

Russell leaned forward and spoke with conviction. 'According to these angels, if we do not find other homes, planets to settle, we may destroy ourselves. A lot of us already believe that Earth can't take a much larger population.' He breathed deeply. 'And it's hard for us to believe, I know. But according to them, we could have a negative impact on these other universes as well. I think we should take what they said seriously.'

'Exactly,' Rick cut in. 'especially as it fits with our plans anyway. John and I – for us Mars was just going to be the first step.' His face fell as he spoke John's name.

Mohun rubbed his forehead. 'We could still go home and agree not to reveal everything that's happened. Whoever wants to stay, can do so.'

The scientist sitting next to Sarah cleared his throat. 'It would be hard to convince anyone, and it's not just a matter of go or stay. We need a plan; how to deal with the potential threat; how to interact with the gourds.' He looked around the dome. 'How to protect humanity.'

Sima shifted restlessly in his chair. 'You're all still talking as though the decision is ours to make. What gives us the right to conceal what has happened; to take on this responsibility as though we know what is best?' He stared at Rick 'I agree we should make plans, but those plans should be about how we will take this news home to Earth. Let the people of Earth decide what should be done.'

'And if we find when we get there that there is no viable international government? What then?' Rick's voice was even. He showed no resentment at Sima's comments.

'If so, we can face it. We can help get it back. It's not up to us to decide the fate of billions of people.'

There were murmurs of agreement around the circle. Alistair looked at Jeremy and felt an overwhelming homesickness. As well messages and gifts for the crew Rick had brought extended news bulletins about the events on Earth. The viewings had reassured the crew that their families were safe but they had all been shocked by the devastation which the Liberty movement had wrought on mainland USA.

'I agree with Sima,' Vicki said quietly. 'If we don't have any faith in the human race, we are already lost.'

The argument seesawed back and forth, voices became heated and died away. The scientists shifted uncomfortably in their chairs, disturbed by the passion of the Millennium crew.

Rick put his cup down. 'All my life, I've battled with bureaucrats. We can't let them win. They stifle ideas and kill off anything worth doing if it poses the slightest threat to their own petty interests. It's more than fifty years since we first landed on the moon and where are we now? They told us the money was needed for other things: global warming, population control, the war on terror. But how far have we got with any of that? The angels are right. Most of those problems could have been solved if we'd kept up our spirit of exploration. That's where we went wrong.' He stood up. 'You're idealists. I have every respect for the average man but you forget that there are a lot of people who seek power just for the sake of it. Perhaps we get that from these gourds. Like Zeus – they only want to dominate people. There's no purpose, no mission in their lives.'

Alistair interrupted. 'Athena is not like that. She and Cercs and others, they live by a strict code.'

'That may be so; but for what? What have they been doing here for the last two thousand years?' Rick pulled open the hatch. 'I need some air. Remember, if I'd taken the approach you're advocating, I wouldn't have got here and you would all be dead. Scientists, explorers, they're welcome to come, but I'm not waiting around while the bureaucrats wrangle. They're not welcome here. You'd better understand that if you want my help.'

Loren followed him and there was a long silence until Jeremy asked, 'What do you think, Sally?'

Sally started. She had lost interest in the argument and was deep in her own thoughts. She longed to see her birth mother; to find out why she had rejected her and what she could remember about her father. But she knew she was wishing in vain that Thomas would be proved wrong; that she had been conceived some other way. She had to face it and find a new way to live. When Rick had spoken of exploring the universe, using the gourds' technology to prolong their lives she had felt an excitement rise in her. She could go with them. She would not be alone in her immortality. She thought briefly of Hilda and David and her friends on earth. They seemed to belong to the distant past. She wished for a moment that she could see them face to face; to say "Sorry. I can't come home." But how could she? She could never explain why.

'I agree with Rick,' she replied. 'How will we convince anyone on Earth to take us seriously? We've lived through it and it's hard enough for us to believe.' She looked around the circle of faces and paused at Alistair's. 'You think I'm different from you. But none of you know who you really are. Everything we were taught, all our history; nothing is the way we thought it was.' She got up stiffly from her chair, pushed open the hatch and stared out. 'We've opened Pandora's Box and we can't shut it again. We need to think differently, find a new way to do things. If we don't, we won't make it.'

One by one they exited the dome. Ulfarr stood by the Aesir tent, gazing out over the southern ocean, Odin's raven perched on his shoulder. There was no other sign of human activity. The silence was unbroken. The light breeze had smoothed over the footprints in the snowy carpet; the air so clear that they could make out the shape of individual ice bergs, strewn across the horizon. The group watched without speaking as the sun dipped below the bright blue water.

Sally walked slowly down the white slope. The moons had not yet risen and the stars shone brilliantly in the darkening sky. In the silence, in the vast and empty landscape, the stars seemed so familiar, she felt as though she were standing once again in some desert in Australia.

Gradually an immense peace filled her. 'I belong here,' she thought. 'I belong everywhere.' She turned to look back at the watching figures.

'We must go on,' she said.

Acknowledgements

A book owes its existence to many people beside its author. The following people are some of those who inspired and supported me during its writing.

My husband, Ib for his immense patience, and my daughters Hanne Taylor and Ellenor Nielsen, for simply being who they are.

Dr Jonna Hakkila and Dr Jennifer Gasston for cheerfully reading and commenting on the early drafts.

The Wynnum Womens' Group; Ann Bovey, Colleen Jones, Sara Simpson and Sharon Songhurst, for perpetual faith.

Nicole Mayer, Dr Leigh Ellen Potter and Dr Francis Suraweera for inspiring some of the main characters.

My colleagues and friends in the Women in IT (WinIT) project, especially Associate Professor Liisa von Hellens and Jenine Beekhuyzen for helping me think in new ways about technology.

My students, colleagues and friends in the School of Information and Communication Technology at Griffith University, for making my life so interesting.

Jennifer Holdsworth and Deaf Services Queensland for inspiring me to complete Auslan 1.

And the staff in the Gastroenterology Department at the Royal Brisbane Hospital for helping me to stay alive.

All praise, no blame!